New York Times Bestselling Authors

MARY BLAYNEY

"Witty prose." —*Booklist*

"Compelling." —*RT Book Reviews*

ELAINE FOX

"A vibrant new voice in romance." —Patricia Gaffney

"One of the best-written, original, and fun novels to come across my desk in ages!" —M. L. Gamble

MARY KAY MCCOMAS

"An introspective and irresistible story." —*Publishers Weekly*

"A remarkable talent." —*RT Book Reviews*

R. C. RYAN

"Delivers it all—with page-turning romance." —Nora Roberts

"These not-to-be-missed books are guaranteed to warm your heart!" —*Fresh Fiction*

DOWN THE RABBIT HOLE

J. D. ROBB

MARY BLAYNEY

ELAINE FOX

MARY KAY McCOMAS

R. C. RYAN

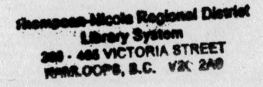
JOVE BOOKS, NEW YORK

JOVE

An imprint of Penguin Random House LLC
375 Hudson Street, New York, New York 10014

DOWN THE RABBIT HOLE

A Jove Book / published by arrangement with the authors

ISBN: 978-0-515-15547-1

PUBLISHING HISTORY
Jove mass-market edition / October 2015

PRINTED IN THE UNITED STATES OF AMERICA

10 9 8 7 6 5 4 3 2 1

Cover images: "Landscape" by Petar Paunchev / Shutterstock;
"Hat" by Albund / Shutterstock.
Text design by Kristin del Rosario.

Penguin
Random
House

CONTENTS

WONDERMENT IN DEATH

J. D. ROBB

I shall not commit the fashionable stupidity
of regarding everything I cannot explain
as a fraud.

CARL JUNG

We're all mad here.

LEWIS CARROLL

CHAPTER ONE

The dead were his business.

Over the years, he'd built a tidy fortune—though it was never enough, never quite *enough*—exploiting the dead and those who loved them.

He loved his work, reveled in it, and all the bright and shiny things his efforts amassed. But over and above the profit, or at least running through the dollars and euros and pounds, was sheer glee.

A man who didn't laugh himself sick seven times a day didn't know how to live.

One of his greatest amusements—and in truth he had so many—but one of his greatest was when the time came around to turn the living into the dead.

That time had come around for Darlene Fitzwilliams, she of the ebony hair and haunted blue eyes. Such a pretty creature. He'd thought so on their first acquaintance, and had thought the same a number of times over the past five months.

He might have kept her longer, as he did love pretty things, but she had committed the greatest sin.

She'd begun to bore him.

She sat now in the cluttered, colorful parlor of his cluttered, colorful house, as she had once every week for four and a half months. She called him Doctor Bright, one of his many names and as false as all the rest.

"Doctor Bright," she said after sipping the tea he always provided, "I had a terrible argument with my brother this afternoon. It was my fault—I missed an important appointment with the lawyers regarding the estate. I just forgot. I was distracted, knowing I'd be coming here, and I forgot. Marcus was so upset and impatient with me. He doesn't understand, Doctor Bright. If I could just explain . . ."

Bright lifted his dark, dramatic eyebrows. "What did your father say, dear?"

"He said it wasn't time." She leaned forward, all that hope and faith (and how tedious that had become) glowing on her face. "I'm so anxious to talk to him and Mama again."

"And you will, of course."

He sipped his tea, smiled at her. "Drink your tea. It will help open you to communications."

She obeyed, biddable, boring girl.

"It's hard not to tell him. And Henry."

The tea made her talkative, a little giddy. The effects had amused him initially. Now he saw her as an excitable little mouse, scurrying everywhere at once. And he wanted to whack her with a hammer.

"I'm going to meet Henry tonight," she continued. "He wants to set the date, and that's something else I want to talk to Mama and Daddy about. They were so pleased when Henry and I got engaged. And then . . ."

"Transitions, a journey." He played his fingers in the air as he spoke, watched her watch them dance. "Nothing more."

"Yes, I know that now. It's just . . . I want to share this with Marcus, and with Henry."

"But you haven't."

"No. I promised you, and my father. You said I'd know when it was time, and I feel it is. I hate not being honest with the people I love, even for people I love. If Henry and I set the date tonight—that's a kind of journey, too, isn't it? Marriage."

"And do you feel ready for that journey?"

"I do. Coming here, all I've learned, it's shown me there aren't any ends, just other paths. Before I came to you, everything seemed so dark, so final. And now . . ."

She beamed at him, her eyes wide and bright, and just going glassy. "I can never repay you for all you've given me."

"It's my gift to give. Regrettably, at a price."

"Oh, of course." She laughed—giddy, yes giddy, primed by his tea party. Opening her bag, she took out a thick red envelope.

Always red for Ms. Fitzwilliams, with cash (he only took cash) in the amount of nine thousand, nine hundred and ninety-nine dollars sealed inside. He'd told her red protected the offering, and nine was a number of power.

In truth red was his current favorite color (though it was about to be supplanted by purple), and he found all those nines amusing.

Darlene set it, as she'd been instructed, on the silver tray on the tea table.

"And the tokens?" he prompted. He wouldn't touch or count the money. The lovely Ms. March would see to all that. But when the biddable girl took two red pouches from her bag, Bright's fingers itched.

These he took, these he touched, these he stroked.

The desk clock was old, heavy crystal, small enough to fit in the palm of his hand. Its monetary value Bright estimated in the low thousands, but it was worth so much more to him.

He could feel Gareth Fitzwilliams's energy shimmering on it, and his father's before him, and yes, even generations back. So many hands touching, so many eyes marking time.

He opened the second pouch, took out the slim, antique ladies' watch. A tiny diamond butterfly perched above the twelve, and pretty diamond chips circled the face.

Yes, Bria Fitzwilliams had worn it often, choosing it in lieu of more stylish and practical wrist units, clasping it on thinking of her own mother, her mother's mother, and back five generations.

Time marked again, birth to death, death to birth and round and round.

"You chose well."

"They're favorites."

"Strong energy. Strong connections. Are you ready?"

He slipped each pouch in a pocket so he could take her hand, lead her from the room. He could feel the vibrations—excitement, fear? Wasn't it all too delicious?

He led her up stairs he liked for their zigzagging climb, down a corridor he enjoyed as the paint and wainscoting he'd designed gave it the illusion of a slant.

The girl weaved like a drunk, so he had to stifle a quick giggle.

He took her into what he called the Passage Room, where lights glowed blue. She took her seat—a good girl—in the high-backed armchair on the raised platform. The height would keep their eyes level, an essential element to what came next.

"Breathe deep," he told her as a blue mist swirled around the chair. "Slow and deep. Hear my voice."

Behind him a white spiral formed on the wall, began to spin. Lights flashed, strobing colors.

"Open your mind."

A hat seemed to float down, to settle on Darlene's head, its long, red feathers swaying. For a moment it banded tight around her skull, caused discomfort, then that eased, and colors washed the room. She smelled flowers, and her mother's perfume.

"Mama."

"A moment more." Pleased with her quick response, he stepped over to a cupboard, opened it, and chose a hat for himself out of the dozens stored there.

A top hat in bold red, for young Ms. Fitzwilliams.

"Into my eyes, into my voice. Follow both to the threshold."

Her eyes were glass, pinned to his. Helpless, he thought, and this time he did giggle.

He slipped into her mind—so easy now, like sliding on ice—and saw as she saw.

A sun-drenched meadow under perfect blue skies. Birds twittered; a warm breeze fluttered the flowers spread everywhere over the ground.

There, under a tall tree spreading dappled shade on a pretty slope, stood Gareth and Bria Fitzwilliams. Young, smiling, he handsome in his white suit, she lovely in her flowing white dress.

With a happy cry, Darlene ran to her dead parents and embraced them.

Touching, Bright thought, so very touching. He dabbed a mock tear from the corner of his eye and gave her nearly twenty minutes to walk in the meadow.

It was never enough, of course, and she was protesting, reaching out, when the blue mist swirled over the flowers. But it was all he could spare her this time—this last time.

He gave her instructions, made her repeat them twice before he removed her hat, and his own. He led her downstairs where the inestimable Ms. March had her coat and bag—and what was now inside it—waiting.

He helped her on with her coat himself, checked to be sure the recorder was properly affixed. After all his time and effort, he deserved to join the farewell party.

"Once you're in the car, driving away, you won't remember me or this house or anything we've talked about. You'll remember your parents, of course, and all you spoke of with them." He kissed her hand, gallantly. "It's been a pleasure, my dear."

"Thank you, Doctor."

"And where are you going now?"

"To see my brother. We argued. I need to tell him everything and give him a gift."

"That's excellent. Good-bye, Ms. Fitzwilliams."

"Good-bye, Doctor Bright."

She walked out and to the curb, where his own driver held open the door of his town car. He waved her cheerily off, stepped back, shut the door.

And laughing like a loon, did a jig around the foyer.

"Oh, was that too, too precious?"

He grabbed March's hands, and kicking off her practical black heels, she joined him in the dance. Giggling with him, she pulled the pins out of her sensible bun so her long, brown hair tumbled and swirled.

"It's party time, Bright!"

"It's always party time, March!"

They clutched each other, swaying as they caught their breath. "A surprise party," he said, "and we mustn't be late. To the theater, March, and don't spare the popcorn!"

They raced off together to watch the show.

In the car, Darlene felt energized, almost euphoric. The lights of the city glittered like ice. She was warm, almost too warm, in the car, and reached for the tall, slim glass of clear liquid marked *Drink Me*.

Cool and light on the tongue, it made her smile.

She was going to see Marcus. They'd argued earlier, she could hardly remember why. But the why didn't matter. They would make up, and she'd tell him about the dreams she'd been having. Dreams of their parents, and how they'd helped her accept their sudden, tragic deaths.

They were together, away from all pain, all worry, all sorrow.

She felt the same, right at that moment. She should contact Henry, tell him she'd bring Marcus with her. They'd set the date for the wedding.

But when she started to reach for her 'link, a pain shot up her arm.

Because she wasn't supposed to do that, she remembered. She wasn't supposed to talk to Henry yet. Marcus. She was supposed to see Marcus.

She didn't complain when the car pulled over a block from Marcus's building, but got out, began to walk. The frigid January wind whistled around her ears. It was almost like voices.

A new year, she reminded herself as headlights beamed into her eyes. The year she'd marry Henry Boyle: 2061.

Her parents had died in June of 2060. She wanted them at her wedding. She'd dream them there, she decided. She'd explain it all to Henry—no, Marcus; Marcus first. And they'd all be happy again.

"Evening, Miss Fitzwilliams."

She stared at the doorman. He wore a big red heart over his chest and was gobbling what seemed to be a cherry tart.

Then she blinked, and it was just Philip the night doorman in his thick navy coat.

"You okay, miss?"

"Yes, yes. Sorry. My mind went somewhere. I'm going up to see my brother."

He opened the door for her and, God, the lobby looked so long, so narrow, so bright. "Is he alone?"

"As far as I know. He came in a couple hours ago. Want me to call up for you?"

"Oh, that's all right." The elevator doors looked so shiny. She could see worlds reflected in them. She stepped in, had to think very hard to remember. "Fifty-two east."

The ride up made her feel a little drunk. She needed something to eat, she decided. Had she had dinner? Odd that she couldn't remember.

A couple got in as she got out, called her by name.

"Oh hello." She smiled at them, the man with the grinning cat's face and the woman wearing a crown. "I'm going to see Marcus. I have something for him."

She rang the bell on her brother's door, waited with a smile until he opened it.

"I wasn't expecting to see you."

"I know." Just as she knew he was still angry with her. She held out a hand for his. "I'm so sorry, Marcus."

He sighed, shook his head. Closed the door behind her. "I miss them, too, Darli, and we owe it to them to make sure everything's done right, for the estate, for the business, for the rest of the family."

"I know."

"You can't keep closing in, shutting down."

"I know. I know. It's been so hard, Marcus, losing them the way we did, and I haven't handled it well. I haven't done my share."

"It's not about the work," he began, then his eyes narrowed on her face. "Have you been drinking?"

"What? No!" She laughed. "Just tea, lots of tea, and I've got so much to tell you. I needed to talk to them first."

"To who?"

"Mama and Daddy, of course."

"Darlene."

"I needed to *know* they're all right. In a better place. I can *see* them there, and it's beautiful. It's Wonderland!"

"Okay." He set a hand on her shoulder. "Okay."

"I brought you something, like a peace offering."

"Fine. Take off your coat, let's sit down. We need to talk."

"In a minute," she muttered. She opened her bag, stared at the red scarf. Her fingers floated over it, through it, and down to the bright red rose beneath.

"For you," she said and pushed it at him. In him.

He looked at her so strangely, but then he wasn't the sort of man who expected a flower. Delighted, she pulled it back, pushed it at him again.

And again, until he sprawled in the meadow covered with red roses.

"I'll get Mama and Daddy now, so you can talk to them. Sit right there!" She raced across the meadow, pushed past long, flowering vines that barred the view. And climbed to the top of the hill.

She saw her parents dancing by a silver lake and, laughing, flew toward them.

And flying, never felt the fall.

CHAPTER TWO

Instead of enjoying a rare night off sprawled out with her ridiculously sexy husband watching a vid where lots of stuff blew up, Eve Dallas stood over death.

She'd pulled rank—a favor for a friend—to take primary on what, on the surface, struck as a murder/suicide. Sibling rivalry taken to extremes.

The friend was currently in the kitchen area of the crime scene—the swank Upper East Side penthouse of the late Marcus Elliot Fitzwilliams—with her own pretty sexy husband. And the uniformed cop who kept them in place.

Eve studied the silver shears deeply embedded in the victim's chest. Cause of death might have been apparent, but she opened her field kit, crouched to do her job.

"Visual identification of Fitzwilliams, Marcus, confirmed with print match on scene. Victim is thirty-six, single Caucasian male, owner and only listed resident of this unit. Employed CEO and president of Fitzwilliams Worldwide."

She took out microgoggles, lifted one of the victim's hands with her own sealed ones. "No visible defensive wounds, no signs of struggle. COD, three puncture wounds to the chest. ME to confirm."

Bled out right here, she thought.

"An attempt to resuscitate the victim resulted in some compromising of the scene."

Rising, she crossed over to the open terrace door, studied the bloody palm print on the glass. Running it, she ID'd the victim's sister. Who was even now splatted on the sidewalk below.

Eve stepped out into the cold, looked down to the street, the police barricades, the crowd lined up behind them.

The icy wind dragged at her short, choppy brown hair, had her sticking her hands in the pockets of her long leather coat to warm them.

"Long drop," she muttered.

And since she'd gotten a report from the first-on-scene, she knew Darlene Fitzwilliams had taken that long drop less than ten minutes after the doorman had let her into the building.

She'd talk to the doorman herself, but for now . . .

She wandered back inside. "She comes in. Not much time for an argument or to get heated up. Plus, who carries a pair of scissors that size in a handbag? Stabs the brother in the heart, three times, walks over, goes outside, jumps."

Eve scanned the room.

Rich, tasteful, with some humorous touches, like the pencil sketch of a frog wearing a crown.

She'd have her partner do a solid run on both of the dead, and the family business, when Peabody got there. But for now, she'd get a sense of things from Doctor Louise Dimatto and Charles Monroe.

The kitchen—a lot of steel and glass—flowed into a lounge area—lots of leather and wood. Charles and Louise sat hip-to-hip on a long, low sofa the color of fog. He had his arm around her shoulders; she had her head tipped toward him.

She'd changed her hair, Eve noted, wearing the gentle blond in a straight, chin-length deal, sharply angled.

And she'd been crying, which made Eve uneasy.

While Louise looked delicate, Eve knew her to be tough as they came, strong enough to defy her wealthy, conservative family and start her own clinic, run a mobile medical that serviced some of the diciest areas in the city.

But now she was pale and puffy-eyed, and fresh blood stained her elegant blue sweater.

Her eyes, nearly the same color as the sofa, met Eve's.

"Dallas. I couldn't save him. Marcus. I couldn't save him."

Eve nodded to the uniform standing by to dismiss her, then, nudging a shallow bowl of wooden balls aside, sat on the table to face her friend.

"I'm sorry. You knew Marcus Fitzwilliams."

"We've known each other since we were kids. We even dated awhile. Our families . . . There was some hope we'd make a match of it, but we didn't suit that way. We've been friends for most of our lives. You met him—Marcus and Darlene and their parents—you met them at the wedding."

"Okay." Eve had a vague recollection of the man she'd just examined dancing with Louise, lifting her off her feet with a laugh, spinning her around.

"It was only a few weeks later—we were just back from our honeymoon, Charles and I—when Gareth and Bria, Marcus's parents, were killed."

"How?"

"It was an accident." Charles spoke now, using his free hand to grip Louise's. "Rain-slick road, a semi lost control, overturned. Eight people were killed, the Fitzwilliams among them."

"They were so close," Louise murmured. "It crushed Marcus and Darlene."

"Take me through tonight."

"We were coming over, just for drinks. To catch up. We've all been so busy, and we wanted to catch up with each other." She closed her eyes. "And he wanted to talk to me about Darlene—as a doctor."

"Why?"

"He was worried about her. She wasn't coping well. She'd closed off from friends—I can't count the times she's put me off in the last few months. There's considerable to deal with, the business, the estate, but Marcus told me she was dragging her heels at every turn. She's engaged—a great guy—but she'd been drawing back from Henry, too. She'd been secretive. Darlene's always been so open—naively so, really—but that changed."

"And that caused friction between them, between the siblings?"

"Some, yes. But not—" Louise shook her head, took a steadying breath. "They loved each other, Dallas, they're friends as well as family. Darlene was going through a difficult period. They argued. Marcus told me they had a shouting match just today when—"

"Today?"

"She missed an appointment, regarding the estate. And not for the first time. An estate is complex and broad-based and takes a lot of time and work to handle. Marcus felt, and I agree, that settling it, closing it, was important for Darlene. It would help her reach some sort of closure. But she put up a lot of roadblocks. She'd say . . ."

"She'd say what?"

"She'd say she needed to talk to her parents before she signed off on anything."

"Her dead parents." Sitting back a little, Eve laid her hands on her thighs. "Was she using?"

Louise sighed. "I've never known her to, and I've known her most of her life. Henry—her fiancé—told me she was using some sleep aids. Herbal-based, nothing heavy."

The scene, Eve thought, and the players in it read loud and clear. "She argued with her brother today, came here tonight. You were coming over. As far as you know she wasn't expected."

"She wasn't. She was supposed to meet Henry for dinner, about eight. I hate how this sounds, but he was going to contact me, let me know her mood. We thought a kind of intervention. If it seemed right, Henry would bring her over here, and we'd talk to her together. All of us who loved her."

"Henry Boyle. Where is he now?"

"You said I couldn't contact anyone, so . . ." Tears rose up in Louise's eyes again. "He must be waiting for her. He doesn't know she's— I know how it looks." Some of that toughness came through as Louise leaned forward, gripped Eve's hands. "I know it looks as if Darlene came here and killed Marcus, then herself. It's not how it looks. I *knew* them, Dallas. There's something else here."

"What time did you get here?"

"About . . . eight fifteen, eight twenty?" She looked at Charles for confirmation.

"Yes, close to that. When our cab pulled up there was already a crowd, people shouting. The doorman told us it had just happened. Just minutes before. He was pretty shaken up, told us he'd just spoken with her about ten minutes earlier, and she'd gone up to see Marcus."

"There was nothing I could do for her." Louise drew in a breath. "Nothing I could do."

"We ran in," Charles continued, "both of us thinking of Marcus. Security let us up—they know us, came with us. Marcus didn't answer, so they bypassed."

"He was on the floor. I tried to— Maybe if I'd had my medical bag."

"Louise." Charles pressed his lips to her hair.

Turning into him, she squeezed her eyes shut. "No, I couldn't have brought him back. He was gone, but I had to try." She looked down at the blood on her sweater. "He was family to me. They were family."

"We contacted you," Charles said. "Right away. We didn't touch anything but . . . but Marcus, and contacted you."

"Was Marcus involved with anyone?"

"No, not right now. For the last several months, he's been focused on the family business, the estate, the Fitzwilliams Foundation."

"Who gets the money now?"

"I don't know." Because her voice was thick, Louise cleared her throat. "There are aunts, uncles, cousins. Many of them are involved in the business, the foundation."

"Do you know who I'd talk to about that?"

"Ah, probably Gia Gregg—the family attorney. My family's, too. She'd know."

"Enemies?"

Louise shook her head. "I can give you a list of friends, family. I don't know enemies—though I'm sure he had a few. He was a tough and exacting businessman. He'd been groomed to run the family empire, and he didn't suffer fools. Someone set this up, Dallas. Someone set this up to make it look as if Darlene killed him, then herself. I'm telling you, that's impossible."

Eve pushed to her feet. "Make me a list. Friends, exes, family, coworkers. Anyone you can think of, and their connection to both Marcus and Darlene. I'm going to have you taken home."

"Home? But—"

"There's nothing you can do here." Harsh as it was, it was true. "You called me for a reason, now trust me to take care of your friends."

"I do." Clinging to Charles's hand, Louise rose. "I trust you'll find out who's responsible for what happened here. You need to trust me. What you see here is a cover."

She rode down with them, arranged for a black-and-white to drive them home.

Then she ducked under the barricade. As she approached the body, Peabody pushed her way through the crowd of gawkers.

"Sorry, Dallas. Twenty-minute delay on the subway." Peabody pulled her pink and green hat—with bounding pompom—farther over her dark flip of hair as she studied what was left of Darlene Fitzwilliams. "Wow. Long drop."

"Fifty-second floor."

"Really long."

"I gave her a cursory look when I came on scene, so I'll finish her. I've already done the one upstairs—her brother. Multiple stab wounds, heart area. Big pair of scissors. Talk to the doorman again, see if he wavers in his statement. He says he talked to the sister here, let her go up to see her brother. Some ten minutes later, she came down, the hard way. Security—along with Charles and Louise—"

Peabody's head swiveled back. "Charles and Louise?"

"They were coming to visit the brother—old family friends of Louise's. He was dead when they went in."

"Oh man." Peabody's dark eyes reflected sympathy. "Are they still here?"

"I just sent them home. This one has a fiancé I need to contact who's apparently waiting for her. She's going to be really late for dinner."

"I'll say." Peabody tipped her head back, looked up. "Murder/suicide."

"It sure as hell looks like it. Louise gauges that as impossible. Talk to the doorman, any other wits you can find. We treat it as undetermined until otherwise."

Opening her field kit, she knelt beside the shattered body, and put aside what it sure as hell looked like.

CHAPTER THREE

Eve officially identified the body, determined time of death—
within two minutes of the first victim. Cause of death was
brutally apparent, but the ME would determine if there were
other injuries, injuries incurred before flesh and bone met
concrete.

No sign of struggle, no break-in, she thought. If the doorman stuck to his story, he'd opened the door for Marcus approximately two hours before his death.

No one except the sister had come calling.

The apartment security showed only the sister at the door,
only she going inside.

Sitting back on her heels, Eve played it through.

Sister, depressed, unable to cope with parents' sudden
death, friction with brother. Arguments, including one that
day. Suffers a breakdown, goes to brother's apartment, stabs
him, crosses over to the terrace doors—leaving a bloody
handprint—walks out, climbs up, jumps off.

She could see it, just that clearly. And she could hear Louise's voice telling her it wasn't possible.

"Okay, Louise."

Who else had motive? A lot of money and power at stake. The murder weapon. Determine if the scissors belonged to the sister, the brother, or who else. Tox report. Maybe, despite Louise's belief, the sister leaned on illegals to get her through.

Who else had access to the penthouse?

"Bag her," she ordered the waiting morgue attendants, and started to rise when she saw something in a pool of blood.

"Hold it." She pulled out tweezers and lifted bits of shattered plastic, and what she recognized as a mini lens, in pieces.

Just why would Darlene Fitzwilliams have worn a recorder? Eve wondered as she sealed the bloody pieces into evidence.

Sealed bag in hand, she pushed to her feet. "Tag her for Morris—flag tox as priority. Same with the one inside."

Peabody jogged back to her. "The doorman's solid on it. He did say she looked a little off—distracted. And I talked to this couple who got in the elevator on fifty-two as she got out. They live on that floor, know both the DBs. They said she looked right through them even when they spoke to her. Like she was in a trance."

"She was wearing a mini recorder." Eve held up the evidence bag.

"It didn't handle the fall any better than she did. Why would she have been wearing one?"

"Good question. When did the wits see her?"

"They passed just a few minutes before she came down—without the elevator. They ended up walking about a block when the woman remembered she'd forgotten the little gift she'd gotten for the friends they were meeting. So they backtracked. They hit the lobby about the same time she hit the pavement."

"I've flagged her tox, given that a push. Have the Electronic Detection Division go over all the electronics, including security. Let's take another pass upstairs, and I want another look at his feed, her at the door."

As they started toward the lobby, Eve turned in the direction of shouting, saw a man struggling against the two uniforms who held him back.

After passing the evidence bag to Peabody, Eve crossed over to the barricade. "What's the problem?"

"Lieutenant, this guy—"

"Darlene! Let me through, goddamn it, I need to see Darlene. The media flash said— Darli!"

"Who are you?"

He stopped fighting long enough to catch his wind, but his eyes remained wild. "I'm Henry Boyle. I'm Darlene Fitzwilliams's fiancé. Let me through."

"Mr. Boyle, I'm Lieutenant Dallas. You need to calm down and come with me."

"I want to see Darlene."

Eve nodded to the uniforms, who let Henry through the barricade.

"I want to know what's going on. I need to—" He stopped dead, every ounce of color leaching from his face as he saw the body bag being lifted into the back of the dead wagon. "Who is that? What's happening?"

Eve took a firm grip on his arm, pulled him toward the lobby doors and inside. She took him to the far side, ordered him to sit.

"Go up, get started," she told Peabody. "I'll take him. When the sweepers get here, make sure they take that recorder, get it to the lab."

"Are you sure you want him? He's going to break."

"Yeah. I got it." She dragged over another chair, sat facing Henry Boyle.

He already knew. He was clinging to the slippery thread of denial, Eve thought, but he already knew. She cut the thread, fast.

"Mr. Boyle, I'm sorry to tell you that Darlene and Marcus Fitzwilliams are dead."

"That's not possible. I'm meeting Darlene for dinner. She's running late, and the media flash said . . ."

He looked toward the doors, the lights, the barricades, the body bag.

"Oh God." He started to lurch up. "Darlene."

"Sit." Eve pulled him down again.

"The media flash said murder/suicide. That's insane. That's absolutely insane."

Goddamn leaks, Eve thought. "We haven't determined murder or suicide. Where were you between eight and eight thirty?"

"What? I don't know. What time is it?" He looked at his wrist unit, and started to shake. "In the restaurant. In KiKi's—it's on Third. She was late, she didn't answer her 'link. Marcus didn't answer his. Darlene . . ."

"When did you last speak to her?"

"This morning, before I left for work. We live together. We're getting married. We haven't set the date, but . . ."

Tears rolled. Eve thought his eyes were still too shocked to realize they wept, so the tears just spilled down his cheeks.

"How would you describe her mood?"

"She's been struggling—her parents' death. But she seemed a little steadier this morning. But we talked later, on the 'link, and she was upset. She and Marcus had an argument. She hadn't gone to the lawyer's office for the estate meeting. She'd promised him she'd be there, and she hadn't gone. Papers needed to be signed, so Marcus was frustrated. I spoke with him, too. Mediating, I guess. They'd never hurt each other, not this way."

He began to rock now, then just dropped his head in his hands and wept.

Eve rose, ordered a uniform to find coffee somewhere, and gave Henry time to compose himself.

And did her best to block his view when they brought the body bag down from the fifty-second floor.

The doorman came up with a go-cup from the staff break room.

Henry cupped his trembling hands around it. "I can't understand. I keep thinking, no, this isn't real. I kissed her goodbye this morning. She's been distant and distracted for a while now, but she kissed me back. She held on to me, and told me she loved me. Just this morning."

"Was she taking any drugs? Any medication? Any illegals?"

"She used some sleep aid—a natural herbal blend. And she'd taken an antidepressant for a while, right after her parents died, but she threw it away last summer. She didn't like how it made her feel. I've known her for five years, and lived with her for two now. She doesn't do illegals."

He drank some of the coffee, set it aside. "I know who you are. I mean, we've met. At Charles and Louise's wedding. You had their wedding at your estate."

"Yeah, I remember."

"I work for Roarke."

That she didn't remember—or hadn't known. "As what?"

"Architectural engineer, rehabilitation specialist. New York branch. Lieutenant Dallas, what they're saying on the media reports, it's not true. Darlene and Marcus fought like any brother and sister, but they loved each other. And Darlene, she's gentle. She's gentle and loving and compassionate. Someone did this to them. You have to find out who did this to them."

"Working on it. Did she use a lapel recorder?"

"What? No. She didn't have one. Why?"

"Just details." Puzzling ones, Eve thought. "Is there someone you'd like me to contact for you?"

"The two people who mean the most to me in the world are gone."

"Louise?" Eve suggested.

"I— Yes." He swiped at his eyes. "Do they know? I should talk to them. I should—"

"They know." Rising again, Eve contacted Louise, got the go-ahead. "I'm going to have you taken downtown, to Louise. She'd like you to stay with them tonight."

"She loved them, too."

"Who didn't?"

He shook his head. "Marcus ran a tight ship, from what I know, and people who have a great deal of money can inspire envy or contempt. But I don't know anyone who disliked either of them enough to hurt them."

"Who'll be running the tight ship now?"

"I'm not sure. I'd guess their uncle—Gareth's younger

brother, Sean. He and his wife—second wife—are based mostly in Europe. He runs their resort business over there. I don't know that much about it. Darlene's primarily involved in the foundation work. Marcus handled the reins of the businesses."

"All right. I need to go through her things."

He stared, blankly, with red-rimmed eyes. "Her things?"

"You said you lived together. I need to have access to your residence and go through her things. Your electronics."

"We're on First Avenue. I can take you."

"I can get there. Your permission makes it smoother."

"Whatever you need to do. I can give you my key swipe, my access codes."

"I have a master. If you think of anything else, let me know. Louise knows how to contact me."

"When can I see her? Please. When can I see Darlene?"

"I'll let you know."

"I kissed her good-bye this morning. I didn't know it was going to be the last time." He slid his hands into his pockets, drew out a pair of dark gray ladies' gloves. "Darlene's. She left them on the table by the door this morning. I saw them when I got home tonight to change for dinner. She's always doing that. I put them in my pocket for her. It's cold out."

Eve carried his grief upstairs. It weighed on her as she studied the blood on the floor of the penthouse.

"All the electronics tagged," Peabody told her. "I scanned them—and there's a conversation between the male vic and Louise about coming over tonight and setting up what they called a mini intervention with the sister. Two conversations with the fiancé—who also left a v-mail about nine, saying Darlene was running late and didn't answer her 'link."

"Jibes with his statement."

"Her 'link's in the handbag we're taking into evidence. Several v-mails and texts from the brother about her being late, then missing this meeting. A conversation with the fiancé and two v-mails and two texts from him asking where she was, asking her to get back to him. E-mails that appear to deal with business again—the foundation stuff.

"No illegals," Peabody continued, "no evidence of another occupant. Sweepers took a good look at the security, and agree with you. No break-in. But EDD will give it the once-over. He's got some cash, and the place has plenty of easily transported valuables—e-stuff, art, jewelry. We came up with two safes. One in the bedroom, one in the home office. EDD to access."

"Okay. I want another look at the on-door security feed."

"I had a look myself."

Eve accessed the viewing screen through a panel by the main door.

"I ran it back to this morning when the vic left—oh-seven-thirty-eight," Peabody said. "According to his calendar, he had an eight o'clock meeting at his HQ. Nobody came in or came to the door until he returned at eighteen-sixteen. Alone. And no other approach until the sister. Here. Twenty-oh-three."

Eve watched Darlene step to the door, press the buzzer. Smile. Watched her mouth move as the door opened, and she stepped inside and out of cam view.

And Eve ran it back, watched again.

"No illegals. They all say nope, she never did illegals. Look at her eyes, for Christ's sake."

"Sure looks high."

"Looks ready to fly, and I guess she did. Assess, Peabody."

"We don't really have all the data."

"Assess with what we have. What's your gut?"

Peabody sighed. "My gut says Darlene Fitzwilliams suffered a breakdown, likely self-medicated. Guilt, grief, said medication, exacerbated by an argument with her brother over the dead parents, turned that breakdown violent. Impaired by substance or substances as yet unknown, she stabbed her brother, then jumped off his terrace. Sad to the tragic."

"It plays."

"But?"

Eve wandered the room—wealthy, privileged, but not fussy, she thought. The sort of place, yes, where friends and family would be comfortable.

"My head agrees with your assessment, given current data. My gut . . . My gut may be overly influenced by the unrelenting insistence of someone I trust and respect that my head's wrong." Eve turned around again. "And unless I'm mistaken, those broken, bloody pieces in that evidence bag used to be a lapel recorder. Who was watching?"

"That's creepy."

"Hang here for the sweepers—and make sure they take that evidence bag to the lab. Tonight. Then go by Central on your way home, write it up. Write it up straight. I'm going to go by Darlene's residence, take a look at her things, at her lifestyle. The fiancé gave me clearance."

"You don't want me to come with?"

"I want the report in. It's so fucking clean and simple. I want to see it written up, see if there are holes to poke through. I can't do that if I write it myself. Then go home, catch a few hours. We'll probably take the lawyer, this Gia Gregg, first thing in the morning. I'll give you the where and when. Figure on oh-eight hundred."

"Will do."

Eve pulled out her 'link as she headed down to the lobby. Roarke filled the screen, made her wish she was home.

"I figured you hadn't hit the rack yet."

"I'm waiting for my wife."

"You're going to wait awhile yet."

His eyes, so breathlessly blue, stayed on hers. "I knew them a little."

"The Fitzwilliams."

"Yes—the media's having a rout over the salacious idea of murder/suicide in the gilded halls of the wealthy and powerful."

"Fuck the media."

"I'm sure others feel the same. You met them yourself—at Charles and Louise's wedding."

"I've been refreshed. What's your take on the salacious idea?"

"I didn't know them well enough to have one. How's Louise?"

"Handling it. And she'll be distracted, as I sent the sister's fiancé down to her. Henry Boyle. He works for you."

"He does, and for a number of years now. A smart, creative, interesting man. I know he was mad about Darlene."

She'd seen the love; she'd felt the grief. "I'm about to turn their residence upside down to see if I can find the reason this is murder/suicide or the reason it's not." She stepped out in the lobby. "Did you watch the rest of that vid?"

"I didn't, no. It's not nearly as entertaining without you."

"We'll get back to it. Anyway, don't wait up."

"I won't."

She clicked off, stepped outside, glanced at her wrist unit.

Nearly midnight, she noted. It looked like the day would end and the next begin with murder.

CHAPTER FOUR

Eve considered double-parking, then homed in on a spot across the street. She hit vertical, took the short flight crossways over traffic, executed a quick one-eighty, then dropped down.

Not bad, she decided as she got out. Not half bad.

Since traffic was fairly light, she gauged it, jaywalked—more jay-jogged—back across the avenue, then hiked the three-quarters of a block to the pretty white-brick townhouse where her victim/suspect had co-habbed with Henry Boyle.

It shouldn't have surprised her to see the ridiculously handsome Irishman sitting on the top of the three steps leading to the front door.

"I believe you just broke several traffic laws, Lieutenant."

"Maybe."

She stood at the base of the steps just looking at him, the way the wind ran through that black silk hair, the way that beautifully sculpted mouth curved just for her.

She wondered how many people could claim to have a spouse, a partner, a lover sitting out on a cold, windy January night waiting for them. Not many. And if you added in how gorgeous that spouse, partner, lover looked doing it, that number whittled down to one.

Just her.

"Why aren't you home in the warm getting some sleep?"

"I'll tell you," he said, with the Irish a gilded thread woven through the words. "I debated my choices. Going off to bed without my wife, or coming out to join her." He rose, tall and lean. "I found it an easy choice, even without the added incentive of poking about in other people's belongings."

He'd enjoy that part, of course, she mused; had built the foundation of his empire doing just that as a Dublin street rat.

She climbed up until they were eye to eye. "Did you mess with the locks, ace?"

"I didn't, no. As yet." Still smiling, he brushed his lips to hers. "Would you like me to?"

Her master would get them in. His skill would get them in quicker. And it was freaking cold.

"Go ahead, have some fun. Tell me about Henry Boyle," she said as Roarke went to work.

"Bright, as I told you. Talented, creative. Earned a promotion about ten months ago. He's done good work—and I have him in charge of engineering on the youth shelter. I like him quite a bit."

So saying, Roarke opened the front door and gestured Eve in. In the dim light of the foyer, she saw the security panel blinking.

"I didn't get his codes," she began.

"Please." Roarke only shook his head as he scanned the panel with some little tool, which had the light blinking off then going steady green.

"It's a nice system," he commented.

"One of yours."

"It is, which made that simple."

He glanced around the foyer, one that spilled seamlessly into a living area with cozy conversational groupings, a small glass-tiled fireplace and art of various European cities. She recognized Paris, Florence, London. Wondered a bit that she'd actually been to those places.

"Lights on full," she ordered, and wandered into the living area. "Casually urban," she decided.

"What does that tell you?"

"Just that it's a comfortable space for a couple of city-dwellers. The art's probably originals, and some of the dust-catchers are likely important. But it doesn't come across as 'we're really rich.' Then again, I guess he's not."

"He does well—and earns it."

Roarke glanced around himself, noting she'd been right about the art.

"But no, he wouldn't have her generational fortune. I met her a couple of times—before the wedding. I recall having a conversation with her about philanthropy. She was very dedicated to her work in her family foundation. And I would say she and Henry were very much in love, and nicely suited."

"How did he get along with the brother?"

"Very well, as far as I know. Is Henry a suspect?"

"Right now I have what reads as murder/suicide. He wasn't there—I checked his alibi on the way over. And he has no motive I can see."

"But."

"But both he and Louise—with Charles backing her—insist it couldn't be what it reads. So . . ." She looked around. "Plus I found what appear to be pieces of a busted-to-shit lapel recorder beside the body. Who wears a recorder when they're about to commit murder/suicide?"

"Some might want it documented—last words and so on—but jumping from the fifty-second floor would eliminate that."

"Exactly. I'm going to start in the bedroom—must be upstairs. Why don't you take the electronics?"

They started up together, then Roarke turned into a room serving as a home office. Comfortable again, Eve concluded on a quick glance. Organized without being obsessive about it. A coffee cup left on the desk, sketches pinned to a board, an ancient pair of skids—his—in a corner. A data and communication unit with an auxiliary comp. One large wall screen.

As Roarke took off his coat, she moved on.

A guest bedroom: soft, soothing colors, and the required—
for reasons she couldn't fathom—mountain range of pillows.

She found the master—a little more elaborate here. The
bed, a soaring four-poster, struck her as an antique, while the
set of chairs in the sitting area with their silky blue and silver
print hit solid contemporary. Wood floors, a silver area rug,
a sweep of blue—silky again—to frame the windows. The
fireplace was a long, narrow rectangle inserted into the wall
across from the bed.

Clear glass lamps vied with a painting of blue and white
flowers in a thick, deeply carved silver frame. Real flowers—
white lilies—speared out of a massive urn that looked as old
as the bed.

She tried the closet.

It had likely been another bedroom at one time, gutted and
outfitted as a massive closet. Henry's clothes ranged along
one side—slightly jumbled, and with plenty of room for more.

Hers, on the other hand, were double tiered, with the back
wall reserved for countless pairs of shoes. Eve noted the
comp, had seen its like before. Darlene could consult it when
choosing an outfit, could use it to revolve the clothing from
day wear to evening to sports.

Apparently she'd taken wardrobe as seriously as philanthropy. And since Eve herself was married to a man who did
the same, she couldn't be too critical.

A large counter lined with drawers stood in the center of
the closet. Eve opened a drawer at random and counted over
a dozen bras.

Why does one set of tits need so many? she wondered, and
began to rifle through them.

The drawer below that held sweaters—she didn't bother
to count these—and below that was stylish gym wear. In the
bottom were the leggings, sweatpants, and T-shirts that told
her the woman had worn regular clothes at least some of the
time.

She moved down, top drawer middle: panties, and plenty
of them, skimpy, lacy, colorful, all neatly folded.

And at the bottom of the stack—where a male co-hab was unlikely to go—she found a silver card case.

Inside she found business cards for psychics, sensitives, mediums, tarot readers, spiritualists.

"Interesting," she murmured. "Why hide these from Henry?" She took out an evidence bag, dropped the case in.

Under another stack she found a few brochures—the same deal—with rates for readings and consultations, and with testimonials from satisfied clients.

By the time Roarke joined her, she'd finished the closet.

"I can't say I've found anything helpful," he told her. "Nothing on his office electronics, the house electronics and 'links that seems to apply. Her office is on the next floor, and what strikes is what's not there."

"What's not there?"

"She has it set to automatically delete any searches twice daily."

"And you let that stop you?"

He gave her a quiet look. "Hardly. I can tell you the vast majority of her searches fell into the area of research for her work. Running organizations that applied for a grant, that sort of thing. But she's spent considerable time doing searches on the afterlife, on communicating with the dead, on those who claim to serve as a bridge between this world and the next."

Eve nodded. "Like this?" she asked, and upended her evidence bag on the bed.

Roarke studied the brochures, pamphlets, business cards.

"Yes, like that."

"She had these hidden—underwear drawer, and inside an evening bag. It's quite a collection. New York, New Orleans, Arizona, Europe—Western and Eastern. I'm going to say she contacted at least some of these, paid visits. And the fact she hid it means she wanted to keep it to herself, and/or friends and family disapproved."

"She suffered a great loss, and looked for comfort."

Eve plucked up a brochure. "Nutritional Psychic. A grand buys you an hour consult where Doctor—and I bet that's a loose one—Hester will recommend which herbs and berries you should consume in order to open yourself up to messages from the dead."

She tossed it down, picked up another. "Now this one's a bargain. Initial fifteen-minute consult's free. During that consult Lady Katrina and her spirit guide, Ki, will determine if you have what it takes to pass through the portal."

She tossed that down as well.

"I'm also betting when I check her financials I'm going to find big gobs of money pissed away on this crap."

"I tend to agree with you regarding Doctor Hester, Lady Katrina and Ki, but we both know there are legitimate sensitives."

"Who talk to dead people."

He flicked a finger down the dent in her chin. "You do."

She rolled her eyes. "I dream about them—small wonder."

"Agree there as well. And no, I wouldn't put my money on any of these holding conversations with the dead. I'd say the dead speak if and when the spirit, we'll say, moves them."

"Don't go all Irish on me."

"In the blood and bone. Still." He laid his hands on her shoulders, sensing her frustration. "I see where you're going, and it makes perfect sense. She got herself overly involved here, and it maybe fell under the influence of someone not just illegitimate but dangerous. But how could that influence be so strong, Eve, to have her kill the brother she loved, and herself?"

"I don't know yet. But it's an angle. She had a good life here. You can feel it." She poked at him when he lifted his eyebrows. "That's not psychic mumbo. You just have to look around, and you get it. She had a good life here, a man she loved, work she loved, family, a place. She took a kick to the gut, I get that, too. Either grief twisted her up to the point she had a psychotic break, or someone twisted her up in it."

"You'll find out which."

"Yeah. Either way, she won't be crossing the bridge and coming through the portal to tell me. We work it."

She rebagged her evidence.

"Got another hour in you?" she asked with a glance up.

"What did you have in mind?"

"I want to go through the rest of it before Henry comes back. Plus, I didn't find any snazzy jewelry, and she's bound to have it, which means a safe. You find the safe, and I'll go through the rest of the place."

"And finding it, do I open it?"

"Yeah, you open it."

He flashed a grin. "This is much more fun than sleeping alone."

CHAPTER FIVE

She dropped into bed at two a.m., with the muttered request that Roarke wake her at six if she slept through. He was better than any alarm.

With a low fire simmering, the cat curled into the small of her back, and Roarke's arm wrapped around her, she tumbled straight into sleep.

The dead had a lot to say. In dreams, she thought, dreaming. And that was different from believing you could walk over some magic golden bridge into the afterlife and have conversations with vics.

No golden bridge for her. She sat in Interview A, with Marcus and Darlene Fitzwilliams seated on the other side of the scarred table.

"What gives?" she asked.

"I love my brother. I'd never hurt him."

"It's pretty clear you did."

"I've never hurt anyone in my life, not on purpose. You were in my house. What did you see?"

"It's all right, Darli." Marcus draped an arm around her shoulders, pressed his lips to her temple.

She'd seen that, Eve remembered. A photograph of just that, in a frame. Another when they'd been teenagers— Darlene riding on Marcus's shoulders as he hammed it up. Her in a bikini, Eve remembered, him in swim trunks, up to his waist in a blue sea.

Other photos, many photos. The siblings, the parents, Darlene and Henry, Marcus and Henry. Holiday photos, casual photos, formal photos.

A life in frames.

"You had secrets," Eve said.

"Everyone has secrets."

"And some people kill to protect them."

"Do I look like a killer?"

"Mostly killers look like everybody else. You jammed scissors in your brother's heart."

"I couldn't." Darlene gripped the handle of the shears now buried deep in her brother's chest. Yanked them free. "I'd kill myself first."

"You killed yourself second," Eve pointed out. "Grief can mess you up."

"How do you know? You've never lost anyone. You don't know my grief, you don't know my sorrow. My parents were angels. Yours were monsters."

Darlene drove the bloody points into the table. "You're surrounded by evil. How can you see through it to what's good?"

"You just have to look hard enough."

"Then look! I was going to have what you have. I just wanted answers. That's no different than you. I wanted what you want."

Eve opened her eyes and looked into Roarke's. "This. She wanted this."

"You've a few minutes left to sleep, but you dream so hard."

"She wanted this, and she had the person who wanted to give it to her. Why end everything? Gotta look deeper."

"All right." He kissed the brow she'd furrowed.

She laid her hand on his cheek. "Sometimes you don't have to look very hard."

"For what?"

"For what's good. You're right here." She tipped her face up, touched her mouth gently to his. "And when things aren't so good, you're still right here."

"Always."

She eased over so her heart lay on his, so her mouth lay on his. The only bridge she needed, she thought, was the one that led to him.

Her body, warm, smooth, fit so perfectly with his. His lanky, leggy cop. They could fill each other with love, with light, a kind of awakening after the long, dark night.

It touched him, the tenderness of her hand on his cheek, the sweetness of her fingers sliding through his hair. As much a lifting of the heart as arousal. He gave her the same; soft and easy, slow, dreamy kisses as desire roused.

He shifted. When he covered her she opened. She welcomed. She enfolded.

With their mouths meeting again, again, their bodies moved together, a rise and fall, rise and fall until that final peak.

And the quiet, sighing slide that followed.

SHE THOUGHT OF IT LATER WHEN SHE STOOD IN HER HOME office, studying the murder board she'd set up.

Darlene had wanted that—not just the sex; the connection, the continuity. And Eve had seen that connection in photographs in the townhouse.

Eve glanced over to a photograph of her and Roarke, taken by some enterprising paparazzo. They'd taken down the bad guy, and were both a bit bruised and bloody—a contrast to the glittery evening clothes. And they grinned at each other.

The connection was there, clear to see.

Who'd give that up and jump off a building? You'd have to be crazy—and that might be the answer. If she was sane, the logical answer was Darlene had been pushed. One way or the other.

She texted Peabody with a change of plans and told her

partner to meet her at the morgue at oh-nine-hundred. Meanwhile she split the list of reputed psychics, gave Peabody half to run.

She'd start on the others, but first she wanted a look at Darlene's financials. That might tell its own tale.

TEN MINUTES LATER SHE WAS UP AND CROSSING TO ROARKE'S adjoining office.

"I know you're busy."

He glanced over from his wall screen and the schematics on it. "I've been busier."

"It's a money question."

"I'm never too busy for that."

"I'm looking into Darlene's financials. For the past eighteen weeks—including the morning she died—she withdrew nine thousand, nine hundred and nine-nine dollars from her personal account. I'm reading it as cash."

Roarke sat back. "Isn't that interesting."

"There's other activity. Deposits, transfers, other withdrawals—one every month for five or six thousand. But eighteen weekly for that amount's a flag for me."

"One dollar more, you hit ten thousand and the IRS might do a sniff. Blackmail springs to mind, but with what you found last night, another idea leapfrogs over it."

"Somebody's been taking her for a ride for four and a half months. Parents died seven months ago. I need to find out when she started hunting for psychics, but that's what rings. She has another personal account—years old. This one? She opened it about five months ago, and not at her usual bank. I think she was hiding this, just like she was hiding the business cards and pamphlets."

"I'd agree, but if you're angling from that to whoever she was paying somehow pushing her to murder/suicide, why? Forget the how for a moment. Why? A dollar shy of ten large a week is a very nice income from one source."

"Maybe she'd decided that was it." Demonstrating, Eve swiped a finger through the air. "Maybe she'd figured out whoever she was paying was full of bullshit, maybe argued, threatened. Could be this bullshit shucker figured out a way to get more if he eliminated her, and her brother. A lot of ropes to tug there." She jammed her hands into her pockets. "I need her tox." She hadn't given Morris enough time, and found that frustrating. "I need how. She was high, and everyone says she didn't use, but damn it, she was high. So maybe she didn't know she was using. Still doesn't tell me why she'd kill her brother. If we stretch it to mind manipulation—not a big stretch since we've dealt with it before—it still doesn't explain the why." She'd taken a turn around his office before she caught herself. "Sorry."

"I never tire of watching you work."

"I'm working these angles because two people who loved her insist she couldn't do what she did."

"Not just because of that."

She blew out a breath. It could be disconcerting to have someone who knew her inside and out.

"No, not just," she admitted. "My sense of her, too. Money's part of it. Gia Gregg—lawyer. Do you know her?"

"Not personally, but she has an excellent reputation. Specializes in estate law, high-end clients."

"Too early for her, too. I'm going to get out of your hair, go on in. I can start running the list on the way, and maybe get lucky and push Morris on the autopsy."

"Would you like me to look for more?"

"More what?"

"Money, darling."

"You can give it a glance if you have time. Thanks. I'll be . . . communing with the dead for a while, one way or the other."

"Give them my best or my worst, depending. And take care of my cop."

"I can do all that. See you later."

She started her run on the psychics at the top of the list as she drove downtown, letting the in-dash do the work. She eliminated one straight off, as he was doing time for fraud.

Two others had done time. Eve bumped them down, figur-

ing Darlene had enough brains and certainly enough resources
to have gotten the same information. And while she might
have been gullible, she didn't strike Eve as brick-stupid.

She toggled that with Darlene's travel. Though she had
flown to Europe twice in the last six months, there was nothing for the last eighteen weeks.

Eve bumped down anyone on the list out of the country.
But she'd check with Henry Boyle, and with Darlene's office,
just to be sure she hadn't snuck any travel in that didn't show.

She continued the runs as she walked through the white
tunnel of the morgue—and tried to resign herself to spending
a good chunk of her day talking to woo-woo shovelers.

She found Morris with Darlene's shattered body, and with
the brother laid out on a second table.

"Jumpers or floaters," she began, "which is worse?"

"Floaters go on a sliding scale. The longer they're in the
water, the higher they rate."

He wore a steel gray suit today, paired with an electric blue
tie. He'd gone silver with the cord that twined through his
single thick braid of black hair.

And he looked, she thought, both rested and alert.

"Jumpers," he continued. "We can judge them on a sliding
scale as well. The higher they go, the higher they rate."

"Fifty-two floors. She rates pretty high."

"She does. Years ago I had a jumper—literally. A skydiver."

"Why do people do that?" It absolutely baffled her. "People actually pay to do that."

"It's exhilarating."

"You?" Surprised, she frowned at him. "You've jumped
out of a plane? On purpose?"

"An amazing sensation. I'm quite a fan of sensations."

"Jumping out of a plane would give me a sensation of insanity."

"Only if you did it without a chute. My skydiver, however,
ran afoul of his business partner, who'd sabotaged his chute.
His fall of thirteen thousand feet puts him at the top of my
scale. Not as far for her, but the results . . ." He glanced down,

quiet pity in his eyes. "She was a lovely young woman before that last step."

"Yeah, and lovely young women are more inclined to pills for self-termination. What can you tell me about her?"

"At this point I haven't found any injuries prior to that last step, but it's going to take more time to be certain, given the state of her."

"It's the tox I'm most interested in right now. She and the brother? Friends of Louise's."

"Ah, I'm sorry to hear that."

"Louise, Charles, and the woman's fiancé—who looks to be in the clear on first pass—are all adamant she didn't use. But the security feed on the brother's door and two wits who saw her get out of the elevator all say she looked high on something."

"I can tell you that before that last step, her liver, kidneys, lungs, heart showed no signs of abuse or disease. She wasn't a habitual user. Her stomach contents? Tea, sugar cookies— real sugar—and about two ounces of white wine."

She caught the inflection. "And?"

"The blend of tea to start." He gestured to his comp screen, brought up some sort of colored chart with a lot of words she didn't understand. "It was a chamomile base—harmless enough—but laced with other elements. Valerian, for one."

It rang a bell. "A sedative, right?"

"Yes, it can be used as one. Peyote."

"Hallucinogen. Shit. Is this like the Red Horse?"

"No. I remember that too well, and this wasn't the same. Nothing in this would trigger violence. But there are elements here and in the other stomach contents I can't identify. I've flagged it top priority for the lab, as requested. They're minute traces, nothing debilitating. It may be that the combination of them caused such violent effects."

"If we weigh in the insistence she didn't use, it leans toward her being dosed." Eve circled the body. Had she known she was falling? Eve wondered. Had she seen the ground rushing up?

"Where'd she get the scissors? That's a question. Not the sort of thing you carry around in a purse—they were huge."

"Shears, actually," he corrected. "Nine-inch blades. I did a quick exam of his wounds. And I'd agree, it's not the sort of thing most women carry."

"And no reason I can see why her brother had them sitting out where she could grab them," Eve said. "He had kitchen scissors—in a knife block—and a pair in his office, desk drawer. Which makes it lean premeditated. For somebody."

Eve turned from Darlene, stepped over to Marcus.

"She was smiling," Morris said.

"I'm sorry?"

"When she rang his buzzer. She was smiling—glassy-eyed, yeah, but smiling the way people do when they're ready to say, hey, sorry about that. And nothing I get in my read of her says she had that kind of chill. That she could stand there, smiling, with a pair of nine-inch blades in her purse she intended to jab into her brother's heart."

She shook her head. "There wasn't enough time for them to have a serious argument. Five, six minutes after she went in, he's bleeding. Then she went straight out to the terrace and off. She was dosed, that's my read on this. Who wanted her dead? Her and her brother."

"She can't tell me that."

Eve let out a half laugh. "She believed she could. She was seeing psychics, mediums, all that crapola. Parents killed in an accident last June, and she's got a secret stash of business cards and info on talking to dead people."

Now Morris smiled. "I talk to them all the time. So do you."

"Ever have them talk back?"

"In their way." He touched a hand, gently, to Darlene's shattered shoulder. "I talk to Ammarylis often."

Eve slid her hands in her pockets. Morris had lost the love of his life the previous spring. "I'm sorry, Morris."

"No, it's a comfort. I hear her voice quite clearly at times. She picked out this tie, just this morning."

Not sure how to respond, Eve said, "Okay," and made him laugh.

"I reached for a gray one, as it matched my morning mood. I heard her tell me to wear the blue—the bold blue. So I did, and it lifted away the gray. Young Darlene was looking for answers, and comfort, I suspect. There are those who can give both—and those who exploit grief and naivety."

"I'm going for door number two on that one, as the one she walked into led her to that long fall."

CHAPTER SIX

Eve was halfway through the tunnel heading out when Peabody came in.

"I'm not late!" Automatically quickening her steps in her pink, fussy-topped boots, Peabody checked her wrist unit. "I'm not late."

"No, I was early. No sign in the female vic of habitual drug use. But she had valerian, peyote, and some as yet undetermined substances in her system—mixed, it appears, with tea and cookies."

"You think somebody drugged her? But murder/suicide takes—" Peabody's eyes popped. "Shit! Red Horse."

"Not according to Morris. Not the same." And they could all be grateful for it. "Ingested, he believes," she added as they walked out to the car. "He's going to crack the whip at the lab so I don't have to. We wait on that. Where did she get the scissors—shears, Morris called them?"

"Dressmaker shears." Peabody climbed into the passenger seat, belted up.

"Dressmaker?"

"Broad term, I guess. I have a pair I use when I'm doing some sewing, or a craft project."

"I went through her residence. I sure didn't see any signs she did the crafty. No sign in the brother's place he'd have use for that sort of tool. And if it didn't belong to either of them, where did she get it?"

"Is it *it* or *them*? Shears, scissors—it's like plural, probably because of the two blades, but it's still just one tool, so . . . never mind," Peabody finished when she caught Eve's cool stare.

"We're going by to talk to Louise and the fiancé. I want to know if she owned those shears. She had to have an assistant, an admin at work. Dig it up, check with whoever that is if she had something like that, or access to it, in the office."

"How about the psychics?"

"On the slate."

"A pair of mine are in the wind. Bench warrants out on them—co-habs, partners. Fraud and theft. He'd rifle through purses and wallets, help himself, while she held a séance. They've been running that scam or others for about five years. They pack up and move off fast, pick another spot, try another variation with new names."

"Darlene ran backgrounds—not a complete idiot—so that should've popped. We're going to factor in the drugs, look for somebody who hypes the use of herbs to help open the portal."

"The portal?"

"A couple of the brochures used that one. Bridge, portal, channeling. They've got a patter, and there's a sucker born every second."

"Minute. Born every minute."

"In my world they pop out every second, and Darlene Fitzwilliams reads like one. She stabbed her brother three times in the heart, didn't waste a minute, then didn't waste a minute jumping off the terrace."

"It looks like that's what she went there to do."

"Yeah. What if she thought she was doing something else? It's not Red Horse, it's not Jess Barrow's version of mind-control VR, but we've dealt with fatal delusions before. She was smiling," Eve added. "That 'I'm sorry, and I know you'll forgive me' smile. She wasn't pissed or afraid, she wasn't nervous. A woman who's never committed a criminal act, who's lived a responsible life, goes to her brother's door intending to kill him and herself? I should be able to see some nerves. Or at the very least, resolve."

"Not if someone put the whammy on her. I know what you're going to say," Peabody continued in a rush. "There is no whammy. But there sort of is, or could be, when you factor in the drugs."

"Drugs are drugs, and not a whammy."

"They assist the whammy, that's what I'm saying. Make her more susceptible. Then?" Peabody lifted her hands, flicked her fingers out. "Whammy."

Eve disliked the idea of the whammy, but had to acknowledge it fit. "And what form would this whammy take?"

"Maybe it's like internal VR, or brainwashing. Brainwashing is a true thing. Documented."

"I'll give you brainwashing," Eve said as she looked for a parking space on Charles and Louise's pretty street. "Internal VR makes no sense. But some form of brainwashing paired with drugs. When Cerise Devane jumped off the Tattler Building a couple years ago, and I sat there on the ledge trying to talk her in, she was perfectly lucid. She knew who I was, who she was. But she was compelled to fly off that ledge—thought I'd enjoy going with her. So maybe that sort of mind-control paired with drugs, with brainwashing. Maybe a whole new fucked-up way to make people die.

"But why—that's a key. What's gained?"

"A lot of money's at stake now."

"Yeah, and greed's a favorite for a reason."

Eve looked down the street toward Louise's home when they got out of the car.

The doctor and the former licensed companion were building a good life here, a happy, settled one. On the surface, it had looked the same for Darlene and Henry. Nice house, comfortable and settled.

As shattered now as Darlene's bones.

"Sometimes people get off on fucking things up. Not much of a motive," Eve said, considering. "But some people do."

"Somebody who had a grudge against Darlene or Marcus or Henry Boyle," Peabody speculated. "Or the Fitzwilliamses in general."

"Possible," Eve said as they walked. "The parents—straight accident. I checked it in and out, so their deaths aren't connected—not in an overt way. But months later both of their children are dead, so . . ."

"A family member who wants more, taking advantage of Darlene's vulnerability."

"Yeah. You've got to look at it." She went through the little gate, down the short walk through what had been a garden in the summer, and up to the front door of the dignified brownstone.

Louise answered. She wore leggings and a black sweater—and shadows under her eyes.

"Dallas, Peabody. You have news?"

"Not really, but some questions."

"We're in the back. Charles and I cleared our schedules for the next couple of days. We want to be here for Henry. Marcus's uncle's on his way here from Europe. The family has a pied-à-terre here, and there's the estate on Long Island. Gareth and Bria's New York home," she explained. "It came to Marcus and Darlene. That was one of the things they were to talk about . . . God." She rubbed her hands over her face. "Sorry, none of that matters. Come on back."

"It all matters. Were they going to sell the Long Island house?"

"No, I don't think so. It's been in the family five, maybe six generations."

The kitchen and great room sprawled over the back of the house with views of the patio beyond through wide glass doors.

Henry pushed up from his chair, misery and hope warring on his face.

"You know what happened? You know who did this?"

"We're investigating, Mr. Boyle. We have more questions."

He sat again, shoving his hands through his hair. "Henry, just Henry. When I woke up, there was a moment I didn't remember. I could smell her hair. I could smell her. Then I remembered, and it was gone. Even that was gone."

Louise bent over, kissed the top of his head. "I'll make fresh coffee."

"I'll get it." Charles brushed a hand down her arm, crossed over into the kitchen.

"Henry," Eve began, "did Darlene own a pair of dress-maker shears?"

"Dressmaker shears? No. She didn't sew."

"Maybe she—or you—had a pair for some other project. You did a lot of the rehab on the townhouse yourself, right?"

"Yeah. I helped design it—with plenty of input from Darli. She had definite ideas about how it should look. We did some of the painting, refinished the floors—we wanted our stamp on it. But we didn't use anything like shears. The only specialty shears we have are poultry shears. Darli bought them last year when she got it into her head to try making coq au vin." His eyes lit for a moment. "That was a disaster. Fun, but . . ." The light died. "They're in the kitchen somewhere, I guess."

She'd seen a weird pair of scissors in a kitchen drawer.

"Maybe she had something like that at work."

"I can't think why. I don't see what . . ." He trailed off as Louise took his hand. Eve saw when realization hit him. "Is that . . . That's what killed Marcus."

"Would he have had a pair?"

"For *what*?" Color flooded back into his face—anger now. Denial was over. "He didn't sew. He didn't make things. For Christ's sake, I bought him a set of screwdrivers as a joke, because as smart as he was, he could barely change a light-bulb. They weren't handy people, Dallas. They were good people. Generous people. Loving. If you'd spend five minutes *listening* to me, you'd know she didn't do these things. Why aren't you—"

"Henry." Louise said it softly, drawing their joined hands up to her cheek. And he deflated.

"I'm sorry. I'm sorry. I know you have to ask questions. I just . . . I smelled her hair. Now I can't."

Charles brought in a tray with a tall white pot and five oversized white mugs. He set it down on the table, sat on the arm of Henry's chair while Louise poured the coffee.

"I didn't get into this last night," Charles said. "So I'm going to say this to you now, Henry. I've known these two women for a while now. If anything happened to Louise, I'd want these two women looking after her. I'd want them looking for the answers. Because I know they'd find them. Answers won't bring Darlene and Marcus back, but having the answers will matter to you."

Nodding, Henry took a mug from Louise and, as he had the night before, cupped it in both hands. "I'm sorry."

"Don't worry about it," Eve told him. "I went through Darlene's things. I found these hidden in a drawer in the closet."

Eve opened the file bag, took out the evidence bag, showed the cards and pamphlets.

"I don't understand. Hidden?" He took the bag, read through the plastic. "She had all these? Psychics, tarot readers? What would . . . Mediums." He closed his eyes. "She hid them from me. She couldn't talk to me about it, so she hid them from me."

"She never mentioned her interest in this area?"

"God. About a month after her parents died—she and Marcus were in grief counseling, but she stopped going. I asked her why she'd stopped, and she told me she wanted to explore another avenue. She hadn't been able to say good-bye, had questions she needed to ask them, so she'd gone to a sensitive. A friend of a friend had a friend, that sort of thing. I was . . . tolerant. I probably showed how fucking tolerant. The sensitive she went to didn't have the capabilities to communicate with the dead."

He waved his hand by his ear as he used the phrase. "But she had some recommendations. I said something like I thought grief counseling would be more beneficial than tossing time and money at some gypsy with a crystal ball.

"I don't believe in that sort of thing, so I dismissed it all. I—I dismissed *her*. So she hid all this from me because she felt I wouldn't understand or approve."

"Was she going to someone?" Louise asked.

"We're looking into that, but we do know she withdrew cash weekly from a new private account she set up a few months ago."

"A new account?"

"A new account in a different bank. Every week she withdrew nine thousand, nine hundred and ninety-nine dollars."

"Ten thousand a week?" The stricken guilt on Henry's face shifted to puzzlement. "For how long?"

"Including the withdrawal she made yesterday morning, eighteen weeks. Do you know of any reason she'd want or need that much cash?"

"No. Just no. She'd have some cash, sure, but Darlene preferred using plastic. She'd have a clear record monthly that way. She was generous, and she didn't deny herself either, but she was raised to know where her money went."

He pointed to the evidence bag. "One of them. One of them was scamming her. Scamming her." He shoved forward in his seat. "Marcus must have found out and threatened to go to the police. That could be why he wanted to hold the intervention, Louise. Because he found out some fake medium was scamming Darlene."

"Henry, he would've told me," Louise said.

"But it makes sense," Henry insisted. "It finally makes sense. This medium got into Marcus's apartment somehow, and killed Marcus. When Darlene got there, he forced her onto the terrace, pushed her over. You have to find him," he said to Eve. "You have to find whoever she was paying. That's who killed her, killed Marcus. You have to find them."

"I intend to. Do you know if she took any trips, did any traveling in these last eighteen weeks?"

"I know she didn't. She was supposed to go to East Washington last month and to London, ah, about six, eight weeks ago—both trips she sent her assistant in her place, and handled her part via 'link conference. She said she didn't want to leave home. Just couldn't leave home."

"One more thing. You've all said she didn't use—and that's bearing out—but did you notice any changes in her behavior, any signs she seemed impaired over the last weeks?"

"She started sleepwalking."

"Henry, you never told me."

He shook his head at Louise. "She asked me not to say anything. The first time—maybe three months ago—I found her downstairs, in the kitchen, middle of the night. She was making these pouring motions. I asked her what she was doing, and she looked at me. Through me, I guess, and said she had to pour the tea for the tea party. It was kind of funny, really, and she woke up as soon as I touched her. She didn't remember getting up."

He set his untouched coffee down. "A few weeks later, I woke up, heard her talking. She was crawling under the bed, calling out to someone to come back. I thought she meant her parents—that she was having a stress dream about them. I tried to coax her out at first, and she laughed. She laughed, and said she wanted to go down the rabbit hole. She wanted to see where he'd gone. She woke up again when I took her hand."

"And didn't remember?" Eve prompted.

"No. She was baffled, and a little embarrassed. It happened one more time about two weeks ago. I woke up, and she was sitting on the side of the bed staring at me. I asked her what was wrong. She said—it was like a riddle. Ah, she said: *Why is a crow like a desk?* I think."

"A raven?" Louise asked. "Why is a raven like a writing desk?"

"Yeah, that's it. A raven."

"It's from *Alice in Wonderland*, the book. And the riddle has no answer. The rabbit hole, that's an Alice reference, too. And the tea party could be the Mad Hatter's tea party."

"Was she a big fan of that story?" Eve wondered.

"I don't know," Henry told her. "Not that I know of, especially. Maybe it's something she read as a kid, or her parents read to her. So it reminded her of when they were alive, when everyone was safe? I don't know."

"All right." A question for Mira, Eve supposed, the department's head shrink. "We'll get back to you," she said as she rose.

"Isn't there something I can do?"

"We'll go be with the family," Louise told Henry. "In a little while we'll go be with the family. I'll walk you out," she said to Eve and Peabody.

Eve waited until they were out of Henry's earshot. "There were sedatives and hallucinogens in her system. A bunch of long, complicated names, and some elements we have to wait for the lab to ID. Being as you're a doctor, I'm telling you I'll clear you to talk to Morris and Berenski if you think you can be any help putting that part together."

"She might have taken a sedative, but I can promise you, she wouldn't have taken a hallucinogen, not knowingly. The sleepwalking—three incidents Henry knows of, which doesn't mean there weren't others when he didn't wake up. That's a concern. As is the money, and the fact she hid all those cards from Henry, didn't tell Marcus. She didn't tell him, or he'd have told me when he asked us to come over, possibly talk with her."

She gripped Eve's hand, then Peabody's. "Someone manipulated her, fed her drugs, caused her to kill Marcus and herself. Why?"

"Find out what she ingested. Leave the rest to us."

CHAPTER SEVEN

Considering the herbs and sleep aids, Eve made the psychic nutritionalist the first stop. Doctor Hester housed her business in a street-level shop in Soho, tucked between a health food store and a bakery.

She'd go for the bakery every time.

The reception/retail area held shelves full of apothecary-style bottles, instructional and motivational discs, candles and crystals.

The girl at the counter sported multiple visible piercings: ears, eyebrow, nose. And a tat of a winged dragon on the back of her right hand.

"A bright and healthy morning," she said, each syllable heavily weighted with the Bronx. "What service can we provide for you?"

"We're looking for Doctor Hester."

"Doctor Hester is preparing for a consultation. If you'd like to book—"

Eve pulled out her badge, held it up.

"We're fully licensed in accordance with all city, state, and federal laws."

"That's not my worry right now. Get your boss."

"Hang a minute." She slid off the stool and went through a door behind the counter area.

Eve watched Peabody ease over toward a section of metabolism boosters.

"Don't even think about it."

"Easy for you when your metabolism runs like a rabbit, and mine's a slug on Zoner. Besides, they're all natural products."

"Nature's a vicious bitch."

A woman came out—short, lavender hair that matched her eyes, a deep purple dress that flowed to her knees. Her data listed her at fifty, Eve recalled, but the perfect, unlined skin carved ten away.

"What can I do to help you?"

"What can you tell me about Darlene Fitzwilliams?"

"Ah, a tragedy. I heard a media report. You're looking for answers. Seeking death is rarely an answer."

"Was she a client?"

"I don't remember her."

"She had your business card, a pamphlet, and a bottle of your Natural Rest."

"I see. Casseopia? Would you check, please?"

Casseopia settled on the stool again, swiveled to her counter comp. "Darlene Fitzwilliams, fifty-minute introductory consult, August three of last year. No follow-up on record."

"Would you pull my notes on that?" Hester gave Eve a quiet smile. "A single consult. It's difficult to remember the details."

"I figured you'd . . . intuit that sort of thing."

The smile never wavered. "My gift is one that intuits, as you say, the inner person. Such as . . ." She turned to Peabody. "You shouldn't worry so much about your weight. Good nutrition, regular exercise, of course, but you have a very healthy, robust body. Your perception of your body is harsher than the reality."

"Really?"

"Natural metabolic boosters such as chen pi, sheng jiang,

rou gui can be helpful. But you're young, healthy, and active. It's the sweet tooth," she added with a knowing smile, "that challenges you."

"Your notes." Casseopia offered Hester a handheld.

"Thank you. Oh yes, so sad," she murmured as she read. "The loss of her parents, so sudden and tragic. She wasn't sleeping or eating well—all that stress and grief. I did recommend a sleep aid, and a nutrition plan, and suggested additional sessions to work on emotional healing and acceptance. But . . ."

Hester lowered the handheld. "I remember her now. She wanted to contact her parents."

"Her dead parents."

"I understand the skepticism. Contact with those who have moved on in the cycle is not my gift."

"Your pamphlet says otherwise."

Hester shook her head. "I can assist, and there are certain herbs and practices that can open and enhance the gift if one has its root. I didn't sense that root in her, and couldn't ethically encourage her. She took the aid, and the plan, but didn't contact me again."

"She came in a couple more times," Casseopia said. "I checked for you. She bought more Natural Rest in October and again in December. Purchased some candles and some bath salts."

"I wish I could have given her more, but I didn't have the answers she looked for. I'm afraid I don't have the ones you seek either."

"Anything in here that causes hallucinations?"

"I don't traffic in hallucinogens, even natural ones. I believe reality is to be embraced."

"The Natural Rest stuff, could it cause them in combination with other herbs?"

"I would have given her a list of herbs, foods, medications to avoid while taking the product. I wouldn't have recommended it if she had been a proponent of altered-reality substances. She was clean, Lieutenant, as both of you are."

"If you can tell that by looking, we could use you in Illegals testing."

"That's not my path. I hope you find the answers you need on yours."

"She seemed pretty straight," Peabody commented when they walked out.

"For a psychic nutritionalist. No buzz anyway, but we'll see what the lab says about the sleep aid. Meanwhile, we've got a couple more right in this area, then one in the East Village. And I want to talk to the lawyer. See if you can get her to come in, save us a trip uptown."

THEY INTERVIEWED THREE PSYCHICS—WAKING UP ONE WHO claimed to commune with spirits only between the hours of midnight and five a.m.

"Nothing there." Eve got back in the car, aimed it toward Cop Central.

"The second one we talked to? Mikhal Lombrowski? He was the real deal. The others, maybe they had something, but mostly they were looking to score. He was genuine."

"Why him?"

"My dad's a sensitive, and he kind of reminded me of my father. He wanted to help her—that's what came through for me—but he couldn't give her what she wanted, so like she did with Hester, she cherry-picked, and moved on."

"I tend to agree. It's also telling that she went to all of these before she started making those weekly withdrawals. We need to find the one she settled on."

As she pulled into Central's garage, Peabody glanced at her signaling 'link. "Huh. The lawyer's on her way in. We don't get that kind of result often."

"Set us up a conference room and give Dickhead a goose on the tox."

"You want me to goose Dickhead?"

Eve thought of the chief lab tech. "It'll throw him off coming from you instead of me. Maybe we'll get happy results there, too."

She needed to set up the board and book in her office, write everything up.

And if she didn't have the tox results within an hour, she'd personally go to the lab and sit on Dick Berenski's egg-shaped head until he produced.

She turned in to Homicide, noted all her detectives and cops were present. "Is there no crime today?"

Baxter, feet on his desk, a 'link at his ear, grinned at her. "Tying one up now, LT. The asshole Trueheart and I took down bright and early this morning's down in booking."

She glanced at Trueheart, who'd soon be ceremoniously awarded his gold detective's shield. Obviously Baxter had dumped the paperwork on his partner.

She glanced across the bull pen to where Santiago sat morosely under a big black cowboy hat with a shiny silver band. "How much longer do you have to wear that?"

"A bet's a bet." Behind him, Carmichael smiled smugly. "And he lost."

"I went double or nothing with her—it's a sickness."

She decided not to comment on Jenkinson's tie, because it looked like an explosion of radioactive waste. Instead she escaped to her office, set up her board. Armed with coffee, she sat at her desk and wrote everything up, in detail, adding a query to Mira.

Then, with more coffee, she put her boots on the desk, her eyes on the board and let her brain play with theories. And, still thinking, she pulled up an incoming from Morris.

"Dallas."

She held up a finger to hold Peabody off, finished reading. "Morris found traces of peyote, cannabis, phencyclidine, and mint inside the female vic's nasal passages, sinuses."

"She inhaled it?"

"Inhaled this—he believes in vapor form. Ingested more in liquid form. What about the lab?"

"Berenski says he'll have the final when he has it—then I played the innocent underling card, said how you were all over my ass, complimented that weird facial hair he's been growing lately. He said to give it another twenty."

"Good job. If she wasn't taking this crap voluntarily, some-body was doing a hell of a number on her. Morris confirms, even without the elements we haven't nailed down, she'd have been in a euphoric and altered state."

"Maybe she didn't know what she was inhaling and ingesting, or maybe whoever mixed all this up told her it was what she needed to communicate with her parents."

"Either way, whoever gave it to her is responsible for two deaths."

"Her lawyer's here—the family lawyer, I mean. I had her taken to the conference room."

"Let's go dig out who stood to gain."

Gia Gregg sat ramrod-straight at the conference table, talking on an ear 'link. She gave Eve a nod and continued her conversation. She wore a black suit, sharp as a scalpel, and her hair in a dark crown of tight curls with shimmering red highlights. It suited her coffee-regular skin and her cool green eyes.

She completed her conversation, then removed the ear 'link and slipped it into a pocket of her jacket.

"I'm sorry. It's a difficult and busy morning."

"We appreciate you coming in."

"Sean Fitzwilliams has arrived in New York. I spoke with him before I came in, and he instructed me to give you my full cooperation. The family is, understandably, devastated. And they want answers, Lieutenant, Detective, because no one who knew Darlene believes she did what the media is gleefully claiming."

She took out a notebook, set it on the table. "I intend to take careful notes of our conversation, as I and my clients also want answers. Have you any leads?"

"Our investigation is active and ongoing." Eve sat, took the lawyer's measure. A solid rep, Roarke had told her, and he would know. Her own research indicated Gia Gregg had represented the rich and richer with a steady hand for more than three decades.

"At approximately eight thirty last evening, Darlene Fitzwilliams entered her brother's apartment. Within minutes she stabbed him three times in the chest with a pair of nine-inch shears and immediately walked out to the apartment's terrace and jumped to her death."

"I don't believe that."

"It's fact. However," she added before Gia could protest, "our investigation leads us to believe Miss Fitzwilliams was under the influence of a hallucinogenic cocktail."

"Darli— Miss Fitzwilliams did not use. In fact, part of her work in the Fitzwilliams Foundation supported rehabilitation and education centers for illegals abuse."

"The final toxicology report is still forthcoming, however, the preliminary has already identified several substances in her system, including valerian, diazepam, peyote, phencyclidine, and cannabis."

Gregg's eyes widened at the length of the list. "Then someone dosed her without her knowledge or consent."

"That may be. If she consented, it's highly probable she did so in the belief the substances would aid her in communicating with her parents. Were you aware she'd been seeking the help of psychics and mediums for that purpose?"

"Not until this morning. I've also spoken with Henry, her fiancé. He told me what you found in her closet, and about the bank account, the withdrawals. Someone used her grief, someone did this to her and Marcus."

"At this point, with the evidence we have, I agree with you."

Gia's shoulders relaxed for an instant. "We need to issue a media release. Darlene's reputation is being—"

"We're not going to do that. Her reputation isn't my concern. Finding whoever provided her with illegals, whoever convinced her to take them or gave them to her without her consent is. Who stands to gain by their deaths?"

"Both Darlene and Marcus leave a considerable estate in their own rights, and have numerous beneficiaries. The foundation itself would be the largest for both."

"Who gets the biggest piece of the pie?"

"Before their parents' death, we had a meeting—the four of them—regarding updating their estate plans, beneficiaries. Darlene chose to leave ten million to Henry on the event of her death, as well as her share of the home they purchased."

"Funny he didn't mention that."

"He doesn't know. Darlene was also firm on that stipulation. He's a proud man. He was raised by a single mother who worked very hard to support him and his sister. He was able to go to college and grad school because of her hard work, and his own. Scholarships, interning. He made his own. And you can trust that when it became apparent he and Darlene were serious, her parents did a thorough background check on him." Gia sighed. "He's a good man. I'm very fond of him myself. He loved her. The money? It didn't play a part for him—in fact, it was an obstacle initially. I'm also aware he works for your husband, who would also have done a thorough background on him. Henry wouldn't work for Roarke in such a key position if he weren't ethical and clean."

"She had a lot more than the ten."

"Yes. There are individual bequests to family members, most sentimental rather than monetary. Marcus, for instance, left Darlene his apartment. There's a difficult area here, as he predeceased her."

"By a couple minutes."

"By seconds would amount to the same, legally. He left most of his property to her, so—though I will study on this—it appears this will flow into her estate. As I said, the bulk goes to the foundation, and to individual organizations the foundation supports. Darlene earmarked several for single bequests or for continuing grants."

She took a disc from her bag, offered it. "I have a list for you, though I can't see how it applies. Darlene researched and investigated all grant requests. She, Marcus, Sean, and two other foundation officers would then review and vote on the grants."

"They—these officers, staff—draw a salary?"

"Yes."

"Who runs the show now?"

"Sean would be acting president, and acting CEO of the business. I can also tell you these aren't positions he wants. He and his wife are well settled in Europe. His youngest child is in school there, his oldest—with his first wife—lives minutes away with his own wife and children. The loss of Darlene and Marcus is shattering, and so close to the loss of Gareth and Bria. It's going to take time and work to restructure the positions, the responsibilities."

"Best guess?"

"They'll try to keep it in the family. I would recommend they divide both Marcus's and Darlene's positions. Several candidates stand out, but none of them would kill for the job."

"People kill for all sorts of reasons," Eve said. "Maybe one of them told her about a medium, guided her where they wanted her to go. Who was she close to? Who would she tell when she decided to go this route?"

"Marcus, and obviously he didn't know. Henry, the same. And Louise Dimatto, whom I know you're aware was a close family friend. Darlene had other friends, of course, but those three were her foundation. If she told none of them, she told no one. I wish she had. I wish she'd talked to me. We had a good personal relationship."

Tears swam into her eyes, and she paused for a moment until she'd controlled them.

"If she'd come to me, I might have been able to help her. I could have used my resources to find her the right person, someone gentle and kind as well as gifted."

"So she could talk to her dead parents."

"While I may be a bone-deep skeptic on such matters, I discount nothing. But I know this: If she'd been able to reach them, they'd have told her to move on with her life, and they'd never have suggested she use drugs. So I have to conclude she didn't reach them."

"We're going to agree on that."

"The family requested I ask when they can have Marcus and Darlene."

"We'll release the bodies as soon as we can."

"Sean—particularly—would like to see them. Henry, he needs to see Darlene."

"No, he doesn't." Eve gentled her tone, just a little. "No one needs to see Darlene as she is now. Trust me on that."

"They'll insist."

"Let me talk to the ME, see if anything can be done to . . . minimize the damage."

"That's very kind of you, and much appreciated."

"You're going to be with the family. If you get any sense, hear anything that leads you to believe someone played a part, I want to hear it."

"You can depend on it. I won't, but I also won't withhold any information that pertains to their deaths. They mattered to me, Lieutenant, as much more than clients."

CHAPTER EIGHT

Obviously complimenting Dickhead's excuse for a goatee worked, as Eve had his report in her inbox when she returned to her office.

The minute she read it, she sent a copy to Mira, then headed out.

"Dallas?" Peabody called from her desk. "Are we back in the field?"

"I need Mira first. Work out the best route to hitting the rest of the psychic list. I'll be back in ten."

She had to get through Mira's snarly admin, but she needed answers. Louise was an option, she thought as she jumped in an elevator despite the crowd inside. She'd given Louise the data mostly to keep her busy, but she'd be a good source.

Still, she was strictly medical, and Mira was both a medical and a head doctor. And a superior profiler.

By the time Eve made it to Mira's office, she was ready to attack. It came as a slight letdown to see the admin's desk unoccupied and Mira's office door open.

"Did someone slay the dragon?"

Mira glanced over. "She's still at lunch. I've only gotten back myself now. Your toxicology report—"

"Have you read it?"

"I just reviewed it. Sit."

"No, I'm revved up, need to get back in the field. That combination inside her—inhaled, ingested—that's extreme."

"Yes. Even in these minute amounts, and particularly when combined with regular use of this sleep aid. The aid itself is perfectly harmless, and potentially beneficial, but no sensitive, no legitimate one, would combine these other substances, even not knowing the client was taking a valerian-based holistic."

"She'd hallucinate."

"She would have been very susceptible to hallucinations, yes. I'm having tea."

"No, please. I mean go ahead, but I don't have time for it."

In sapphire blue heels to complement her winter white suit, Mira ordered blue tea from her AutoChef.

"Not only would she have experienced an altered state— a sensation of extreme well-being—but a kind of spacial confusion. I'm surprised she was able to navigate to her brother's apartment."

"The doorman said she walked to the building. Maybe whoever gave her this crap transported her close to the building."

"I don't believe she could have driven herself in this state. Eve, I've never seen this combination of drugs—herbal and chemical, but with some of the derivatives sometimes used to aid in hypnosis, to relax the patient, help open them to suggestion. Some practitioners use small doses to aid in weight loss, rehabilitation of substance abuse, even anger management. But this combination?" Mira took a sip of tea from one of her delicate china cups. "I would want to do a full analysis myself, but I believe this would have left her open to post-suggestions with hallucinations and altered perceptions. The addition of phencyclidine?"

Eve wasn't a chemistry whiz, but she was a cop. "That's the base element for Zeus."

"Yes, and while this amount and combination isn't Zeus, it could cause someone to harm themselves. To burn themselves—even set fire to a building mistaking a flame for a flower, for instance. Or cut themselves believing a knife was a bar of soap. To fall, seeing a drop off a building as a set of stairs."

"She stabbed her brother three times. She might have thought she was giving him a love tap. She fell fifty-two floors, maybe thinking she'd sprout wings and fly." This fit, Eve thought. This worked for her, both brain and gut. "We may never know, but it's pretty damn clear somebody fucked her up, and if she needed help getting to her brother's place, they wanted him dead, too."

Nodding, Mira brushed back a curve of rich brown hair. "Look for someone who's skilled. This combination took time and practice to perfect. Someone also gifted. It's very likely they are indeed a sensitive, as they read this victim very well. They also gained her trust, and I would say gained it quickly.

"It's most likely a male—she would see a male as authoritative, experienced. Probably between forty and sixty. He's experienced, he's studied, and she wouldn't have been as susceptible to a younger man."

"Misses father, depends on older brother."

"Yes. Your killer is a sociopath who exploits his own gift. He's organized and intelligent, and enjoys having control over others, and looks for gain. He likes to live well. He may also be a psychopath, finding pleasure in causing death, yet he has no direct hand in the killing."

"I found pieces of what the lab's confirmed was a lapel recorder near her body."

"Ah." Mira nodded again. "No direct hand in the killing, but a desire to watch. To kill, essentially, without being there or getting his hands bloody. He's unlikely a physical sort. A manipulator."

"She was sleepwalking."

Mira frowned over her tea. "The sleep aid should have prevented that."

"The three times her fiancé found her at it, she was doing

or saying weird things. Pouring tea for a party, down in the kitchen; crawling under the bed saying she needed to go down the rabbit hole. Sitting on the bed, waking him up with a riddle about a raven and a writing desk."

"*Alice in Wonderland*."

"That's what Louise said."

"Interesting." Mira sat back in her blue scoop chair, sipped more tea. "A sort of test, I'd think, laying a base for the post-hypnotic suggestions. An interesting choice. A kind of surreal story filled with a young girl's bizarre adventures. Some interpret it as drug-based—the hookah-smoking caterpillar, the mushrooms that cause Alice to grow, and so on. He may be an addict himself. A combination of psychic abilities and hallucinogens would give him a heady sense of power."

"He kills—or rather causes another to kill because he can, and because it gives him a sense of power. Watches, from his . . . client's point-of-view—that gives him a front-row seat."

"Yes, and Alice again. Perhaps delight; a childish delight in watching the murder and suicide he's manipulated."

"He's probably done it before."

"It worked so seamlessly, really, it's difficult to believe this was his first."

"Then I'd better find him before he sets the next one up." Heading back, she switched from elevator to glide, moving briskly, and spotted Roarke the minute she turned in to Homicide. He sat on the corner of Jenkinson's desk holding a conversation that had her detective grinning.

When he saw her, he rose, strolled over. "Lieutenant."

"Are you here to report a crime?"

"No. I had a meeting nearby and took a chance my wife might be about. And here she is."

"Not for long." But she considered her options. "How much time do you have?"

"That would depend."

"If you've got an hour, maybe two, I'd split Darlene's list with Peabody."

"Then I've got an hour, maybe two."

"Good. Hold on a minute." She stepped over to Peabody's desk. "See if Feeney can spare McNab. If so, take him with you and check out the last half of Darlene's list. If McNab can't do it, take Uniform Carmichael. Roarke and I will work on the first half."

"Sure. I'll tag him now."

"McNab or Carmichael, Peabody. Good eyes and experience. We're looking for a sociopath with at least some psychic abilities, one who may be an addict. An interest or obsession with *Alice in Wonderland* is likely, so look for any sign of that. Psychopathic pathology's also very probable."

"Solid backup because he could try to put the whammy on me."

"Solid backup." Eve left it at that, turned away, and noted that Roarke must have slipped into her office and back, as he held her coat.

"Thanks. Report after every meet," she told Peabody, and strode out, swinging on the coat as she walked.

"You probably know more about this *Alice in Wonderland* stuff than I do."

"I know the story," Roarke said. "I've read the books, and seen a variety of vid interpretations."

"Like I said, you know more than I do, so you'll be handy. The person we're after likely knows a lot about it, too. You might catch something I'd miss."

"Such as a white rabbit or mad hatter?"

"If you say so. I'll drive," she said when they reached the garage.

"You don't know the story?" he asked her.

Her childhood hadn't been prone to bedtime stories. Then again, she thought, neither had Roarke's.

"Some kid falls down a rabbit hole, which makes no sense because rabbits are a lot smaller than kids. Weird stuff happens."

"It's considerably more entertaining than that. Though it was written as a children's story, it has fascinating symbolism, intrigue, social commentary."

"Whatever it's got, somebody who may have psychic

abilities and certainly has access to and knowledge of hallucinogens is using that knowledge, and those possible abilities, to kill. And at least with Darlene Fitzwilliams, some of this Alice stuff played in. It's unlikely she was the first," Eve continued as she navigated traffic. "But I can't run like crimes. I can't know if it's a murder/suicide trend, just murder, just suicide. Or maybe ruled accidental when somebody walked in front of a maxibus because they thought they were chasing that white rabbit thing."

"People will ruin everything, won't they? A beloved story becomes twisted to kill."

"Something strikes you Alice-like, let me know." Unwilling to take the time to hunt up street parking, she pulled into a lot. "There's two within walking distance."

They got nothing from either, then backtracked to the parking lot. Eve headed across town to the East Village.

"It strikes me how much of your day is routinely spent doing this. Talking to people who turn out to have no connection to your case or who may give you another line to tug."

"That's why they call it a job. This next one? Goes by the name of Madam Dupres. She even had her name changed legally. But she started out as Evelyn Basset, born in Yonkers, fifty-four years ago. Some twenty-five years back, she had a pretty thriving business."

This time Eve hit on a street spot and zipped into it at an angle and speed that had Roarke's eyebrows lifting.

"Had a rep, had a screen show, made a bunch of money, and lost it all when her husband-slash–business manager ran off with her assistant. He'd also gotten her to sign over the bulk of her earnings along the way, so he could—legally, if not ethically—walk away with the dough."

"I imagine her reputation suffered."

"You got that." Eve stepped onto the sidewalk with him, gestured north. "Who wants to shell out for a psychic who doesn't know her spouse is screwing around on the side and who's going to end up leaving her broke? Part of her thing was connecting people with dead loved ones."

Eve stopped in front of a Ukrainian restaurant, nodded at

the sign on a skinny doorway. "Now she runs her shtick out of a second-floor apartment over this place." Eve pressed the buzzer, mildly surprised when it buzzed back seconds later to unlock the narrow door. "The thing is," she said as they went into a dim stairwell, "she's clean. No criminal, no litigations I could find. In fact, she worked with cops numerous times in her heyday. Specialized in finding missing kids—the reports claim she was instrumental in locating a number of them. So I figure, if Darlene did her due diligence, this is one she would have come to."

The entrance to apartment 200 boasted a bold red door and a brass knocker in the shape of a dragon. Eve took the dragon by the tail and knocked.

The door opened.

The name had given Eve an image of turbans and colorful scarves, but Madam Dupres stood about five-foot-five in a simple dress as boldly red as the door with her dark curling hair loose and unstyled. A number of large and glittery rings adorned her fingers, so that was something.

"Lieutenant Dallas. Roarke."

"That's right."

She smiled as she stepped back. "No mind reading necessary. I recognize you. Please come in."

The apartment—surprisingly spacious; Eve saw it ran the length and width of the restaurant below—reflected a quiet taste and elegance. A collection of crystal balls in a wall case caught the sunlight and seemed attractive rather than occult.

"I don't read anyone without permission," she said. "So discourteous. You'll have to tell me what I can do for you, but first, please sit. It's coffee you prefer, isn't it? I'd be happy to serve you."

"We're fine." Eve took a seat in a high-backed chair with curved legs while Roarke took its twin, and the madam settled on a long, low couch.

"I've read of your work—both of you—and very much enjoyed Nadine Furst's book on your investigation of the Icoves. It's my sense you don't generally seek the services I provide."

"We're here on official business. Did you know Darlene Fitzwilliams?"

"Fitzwilliams?" Madam Dupres's dark eyes narrowed. Her index finger went to her right temple, pressed. "Darlene. Why?"

"Last night she stabbed her brother to death, then jumped off his fifty-second-floor terrace to her own death."

"Death? Two deaths?" Now all four fingers pressed, and her color drained. "What time? Could you tell me what time they died?"

"Between eight and eight thirty last night."

"I . . . I've been in meditation. I was disturbed, felt something dark crowding me. Shortly after eight last night."

"Is that so?"

"I dreamed of death—a waking dream—so much blood, such grief. There was no ignoring such grief, so I went into meditation, inside a circle of light."

"Are you going to tell me you know why Darlene killed her brother and herself?"

"Fitzwilliams?" Pain clouded her eyes. "I don't . . . Was she— I'm sorry, terrible headache." She got to her feet. "It came on so quickly. I need to take a blocker. I want to help, but . . . She was young, wasn't she? Very beautiful and young and in love and sad and— I'm sorry. If you'll excuse me for just a moment."

She walked away quickly, turned in to a doorway.

"Meditation, circle of light." Eve pushed to her feet. "She knows something. Your bullshit meter's as tuned as mine. What's your take?"

"The pain was real."

"Yeah." Frustrated, Eve jammed her hands in her pockets. "Yeah, it was. We'll give her a minute. There's something . . . She avoided a yes or no. Did you know her or not? And she damn well did. People don't go pale and sick over the death of a stranger."

Impatient to get back to it, Eve looked around. "The place looks normal, quiet and normal. Where's all her trappings?"

She circled the room, glancing at crystals, candles, then angled to look into a neat kitchen with white cabinets.

"She's taking too long."

Suspicion rose up to twine with impatience. Eve crossed to the doorway, saw the pretty bedroom beyond. Across from it another doorway opened to a kind of cozy sitting room, with dozens of white candles.

Circle of light, she thought, and started to step into the bedroom, to call again, when she heard the sound of breaking glass.

She charged in, tried the closed door, found it locked. As Roarke rushed in behind her, Eve kicked the door once, cursed, kicked it a second time.

Dupres lay on the white tiled floor of the bathroom, blood pooling around her from the deep gash in her thigh.

"Call for a bus!" Eve shouted.

Grabbing towels, she kicked the shards of broken mirror out of her way, crouched down to bind the towels on the wound.

"She's bleeding out—gashed the femoral artery. For Christ's sake."

"On their way." Roarke took another towel, wrapped it around the deep gash in Dupres's hand.

Dupres's eyes opened, stared into Eve's. "Beware the Mad Hatter."

"Who is that? Give me a name."

"Lies, all lies. All his words, even his name. Dark is his truth. Death is his joy. I sent her to him. I sent her to her death. He'll seek yours now. Beware the Mad Hatter," she repeated, and the eyes staring into Eve's died.

CHAPTER NINE

Having someone die under her hands pissed her off. Having someone die under her hands during a damn interview added a whole new level to pissed.

She watched the MTs pronounce Dupres and wished she had something handy to kick into pulp.

"There was nothing you could have done," Roarke said.

"I let her walk off, walk out of sight to get a damn blocker."

"The pain was real," he reminded her. "You'd need to be psychic yourself to have known she intended to kill herself."

"Yeah." Eve loosened the fists she'd balled into the pockets. "The pain was real," she repeated, and yanked out her 'link to contact Morris.

"I'm sending one in to you."

"I'm sorry to hear that."

"Self-termination—broke a mirror, jabbed a shard into her femoral artery."

"That would do it."

"She had a severe and sudden headache a minute before she did it. It came on during the interview when I asked her about Darlene Fitzwilliams. I think we're dealing with the same thing here. Drugs and mind-control. Some sort of post-hypnotic trigger. Look for any similarities with Darlene Fitz-williams, will you?"

"I will. Mira might be helpful here, as she's trained in hypnotherapy."

"I've talked to her, and will again. Do me a solid, send the dead wagon." She gave him the address, signed off. Then immediately tagged Peabody to have her and McNab report to her.

"Dupres was a link," Eve said to Roarke. "We're going to turn this place inside out, find out where Dupres sent Darlene Fitzwilliams. Mad Hatter, my ass."

"But you're considering the fact both dead women made references to *Alice in Wonderland*."

"Yeah, yeah."

"I'll start on the electronics while you consider."

"McNab can handle it. This is going to take longer than the hour or two I asked for."

"She died on my watch as well, Eve." Roarke took her hand briefly. "I'm fully in it now."

Understanding, she started her search in the bedroom.

Dupres had a conservative wardrobe—nothing extravagant, but good fabrics, good quality. The same ran true with jewelry, accessories. Nothing there shouted mind-reading psychic who talks to dead people.

No sign, Eve noted, anyone else had spent any time there—no sex toys or enhancements, no men's belongings. No women's belongings, she noted, other than what appeared to belong to Dupres.

Oddly, in the underwear drawer, like at Darlene's, she found a small notebook. A paper book with a good leather binding. She frowned as she paged through, and was still standing there reading when Peabody stepped in.

"The morgue's right behind me," she said, and glanced into the bathroom. "That's a lot of blood."

"Gashing the femoral artery will empty you out pretty fast."

"Why kill herself if she'd drugged Darlene into murder/ suicide? Did she try to . . . you know?"

"Put the whammy on me? No. And I don't think she killed herself because she worked Darlene into killing. I think the same person who did that, did this."

"But . . . you were right here. Was she high?"

"Didn't appear to be, and that's troubling. But it fits for me."

"What's that?"

"It's like a diary, but not. Just observations, thoughts, little poems. She mentions bad dreams, headaches, memory blanks. Sleepwalking."

"Like Darlene."

" 'The Mad Hatter and the March Hare hold their tea parties, but the tea is blood. The Dormouse sits in the corner, counting the money.' What's a dormouse?"

"I don't know, exactly. It's another character in the story."

"Figured. And here, the last thing she wrote. 'Day and night, darkness bright, he has the sight and feeds it on their sorrow. Bright and mad, deceiving sad, take what they had and bring them death tomorrow.' "

Eve glanced up. "Then she writes 'WHY CAN'T I RE-MEMBER?' in all caps, and circles it again and again."

"So he used her, probably to solicit rich clients—the dormouse counting the money—and somehow blocked her memory of it."

"Something like that," Eve agreed. "But the keys here are 'he.' So it's a man, like Mira predicted, and more, there are three. If we take this literally. Mad Hatter, March Hare, Dormouse. Three of them working this."

"It's weird to the mega. Where do you want me to start?"

"Take the kitchen," Eve told her as the morgue team did their work. "We're going to send samples of any tea, coffee, herbs—hell, pretty much any consumables. And we'll get the sweepers in here, in case there's anything."

McNab, who could've passed for a weird psychic in his sunburst shirt and the hip-swinging vest covered with neon blue stars, came to the doorway, then sidestepped for the morgue team and body bag.

"We may have something."

"What something?" Eve demanded.

"We found a memo cube in the room across the hall. A recording. Roarke says it's your vic's voice. It's weird, like she was in a trance."

Eve nudged by him and went into the room where Roarke stood working his PPC.

"Her circle of light," he said.

"Yeah, I saw that. This cube?"

When he nodded, she picked it up and activated it.

"In my circle the door is closed. Nothing passes through. Safe and quiet mind, safe and quiet mind. Too much blood! Too much. What have I done? Help me see. Blue smoke, blue light. Too many voices. Quiet, be still."

Just breathing now, long, deep, a shuddering breath, and more steady ones.

"Blue smoke, blue light. See through it. See true. Bright, bright, bright. Not true. A lie, another lie. I am not weak."

Weeping now, the words thick with tears.

"I found my strength after the lies. These are just more. I didn't see. I didn't know. Bright. It hurts to see. It hurts to know. Blood on my hands. So much blood. Bright blood. A lie, see through the lie to truth. Simon. Zacari. Roland. Carroll, and more and more. One truth in the lies. Where is the truth? All are death. That is the truth.

"Now rest, just rest, mind, body, spirit. Know his truth is death, and don't follow."

"Peabody, run those names and all combinations. Simon, Zacari, Roland, Carroll—add *bright* into them. She says bright too often for it not to mean something."

"I already am." Roarke continued to work his PPC. "Give us a few minutes here, it's a dicey job on a handheld."

"McNab, tag Feeney. Let him know we need the lab. It'll go faster at Central."

"Considerably," Roarke agreed.

"We'll load up her electronics, take them with us. Let's

move. Peabody, let Dawson know the sweepers need to send samples of anything she'd have consumed to the lab. Officer . . ." She read the name tag of the uniform on the door. "Kinsey. Hold here for the sweepers."

"Yes, sir."

They hauled down Dupres's tablets, 'links, desk comp.

"Roarke, narrow the search, crossing the names with psychic and/or medium work and licenses."

"I didn't just come down in the last shower of rain," he replied, and slid into the passenger seat.

"What does that even mean?" She gauged the traffic, cursed it, then shot away from the curb. She felt the first real crack in the case, needed to widen it—and snarled at the fat, sticky knot of vehicles in her way.

"I'm going in hot," she announced, hitting lights and sirens.

In the back, Peabody said, "Oh boy," and clamped her hand on McNab's. Focused on the work, Roarke simply tightened his seat belt without glancing up.

"I might have something on Zacari. One Anton Zacari, lived and worked as a spiritual consultant in Prague from 2049 to 2052. Closed up shop, relocated to Kashmir."

"Where?"

"Himalayas, darling. And there he went missing on a mountain trek, and is presumed dead."

"The dead don't kill." Judging an opening, she punched for more speed. "Got an image of him?"

"I do. Age forty-eight when he dropped off the grid. No marriage, no co-habs, no criminal. Hmmm."

"Try an image match with the other names," she began, then caught his quiet stare as she hit a fast vertical to circumvent vehicles that wouldn't get the hell out of her way. "Fine. If you're so damn smart, why aren't you a cop?"

"You've just answered your own question. Image matches will go smoother and faster in the lab, but I've got something here on Roland. Angus Roland, spiritualist, Edinburgh, 2045 to 2048. Relocated to Istanbul, where he drowned in a boating incident in the Sea of Marmara. Body never recovered. Isn't that interesting?"

"It's bollocks, that's what it is. Image?"

"At a glance, no match, but . . . with a bit of work. Ages are wrong by a few years, but only a few."

"Changes appearance and ID, fakes death after a relocation. The world's his sick playground." Eve ignored the wide eyes of a pedestrian foolish enough to try to beat the sirens, swung hard to miss said idiot, then zipped back to avoid a collision with an oncoming Rapid Cab.

"Stop muttering, Peabody," Eve ordered.

"She's praying, Dallas." She caught McNab's grin in the rearview. "This is some wicked ride."

She hit vertical again, did a kind of midair, two-wheeler turn to take the corner tight enough to have the glida-cart operator doing business on it scramble back.

"Wasn't that close," Eve said under her breath. "Glorified grifter, that's what he is. If the other names don't run the same, I'll kiss McNab's bony white ass."

From the backseat, McNab snickered. "How can I lose?"

The comment pulled a reluctant laugh out of Eve as she arrowed toward Central's garage. And with a scream of tires and a squeal of brakes, she shot into her slot.

"Thank you, Jesus, Buddha, and the goddess Morgana." On shaky knees, Peabody climbed out. "I covered my bets."

"Lab." Eve doubled-timed it to the elevator. "Three or four years in one location. How long's he been in New York? How long does he stay after he scores?"

She rode up to her level, cops and staff and civilians clambering on and off. "I need five in my office." She bulled her way off. "I'll be right behind you."

"She needs to put Dupres on her board," Roarke commented. "Acknowledgment."

"We'll get him." Since Eve wasn't there, McNab wound his arm around Peabody's shoulders, gave her a squeeze. "On the scent now."

When they got off and turned toward the lab, e-geek Callendar crossed paths. She wore a hat with snowmen dancing around the brim and a scarf of purple, yellow, and green in lightning bolt stripes—both courtesy of Peabody's talent with yarn.

"Yo. Heard you caught a hot one."

"Scalding. You out?"

"Was. Scalding?"

"Total," McNab confirmed. "Multi-search, single name cross, global, image matches with variance. Background, deep, on the bogus front—missing and presumed."

"True? Psychic deal, yeah?"

"True. Fresh DB on the slab."

"Want assist?"

"Won't say no."

"All in." She pivoted, walked with them to the lab. She gave Roarke a sunny smile. "Dallas?"

"Had to make a stop. She'll be along."

"Chill."

When they reached the lab, Callendar pulled off her green coat with its purple sleeves and unwound her scarf. Under it she sported a cap-sleeve sweater in puce over a long-sleeve turquoise tee, lime green baggies, and buttercup yellow knee boots.

Between her and McNab it looked as if neon had invaded the planet. Then Feeney stepped in wearing his habitual shit brown jacket and wrinkled beige shirt. The contrast only made the neon glow more fiercely.

He scratched his fingers through his wiry mop of silver-threaded ginger and studied the transported electronics with his baggy, basset hound eyes.

"Callendar, let's you and me give these toys a what-for while the others get set up."

"Aye, aye, Cap'n."

Roarke found it surprisingly easy to fall into work rhythm with a lab of cops. He shifted away from that work for a moment and ordered three large pizzas with a variety of toppings. His wife would mutter about it, but she'd eat.

In the shorthand geek-speak that made Eve's eyes glass over, he and McNab worked out a plan of attack and, with Peabody on auxiliary, settled into it.

Through the glass walls of the lab, Eve noted the sharp and colorful Callendar chair dancing as she worked beside Feeney. Peabody huddled over a comp while McNab stood, that bony white ass tick-tocking, and Roarke—suit jacket shed, sleeves rolled up, hair back in a leather thong—sat on a stool dancing his fingers over a keyboard and a touch screen.

She stepped in and frowned at the chatter. Why couldn't geeks just speak regular English?

"Status?"

"We're running deep on your vic's e's," Callendar told her. "In case something's buried or pinched."

"Doing background, underlayment," Peabody said, "on the two Roarke pulled."

"Image matches on auto." Roarke continued to work. "Analysis of facial elements, probability run on possible re-construction."

"Got reports on the missings and presumed," McNab added. "And jiving into search and cross on remaining names."

"And there. See it?"Roarke asked.

McNab shifted toward Roarke. "And there's the bingo. Collect the stuffed elephant."

"Carroll, Niles George, licensed psychic and hypnotherapist, London, 2039 through 2044. You could toss this image in the mix, Ian."

"All about it."

"A bit of trouble here."

"Yeah, I see that." Eve stepped closer to read the data on the screen. "Had a client walk out of his place, go to her son's place, and, Jesus, set fire to it. The son, his wife, and two children got out. The client didn't."

She felt the pieces fall into place as she read on. "Hallucinogens found in her system. By the time they traced her steps back to this Carroll—and you have to wonder about anybody with three first names—he was in the wind. He could blow pretty far with the three-quarters of a million he'd pulled from the dead client over six months. Some other clients dumped another five million and change on him during his London stint."

"See here?" Roarke brought up another report. "The son was taking legal steps to take over his mother's finances, citing mental and emotional instability."

"Which gives Carroll—or whatever the hell name—motive to get rid of the son, and the client while he's at it. Drain them, eliminate them, and blow. He doesn't just blow, doesn't just shift away from one client to an easier mark, because deluding the client into killing a loved one is part of the whole. Maybe his end game."

"His name wasn't Carroll." Peabody swiveled on her stool. "Niles George Carroll with that ID number didn't exist before 2038. It's pretty good fake data, but there are holes, and when you go into them, it falls apart."

"Got more names here." Feeney leaned back in his chair. "Dupres encoded them, sandwiched between other data."

"Looks like she did the input about three this morning," Callendar added. "The way it reads, Dallas, these are all pre–your bogus Carroll dude. Six in total."

"Let's throw them in. Which is the first?"

"First, if we figure this is chrono order, is Ravenwood."

Eve pulled up a stool next to Roarke's.

"I can run it," he began.

"Yeah, do that. I'm taking Bright. If this is chrono, and Bright wasn't just a rhyme, this could be who he is now."

"Hit on Simon." McNab did his little boogie. "Got your pattern, clear as they come. François Simon, psychic advisor and spiritualist, New Orleans, 2053 to 2057, went missing on a sabbatical to South America. Presumed dead."

"Three to four years, each spot habitually," Eve said as she worked. "He's still here, but probably not for long. Callendar, I want you to—"

"Run a search for murder/suicides each location just prior to the fuckhead's exit. On it."

Roarke hit on two others, with the pattern holding.

When the pizza arrived, Eve did indeed mutter—but grabbed a slice of pepperoni. The lab might have smelled like a pizzeria, with a sugary topping of fizzies, but the work got done.

"Louis Carroll Ravenwood," Roarke announced. "McNab, do a double, would you, to confirm this is the first?"

"Can do."

"Daresbury, England—which, as I've spent a little time boning up on Lewis Carroll—was where Carroll was born and raised."

"Not a coincidence," Eve stated.

"I'd say not. Spiritualist, offering readings, consultations, séances, and past-life regressions; 2022 to 2028."

"His longest stint."

"It seems. Pulling related data, I have an article or two. He claimed to be a connection of Carroll himself, through one of Carroll's sisters. And was called to Daresbury by Carroll's spirit, whom he also claimed to channel. He worked with his sister, not surprisingly called Alice."

"There's no sister mentioned in any of the other data on the other names."

"Wouldn't be," Roarke confirmed, "as she died in Daresbury in 2028. Suicide."

"Bang." Eve's eyes narrowed. "Mira will make buckets of shrink juice with that."

"And more so as it was discovered Alice Ravenwood had been an addict with a taste for meth and LSD. She suffered from acute depression and, after lacing a pot of tea with sedatives, served it to herself and her brother. She died; he nearly did. He left Daresbury soon after. There's nothing on him, under that name, past that."

"I want to see the police report. Maybe he dosed the sister. Either way, it gave him his springboard for all the rest. Crazy bastard skins the clients, then picks one to re-create the— Fucking A, I've got him. Carroll Bright. Claims to be a 'Doctor of Paranormal Studies.' I've got a goddamn address."

CHAPTER TEN

Bright sighed as he entered the lovely parlor where Ms. Harriet March was setting out the service for tea.

"My dear March, the time has come for us to move on. How do you feel about Budapest?"

"Hungry for goulash."

He chortled, giggled, slapped his thighs. "That's the spirit! I've given notice. We'll begin packing after our session with the delightful Mrs. Melton."

"Our Mouse signaled they're on their way."

"Excellent."

"And will Mrs. Melton join her sister in the Wonderland?"

He smiled at the avid look in her eyes. He'd been right to keep her. He'd sensed her potential when she'd first come to him—seeking communication with a lost love. A shadow of darkness inside her, so easily deepened with time and patience.

And of course the tonic she'd become so fond of.

"She and her husband will make their journey tonight, even as we make our own."

Eyes shining, she clapped her hands. "We've never sent two clients down the rabbit hole so close together."

"Isn't it fun! Our time in New York has been so lucrative, and we waited so long for the first to go. I thought sending another would be our little farewell party. And there she is now! Would you get the door, Ms. March?"

"Of course, Doctor Bright. The tea and cakes are all prepared."

Naturally, he thought, and swallowed the little tablet that would offset the tea. He checked himself in the mirror—his favorite looking glass had traveled with him around the world. And he decided he'd use his favorite top hat for this last session in New York.

Then he turned to greet the marvelously wealthy and wonderfully hopeful Mrs. Melton.

She came to him, both hands outstretched. "Oh, Doctor Bright, I've so looked forward to today. I'm so anxious to speak with my sister again."

"There's nothing like a sister," he said with a wide, wide grin. "Let's have some tea."

It would, he thought, be a lovely party.

EVE PLANNED HER APPROACH CAREFULLY. SHE AND PEABODY would go to the house, gain access.

She circled the conference room where she'd assembled her team. "I want him in the box. Once we get him out, the search team—with the warrants—goes in. The detectives from Illegals will handle the search for the drugs. McNab and Callendar take the electronics. And since the expert consultant civilian wants in, he's on finances. We want to establish Fitzwilliams paid him that nine thousand, nine hundred and ninety-nine dollars a session and do a secondary check to see if he scammed his way into her will, probably through the foundation.

"Look for false IDs—licenses, passports—and a client list. Check for recordings of the Fitzwilliamses' murders, and any others." She glanced around the room, nodded. "Peabody."

"Set."

"Let's hit in."

Roarke moved up beside her as they headed out. "He must have abilities. He'll try to read you."

"I know how to block. Peabody's father's a sensitive, and he taught her how to filter. She's anxious about it, but we've got to go in. I want to see his place, see his reactions before we bring him in."

"He's not working alone."

"Thought of that. This is what we do, Roarke."

He knew it, all too well. "It's one thing when your body's on the line. This is your mind as well, so have a care with both."

"Plan to." She separated from him in the garage, got into the car with Peabody.

"I'm a little nervous," Peabody admitted. "What if he tries to put—"

"Don't say whammy."

"What if he tries to put the thing I'm not saying on us?"

"Think about sex with McNab."

"Huh?"

"Didn't you say your father told you to fill your mind with other thoughts, confused and jumbled? Do that. Nobody's going to want to keep pushing in if all he gets is you and McNab and sex."

Catching Peabody's smile, Eve hissed. "Not now. Stop thinking about it now. It creeps me out."

"Just practicing." Happily, Peabody practiced all the way uptown.

Rather than search for a space, Eve flipped up her On Duty light and double-parked. She didn't think this first stage would take above fifteen minutes.

"Wow, this place is really beautiful." Peabody studied the wide, three-level townhouse as they approached. "It looks sort of European. I bet it's on the historic register. One of those great old buildings from the nineteenth century that survived the Urbans."

"We can admire the architecture later." Eve had been

studying it as well. Doors, windows, exits. She doubted her quarry would rabbit—a loss of control and power—but she wanted the layout.

"Cop face—no bullshit, straight out."

"Sorry, I'm thinking about sex with McNab."

"I could learn to hate you," Eve threatened, and rang the bell.

Palm plate, cams, police locks, she noted. She stared stony-eyed ahead until the voice came through the intercom.

"Please state your business."

Not a computer, she thought. Not with that squeaky tone. So, at least two to take on.

"NYPSD. We need to speak with Doctor Bright."

"Doctor Bright's unavailable. Go away, and come back later."

"You can open the door, or I'll stand right here until I get a warrant to open it myself."

And if he didn't, she'd use the warrant she already had. But the door opened a crack. She had to look down a half a foot to meet the eyes of the man with a wild thatch of brown hair. Those eyes had the pinkish tint of a funky junkie.

"The doctor can't talk to you now."

Eve solved the first problem by getting her foot in the door, nudging it open a little wider. "Who are you?"

"I'm Dorbert Mouse. Who are you?"

"Lieutenant Eve Dallas." Dormouse. It suited. "Why don't you tell Doctor Bright I'm here, along with Detective Peabody?"

"Because he can't be interrupted when he's communing with the Other Side!"

The quick excitability spoke of something in addition to the funk.

"He needs to commune with us." Eve nudged the door wider still and saw the brightly colored painting of a hookah-smoking caterpillar curled on a toadstool.

"Nobody invited you! Go away!"

"Look Mouse—or is that Dormouse?"

His pink-rimmed eyes filled with rage. His nose twitched

manically. "You can't see my whiskers! They're not for you to see."

He kicked her, the move so unexpected his foot connected with her shin before she anticipated it. Then he ran, bolting up the steps.

"Shit. Call the e-team in for backup," Eve ordered, and pulled her weapon as she gave chase.

He bounded up, with her and her aching shin in pursuit, and Peabody coming up behind her shouting for the e-team to move in.

He made a fast turn on the second-floor landing and vanished. But not before Eve caught the movement of a wall panel sliding shut.

She tugged at it, got nothing, then ran her fingers along the carved chair rail. When the panel slid open again, she grabbed a statue of a white rabbit with an oversized pocket watch and used it to prop the panel open.

Inside, in half light, she saw crooked steps leading up, and leading down. She closed her eyes for a moment, heard the sound of feet scrambling.

"Up," she said. "Watch your step."

She went up two at a time and caught sight of the shin-kicker darting down an oddly slanted corridor toward a closed door. Blue light leaked under it.

At a full run she hit the door seconds after he scurried through and went in low, weapon sweeping.

Mouse jumped up and down in the blue light, the blue fog, squealing about his whiskers. A woman with long, dark hair giggled and twirled just outside the fog. She stopped when she saw Eve, and her face filled with rage.

"Off with her head!"

To Eve's bemusement, the woman hefted fisted hands over her head as if brandishing an axe, then charged.

Because there was yet another woman—older, sitting in a chair blanketed with that blue mist, her head cocked under a feathered hat, her eyes glazed and glassy, Eve took the quickest route.

Two short, hard left jabs put the charging woman down.

"Stay out of this blue stuff, Peabody."

She caught a movement, saw through the blue curtain the tall, thin man in a purple top hat. Eyes wild, and yes, she supposed, mad with it.

She pivoted toward him as the world went as mad as his eyes.

Lights flashed, bright, multicolored lightning, while crazed laughter boomed. The floor seemed to tip right, then left, as she struggled to keep her balance. Images bloomed in the fog—a grinning cat, the caterpillar that puffed out more smoke, a fat white rabbit with a glinting pocket watch.

And the man in the top hat, who chortled gleefully while he poured tea into cups.

A pretty blue bottle sat on a table, a white light beaming on it. A large label dangled from it.

It said: *Drink Me.*

And it was tempting.

Out of the corner of her eye she saw Peabody step forward, start to reach out. And snapping back, Eve grabbed her arm, yanked.

"Don't."

"But it says!"

She saw now they'd stepped too close, that the fog twined around them. Feeling light-headed, she shoved Peabody clear, stumbled back.

She thought she heard voices echoing, and running feet pounding. More coming to the party.

She barely swallowed down the giggle that rose to her throat and aimed her stunner at what she hoped was the man in the hat and not some illusion.

"Turn this shit off, now, or I'll put you down."

"No need," Roarke said, and the flashing lights fell with a resounding crash—or so it seemed to Eve. The mist crawled back on tiny blue feet to be swallowed up by a gaping mouth in the floor.

"Shit. Shit. I inhaled."

"You'll be all right." Roarke hauled the man in the hat away from some sort of computer. The computer became a fat cat that yawned and stretched, then curled up to sleep.

"Mind taking him?" Roarke passed the Mad Hatter to Callendar.

"No prob. Hey, asshole."

"You're not the White Queen."

"No. I'm an e-bitch goddess. Illegals coming in, Mc-Nabber. I'm bringing in the wagon for this group."

"Yeah, good." He was on the floor, cuddling Peabody, who patted his cheek and smiled dreamily.

"Hi, sweetie! Want to have lots and lots of sex?"

"Yeah, that'd be frosty. How about we get you some air first? What the hell's in that stuff?" he asked Roarke.

"A wild trip, I'd say, but hardly fatal, as the three of these had their share. Best call in the MTs."

"Aw, man, don't call them." Eve waved the idea away with her stunner; Roarke gently took it from her. "I'm fine, we're all fine. Got the bad guys. Somebody oughta do something with the lady over there. She is *out* of it."

"The MTs will see to her." But his wife was Roarke's priority.

"Okay, good. She prolly thinks she's talking to a dead relative."

Roarke put a supporting arm around her waist and led her out.

"I gotta secure the scene and investigate."

"The Illegals detectives can handle that part now." He thought about telling her to mind the stairs, then just solved it by picking her up.

"You're so pretty. The mouse kicked me in the shin." Giggling, she kicked her feet. "I fell down the rabbit hole."

"So it would seem."

"I didn't like it. I like being here with you better."

She was placid enough sitting on his lap while an MT examined her. And perfectly cooperative when he bundled her into the car. As he drove, he could see her start to come back by the way her body lost that pliancy and her eyes started to clear.

"And there you are. Take this."

"What. Jesus." She shoved at her hair, and the raging

headache under her skull, knocking off the snowflake hat she knew she hadn't put on for the trip to Bright's.

"It's for the headache the medicals promised you'd have when you started coming down. And drink this." He passed her a bottle of water as he continued to drive downtown. "Just water. You'll be dehydrated a bit."

Her throat felt as though she'd swallowed sand. She took the stupid pill, guzzled the water. "Bright."

"In custody. All three of them. You dealt with it, Lieutenant, impaired or not. That's the cop in you."

"What impaired me?"

"It's quite a cocktail, according to the lab—as it's the same, assuredly, as what Darlene Fitzwilliams inhaled. Fortunately, you and Peabody didn't have more than a whiff or two."

"Peabody."

"She's right here."

Eve turned around at McNab's voice, saw her partner curled up with her head on his lap, sleeping. "She's okay?"

"They said she'd just sleep it off, and a single exposure like the two of you had wouldn't have any lasting effects." He stroked Peabody's hair as he spoke. "But . . ."

"I contacted Louise—as you'd want her to know what happened," Roarke continued. "She's on her way into Central, as we are, and she'll have a look at both of you."

"I'm fine. I'm starving. I want . . ."

Roarke activated the AutoChef, which produced a large bag of soy chips.

"Oh yeah. Fucker drugged me," she said with her mouth full of chips. "I *hate* that. He's going to . . . Oh, Jesus Christ, there was a woman. In the chair."

"Andrea Melton," Roarke told her. "The MTs transported her to the hospital. She was heavily dosed, and likely routinely dosed. But they know what he used, and they'll treat her."

"I need to talk to her."

"Tomorrow, at least, for that."

"Not for Bright, or whatever his name is. That's for tonight."

"And good luck with it." Roarke pulled into Central. "Want a hand with her, Ian?"

"No, I— Well, maybe."

Together, they got Peabody out, on her feet, where she smiled cheerfully. "Hi! Did we get 'em?"

"Yeah." Eve led the way to the elevator. "We got them."

"Yay! I feel really wooshy."

"Tell me about it."

"Are those soy chips? Can I have some soy chips?"

Eve gave her the bag as they got into the elevator. "Don't you have a headache?"

"No, I . . ." Peabody's entire face winced. "Ow."

"Here we are." Gently, Roarke slipped the pill between her lips and offered her the bottle of water he'd had in his pocket.

"Okay, thanks. He's so pretty," she said to Eve.

"Yeah, I know."

"Mine, too. Sooo pretty. But my head hurts and I'm starving. I'm not supposed to be harsh about my body image, so I'm eating these chips."

"Take her up to the crib," Eve advised. "Louise can take a look at her up there. If she's clear, take her on home. Good job all around, McNab."

"Thanks."

Too tired for the glides, Eve rode all the way to Homicide, gave her partner a last look, and got off so McNab could continue to the crib.

"I need to put all this together, then take on the Hatter and his crazy crew. I don't need Louise."

"I have some lines." He kept hold of her hand as they walked. "And one of them is you'll get checked by a doctor before you finish this. If you argue I'd be forced to mention to your division that you giggled."

"I did not. Shit. I did. I half remember. Fine, fine. But I want coffee, and lots of it. And that's my line."

"Agreed."

She decided it was just as well she'd made the deal, as both Charles and Louise were waiting in her office.

"Let me look at you. Sit."

"Coffee."

Roarke nudged her into her chair and went to the AutoChef while Louise opened her medical bag. She took Eve's wrist in her hand. "Pulse is strong and regular. Follow this light with your eyes only."

Eve rolled them first, then obeyed.

"Peabody?" Charles asked.

"Coming around. McNab took her up to the crib. We're fine."

But Louise still took out a bunch of tools that made Eve scowl. She poked, prodded, scanned, measured. Then nodded.

"You are fine." She took Eve's hand again. "Thank you. Thank you for myself, for Charles, for Henry."

"I haven't finished it yet."

"But you will. He's staying with us for a while—Henry. We can go home and tell him you have the person responsible. It'll help. I'll let you get to it. I want to see Peabody."

Before they left, Charles leaned over, kissed the top of her head. "Thanks for everything, Lieutenant Sugar."

"It's the job."

She blew out a breath when they left. "I probably need you to fill in some blanks spots. When he turned on the light show, I must have been disoriented enough to turn into that mist, just enough. But I had my stunner on him. I remember that."

"You did. Callendar dealt with the other man—the little one—and McNab pulled Peabody out of the mist. You'd knocked her back—I saw that as I came in—but she stumbled into it again. I found the controls, shut down the program, and . . . restrained the suspect. I'm assuming you took care of the woman who was laid out on the floor, sporting a hell of a bruise on her face."

"Yeah, and yeah, okay, I got it. Nice assist, pal. I need IDs on all of them."

"No ID on record for the Hatter. The woman is Willow Bateman—a few minor bumps prior to 2054 when she lived in New Orleans, then off the grid."

"I'm guessing that's when she hooked up, one way or the other, with . . . Okay, the Hatter works."

"The other man is Maurice Xavier. A number of bumps there, and some time in a cage for aggravated assault. He, too, drops off the grid, three years ago."

"Same deal, most likely. I'm going to have the head guy brought up. I think the other two were heavily under the influence, so I'll wait on them. You're going to hang, aren't you?"

"Absolutely."

"Figured. Let me set this up so I can box him in, then shut him down."

"Looking forward to it," Roarke said. "I'll take myself up to EDD, find the money, and help you close the door."

"Have fun with that."

"No question of it."

EPILOGUE

After the Hatter was brought in, Eve took a few minutes in Observation to study him. Tall and skinny, long face, long body, he sat in his prison jumpsuit with a cagey smile on his face and eyes of so pale a gray they seemed almost colorless.

Confident and cocky, she concluded, at least on the outside, but she noted the way his fingers tapped, tapped, tapped on the table as if he played a tune on invisible keys.

"He figures his ability gives him an edge," she said to Peabody. "That he'll read us, and use that to tangle things up."

"Or put the you-know-what on us."

"You can skip this," she reminded her partner. "I told McNab to take you home."

"No way I'm missing this part. Should I think of sex with McNab again?"

"Whatever works." She pulled out her 'link, read the detailed message from Roarke. "The man is good," she murmured. "Three hidden accounts, three different names—all leading back to the Hatter—who, according to Feeney's search, is actually Louis Carroll Ravenwood, born Devonshire, England, in 1999—one sibling, Alice."

"So he was who he was until the sister self-terminated."

"Prior to, he and the sister—big surprise—worked the carny circuit."

Eve looked back through the glass. "Add the money and the false IDs to the whole bunch of drugs Illegals found in his house, and he's not going to look so happy when we're done. Let's go wipe that smile off his face."

He looked over as they came in, and his smile turned into a grin.

"Dallas, Lieutenant Eve and Peabody, Detective Delia entering interview with Ravenwood, Louis Carroll—"

"I'm Doctor Bright."

Eve just kept speaking. "On the matters of case numbers . . ." She reeled off many as she took a seat across from him. "Mr. Ravenwood, you've—"

"I prefer Doctor Bright."

"You've been read your rights," she continued. "Do you understand your rights and obligations in these matters?"

"I understand perfectly, and so much more. How are you feeling?"

"Better than you will. A hell of a lot better than your two pals are. They're getting jittery. That's what happens when addicts don't get their fix. I figure they'll roll on you within twenty-four, but I don't need them. Peabody, why don't you list the illegals found in our guest's home?"

Peabody took out her PPC and crisply read off the report from Illegals.

"Quite a collection." She kept her eyes on his, actually felt him try to probe her thoughts—and pushed her will against his. "That alone's going to get you a nice long stay in a cage. Add in using said illegals on individuals without their consent or knowledge—"

"They come to me." He played his fingers in the air. "They come seeking my help. I give them what they seek. We cross the bridge together, and the crossing requires peace. A quiet mind, quiet, relaxed, still." His fingers played, played, as if stroking a purring cat. "Imagine drifting under a blue sea, under a blue sky. See the clouds, white and soft."

He had something, she thought, and it pulled. But it wasn't enough without the kick of his herbs and chemicals. She leaned closer. "You think you can mesmerize me? You're a fraud. You've been a fraud your whole life. You just figured out how to use a mediocre talent to get rich and feel important."

"Mediocre!" He slapped his hands on the table. "My gift is beyond. My beyond is genius!"

"Your gift is bullshit, Ravenwood. Or should I call you Niles Carroll? Maybe Angus Roland or Anton Zacari or François Simon?"

Something flickered in his eyes—the first hint of fear.

"I have many names. My gift demands it."

"Gift." She snorted. "I've seen carneys with more than you have. That's where you started, right?" She pushed up, moved around the table, coming at him from behind. "Telling fortunes, getting people to quack like a duck at some two-bit carnival? You and your sister."

His body jerked. "Be quiet."

"Golly." Peabody widened her eyes. "You're pissing him off, Lieutenant."

"Am I? Does it piss you off to talk about your sister? Did you feed her the drugs that hooked her, or did she do it to herself? Why did she try to kill you? Did one of your sessions go south? Or maybe you'd just had enough of her, drugged her up good, faked the whole thing so you could kill her."

"She killed herself."

"Like Darlene Fitzwilliams? Like—wait, let me read your mind." She held her hands over his head, swayed. "I feel their spirits reaching out to me. Marian Beechem in London, Fiona MacNee in Edinburgh, Sylvia Garth in Prague."

"Get away from me." He shrieked it, but Eve continued to list names. "All women, like your sister."

"I bet he couldn't bring her back," Peabody said. "She wouldn't come. Not after what he did to her."

"Shut up! Shut your mouth! You can't speak. Your tongue is tied, your throat is closed!"

Peabody's lips clamped together, her eyes widened as she

lifted her hands to her throat. Choked and gasped. Then dropped them. "Nope, I can speak just fine."

Good one, Eve thought. She glanced at her 'link, read Roarke's text. Smiled. Then walked around the table again. "Jesus, the guy believes his own shtick. No good without the tea party and the mists, the lights. The hats? What is it with the hats?"

"Carneys like props," Peabody suggested. "Maybe he'll pull a white rabbit out of one."

"Or a March Hare. But her name's really Willow Bateman, and she'll do all kinds of flips on you."

"Ms. March is loyal."

"To your illegals cocktails, sure. But without them . . . You shouldn't have pitched your pathetic ability against someone like Dupres. She's the real deal, and she gave us everything we needed to shut you down."

"Impossible." He flicked his hands in the air.

"Why? Because you slipped your ugly little mix into her tea leaves? Because you went to her, drugged her, then picked Fitzwilliams out of her client list? And while she was drugged, you planted the order for her to kill herself if she remembered, if she was questioned? Jesus, she lives over a restaurant. Did you really think no one would see you go up to her place?"

"I didn't go! I sent Ms. March."

"Right." Eve sat again. "You sent Bateman posing as a client, and she laced the tea. And Mouse—that's Maurice Xavier—brought them to you. Fitzwilliams now, such an easy mark, and such deep pockets. Wait."

Eve pressed a hand to her temple. "I'm getting another psychic flash. Nine thousand, nine hundred and ninety-nine dollars. Cash. Such a fat fee for you. But . . . there's more. That well-heeled foundation. Millions to pump from that. What's that? What? Yes, I can almost see it. There! The Looking Glass Fund."

"Get out of my head!" The madness was back in his eyes. "You can't see! I want my hat. Get me my hat."

"You really think your stupid hat can stop me from seeing?

The Amazing Dallas sees all, knows all. You had to get rid of them both. Push Darlene to make a twelve-million-dollar bequest to your shell charity, and get rid of them both. For the money, and the satisfaction. Sister, brother, just like you and Alice."

He bared his teeth, all fury now. "I can make you beat your head against the wall until you're dead!"

"Try it." She reared up, pushed her face into his. "Just try it. I'm not drugged and grieving like your victims. You sent Darlene to kill her brother. You gave her the shears. What did she think they were? Candy? Wine? Flowers? Flowers," she repeated when she saw his eyes shift. "'I'm so sorry we argued, Marcus. I brought you flowers.' And she stabbed him in the heart, then she jumped off his terrace, hallucinating, thinking what? She was walking on the beach, stepping into her own house? It doesn't matter, you killed her, killed them both. And for what? For money. For money and entertainment. And to feel powerful."

"I am powerful. I gave her what she wanted, didn't I? She's with her parents. I gave her what she asked for. I deserve the money. I want my money! I want my hat!"

He beat his fists on the table, his feet on the floor. "You'll kill each other before the night is through. I can make you, like I made all the others. You'll cut each other to ribbons. Ribbons of blood. And with blood we'll paint all the roses red."

He took a deep breath, and the shoulders that had come up to his ears relaxed again. "Now, have Ms. March fetch the tea." His fingers played in the air again as he stared into Eve's eyes, smiled. "We're having tea. It's my tea party, and it never, never ends."

"I've got news for you. The party's over."

When they'd finished with him, at least for the night, Eve had him taken down to where he'd be held in the psych section, on suicide watch.

"Mira's going to have a hell of a time with him," Eve said. "We'll take the other two in the morning. We'll see what kind of mood they're in after a night without their particular brand of tea."

She watched Roarke come out of Observation.

"I regret to say, I do believe he's mad as a hatter."

"Probably," Eve agreed. "That's up to Mira, and I don't give a rat's ass if he spends the rest of his life in a concrete cage or a padded room. Either way, he's done."

"He gave me the creeps." Peabody shuddered.

"It didn't show."

"Well, he did, and if it's okay with you, I'm heading home and staying away from you until morning. So we don't end up cutting each other to ribbons."

"For Christ's sake, Peabody."

"Why take chances? I'll write it up, but I'll write it up at home. With McNab sort of keeping an eye on me."

"Fine. I'm going the hell home myself."

"And I'll keep an eye on her," Roarke promised Peabody.

She went to her office for her coat. "He has something." She circled her neck. "Not nearly what he's deluded himself into believing he has—most of it hinged on the drugs. Wherever he ends up, he won't have them, but he needs careful watching."

"He was afraid of you, afraid you have more than he does." Roarke tapped the dent in her chin. "Perhaps you do."

"Not a psychic—just a cop who knows how to read killers."

"I have a hypnotic suggestion of my own." This time, he laid a finger on her forehead. "You want to go home with me and have lots and lots of sex."

"You putting the whammy on me, ace?"

"I certainly intend to."

As they walked out, he pulled the snowflake hat out of his pocket, fixed it on her head.

What the hell, she thought. As hats went, it was warm—and pretty sweet.

ALICE AND THE EARL
IN WONDERLAND

MARY BLAYNEY

AUTHOR'S NOTE

Be advised: this is a time travel! My time-travel world began with Amy and Simon in "Amy and the Earl's Amazing Adventure" in the anthology *Dead of Night*, which is available as a paperback or eBook.

The magic coin, also known as Poppy's Coin, is an element in all the anthologies I have done for Berkley. Their chronology varies, and someday I will do a spreadsheet to figure it out for myself. In the meantime, I hope you enjoy the Earl of Weston's adventure.

A couple of elements to note. The "space-time continuum" is a phrase that Amy Stevens used before she and Simon West traveled back to 1805. It was hardly a reflection of her understanding of science but came from the TV show *Stargate Atlantis*, something she admitted when pressed by Simon. No one really knows (including yours truly) how the coin enables time travel, except for the easiest explanation: "It's magic!" Please suspend your disbelief and enjoy the story.

I always knew that Weston's story was waiting to be told, for he is the "earl" referred to in the title of Amy and Simon's novella. I was delighted when we were given the title *Down the Rabbit Hole* for this book, because his experience of time travel was totally unexpected (unlike Amy and Simon, who knew where they were going), and it was totally out of keeping with his known reality. Thank goodness he had Mr. Arbuckle to help him and someone to share the experience with him.

PROLOGUE

"It's a disaster." Bennet William George Haven West, third Earl Weston, moved about the room as he spoke. The mantel needed paint. The books should be dusted. At least the decanters were full. "A disaster, to put it plainly."

"Come now, Wes, it's not like we are on the edge of complete bankruptcy. We'll find a way out."

Weston loved his cousin and heir presumptive. Ian's use of "we" made him feel less alone and told him everything he needed to know about Ian's loyalty.

"It's almost that bad. These last two days with the estate's man of business have convinced me that while no one will refuse me credit, there is not enough money coming in to make a dent in the bills that have been piling up for the last two years, at least."

"Two years?" Ian sounded shocked.

"Two years. Since the old earl's son and heir died. Apparently my cousin was the only one able to keep his father's generosity under control."

"Uncle Weston was an amazing man. Everyone mourned his passing."

"As did I, Ian. I loved my uncle and benefited from his largesse as much as anyone. He never said no, whether it was to a beggar on the street or to his wife and children." Weston poured himself just a drop more wine and offered the decanter to Ian, who shook his head. "If only his generosity had not extended to every possible investment suggested. You know as well as I do that each was less successful than the one before it."

"When he died—has it been three months already?—I wondered then, and still do, if the news of the loss of that ship brought on the apoplexy that killed him." Ian shook his head, his expression a mix of sorrow and frustration.

They were verging on maudlin ground now.

Weston stood up. "I am off to Westmoreland. The blasted artist is ready to put what he calls 'the finishing touches' on my portrait. The portrait I cannot pay him for."

"Wait, tell me what your man of business had to say about the opportunity to invest in the canals. The new venture that Lord Wedgebrook is so excited about?"

"He said exactly what I expected. That I need to be sure that the investment is sound. The estate cannot stand another failure."

"But it would be your money, not any of the money that is part of the estate."

"As it stands now, Ian, I am the estate. The farms are in wretched condition. The tenants can barely call themselves farmers. The cottages are in such disrepair that no one with any ability will sign on."

Ian shook his head in sympathy. "It's hard to know where to start."

Weston felt for the locket in his pocket. He had thought marrying Alice would be the first step toward the future. With her by his side, anything seemed possible. Now he was almost glad she had refused him. Debt was the last thing she would want in a husband.

The less noble part of him missed her. Missed her quite desperately. How could she say no when he knew her heart was filled with the same love and longing as his?

"Wes, what is it? What has you looking so stricken? Truly, there is way out of this."

"Stricken? Did I? It was nothing, just a moment of grief." Let Ian think it was for his uncle. Move on, he told himself. Thinking of Alice only led to an endless circle of anguish that squeezed his heart and made his head ache.

"I will go to Westmoreland and start there." Weston stood up. "I can close up this house and reduce expenses until next Season, at least. I can sell some horses, and there are some paintings not entailed. The Rembrandt, for one."

"Dear God, Wes, that would be like announcing to the ton that you are on the verge of bankruptcy. Have you thought of marrying an heiress?"

"An heiress? Never!" Weston answered, more sharply than he intended.

"Very well." Ian held up his hands as if in surrender. He stood up. "Feel free to call on me anytime, Wes. I will help you in any way I can. Indeed, I may even know someone interested in the Rembrandt."

"Thank you, Ian." Weston took the hand his cousin offered and clapped him on the shoulder. "No need to rush into it. I will think on it at Westmoreland. Who knows, something miraculous might happen. Yes, a miracle. Something that neither of us can imagine."

Within a quarter hour, Ian was off to his lodgings and Weston was bound for the country. Eight hours more and the earl was less than ten miles from Westmoreland. The carriage rumbled on in the moonlight.

He wouldn't be traveling in the dark much longer. Only a few miles more. The moon was full, the roads were safe, and he had a pistol if he was wrong about that.

He spent most of the trip leaning against the cushions, pretending to himself that he could doze off, but he'd spent the whole of the trip considering ways and means of righting the accounts. In a half-dreaming state, his head was filled with ideas from sensible to bizarre.

Weston fingered the round locket in his pocket and wished the future had a different look. One where he and Alice faced it together, with enough money to make her every wish come true.

He drew a deep breath and a sudden lassitude overcame him, dragging him to sleep just when he thought he might never sleep again.

CHAPTER ONE

"What the blazes is going on?" A hard thump had awakened him.

Weston's first thought was to have a word with the coachman, but when he opened his eyes he wondered if his last visit to deal with the estate's debt had done the job and he was ready for Bedlam.

He was not in his coach at all, but in the library of his town house in London.

He'd left London. He was sure he had. Weston could recall his conversation with Ian and his final words to the major-domo. "Send the overdue bills to Herbert." His man of business knew what to do, and it would not be wise to let the staff know how much to let he was. Not with his sister's come-out within the next year.

Now that seemed to be the least of his worries. As he straightened, he realized he was seated on the sofa, and that there was someone next to him.

And another man stood nearby, wringing his hands in a way that was not at all reassuring.

"Answer me, man. What the devil am I doing in London after riding in my carriage for ten hours?"

"I can explain, my lord. Truly I can. You must calm yourself and allow me to see to the lady. She should be awake by now."

Weston turned to the person beside him. He'd assumed it was a man, given the clothes worn. Pantaloons. Dark blue pantaloons of some coarse material. He leaned forward a little to see her face.

"Alice?"

Alice Kemp stirred, and Weston shook his head, then checked to make sure he still had the locket. At first he could not find it, as he was no longer wearing a coat, but then he felt it at his hip in the pocket of the strange pants he was wearing, surprisingly like the pair Alice had on.

"Maybe insanity is not the nightmare I thought it would be." Alice being next to him was a wondrous delusion.

He was speaking aloud but to himself, a sometimes unfortunate habit, and quite naturally, the man thought Weston was addressing him.

"Oh, my lord, I assure you. You are as sane now as you were yesterday. Something most unusual has happened, and as soon as I am certain the lady is well, I will explain it to both of you."

"Kemp. Her name is Alice Kemp." The earl took her hand and felt for her pulse. Alice's hand was as warm and soft as he remembered, and her pulse was not much quicker than a normal beat.

As he watched, her impossibly long eyelashes fluttered, and he smiled at the green eyes he had never forgotten, any more than he had forgotten how she felt against him.

"Weston?" She asked more than said his name, and as her eyes cleared she moved to a sitting position. "Where am I?"

She brushed at the pants with an expression of disgust, if not outright revulsion. "Showing the outline of my legs is very embarrassing."

"Yes, Miss Kemp, I am sure, but I can explain if you both

will give me your attention." The gentleman was wringing his hands again.

As was typical of Alice Kemp, she went on as if she had not heard him. "Where are we and why am I here?" She looked from the gentleman to Weston. It was not a friendly look. It was more like a glare.

Weston stood up and began to circle the room. The mantel that had needed paint last night was now a green marble. The room looked well-kept and dusted. "Now. I want explanations now."

The man nodded, a series of short rapid movements that showed he was ready to comply.

"First, my name is Mr. Arbuckle. Until today and for many years, centuries even, I have been the caretaker of a magic coin. It was placed into my keeping in the early nineteenth century, where I was born and raised, and I have been responsible for it ever since. I have not always been in control of it, but I have always been responsible for it. But that is another story entirely."

Weston rolled his eyes. If he was not mad, then this man must be.

"Listen, please, my lord." He turned and bowed to Alice. "And you too, miss."

"How do you do, Mr. Arbuckle. I am Miss Kemp. It appears I have been kidnapped and have no choice but to listen to your fantastical story. Luckily, I have always had a fondness for fairy tales." Her disdain was obvious. She stood up and moved to the fireplace and chose the sharpest poker in the lot. "If I do not like what you have to say I want to assure you that I am more than capable of defending myself. Is that perfectly clear?"

Now that was the Alice Kemp he loved. She had a unique way of taking command of a situation. He did his best not to react at all.

"Yes, miss. Yes," Arbuckle said as he took a step back, even though he was not within striking range. "And my story will sound fantastical, but will be amazingly easy to prove."

Alice—he really should try to think of her as "Miss Kemp," but once you have held a woman in your arms and made love to her it was almost impossible to think of her with any element of formality, so "Alice" it was—lowered the poker but moved closer to the library door.

Weston wanted to understand as much as she did. With that, the earl turned to the gentleman and narrowed his eyes. Arbuckle seemed innocuous enough. Portly, with a ring of hair surrounding a bald dome. Eyes a soft if aging blue. He had the air of a man of ideas rather than a man of action. He was not a physical threat, to be sure.

"My lord Earl and Miss Kemp." Arbuckle bowed to one, then the other. "You have both traveled in time from your country home, my lord, to your town house in London. The year is not 1805 but 2005."

CHAPTER TWO

"We have traveled through time. Of course we have," Weston said. "Why did that never occur to me?"

"Weston, stop being sarcastic," Alice commanded. "That is not the way to find answers."

"Indeed, my lord, it is odd, but I can explain."

"Explain away, but can you prove it? How do we know that you are telling us the truth?" Weston walked to the windows that looked over Green Park.

He turned around on his heel. "The park looks just as it did in 1805. The library is the same." The earl reconsidered. Hadn't he just noticed that the mantel was different? "Except for the mantel and that box on the desk and that odd-looking glass on the wall."

"Yes, my lord. The box is a computer, an instrument that transfers information, and the item on the wall is a screen that shows pictures on demand. Would you like to see how they work?"

"Definitely not," Weston said at the same moment that Alice said, "Yes."

"Prove it, sir. Prove we have time traveled," Alice demanded.

"Wait, Alice."

"Wait for what, Wes?"

Alice had called him Wes. Did she even realize it? The verbal gesture inclined him to agree to anything she asked.

"Mr. Arbuckle"—Weston nodded to the man—"before you prove this time travel to us I want to know why we would have made this leap through time. What purpose would it serve?"

"Thank you, sir," Arbuckle said, drawing a deep breath. "Do you see your portrait, my lord?"

Weston turned to the wall—so the artist had finished. It looked a bit different than it had last he saw it. "Indeed."

"Do you see the coin on the desk next to your hand?"

"Yes." There was a coin, a small train and the locket that was in his pocket now. "But when was that coin added? I thought the painting was completed yesterday."

"The man and woman who took your places were sent back in time for the sole purpose of bringing that coin to you."

"Took our places?"

As Weston was about to toss out at least five more questions, Arbuckle raised his hand. "Yes, two people have traveled to your time from theirs. That is, from the time that you are in now. And, my lord, the space-time continuum demands that Miss Amy and Mr. West's physical bodies be replaced while they are time traveling, um, that is, to maintain the balance of space and time."

"That is ridiculous," Weston insisted.

"Absurd it may sound, but truth it is. I want to assure you that this is only temporary. You *will* return to your own time and place. And when you do, you can only go back with . . ." Mr. Arbuckle stopped abruptly and asked, "Did you bring something with you, my lord? Miss Kemp? A belonging of some kind?"

Alice looked down at her new clothing and shook her head. Weston was about to do the same when he remembered the locket. He debated lying, as he was not at all sure that he wanted Alice to know that he still had it, but the situation they were in made such a lie seem petty. He nodded and drew the locket from his pocket. "This came with me, though I cannot precisely say that I brought it."

"Wes," Alice said, and he could not decide if she was touched or surprised until he looked at her. The softness in her eyes was his answer. *Yes, Alice, I have kept it, and I always will, until I can convince you to wear it again and forever.* He spoke with his eyes and knew she understood when she looked away and down.

Alice Kemp was no more his now than she had been a year ago. Or two hundred.

Mr. Arbuckle cleared his throat. "The item you carried, my lord, takes the physical place of the coin they carried. That is the only reason you were allowed to bring something that is not from this time period."

Weston wanted to know why the coin chose that particular item, the locket, but feared the answer would be something to do with the absurdity of time and space continuity or whatever Arbuckle had called it.

Or, he would have feared it if he believed a word of this story. Still, there was the issue of his traveling by coach for hours only to magically arrive where he had started.

And what was so important about a damn coin? Questions. He had a hundred. Weston pressed his lips together and waited for an answer to the first one.

"If you will come with me now I will prove that you have moved through both space and time."

"But I have a dozen more questions," Alice insisted.

"I am sure you both do, Miss Kemp, and I will do my best to answer them, but first I want to establish the truth of what I say, if you please. The changes in London will convince you better than I ever could with words."

Mr. Arbuckle walked toward the door. Weston followed him, anxious to see the proof.

"I cannot go out in public wearing this!" Alice had not moved from the spot.

Both men paused. Mr. Arbuckle did not open the door.

"Miss, I assure you that no one will be at all shocked. The jeans you are wearing are typical for all English women."

"Jeans?" She looked down at the offending garment. "Do they now name their items of clothing?" Her tone indicated that her question was more sarcasm, the kind she had deplored in him.

"Alice. We have traveled two hundred years into the future and you choose to quibble over an item of dress?"

"Quibble!" Now she was insulted. "You know as well as I do that what people wear can seal their fate in society. Beau Brummell has proved that."

"Miss Kemp, please do trust me in this," Arbuckle urged. "No one will think it unusual for you to be out and about dressed as you are. You are wearing essentially what Miss Amy and Mr. West were wearing when they traveled back in time, as they are wearing what you wore. So you see it is perfectly normal."

Weston could not control a burst of laughter. " 'Perfectly normal' are the last words I would use to describe this situation." He turned to Alice. "Come, my dear, have you not always wanted to experience the comfort of men's dress? Now is your chance."

"Dress as a gentleman? Never. No more than you have wanted to dress in skirts, my lord." But with a sigh Alice moved toward the door. "Very well. But I will box the ears of anyone who dares insult me."

"I know that you are entirely capable of taking care of yourself," Weston said, "but I assure you, Alice, that I shall do more than box ears if anyone should insult you."

Alice turned her head away quickly, but not before he saw the hint of a smile.

CHAPTER THREE

As they made their way into the passage toward the front door a woman was coming up the stairs. "Are you done with the tea things, then, sir?"

A servant. This woman was a servant of some kind, but dressed in a way that made it look as though she were trying to copy her betters.

"Yes. We are done." She was looking at him, but it was Arbuckle who answered. "Mr. West and Miss Kemp will be back shortly."

"Very well, sir."

Weston gave a brief nod when the servant glanced at him for confirmation. As the housekeeper moved into the next room to clear the tea table, Arbuckle whispered, "I beg your pardon, my lord, but the housekeeper—Tandy is her name—knows nothing of what has happened. And since you look exactly like Mr. West and not at all like the current earl, I thought it best to address you as him."

"Yes, I see," the earl answered, and then looked at Alice.

She nodded. "We will have to be careful what we say when she is around."

"Which is not that different from our day, is it?"

Alice nodded with a small smile that brought an inordinate amount of joy to his heart.

Turning his attention from Alice, he made his way to the front hall. As they walked down the stairs that circled the entry hall, Weston noted that, while the place looked the same, the decor was different.

"It looks familiar, but parts of it are not at all as I recall," Alice whispered to him, and he smiled at the intimacy, nodding.

Yes, he had no doubt this was his town house. The Rembrandt hanging at the landing proved it. He knew it was the same place, but so much around it was different, and for the first time the earl wondered if Mr. Arbuckle might be telling the unholy truth.

Did he even need to say that the next few hours were the most amazing of his life thus far? He knew the memory of this terrifying, horrifying, incredible look at the future would astound him forever.

There was the obvious. Thousands of horse-free carriages, which Arbuckle called "cars," some large and some small, filled the roads. Conveyances called lorries took the place of carts, but still managed to block traffic as much as the old horse-drawn drays had.

Buildings were tall, huge. The lifts they rode on made stairs unnecessary except for emergencies. There were still pockets of small homes. Mayfair retained much of its nineteenth-century look. Even Berkeley Square was still there, if marred by the hideous building that was the American Embassy.

"What surprises me as much as the change," Alice said at one point, "is how much has remained the same."

Indeed he had noticed that too. London remained a hub of the world. People of all nations were on the streets, some hurried and on business, others shopping at a leisurely pace. He was delighted to see that the Burlington Arcade remained, with some of the same shops he frequented.

And Hatchards!

The bookstore still had pride of place on Piccadilly. Alice suggested they go inside, and Mr. Arbuckle agreed.

There were books displayed in far more dramatic ways than in his day, when stacked books near the door had been the only announcement of new publications. Now there were stands as tall as he was, with bright, even bold, covers. He moved from one to another, running his fingers over the smooth paper covers of three or four different books. No more leather covers. And authors seemed to crave publicity, as their pictures were a prominent part of the back cover.

One of the displays particularly caught their attention. The book was *Alice in Wonderland*, and Mr. Arbuckle explained that it was a perennial children's favorite.

"That could be a story about us, Weston. For this London is, indeed, a wonderland."

The earl turned to their guide. "How did this Alice reach her Wonderland? Was it by time travel as well?"

"No, my lord. She fell down a rabbit hole."

"I did that once too," Weston said with a laugh. "Well, my horse did. He fell in the rabbit hole and escaped unharmed, but it left me more dizzy than clearheaded. For a day I saw two of everything. Was that Alice in Wonderland's experience as well?"

"No." Arbuckle shook his head.

"Shall we purchase a copy?" Alice asked, and made to lift one from the stand.

"You may, if you wish, but you will not be able to take it back with you. If you take something with you, then you must leave something behind. The space-time continuum, you know."

Weston's expression must have looked as confused as Alice's did, because Arbuckle shook his head. "Of course you have no idea what I'm talking about. As I said before you can only go back with what you came with, and that would be the locket. Unless you wish to leave the jewelry behind?"

Weston shook his head. Arbuckle nodded. Nothing was said, but each understood the other.

"If the people pretending to be us must leave the coin, what will they bring back?" Alice asked, as though she had not witnessed the silent commune.

Mr. Arbuckle shrugged. "They will think of something."

"It will be a challenge to see if we can discover what it is they chose to bring with them." Alice's smile hinted that yet another adventure awaited them.

"Indeed," Weston agreed, though he would agree to almost anything when she smiled at him like that. His smile must have been too suggestive, since Alice turned from him and picked up the nearest book, obviously only pretending interest in it. The book was a large volume called *The Annotated Pride and Prejudice*.

He stepped closer as though he wished to look at it with her, when all he really wanted was to inhale the lovely vanilla and rose scent she favored.

Alice dropped the book and moved to the other side of the table, clearly more upset than charmed by his nearness.

In the name of all that was holy, he did not know if his presence was welcome or not. Did she really want nothing more to do with him? If so, why had she been at Westmoreland in the first place?

CHAPTER FOUR

Arbuckle must have sensed the tension, because he announced in a too-cheerful voice, "I think you will be happy to know that Miss Austen's works still sell very well."

"Miss Austen?" Alice asked, grabbing on to the conversational gambit as if it were a lifeline.

"Jane Austen," Arbuckle elaborated, "the author of *Pride and Prejudice*, the book you picked up."

Weston was as much at sea as Alice. He had never heard of an author by that name. "A female author? Most likely she wrote gothic novels, the kind of books in which I have no interest."

"Oh, Weston, do not act so superior, as if you never have read Defoe's satires."

Arbuckle picked up the copy of *Pride and Prejudice* and opened it to the front page. "My apologies. *Pride and Prejudice* was not published until 1813. It seems you have a treat waiting for you. I do believe at first she wrote anonymously, but the Prince Regent greatly admired her work, and eventually she became known to the public."

"The Prince Regent? What happened to King George III?"

Weston felt some concern. A regent meant the king was still alive but incapacitated in some way. "Did his brain fever return, or did another would-be assassin come too close to success? When and for how long?"

Arbuckle waved his hands as if trying to make Weston's questions disappear. "Oh dear, oh dear. I know you cannot change history, as this event was always meant to happen, but I don't know how much we should discuss or if I must watch my words."

Sensing his real distress, Weston nodded. "I will not press you. The king has been ill several times. For the moment I will assume it is another one of those occurrences." Mentally, he decided he would find a history of the last two hundred years and inform himself.

That thought was the launching point for an idea that could make this time travel worthwhile. But this was hardly the place to discuss it, for it would, no doubt, upset Mr. Arbuckle even more.

"Since we cannot purchase anything here I suggest that we leave and find a coffeehouse, Mr. Arbuckle," Weston suggested.

"A coffee shop?" Arbuckle repeated and then smiled. "An excellent idea."

Weston took Alice's arm and was relieved when she did not pull away.

"Yes indeed." Alice laughed. "My head is filled with questions. Everything from wanting to know when did women begin to dress like men, and why did men not choose to dress like women? And what diseases have been cured? How long do most people live?" She shook her head. "My list is endless."

Weston was glad to see that Alice's spirit of adventure had come through time with her. He'd always thought her imagination one of her most appealing assets. It was pure joy to see her flourish here.

Why could it not have led her to see a life with him as Countess Westwood? Instead she had apparently imagined a world where the ton would not accept them as a wedded couple because her own family was socially shunned because of her parents' divorce.

"After I order the coffee, I will answer as many of your questions as seems prudent. You have time, and every visitor to this century should experience Starbucks."

A few minutes later they were seated at a table in a mad-house of a coffee shop. Mr. Arbuckle insisted that they sit and took their orders. "Starbucks' system takes some time to understand. It's as though they have their own language. If you tell me what you would like, I will translate for you. Besides, you have no money with you. You will be my guests."

Arbuckle took their orders and then left them at the table. Weston knew enough to make the most of his time alone with Alice. Or as alone as they could be surrounded by dozens of strangers.

"Alice," he began, resisting the urge to reach for her hand. "Mr. Arbuckle said that we both time traveled from the country house. Why were you there?"

Alice Kemp looked away and cleared her throat. "I had just arrived to accept a position to help your sister prepare for her Season." She shook her head. "Now someone from this time has taken my place. I cannot imagine a woman from 2005 being of any help at all. I fear my efforts at a career are about to be thoroughly compromised."

Weston tried to conceal his disappointment. He'd hoped she might have come looking for him. He tried to find a way to ask what he most wanted to know. In the end he decided to be honest. "Did you know I would be in residence?"

"No," she said. "But then a woman who must make her own way cannot expect to have everything as she wishes."

"That was a dart aimed right at my heart, Alice." He did reach for her hand, but she moved it from the table to her lap. "I wanted to marry you."

"And a marriage with me would have completely estranged you from your family at the least, if not all of society. You saw how badly my Season progressed. My aunt insisted we had to at least attempt a Season to see if the ton might be willing to overlook my parents' behavior, but you were the only gentleman who took an interest, and the ton hardly considered that a mark in your favor." She looked away again and shook her head, obviously refusing to be drawn any further into the old argument, but then added, "At least that Season taught me all I need to know about helping young ladies succeed."

Weston decided it would be best not to pursue the subject until he had something new to fuel the debate. Apparently love was not enough for Miss Alice Kemp. He would change the subject. It was wisdom rather than cowardice, he insisted to himself. "So tell me what you think of this wonderland."

As always, she responded instantly to any question about ideas or observations.

"This wonderland, as you call it, is a cross between shocking and overwhelming. I cannot decide if I am appalled or amazed. I vacillate between the horror of wearing men's attire and how intrigued I am by the way London has grown and changed." She paused a moment, but then went on. "Weston, did you see the conveyances that carried dozens of people? And still the roads are not big enough, just as they are not in our day."

"Yes, and what about the devices that people hold to their ears? I do believe they talk into them. Who are they talking to?"

"Women wear the most amazing shoes. How can they manage on such high heels? And the dresses are so short as to be embarrassing."

He rather liked that part of this world, but was not about to say so aloud.

"And their reticules, Weston! They've grown to the size of a portmanteau."

"What does one need to carry besides a handkerchief and vinaigrette?" he asked.

"In this day and age, who can say?" She looked around the room and leaned closer to him, not quite whispering. "Another thing I noticed is that women are out and about on their own. Not a maid or footman in sight. Do you think it is safe?" She leaned back and answered her own question. "Of course it is or they would not do it."

Arbuckle came to the table with two cups and returned to gather a third. They were not proper cups but made of some kind of fortified paper. The smell emanating from them was comforting and familiar.

Arbuckle placed packets on the table and told them it was sugar, which they were welcome to add to the coffee.

Weston tasted it first, and his eyes widened in surprise. "This is the most amazing coffee I have ever tasted. Where is it from?"

Arbuckle looked relieved. "It is the standard Starbucks blend. Some people think it too strong."

"It's wonderful," Weston said as he took another taste.

Alice reached for some sugar.

"Aha," Weston said. "I knew you would add some. Your taste for sweet things has come forward two hundred years with you."

"And you brought your superiority with you, as well."

He recognized this tendency Alice had to criticize him as a strategy to encourage a distance she wanted and he did not. He knew from past experience that when she was honest with herself and with him that her words were completely different.

They drank in silence for a few minutes, observing the chaos around them.

One couple was having an intense low-voiced discussion at a table next to them. Two others at different tables were reading something on a device in front of them and then tapping wildly with their fingers, one occasionally stopping to run his hand through his hair. They seemed oblivious to the line of people waiting for service or the loud voices of the waitresses calling out the items that were ready.

"Is there a way to copy this business?" He had not intended to speak aloud, but once said, it could not be called back.

CHAPTER FIVE

"Weston, why would you want to copy this business when there are already dozens of coffeehouses in London alone?" Alice said. "And surely you would not go into trade! Apart from that shocking idea, what does this Starbucks offer that is not already available, besides wonderful coffee and good lighting? Neither of which we can bring back with us without altering the continuity of time."

"The space-time continuum," he corrected. Weston turned to Arbuckle. "And what is the space-time continuum?"

"I'm afraid I have no idea." Arbuckle looked profoundly apologetic. "All I know is the magic coin enabled Miss Amy and Mr. West to travel to your home and for you to travel here."

"Exactly what is this magic coin?" Weston asked. "You mentioned it before when I was less inclined to believe you."

"Sir, I can tell you all I know in a few sentences. A shipment of coins bound for India was lost when the ship sank just off the Goodwin Sands in 1810. The ship was found by treasure hunters in 1987, and among the coins was one that was different from all the rest. It grants wishes."

"Do you have proof?" Weston asked.

"It does sound rather like a grown-up fairy tale, Mr. Arbuckle," Alice said with a bit more diffidence than before.

"Yes, it does, miss, and yes, my lord, I have proof. I have seen the coin grant wishes time and again."

"I will take your word, for the moment, but now I want to know how you knew the coin needed to travel back into the early nineteenth century. Indeed, to before it was even minted."

"Ah, my lord, because the coin had to be there to grant the wishes that are the heart of its mission. I was more than relieved when Miss Amy and Mr. West were willing to take it. I worried about how the coin would travel through time ever since I saw it in your portrait when it was loaned to a special exhibit at the National Portrait Gallery."

"I fear this is beginning to sound like nonsense again," Weston said.

"Really, Wes, why do you say that?" Alice asked, her head tilted to one side in a gesture of challenge he recognized. "Is it any more fantastical than the two of us skipping ahead two hundred years?"

Before he could answer Alice turned to their host.

"Mr. Arbuckle," Alice asked, "since you cannot explain the space-time continuity, then how can you be sure the coin can bring them back and return us to our more familiar world?"

"There is no doubt in my mind that Amy and Mr. West will return to their rightful place, as will you," Arbuckle answered promptly. "Because the coin has enabled me to travel through time as well."

"You've traveled through time?"

"Why did you not tell us that sooner?"

Both of them spoke at the same time.

"Until Amy and Mr. West traveled I thought I, as keeper of the coin, was the only one who could do so."

"But you have not traveled back, have you?" Weston hated to point out the obvious, but he needed answers.

"No, because I assume my work here is not done. But I

have complete faith that when the time is right, we will all be where we belong."

"Faith in the reality of space and time travel?" Alice asked.

"The space-time continuum," Weston corrected.

"No," Arbuckle continued, "I have faith in God. My experience has led me to believe that there are dimensions or realms we do not see or understand. But the Divine does, and He makes all things possible."

"Including magic coins?" Weston did not share such a broad view of heaven, earth and all between, but Alice seemed more at ease with an explanation that was based on religion instead of science, for she smiled a little and nodded.

"Do you know when that will happen?" Weston hated to spoil her happy mood, but he could not resist asking.

"I have no idea."

"That seems to be one of your favorite phrases, sir, and it is not at all reassuring." Weston felt compelled to add, "Though I do appreciate your honesty."

"I know it will happen, and it will not matter if you are in the library or in Paddington Station. You will return to exactly where they are standing, and they will return here."

Alice stood up. "So there is no need for us to rush back to the town house? We may explore more of the twenty-first century?"

Excellent questions, the earl thought. If they could explore more he might be able to act on the idea he had had at the bookshop. Namely, did his visit to the future hold a way for him to repair the West family fortunes?

For the first time Mr. Arbuckle hesitated. "I am not sure how wise it is for you to know every detail of modern life."

Alice sank back into her seat, looking quite disappointed.

"But you told us that we cannot change history," Weston reminded him, and not just because he hated to see Alice disappointed. Before Arbuckle could answer, Weston went on, approaching the subject another way. "Tell me, sir, have canals prospered in the last two hundred years?"

"Oh yes," Alice said. "Lord Bridgewater's canal generated many imitators. It was a brilliant way to move coal."

"It may have been brilliant then, but they are no longer used for transport in this country." Arbuckle spoke with regret. "The canals today are no more than pleasant byways where people use the old barges for vacation houses and some even make permanent residences of them. They have no real economic value anymore."

Thank the good Lord he found that out before he invested in them. Perhaps I am using the wrong approach, he thought. "Tell us what has changed lives the most."

When Arbuckle pressed his lips together as though he would refuse to answer, Alice interceded. "Come now, sir, what does it matter? We have been dead so long it can hardly make a difference to the content of space and time."

"Space-time continuum," Weston corrected sotto voce again. Alice merely shrugged at the correction.

Arbuckle nodded. "I suppose you have a point, miss." With his finger on his lips, he seemed to give the question some thought. "I think electricity has been the most significant invention. It is now used to power lights, provide heat in the winter and cooling in the summer, and further powers so much of what we use in daily life."

"Electrical science is of some interest in my time," the earl said, wondering if that was the key to repairing the West fortunes.

"Yes, but the true development of electricity in a practical way does not happen until the end of the nineteenth century."

"Shall we walk among the crowd?" Weston suggested, hiding his disappointment. "Perhaps that will provide inspiration." He spoke the last aloud without intent. Mr. Arbuckle was taking the used cups to a trash bin, but Alice heard him.

"Inspiration for what?"

"A way to repair the fortunes of the Earl of Weston," he answered as he stood to help Alice from her chair. "There must be something here that I can invest in back in our own time."

CHAPTER SIX

As Weston watched Mr. Arbuckle make his way back to them, a conversation from a nearby table distracted him.

"See, Ginny. That girl didn't mind that the guy with her helped her up."

The speaker was half of the couple he had observed earlier having such an intense conversation. Weston was sure the young gentleman had not intended him to hear.

"Yes, but that's the least of it, Bryce. It's not those old-fashioned things like helping a woman put on her coat or opening the door, it's your overall attitude toward my work."

"It's not your work, Ginny. It's the way it consumes you."

With a glance at him, Alice sat back down in her seat, and Weston did the same. Yes, this was a little bit of twenty-first-century drama that he wanted to hear, rude as eavesdropping may be.

"Being a physician takes time," the girl continued.

"But you're done with your residency."

"And now I'm going to spend a year or two as a colleague of the foremost physician in the field of head and neck surgery."

Alice looked stunned. He probably did too. This woman was a physician? Beyond that, she was apparently about to specialize in a field of science he had never heard of.

"So if we want to marry we'll have to wait?"

The girl shook her head. "I love you, Bryce. I want this to work. But your job with the foreign office and mine, well, it makes it hard to have much of a life together."

"Shall we go?" Mr. Arbuckle asked as he came back to the table.

Embarrassed by his eavesdropping, Weston stood up with unnecessary speed. Alice was more decorous but made no demur, and they left the coffeehouse and the little drama behind them.

Alice took his arm and leaned closer and said, almost whispering, "Did you hear that, Wes? That woman, she could not have been much more than thirty. And she is a physician! It's astounding."

"It most certainly is. I'm not sure I would be willing to trust her to care for me."

"And why not?" His comment brought Alice up short, and they stood in the middle of the walk, people streaming around them on either side. "She must have been well educated if she is to work with the best in her field. Do you not believe that a woman can do work with an expertise equal to a man's?"

"I find it hard to believe that times have changed that much."

"Oh, Weston, don't be ridiculous. Look at those things that fly and the machines that hold more information than every book in your well-respected library. If those things are possible, then why not a woman doing a man's work?"

"Shall we move along, my lord?" Mr. Arbuckle suggested. "We can walk to Green Park. It's only a few blocks away, and we can continue the discussion there, if you wish."

They followed behind Mr. Arbuckle, arm in arm, weaving through crowds that seemed to have grown in the short time they were in the coffee shop. As they walked Alice pressed her point. "All these women we see passing are so much better dressed than I am. Based on what we overheard it's most likely that they have positions with responsibility outside of maintaining a home."

"Hmm," was the only response that occurred to him.

"They could be bankers, shop owners." As they waited at the light she turned to a well-dressed woman. "I beg your pardon, miss, but would you tell me what you do with your day?"

The woman looked slightly nonplussed, but shrugged. "I'm the manager of an art gallery in SoHo." As the light changed she hurried off. "Sorry, I'm quite late getting home."

"There, you see, Wes? Though I am not sure what someone who manages an art gallery actually does, the word 'manager' indicates a position of some responsibility."

As they entered Green Park, Mr. Arbuckle waited for them so they could all walk side by side on the wide path.

"Mr. Arbuckle," Alice asked, "is it not true that women do all sorts of work now, work that used to be reserved for men in our time?"

"Yes, miss, that's quite true."

Weston wondered if the change was one-sided. "Next you will tell me that men are giving birth and nursing their young."

Even as he spoke, they passed a park bench where a young man was holding a babe and feeding him with a bottle. Weston's face must have shown the panic he felt, for Alice laughed out loud.

"No, my lord," Mr. Arbuckle reassured him, "men do not give birth, but they are much more involved in child care now than they were in 1805."

"How, um, interesting." Weston did not know whether to be relieved or impressed. "Do men have nothing more important to do than care for puking and mewling infants? Have the women taken all their positions?"

"Oh, Weston, please." Alice's tone made him feel like a fool. "Did you not hear Mr. Arbuckle say that they share the responsibility? I imagine that both men and women work, and sharing domestic duties is the only way they can manage."

Frankly, this struck him as more amazing than cars and computers.

They had come out of Green Park and continued along Piccadilly, arrowing back toward the town house, both of them lost in their own thoughts for the moment.

Weston tried to decide if he would be willing to share "domestic duties" if that meant Alice would marry him. The answer was an unequivocal yes. Ah well, then he was not quite so far removed from twenty-first-century man as he'd thought. But then the problem had never been his willingness to commit to her, but hers to him.

Her obstinate belief that her parents' divorce and her family's social ostracism would extend to him had truth at its core, but he was convinced that the two of them could have persuaded the ton that she was as much a lady as any Countess Weston. And it was probably a fantasy on his part to think that the open-mindedness he was seeing in her was something that would travel back with them.

CHAPTER SEVEN

Sorry soul-searching was becoming an unwelcome habit, but Weston was stopped short of further conjecture by Alice's insistent tug on his arm. "Tell me why all those people are walking into that building. They cannot all have positions there."

Weston had been so lost in thought he had not even noticed that oddity as they turned the corner. "Yes, I see, and at least as many are coming out. But why?"

"They are not actually going into the building, my lord. The building access is also the entry to the Green Park Underground station. The Underground is a train system that runs in tunnels beneath the city. In London, it's the most popular method of moving from place to place."

"I want to see it!" Alice said. "Can we ride on it?"

Mr. Arbuckle hesitated and shook his head. "Not now, miss. It's the time of day when everyone is going home, and the trains and tracks are much too crowded. Maybe later this evening."

"Judging by the number of people pouring in, I suspect

you have the right of it," Weston said, pulling Alice just a bit closer. "I would not like to be separated. From either of you," he added quickly.

They were standing in the shelter of a small, freestanding shop that appeared to exist to meet the needs of those who used the so-called Underground. It did not look like it would survive a strong wind, but it did appear to have occupied the space awhile. As he watched, people purchased packages of food and newspapers.

"At least newspapers still exist and do not appear to have changed that much."

"But the pictures. They are not paintings, and are printed right on the paper. In colors." Alice let go of his arm and picked up a periodical.

Weston examined several of the newspapers that were on display and was brought up short by one that proclaimed: *Vinton to Divorce.* He picked up the paper and handed it to Arbuckle. "Purchase this for me." When Arbuckle hesitated, Weston insisted, "Then give me the money! You told us before that nothing we can do will change the future, as this event was always meant to be, so let me have this."

"It's not that, my lord, but this is hardly a reputable newspaper. There are others that would be more, uh, honestly informative."

"Will they have stories on this divorce that is on the front page?"

"I'm not sure."

"Then let's have this one and we can look on the information box for more when we are back at the townhouse."

"Computer, my lord. It's called a computer."

Weston did not care what it was called, as he was damn sure he would never see one when he returned to Westmoreland. It ranked with the space-time continuum as something he had no need to understand.

Twenty minutes later they were in the library again. As soon as they were seated, the housekeeper brought tea and some small sandwiches and sweets.

"Will you be here for dinner, then, sir?" she asked, with a casual air that reminded Weston of his sister rather than a servant.

With a look at Mr. Arbuckle, Weston nodded. "And have a guest room made up for Miss Kemp."

"Of course." She nodded to Miss Kemp. "Dinner will be served at eight o'clock," Tandy added as she left the room.

"She seems rather more a friend than a servant, does she not?" Alice said.

"Yes, I almost thought I should add a 'please' to my request for a guest room."

"Servants are much more difficult to find these days," Arbuckle said. "The Weston housekeeper has been with the family for near forty years."

Weston nodded. "Then she is family. I will add the 'please' next time. I would not want to create problems for Mr. West."

They sipped tea and Weston ate several of the tasty but too-small sandwiches. As he ate he moved about the room, looking more closely at the modern additions, touching them carefully, anxious to read the paper but wise enough to wait until they were both fortified with some food and tea.

Alice kept to her seat and sampled the pastries. Weston watched as she took a delicate bite, closed her eyes and savored the taste with such bliss that he wanted to capture the taste of it, and of her, with his mouth.

When she reached for a third treat with a guilty glance his way, he raised his tea cup in salute, came back to his chair and took a cream confection himself.

They sat in silence. After finishing his tea, Weston held the newspaper in front of him so that the headline was clear to everyone in the room, especially Alice.

But Alice was engrossed in the periodical she had purchased, called *Vogue UK*, whose colorful pages held her in thrall.

It took him a few minutes to focus on the article that accompanied the headline on the front page. It was one of his less salacious wishes to do just this with Alice: sit in the library, reading what interested them and sharing the best bits, all the while watching the clock until they could retire. Together.

He cleared his throat and gave his full attention to reading about Vinton and his divorce. When he was done he had more questions than answers. "But that's what time travel is all about, is it not?"

He had not meant to speak aloud, but both Alice and Mr. Arbuckle turned to him.

"What is time travel about, Wes?" Alice asked, the magazine spread open to a page of women in gowns cut low and without sleeves. Gowns that showed an amazing amount of the body. Weston considered them with interest until Alice looked at him.

"Are you ogling, Wes?"

He shook his head and cleared his throat, turning away.

"While you were distracted, Weston, I asked what you think time travel is about."

Relieved that she did not pursue her question about ogling, Weston answered promptly, "Questions, my dear. Time travel is all about questions. For everything I learn, ten more questions come to mind."

CHAPTER EIGHT

Weston took a deep breath and directed Alice's attention to the front page of the article he had just finished.

"Do you see this headline?"

She nodded with a frown and looked back down at her magazine. "I can see divorce is as shocking now as it is in our day."

"Not exactly," Weston said. "Vinton is a member of Parliament who, and I quote, 'has built his career on deploring the rising rate of divorce in the country.'"

"Oh," was Alice's only reply.

"It seems Vinton is extremely conservative, and it was a shock when his press manager, whatever that is, announced that he would seek a divorce from his wife of twenty years, as she is about to make public her intention to have a sex-reassignment surgery."

"What!" Alice said, clearly shocked into the curt comment.

"Do you see what I mean about endless questions? Perhaps not all of them are meant for polite company."

"You've gone so far as to introduce the subject; please do not become hesitant now." Alice put her hand out for the paper and Weston handed it to her. She held it up as she read, and he wondered if she was only using it to hide her face or actually reading the article.

"I assume since it's in the paper that changing one's sex is possible in this day and age?" Alice asked Mr. Arbuckle.

"Yes," their tutor of the twenty-first century replied with a slow nod. "But changing one's sex is not common."

"If a woman can become a man, then can a man become a woman?" Alice's expression was neutral. With effort, Weston judged.

"Yes, it can work both ways, miss."

Women could now become men? Weston tried to ignore the disquiet that aroused in him and turned to Mr. Arbuckle. "Does one use a magic coin?"

He thought he heard Alice stifle a laugh, but he could not be sure, as she was once again hiding behind the newspaper.

"No, sir. It requires massive doses of hormones and surgery."

"By all that is holy, you are actually telling me women can become men." Arbuckle had answered them once, but Weston found himself wishing he had heard wrong.

"Yes, my lord, and men can become women."

Alice lowered the paper. "Which change is more popular?"

"I do not know, miss, but I could use the computer to find out." Mr. Arbuckle was a little red in the face himself, and whether Alice noticed it or not, she rejected the offer with a raised hand, as though chasing a fly away. Do they still have flies in 2005? he wondered.

"It says here that Vinton was active in his protests of the divorce rate." Alice pointed to the article.

Weston had known this was a subject that, though painful, would interest her.

"The article implies that the rate has stayed the same for the last few years, but that Vinton believes it is indicative of a moral decay that he thinks is rampant."

"Well, yes, the rate has increased dramatically," Arbuckle explained, "especially from your perspective. I don't know the exact percentage, but I would say forty percent of marriages end in divorce."

"By all that's infamous, that would be forty out of every hundred?" Weston looked at Alice, who was equally astonished.

"But how can that be? Are divorces not expensive anymore?"

"Not as expensive as they were in the nineteenth century."

"And there is no social ostracism?" Alice asked.

"No, miss, not as there is in your era."

"In my life," she said with a breath that was part laugh and part shock.

"Your life, miss?" Arbuckle asked carefully.

"My parents divorced." Alice spoke without emotion in a tone that suggested no more discussion.

"Oh, yes, then I see why this would interest you."

"And no one cares anymore? The marriage ends and people go on with whatever they were doing?" Weston asked.

"Well, it's never so simple. There is almost always pain, and since marriage is a binding contract, the law is involved. But in time everyone goes back about their lives."

"What happens to the children?" Alice asked, obviously distressed.

"The court awards custody to one or the other parent, or, more usually, both."

"If they are not living together, at least I assume they are not living together, then where do the children stay? And the former wife. Does she have a place to live?"

"The children live at one house or the other depending on the custody arrangements."

"Oh, then that's not so bad, then. I spent the Season with my aunt, while my father was in London, you understand, and the rest of time I was with him." Alice relaxed a little.

"And the ex-wife usually is provided for. But not always. Some women actually make more than their spouses, and it's the ex-husband who must be supported. In both cases that stipend is called alimony."

"That is both fascinating and overwhelming." Alice considered for a moment, shook her head and went on. "Can you define moral decay, Mr. Arbuckle?"

The poor man looked as though he could use something stronger than tea.

"Um, I assume they mean the casual attitude toward sex outside of marriage."

Weston shook his head. "It sounds much like the behavior of the ton during the Season and at most house parties."

"It is not that simple, my lord. The issue is a much-discussed topic, but as to your point, the more liberal members agree with you."

Alice laughed. "Best not let anyone hear you've turned liberal, Wes. It could upset the balance of power in Lords."

"Alice, I suspect my views on many things will change after this experience."

They went on to discuss the openness of homosexual behavior and a dozen other social changes that would shock even the most liberal members of the House of Lords.

The three of them entered into a spirited discussion on the issue of moral decay. It was threatening to become a full-blown argument when Tandy knocked on the door to announce dinner. It was a well-timed interruption.

CHAPTER NINE

Dinner was a delicious experience, but completely different from the way the meals were presented and served in Weston's day. There were fewer dishes, and no footmen to hold the serving platters. The chicken Cook had prepared was in a white wine sauce over a concoction of brown and wild rice (he'd had to ask what it was) with roasted asparagus and a mix of green leaf vegetables covered with what he suspected was an oil and vinegar topping.

Salads, as they were called, were new to him, and without the topping would have been more suitable as food for rabbits—though he was careful not to voice that thought aloud. Despite so few dishes, he was replete after a healthy sampling of everything.

Dessert was the most wonderful burnt cream he had ever tasted. The twenty-first-century name for it was crème brûlée, after the French, and if he thought it was delicious, he was sure that Alice near swooned with pleasure at each mouthful. A suitable white wine accompanied the meal, and coffee finished it, offsetting the feeling of fatigue that had been tempting him to abandon the evening's adventure.

"Is it a good time to test the Underground, Mr. Arbuckle?" Alice did not seem to be suffering from the same languor as he.

"Yes, most assuredly. We will take the Underground just one stop, but it will be enough of an experience, I am sure. The speed and widespread use of trains for travel first began in the late eighteen hundreds, but they reached their prime in the last century."

With compliments to the cook, who turned out to be Tandy herself, the three of them left the house once again. The nearest locale to find the Underground was the one they had passed earlier in the day at Piccadilly.

As they went inside and proceeded, quite literally, underground, Alice clung more firmly to his arm. Mr. Arbuckle moved ahead of them with confidence, paused long enough to pay for tickets, and then directed them to the stairs. The moving stairs.

Weston could feel the tension in Alice increase and was sure if he could test her pulse he would find it hammering as hard as his was. Neither he nor Alice stepped onto the moving stairs with as much confidence as the people around them, but no one seemed to care.

"Thank goodness most seem to just ride on these," Alice whispered. "It would test my balance to ride and step down at the same time."

They both watched their fellow travelers.

"They do not seem at all amazed," Alice observed. "Their expressions range from—um—disinterest, I would say, to"—she paused again—"impatience."

"I suspect the impatience stems from whether they have had dinner or not."

She laughed a little, and her death grip on his arm eased just a tad.

As they moved deeper and deeper under London, he wondered aloud, "Do you think this is what coal miners experience when they head into the earth?"

"Possibly, though without as much light. And it certainly is not as clean as this."

"This convinces me that miners are not paid nearly enough."

"We can breathe quite comfortably, Weston. How can that be?"

Instead of answering her, he nodded to the end of the moving stairs, and they both concentrated on stepping off without mishap.

"Part of me thinks that was quite enough adventure," Alice said. "And we haven't even seen the underground transport yet."

A moment after Mr. Arbuckle announced, "It will be loud," the noise level increased dramatically. It took real effort not to cover his ears, as Alice did for a moment. As they walked toward the platform where a few people were waiting, the train charged by them moving faster than anything Weston had ever seen.

It stopped and the doors opened, and they did not need the voice urging them to "mind the gap" to step carefully from the platform into the carriage, one of several carriages connected for a train of considerable length.

Alice leaned closer; in truth she did it to make room for someone who wished to take a seat in the small space next to her. The side of her body pressed into him, and the jolt of lust that echoed through him at even this minimal contact made Weston marvel at his control. When they finally did go to bed, he wondered if their rooms would connect.

The ride was astounding; so astounding that his arousal subsided in the face of this terrifying experience. It felt as though they had been shot from a cannon.

"I devoutly hope the driver knows the correct route," Weston said, turning to Mr. Arbuckle, who nodded.

"The train has wheels, and they run on tracks so there is only one way they can go. These trains can run without a driver if necessary."

"The Oystermouth Railway!" As he tried to form a mental image of carriage wheels locked into a track to convey a load, the words popped into his mind, making the connection. He spoke aloud without thinking.

"What are you talking about, my lord?" Alice actually put some distance between them as she asked. Did she think he had gone mad?

"Alice, they are constructing a system that functions on rails in Wales, but they do not call it the Underground, they call it the Oystermouth Railway. When it is complete they will use it to transport coal from an area where there are no roads."

"I've never heard of it," Alice said. "Have you, Mr. Arbuckle?"

Arbuckle shook his head. Of course I know a little about the development of railways, but not that particular one."

"Not many have heard of it. Yet. The only reason I know it," Weston continued, "is because the estate owns several coal mines that would be serviced by the railway. The trustees are not inclined to maintain the connection because they feel it will cost more than it is worth, and they approached me recently with the suggestion that we sell our interest." He looked around him with satisfaction. "I think not. There is obviously more of a future for railways. More than just carrying coal away from the mines."

As the train pulled to a stop and Mr. Arbuckle rose, Weston and Alice followed.

They reversed their route, stepping onto the moving stairs that went up—a much easier proposition than stepping on to go down. One wasn't likely to fall up the stairs, though he imagined it was possible.

"Mr. Arbuckle, Alice wonders how it is we can breathe so comfortably below ground, and I wonder what fuels these marvels."

"I really do not know the answer to either question, my lord, but in the early days of train travel it was coal that fueled the engines."

Weston nodded. "More and more I am committed to the coal mines in Wales, Alice."

She gave him her attention, and he went on. "They are clearly a fundamental part of the future. And I think it's significant that the Oystermouth Railway is a project that I am already involved in."

"It was your uncle's investment, was it not?"

"Yes, and one that is infinitely more sensible than it seemed. I will not let it go, regardless of what the estate trustees counsel."

CHAPTER TEN

"Are we not still in Mayfair?" Alice asked as they exited the Underground station into a salubrious evening.

"Yes, miss, we are."

"Certainly it would be easier to walk. And cost less."

"Yes, miss, but most people take the Underground much farther than we did. As in your time, only the wealthy can afford to live in Mayfair. I thought a sample of the Underground was all you would need."

"When did train travel become popular, Mr. Arbuckle?" Weston was piecing together a plan and could barely contain his excitement. But before his companion could answer they were all distracted by a man, or boy, who came racing toward them, bumped through them and, without apology, ran on.

"Stop! Police!" A woman dressed in a uniform followed the same route as the boy, but having been prepared, the three of them stood back and let her through.

Weston stared after her, both puzzled and astonished.

"What was that?" Alice asked, raising her hand to her heart, as if that would still the beating that had to match his.

"Someone who the police think has committed a crime," Mr. Arbuckle explained.

"But who was that woman chasing him? Had he stolen something from her?"

"No, by her uniform I would say she is an officer, a member of the Met—the Metropolitan Police Force. They, er, work to keep innocent people safe by apprehending those who break the law."

"But women are allowed to do this?" Alice raised a hand to her head as if trying to hold in an explosion of questions. "I think we had best return to the library. I am not sure how much more of this era I can take."

Weston understood the feeling. He offered his arm, which she took willingly. She was shaking.

"It has unnerved you that much?" he asked with as gentle a tone as he could muster. "Seeing a woman whose main work it is to keep the peace and protect the innocent?"

"Yes, it has. In our time women are the ones who need protection."

"But think of it this way, Alice. What the women of 2005 do is merely an extension of a woman's main work in 1805. True, her obligation in our day exists mainly on a domestic level. In the household it is a woman's task to do the same, to keep peace and protect the innocent." Another thought struck him. "Why, the housekeeper of a big estate wields even more power than the lady of the house, and may even be a better template for what this woman does."

"I see your point, but still find it shocking." Alice drew a deep breath. "You must agree, Wes, this takes protection to another level. I do believe she was carrying a pistol."

They turned the corner, heading in the same direction as the young man and the woman, only to find the area quiet, with no sign of the villain or the officer. It was as though the ripple had faded, and the steady stream of people walking continued as before.

They took what Arbuckle called a taxi, a modern horseless version of the hackney, but significantly more comfortable and much quicker.

Weston asked Tandy for tea, and they made their way back to the library as though there were no other room in the house that would accommodate them.

That suited him well enough. In his day there had been a drinks cabinet in the corner of the room, and he was pleased to find it was still there. He poured himself a glass of brandy and raised the decanter to Mr. Arbuckle, who shook his head. Very well, he would drink alone.

Mr. Arbuckle rose. "I will be leaving you now. I must return to the museum I care for these days and make sure the alarms are set and that the cats are fed and settled for the night."

"You're going to leave us alone here?"

Weston could see that Alice would need something stronger than tea to soothe her.

"Hardly alone, miss. Tandy and her husband are within reach. All you need do is to use the bellpull to call for them."

Weston held out his hand. "Thank you for your service today. I trust that we will see you in the morning?"

"Sooner than that, sir, I will be back this evening. Tandy has assigned me a room in the gentlemen's wing. That way I will be relatively close in case you should need help with anything."

"Very good, then." It was a rather vague explanation, but Weston was reassured that Arbuckle would be nearby. "Does the housekeeper live here too?"

"But wait, please. What will Mrs. Tandy think if I am here overnight?" Alice asked, panic in her voice.

"I do believe Tandy is her Christian name, Miss Kemp," Arbuckle said, with a gesture of apology. "She is used to the overnight guests that the earl and his brother welcome."

"But ladies?" Alice asked, her hand going to her chest.

"Yes, miss." This time he spoke with even even more apology. "It is very common in this time for men and women to be more open about their—oh dear—" Weston heard him whisper to himself. "In 2005 short relationships of an intimate nature are very common. Tandy will think it nothing unusual that you are staying here." He closed his eyes and went on.

"What will strike her as odd is that you and the earl will have separate bedchambers."

"I wondered why she seemed so accepting of an unaccompanied young lady with me all day," Weston said, as Alice seemed beyond words.

"We are lucky, my lord, that you look so very much like the earl's younger brother, Simon West, for he is the one who time traveled with Miss Amy."

"She has worked here for so long, are you sure she suspects nothing?"

"My lord, I am certain that she does not suspect you have time-traveled from the Regency and changed places with Simon. You did it yourself and find it hard to believe."

Weston nodded. It was a good point.

"Was Miss Amy Mr. West's most recent short relationship?" Alice managed to choke out.

"No, Miss Kemp. They traveled as friends only."

The earl suspected that Mr. Arbuckle wanted to say more but held the thought. If it was about the prospects of that time-traveling couple's relationship remaining chaste, then Weston was glad he did not add to Alice's upset.

Mr. Arbuckle bowed again and made his exit as if he dreaded any more questions. A profound silence surrounded them. Weston moved around the room aimlessly, too restless to sit.

Alice sat down with a less-than-graceful thump and reached for her tea, then looked at him. "What does brandy taste like, Wes?"

Without answering, he added a dollop to her cup and she sipped. "Oh!" She swallowed again without a second sip. "Rather soothing, actually."

"Without the tea it burns more but is equally comforting."

"Why, then, are women discouraged from drinking it? Why is tea our only choice?"

"I have no idea, Alice. As far as I am concerned you may have all the brandy you would like."

CHAPTER ELEVEN

"Do you want the truth, Weston? Do you really want to know how I think of you?"

They were working their way up the flight of stairs to the bedroom wing. At least he hoped it was still the bedroom wing.

Alice was speaking clearly, and that had fooled him into thinking that her tolerance for brandy was more than anticipated. But now she was hanging on to the railing as if it were a lifeline. That was just as well, as she had already missed one step.

He made a mental note that her capacity for drink was about what you would expect for such a delicately boned woman. Virtually nonexistent.

"No, Alice, I do not want to know what you think. Not tonight. What you need right now is a bed."

They were at the top of the stairs and he saw, with relief, that the double doors of the master's suite were just ahead, as they had been in 1805.

"Yes, that is exactly what I need. A bed with you in it."

"Alice!" He could not keep the surprise from his voice. "Do you realize what you are suggesting?"

She wrinkled her face and laughed at his dismay. "I am just being honest. I suspect the brandy is, in fact, a truth serum and men do not want women to drink it for fear of the truths that they will hear."

He opened the doors to the master suite and walked into the salon that the earl and countess shared, with their bed-chambers on either end.

"It's quite lovely, Wes." Alice walked around the room, bouncing off a chair and almost knocking a figurine from a useless stand that was not quite in the corner.

"Do you think there is a loo near here? It is one twenty-first-century improvement that I can praise."

He led her to the door that was slightly ajar and, indeed, it was a bathing chamber. He pushed her in and closed the door, hoping she would not faint dead away.

As he examined the china figurine on the mantel and the ivory combs and brushes on the dresser, he heard some un-mistakable gagging sounds.

A few minutes later she opened the door and leaned her head out. "You, sir, are a monster. Why did you not tell me brandy would make me sick?"

"You drank too much, for which I will take full responsi-bility, my dear. But you do feel better now, don't you?"

She closed one eye and appeared to give it some thought. "Yes, I do."

"Then rinse your mouth out and come to bed."

She smiled at the idea, shut the door and completed her ablutions.

He hurried to the bathing chamber that was designed for his use and freshened up. He could not imagine sleeping in his clothes, so he stripped out of them and donned a robe that was hanging on a hook at the back of the door.

The salon was empty, and he walked over to the countess's side of the room and looked into the bedroom. The bed was untouched. With a mix of irritation, amusement and curiosity he headed for the earl's bedchamber. He opened the door and saw a distinct little mound under the covers, and discovered the most amazing thing about the love of his life.

She snored.

Weston could not resist slipping into bed beside her. Maybe it was not what a true gentleman would do, but he was not perfect. She had not taken her half from the middle so he considered that as good as an invitation. They would only sleep together, if that was what she wanted.

He tried to ignore the sweet little snores and instead remembered that amazing summer afternoon in the Lake District at a house party where they had met after her not very successful London Season. It was the first and, he thought with regret, the only time they had made love.

The boathouse was not meant for boats at all but was designed for seduction. Never had it been more clear than the day they had raced there to escape from a storm. The weather had threatened all day, but the rain had held off until they were just far enough from the main house to make the little one-room boathouse a safer place in a storm.

"Even nature is on our side," Alice had whispered between kisses that convinced them that they needed to lie on the lounge to fully enjoy them. Their bodies pressed together in imitation of their lips.

It seemed as natural as the rain to undress each other in between kisses. Eventually the urgency of their caresses compelled them to rush removing the last bits of clothing. They paused for no more than a breath and came together in a heated coupling that had him forgetting she was a virgin.

Apparently she forgot too, as she made no sound of pain but rather surrendered to him with a moan of pleasure that escalated to a crying gasp as she crushed him to her and welcomed his seed.

There was never a moment of regret, for either of them. In a few weeks they learned there was no need to marry, which he regretted, though Alice swore that would never have been an option.

It was the beginning of the end for them. The first argument that could not be resolved. He could not recall the exact words, but could still recount them closely enough for it to act like cold water on his lust. "You would rather have a bastard child than marry me?"

"Not really. An ill-born child does not have an easy life if they wish any entrée to society, even country society."

"Then why?"

"I will not ruin your place among the ton, and in Parliament where you have such great responsibilities, by leg-shackling you to someone so far beneath you, the daughter of a divorced couple."

"That is not a burden you should have to bear."

"This is an absurd argument, my lord. I am not carrying your child, so it is a moot point."

Absurd it might have been, but on it went until it became clear that neither one of them would give their ground.

So that hour in the boathouse was the one and only time they had made love. No, neither of them regretted the act, but it had brought too dangerous a subject to the fore, and had crushed his hopes of marrying her. It was better to avoid the action.

In the end the frustration of love unfulfilled had made living near each other too much to bear. He had gone off to London and she had left for Yorkshire and her first position preparing young ladies for their come out.

Now they were beside each other, but miles apart in all that mattered.

As he had the thought she turned toward him, her eyes open but still half asleep. "I did not mean to sleep in your bed." She made to rise but he stopped her with a gentle hand on her shoulder.

"Nothing will happen that you do not want." He meant that even as he wished that she would want what he did. "I do suspect the brandy left you confused."

"Never say that word to me again. Brandy." She shuddered and closed her eyes as he watched her. "I may have been confused before, but now I feel fine. Even the headache is gone."

"Lucky you, Alice. That is not the norm."

She gave him a look that said her episode in the bathroom had been punishment enough.

"Can you guess how many times I have wished for this, Wes?"

Now there was a change of subject, but he was not sure the subject was a wise choice.

"Us in bed together? I imagine that I have wished for it at least as many times as you have." He would wait for her to decide how much more it would be than lying side by side.

She raised her head and, oddly, kissed his shoulder. Then she moved away and turned her attention to the ceiling.

"They no longer have bed curtains," she said, changing the subject.

"No, the rooms are warm enough that they do not even need a fire, either," he said, following her lead.

"Without curtains, sleeping feels so much more public to me."

"This from a woman who made love in a boathouse." He knew it was the wrong thing to say.

"I am not talking about making love!" she snapped.

"It's all I can think about."

"You know, Weston, you know," she repeated the words with emphasis, "from our one experience that making love makes our world even more complicated."

Yes, it did. Making love satisfied him, them, physically, but to be satisfied emotionally was something else entirely.

"Only because we allow it to complicate."

"Perhaps for a man the act is simpler. For a woman it means a kind of commitment. At least for this woman it does."

"Then make the commitment, Alice. Say you will marry me. That one yes will be as binding to me as any said before a vicar in a church."

She did not answer him with words. Alice pushed the covers back, slipped from the bed, gathered her clothes and then faced him. "I wonder if women today feel less of an emotional commitment when they make love? Weston, in all the ways that matter I have been yours since that first time we were together. You are the one and only man I will ever love.

But the very act of marrying you would mean living with the constant reminder that I am not your equal and never will be."

Alice left the room, and he was smart enough not to call her back or follow her. One moment of honesty was enough for tonight. She loved him. Would love him forever. He held that thought as closely as he wanted to hold her. And actually fell asleep smiling.

CHAPTER TWELVE

Mr. Arbuckle was waiting for them in the library. Weston wished he had been with them at breakfast, a meal made awkward by the housekeeper's nonchalance and Alice's embarrassment. Her discomfort made him so restless it was all he could do not to stand up and prowl the room.

"Good morning!" Mr. Arbuckle announced, rubbing his hands together as if he were preparing to share a special treat. "Is there something specific you would like to do today?"

"I want to go back to my proper time and place," Alice announced. Her discomfort dimmed some of Mr. Arbuckle's enthusiasm.

"I am afraid I have no control over that. The coin does, and it is most certainly at the earl's country house, Westmoreland, far out of our reach."

"Alice, try not to worry so much."

"Oh, Weston, that is so easy for you to say. My whole livelihood depends on creating and maintaining a good packet of references. I am so afraid that Miss Amy, despite her best intentions, is ruining the profession I have nurtured so carefully."

"This is not easy for me to say, my dear." He sat across from her and leaned forward. "My uncle left the estate a financial disaster. I have been trying to find a way out of the mess." He looked at Arbuckle and smiled. "But if I am right, then the coal investment will be the solution. It makes me more willing to believe that the gift of this time travel has not been all one-sided."

"And, so it is, my lord," Arbuckle agreed. "As I told Miss Amy and Mr. West, this passage through the space-time continuum was always meant to be. What happens here and in 1805 is part of the long-accepted history of your family. You are not changing history in any way."

Arbuckle stepped closer to Alice. "That is true for you too, Miss Kemp. There is something in this experience that will enrich your life, make it better, make it happier, make you wiser. The magic coin does not deal in misery or unhappiness, nor does it only affect one person. It grants wishes, and one rarely wishes for bad things, now, do they?"

"But we did not wish on the coin," Alice pointed out with unnecessary asperity.

"You will have a chance to make a wish when you return, and in doing so you can use the insight you have gained in this century to make your world as you would wish it."

"The world I wish and the world in reality are two very different things."

"Have faith, Miss Kemp. Have faith that the coin will make your heart's dearest wish come true."

She looked at the earl with a question in her eyes.

"Yes, my dearest love, if your wish is to find a life together as man and wife, then my wish is the same."

"How can you put that before your family and the estate's needs?"

He shrugged. "Because with you anything is possible."

Mr. Arbuckle found his hat and bowed to them. "I will leave you to discuss the details of your future. If you should leave before I return I must say that knowing you has been both a pleasure and a unique experience."

"The feeling is most assuredly mutual," the earl said, and

Alice nodded in agreement. "When you return to the nineteenth century please come to Westmoreland. You will always be welcome."

"Thank you, my lord," Arbuckle answered, smiling with delight. "I will see you again then, if not tomorrow morning."

When he left and it was the two of them alone, they sat together on the settee, holding hands as they had not since they arrived in this time and place.

"This moment is perfect."

"Yes," the earl agreed. "I was thinking the same thing. I wish this was our future."

"Oh, so do I, Weston. So do I."

Suddenly overcome with an amazing fatigue, they both fell asleep, and their dreams took them home.

AS HE AWAKENED, THE EARL RECOGNIZED THE DISORIENTA-tion, the odd sense of travel with his mind as much as his body, that he'd felt the day before. Weston was not surprised when he opened his eyes and found he was on the settee in one of the salons at Westmoreland, surely in his own time.

Alice was beside him, her head on his shoulder, still sound asleep. He smiled and decided to wait for her to join him in 1805. He looked around the room, at the spot above the shelves that would hold his portrait, where the painting of Venice by Guardi currently hung.

Or should have.

The space was empty, the wallpaper a bit less faded than what surrounded it. Someone had stolen the Guardi! Or had the trustees taken it upon themselves to remove it for sale, to pay the most egregious of the estate debts?

"What is it, Weston?" Alice whispered to him, obviously having woken up and followed his gaze.

"There should be a painting there, and I have no idea why it's been moved. I will have to investigate or have someone do it for me. What I want to do most now, besides kiss you, is find the coin that has been at the heart of this bizarre adventure."

"You certainly are not kissing me." Alice stood, a little unsteady on her feet, but paused a moment and then straightened, smoothing her gown. "Thank goodness I am wearing my own clothes!"

"I rather liked the jeans we wore. They were comfortable."

"But hardly appropriate for 1805. Nor is my presence alone with you. I must leave this room at once." She smoothed her hair and looked at the door as if someone would burst in at any moment.

Did she learn nothing in the twenty-first century? he wondered. "Very well, preserve your name for now. But I know you love me, and with that magic coin Arbuckle insists anything is possible, even having you agree to marry me."

She would have argued, but he took her by the shoulders and turned her around. "If you take that door, it will lead you into a room that is almost never used and you can come out into the passage. Tell the footman you are newly arrived and have lost your way to Lady Anne's chambers. You will have the day with my sister, and then I will see you at dinner." He twirled her back around and pressed a kiss to her mouth; a kiss that left no doubt of his intent.

Alice merely shook her head, though Weston thought he saw the ghost of a smile before she gave him her back and hurried to the connecting door.

He watched her leave, the future firm in his mind, then folded his arms across his chest and waited for the magic coin to find him.

In the meantime he decided he would circle the room and try to recall if anything else was missing. He didn't think anything was.

It was not long before there was a scratch at the door. The butler came in at his "Enter."

"My lord, I have been trying to find you for the past hour."

"Really, Stepp, I thought you knew my every move."

"Yes, sir, but you have been so unpredictable lately."

"I have?" And he could just guess why. Simon West had had no Arbuckle to help him adjust to 1805.

"I'm sorry, my lord, but yes."

Weston nodded and moved to sit behind his desk. Not that he was tired, but he had a feeling that it would be a while before life returned to normal, if it ever did. Sitting at his desk reminded him that he was the final arbiter of all that happened at Westmoreland. And something must have happened, besides the disappearance of the Guardi, or Stepp would not be looking so, um, tense. Yes, tense. He usually never betrayed his sensibilities.

"You have found me now, Stepp, and you have my full attention. What is it that you need?"

"Thank you, my lord." The man bowed with some formality, which was hardly the norm. "I would never bother you with a domestic issue, but this involves money. A coin, to be precise. And, oh, my lord, Lady Anne has dismissed her maid." As Stepp spoke he placed a coin, the magic coin, on Weston's desk.

Weston did his best not to grab the coin and shout for joy. He barely contained his smile. "What a relief," he thought, aloud, unfortunately.

Stepp looked shocked, and Weston hurried to assure him. "The coin, Stepp. The coin is mine. I brought it from London and somehow it disappeared. I am so relieved that someone found it." Now he did pick it up and tuck it in his pocket. Please God, it would stay there until he had addressed the other, and to Stepp, far more important issue.

"As for Lady Anne and her maid. Am I right that my sister's maid is your daughter Martha?"

"Yes, my lord," Stepp acknowledged without any emotion.

"Did Lady Anne give any explanation for Martha's dismissal?"

"Not much, my lord." The butler spoke with asperity, then seemed to recall to whom he was speaking. "I do not mean to sound rude, sir. It was something to do with the coin. One of the maids found it, Martha took it, and it went awry from there."

"I am sorry it has come to that," Weston said as he felt the beginnings of a headache. "I will talk with Lady Anne and Martha and see what I can do to help."

"Thank you, my lord. But you had best know right away that both Lady Anne and her maid are adamant about never working together again."

"I understand, Stepp. Two strong-minded women."

"Yes, sir. I do think you understand." Stepp drew a deep breath, which did not seem to ease the rigidness of his posture. "There are one or two other issues that would benefit from your attention. If you do not think it too impertinent."

"Never, Stepp. Please go on."

"First, the coin, my lord. It bears the date 1808, but quite it is only 1805. How can that be?"

CHAPTER THIRTEEN

"Ah, yes." Weston prayed for inspiration as he pulled the coin from his pocket. "Well, you see, Stepp, the coins are being minted for use in India, as you can probably tell by the foreign wording on it."

Weston handed him the coin so Stepp could examine it. "Yes, sir, I noticed that. Everyone has."

"The coin has no value in itself. It is a medium exchange like the paper currency the government is trying to have us use now."

Stepp nodded.

"The estate has interests in mines in Wales, and the ore from those mines is being used to mint these coins. This is a sample given to me as a gesture of . . ." He hesitated, trying to think of the right word. Stepp was hanging on every detail and, no doubt, this would be the official explanation spread belowstairs.

"The project managers gave it to the trustees and thence to me as a gesture of goodwill and commitment to the process." In fact they had sent a small, toylike train, but Stepp did not need to know that.

"Thank you, my lord. There has been much speculation belowstairs, up to and including the absurd idea that it is a magic coin."

Weston smiled and shook his head.

"Would that all headaches were as easily cured," Stepp said, as he handed the coin back. "Next, my lord, you may not know, but Miss Kemp has been unavailable and sent a replacement, a Miss Amy Stevens. I have no doubt, sir, that Miss Stevens did her best but even I am grateful that she is only temporary. I do hope Miss Kemp will return soon."

"I do believe that she will be arriving today."

"Indeed!" Stepp's relief was profound. "Thank you, thank you very much, my lord." The butler did relax now and nodded. "I suspect that Lady Anne's upset with Miss Stevens had much to do with Martha's abrupt dismissal. I am certain that Miss Kemp's arrival will ease Lady Anne's sensibilities."

"I'm sure," Weston lied. He was not sure at all. If the day proceeded as he hoped, Alice would be his fiancée very soon, and not someone Anne could order about.

As he spoke, he realized that Martha's dismissal was probably something for which he and his fellow time travelers were responsible. He must do something to help the maid find a new position.

The idea struck him at the same moment that the coin glittered a brighter gold. Give the servant the coin and send her out to fulfill wishes. Who could resist such a task? Of course, convincing her of the truth of its magic would have to come first.

Stepp had turned to leave the room and literally swayed on his feet. "My lord, where is the Guardi painting that should be hanging on that wall?"

Dear God in heaven, when would this confusion end? The painting. Where *had* it gone? Had it time traveled? The thought was cynical, but the weight of the coin in his pocket gave him the answer. Weston suddenly knew what had happened to the painting. It was with Miss Amy and Simon West. The painting was what they had taken with them to the twenty-first century when they left the coin behind. So, again, he opted for the truth, or a version of it.

"I do believe it has been stolen."

"Stolen!"

"Yes."

"But by whom?"

"I will tell you more when I am certain." *That is, as soon as I think of some way to explain the theft.* "In the meantime make a notation in the journal you keep that the painting has been stolen."

"I will do as you wish, my lord." Stepp left the room, to find a glass of brandy, no doubt. It's what Weston wanted. He thanked God and the magic coin for the inspiration of the last few minutes and then begged those same powers not to abandon him anytime soon. He still had more than one person's world to set right, and he could see he would have to speak carefully to ensure that all the loose ends were done up.

He made a mental list. First, talk to his aunt dowager about the changing times. To him it was a formality he owed his uncle as his heir. His wife, the dowager countess, would need to know that changes were coming. Her support would be welcome but, he reminded himself, not essential. She would be a challenge and best tackled first.

Second, inform his sister that he had every intention of making Alice Kemp his wife and that she would be introduced to society by her sister-in-law rather than assisted by a hireling. Yes, that was the approach to take, but still it would not be easy to convince his status-conscious sister that her servant would be elevated above her by marriage.

Third, put the coin, the locket and the train in the portrait to inform the future that all had gone as he had planned. Perhaps best to do that last, when it was indeed proved that all *was* going his way. No, he would do it as it came to him. And embrace the conviction that his future with Alice was secure.

The two last items were the most important of all. One, he would be sure that Alice had her wish, and two, trust that it would be the same wish he held so close to his heart. That they had a future together, and love was the key.

If convincing the dowager that Alice was to be made welcome would be a challenge, then convincing Alice herself would be an even greater one.

CHAPTER FOURTEEN

Finding the dowager was easy. At this time of day she would be walking through the garden, dictating to the gardeners—the only place at Westmoreland where she still had authority.

"Good morning, Lady Aunt," Weston called out, loud enough for half the garden to hear.

"Weston," she said, quite formally.

"The gardens do appear to be ready to make quite a show." It was the best that could be said of the space where tulips were the only flowers ready for a vase. "The bulbs from the Dutch seem to be thriving."

"Yes," the dowager agreed, "the expense was well worth it. My husband understood those things."

"The blooms remind me of him every time I see them."

Those ungodly expensive bulbs were another example of his uncle's misguided generosity.

"What do you want, Weston?" The dowager sat herself down on the bench and looked up at him. "I cannot imagine you came out here to discuss the garden."

To the point, he thought. "Very well, though it is always good to share a lovely day with you."

The old lady's "Humph" told him that he had overdone it with that heavy-handed compliment.

He sat down next to her but was not so bold as to take her hand. "Times are changing, Lady Aunt, and to survive we must change with them."

Her body tensed; he did not need to be holding her hand to see that.

"Please listen," Weston continued. "Times are always changing. King George has remained loyal to his wife and all their children for all these years. That certainly is different from previous monarchs."

"And he has gone mad for it."

"Perhaps that is not the best example," Weston acknowledged. "We no longer need to fear smallpox, and more and more men and women are marrying for love rather than money or power." Before his aunt could reply he stopped her with a raised hand. "This is my way of telling you that I have every intention of marrying Alice Kemp. We love each other and want a life together. The only thing that is keeping her from accepting my proposal is your disapproval." That was a slight exaggeration, but his aunt's opinion was a factor.

"You want my approval?" She looked surprised.

"I value it above most things, but I must tell you that with or without it I will do my best to convince Alice to be the next Countess Weston."

The old lady sat very still for a moment, and then allowed the smallest of smiles. "About time, Weston. About time that you actually believed that you are the earl and what you want is what will be."

It was his turn to look surprised.

"I am not saying that I will welcome her with open arms," the dowager added. "She will have to prove herself worthy. But I will do nothing to hinder the proposal."

Weston took her hand and kissed it. She pulled it from him as quickly. "There, you see! You are being obsequious again! It is your right! I am nothing more than an old lady sitting among the tulips waiting to die."

"Nonsense, madam." He stood up and bowed to her. "You are the keeper of an old and ancient title and I value your willingness to pass it on to the woman I have chosen."

Her smile grew to almost a grin. "Now *that* is well said, nephew."

They parted on such good terms that Weston was convinced that the coin had more influence than even Mr. Arbuckle knew.

The conversation with his sister was next. He found her in the small music room, playing Bach. He was relieved. Bach meant that her world was ordered and as happy as it ever could be. If she had been playing Beethoven he would have left the room and waited for another day.

He took a seat, knowing full well that interrupting her would not be in his best interests. Less than a minute later, she played the final notes and looked over her shoulder at him.

"I doubt you have come for music appreciation, Weston. And I can go further and guess that you have come to plead for me to reconsider Martha Stepp's dismissal. I will not."

She turned back to the pianoforte and began shifting the music sheets. Dreading Beethoven, Weston came over and sat on the bench beside her, facing the opposite direction.

"Anne, I respect your decision to dismiss your maid. I know it must have been difficult for you."

"No, it was not," his sister said, raising her chin a little. "And I do not regret it."

Anne never made anything easy. He could not imagine how she would ever find someone who would be able to bear her moods. "Yes, be that as it may, I trust you will allow Miss Kemp to help you find a new dresser."

"Yes." Anne drew breath. "She certainly is an improvement over that person she sent as a substitute when she was delayed. At least she had a reasonable explanation for her delay."

Anne began to fiddle with the sheets of music in front of her again, and a thought occurred to him.

"Sister, dear, do you even want a Season? Do you even want to go to London; and if you do, then why?"

"Of course I want to go. And finding a husband is what the Season is for."

Hmm, he thought, not exactly enthusiastic about finding a spouse. He thought about the women he had seen in the twenty-first century and wondered if there was a way for Anne to have what she truly wanted.

"I do believe there could be more to the Season than husband hunting. If that were just a side interest, then what would you really like to do with your time?"

He looked at her as she furrowed her brow and stared into the middle distance as if trying to find an answer.

"Music. I would spend all my time attending musicales and operas and meeting composers." She spoke with a kind of defiance that made him realize how rarely anyone took her seriously.

He smiled at her and nodded. "Then that, my girl, is what you shall have. You do not have to go to Almack's once if you would rather not, and, I would think, one ball a week would satisfy your more traditional relatives."

This next sigh was more like a huff. "You are not serious."

"I truly am. I have had a recent experience that convinces me that living the life we want is more important than bowing to the conventions."

"I suppose this is what comes when one unexpectedly inherits a title," Anne said. "*My* father would never have even considered such an idea."

"Well, your father held the Earldom of Uxbridge, one of the oldest in England. Let me remind you, however, that our mother was the one time in his life when he gave in to his heart. He had no need to make a second marriage. So even he had a moment of doing what he wished rather than what he must."

They rarely spoke of their different fathers, of their mother's two marrages. His father was no more than an earl's second son without even "Lord" before his name. Anne's father had been an earl.

Lady Anne had always held her title over him, and then fate had intervened, giving him a title he had never expected.

Now, if he chose, he could hold his title over her. But he did not so choose. He wanted only one thing now.

"But what will we tell Miss Kemp? She expects to lead me through a typical Season."

"Miss Kemp will be part of your Season, but—and brace yourself for this—she will be doing so as my wife, as the Countess Weston."

It had just the effect he expected. It took him some time to convince his sister that if she could live life as she chose, filled with music first and foremost, then she could certainly grant him permission to do so himself.

"But we know nothing about her."

"I do, Anne. I met her in London last Season and we came to know each other quite well. I proposed to her then but she refused, as she thought my family would take offense at my connection to a woman whose parents were divorced."

He made himself stay relaxed and waited for the explosion.

"Divorced? Truly?" She thought a moment. "How have I never heard of it?"

"You have not been to London." Weston put a hand on the instrument she sat before. "And music is all you truly need, Anne."

She nodded her agreement and was silent a moment. "So, her parents were divorced. How very awkward."

It was not the reaction he expected.

"Is that all?"

"I am not an idiot, Wes. I gather that her influence is what has led you to a more, shall we say, open mind about my Season. I expect you brought her here for more than my education."

"Do not insult her, Anne. She is as much a lady as anyone with a title."

She actually patted him on the arm. "I do not mean any insult, brother, only that I see your motives more clearly now."

He stood up then and gave her a formal bow. Best not to let this go on any longer or they would wind up hugging each other. "Thank you for your support, my lady. I look forward to sharing the Season with you and my countess."

A shake of her head was Anne's only answer. As he left
the room he heard her begin to play something lighthearted,
perhaps even happy. Definitely not Beethoven. The notes sang
through the air and touched his heart so deeply that he
laughed. He laughed out loud.

CHAPTER FIFTEEN

Weston thought the portrait artist would be the easiest of the lot. More fool he.

"My lord, you cannot be serious! The painting is virtually complete. To add elements such as these will require a complete reconsideration of the composition so that the eye views what is important."

As far as he was concerned, the train, the locket and the coin were what was important, but he knew better than to tell that to the man.

"I understand that this may entail more time than anticipated. I am willing to consider additional support if that makes the decision easier for you."

The artist brightened a little at that suggestion. "I do have other commissions."

That may or may not be true. The trustees had found him, and insisted the portrait be an immediate priority. Clearly they feared the third earl would die before his portrait was done, as his uncle, the second earl, had.

"I trust they will understand your commitment to excellence."

The artist smiled a little and picked up the coin. Weston felt a moment of panic but the man merely looked at it, then set it down. Weston wondered what the man might have wished for, had he known it could grant wishes.

"All right, my lord. It will be a challenge, but I can rise to the occasion. Can you tell me what these items symbolize so I can cast them in the proper light?"

The locket was easy; the others took a moment of thought. "The locket symbolizes the love of my life. The train car is the future of England, and the coin, well, the coin represents all that we wish could be."

The artist nodded as though he understood perfectly. "I will consider, my lord, and let you know if I need you to pose again."

Weston grimaced. He hadn't considered that possibility, but it was too late to back out now.

He left the conservatory and sent one of the footman to ask Miss Kemp to join him in the library. It seemed to take forever but he suspected that was only his imagination.

He was not going to tell her that he had already told his aunt and his sister that he was going to marry her, nor that he'd included the locket in his portrait. He would tell her he loved her and that he hoped the twenty-first century had shown her, as it had shown him, that anything was possible where two hearts were as one.

He paced the room while he waited, touching items at random; a porcelain figurine on the mantel that reminded him of his sister, one of the leather-bound books that looked as though it was frequently pulled from the shelf, the velvet softness of a tulip in one of the arrangements that appeared on a regular basis. His aunt's doing, no doubt. How many rooms did she fill with flowers?

Why should a trip through time awaken in him the realization that he did not know his household, his family, or his world as well as he should? Because he now knew how temporary it was? How easily space and time could be shifted to a different reality?

Weston doubted that he would ever time travel again, but

once was enough to change his view of this world and to realize that the future was, in some part, up to him.

The footman opened the door and Alice entered. She came to him, smiling a little but with her hands folded neatly at her waist and not the slightest sign of nerves.

"Thank you for coming, Miss Kemp." He gestured to the footman to leave the door open.

"Thank you, my lord, for considering the proprieties."

He nodded. "It's nice to see you smiling," he began.

"I do believe that Mr. Arbuckle's Miss Amy did me a favor. Lady Anne is so relieved to have her gone and me in her place that she has yet to find fault with any of my suggestions."

"About that, Alice, there have been some changes in the last hour. I talked to Anne about what she truly wants from her London Season. What she *truly* wants." He went on to explain his sister's true wishes and how he was going to permit her to have the Season she longed for.

Alice took it all in and stayed silent almost a minute. Well, for thirty seconds, at least. "Does that mean there is no place for me here now?"

He took a step closer to her, but when she stiffened just a little he did not reach out for her. "There is a place for you here. If there is one thing I learned in the future it is that times change, but they can only change if someone sets the change in motion."

"Yes, divorce is so commonplace in the future that it seems absurd that it spells social ostracism here."

"And we can begin that change if we set it in motion by marrying and announcing to the world that love is more important to us than social acceptance."

"So our possible marriage is going to change how the Regent and the ton view marriage and divorce?"

"I have no doubt of it," Weston said, ignoring her skeptical tone. "If we show the world that we mean to be a part of society despite your parents' behavior, then I am convinced that eventually they will accept us."

Alice nodded but was still not smiling. "And given that Lady Anne's true reason for her Season is to enjoy music and not necessarily to find a match, we need not worry about how our marriage will affect her prospects?"

"Exactly."

"Weston, darling man, I would marry you in a minute if the reaction of the world were my only concern."

As she spoke, Alice took a step back; several, in fact. Her voice was so full of regret that Weston was afraid, actually afraid.

"What society would think was a logical reason to refuse you before, but now, the reality of the future has made me see it differently." She drew a deep breath and shook her head. "The real reason is far more personal."

"Tell me." He was angry now, and he knew it showed in his voice.

"I will." With another breath she began. "Do you know how many times my aunt told me I was just like my mother? Just like her." Alice closed her eyes. "The very thought terrifies me." She put her hand on her heart. "It fills me with a soul-wrenching fear that I will commit myself to you and then make your life, our lives, a living hell."

"Alice, I cannot imagine that happening." Though he could see by the fear, the pain, in her eyes how real it was for her. "We love each other. Your mother's marriage was presented as a fait accompli. I can only wonder why someone with her spirit agreed to it."

"Wes, you're thinking like someone from the twenty-first century. The marriage seemed ideal to her. A husband with wealth and position. A fabulous country home and a town house in London. She assumed that she would provide him with an heir and then be free to find entertainment elsewhere. No one, *no one* warned her that his jealousy was so easily aroused. No one suspected that every physician they consulted would tell her that after me there would be no more children. The divorce, when it came, was almost as businesslike as the marriage proposal. My father wanted an heir and would give up my respectability to attain it."

She threw up her hands in disgust. "Based on what we saw

in 2005, I agree that the rejection she experienced is ridiculous. But it is the way it is in this time and place."

Before he could answer her, she went on.

"My whole view of this world is different, now that I have seen the future." She grasped his arms. "Please tell me you agree that women should be free to choose the life they want."

Weston nodded. "Have I ever denied you that, Alice? When you said no I did not press you or go to your father and have him add his support."

"It was never you I feared. I worried endlessly about what society would think. What your sister would say. How your trustees would respond."

"Alice, we completely agree that women should be free to choose the life they want. We agree that means you are free to choose marriage, if that's the life you want?"

She nodded, her eyes filling with tears.

"Honestly I cannot see you as a military officer, as fine as you would look in the uniform." His attempt to lighten the moment failed.

"Wes, I am still afraid that I will fail you."

"I am not. I know Alice Kemp's heart as well as I know my own, and while we may sometimes differ in our views of the world, I have no doubt we will listen and learn from each other with open minds and hearts."

She pressed her lips together for a moment and then laughed out loud. "How can you know me so much better than I know myself?"

"So you will consider marriage?" He was afraid to say it aloud, to give words to his hope. Before she answered, Alice walked over and closed the door.

She came back to him, wrapped her arms around his neck and kissed him lightly, which was just as well, since her touch was a wild distraction.

"Yes! Yes, I will marry you, my lord earl!" She leaned back in his arms. "To be married to you, to share a lifetime, is all the wonderland this Alice could ever want." She laughed out loud again. "Oh dear heaven, it feels so wonderful to say it. To admit it is what I have always wanted."

They sealed their agreement in the traditional way, so it was quite a little while before Weston brought up his next item for discussion.

"The coin, Alice." She was tucked against him on the sofa, and he thought she might have fallen asleep. "The very magical coin." He felt her nod and kissed the top of her head.

"Did you ever actually wish on the coin, Wes?"

When he shook his head, she nodded. "Neither did I."

"And I am not going to start now, since I already have my heart's fondest wish."

"There are any number of practical things we could ask for."

"If you want to make a wish, I will fetch the coin from the conservatory where the artist is finding the proper place for it in my portrait."

"You are having it added to the portrait? What a wonderful idea." Alice sat upright and patted her hair, which did nothing to make it look less tousled. "It will let Miss Amy, Mr. West and Mr. Arbuckle know it is now firmly entrenched in the nineteenth century."

"Yes, thank you. I think they will appreciate it."

"Let me think about a wish for a day or so. I am so happy now that to ask for more seems selfish."

"Only a day or so, Alice, if you please." He narrowed his eyes, considering his decision once again. "I want to send the coin on its way. I want it to go somewhere, anywhere else but here."

Alice laughed. "You do not want to have a tussle with it over who is actually in charge?"

"You could put it that way. Not to put too fine a point on it, I am afraid of what will happen to Westmoreland if wishes run rampant."

"But how will you, as you said, 'send it on its way'?"

"Anne's disgraced lady's maid will be leaving Westmoreland. I thought that we could ask her if she would like to take charge of it, after explaining its peculiarities, of course."

"Of course." Alice thought about it. "What in the world makes you think she would be interested?"

"I hate to admit it, but I was holding the coin when the thought came to me. According to the butler, Martha has held the coin too. I suspect she made a wish."

"Oh dear," Alice said, raising her hands to her cheeks. "I see why you would rather the coin be somewhere else."

"Thank you," Weston said with real relief. He felt as though he were somewhere between a fool and a coward.

"I would suggest that you give Martha some financial support. Quietly, so no one thinks unkind thoughts. It may be a while before she is able to find another position."

"An excellent notion. And a letter of reference from my soon-to-be countess would help as well." He took her arm. "Let's find her now and prepare her for an adventure so that we can begin on our own."

Arm in arm, they left the library. Weston felt the coin warm his hand and knew they had made the right decision. They no longer needed a magic coin and, for more reasons than one, he would be happy to share its magic. He was certain that he and Alice would have quite enough adventures without it.

iLOVE

ELAINE FOX

For Enrique. And Siri.

CHAPTER ONE

It happened so fast. The dumping. Jeremy and Macy were sitting on the patio of their favorite café, on a strangely balmy day in November, when Macy stood up, said she'd had enough and left.

Well, maybe she'd said a little more than that, but Jeremy couldn't remember exactly, and the gist was the same.

At first he'd thought she was kidding. In general, women didn't dump Jeremy Abbott, though that wasn't why he'd been floored. It wasn't until he saw her shoes heading past the table—he'd been looking at his phone at the time—and glanced up to see her striding toward the patio gate, curls bobbing, shoulders straight, purse bouncing off her hip, that he realized she'd been serious.

He looked back at her seat, half expecting her to still be there because the other scenario was too weird, but the chair canted outward exactly as if somebody had abruptly stood and ended a relationship.

She'd finished her omelet, he noted blankly. In record time. His was still half-eaten on his plate. And moments before, he'd been laughing at some joke she'd made.

Although in retrospect, maybe it wasn't a joke.

The most damning part was that he'd thought things were going well—*really* well. Well to the point of thinking, *Holy shit, maybe this is IT.*

No so for Macy, whose thoughts apparently ran more to the *Exit, stage left* end of the spectrum.

He'd have said he couldn't have been more shocked, but that was before the next thing happened.

He kept an eye on her auburn head as it moved through the crowd, and he tried to stand to go after her. Because it was ridiculous—you don't just end a nearly seven-month relationship with an *I'm outta here* over brunch. Where was the explanation, the *It's not you it's me*, at least a freaking apology for potentially, maybe, possibly hurting his feelings?

But he couldn't. Couldn't go after her, couldn't get out of the chair, couldn't, in fact, do anything except grab hold of the table while the most unbelievable feeling of suction rose through his legs to his torso and up across his chest like a flood tide.

Could he be having a heart attack? He was only thirty-four! Headlines and Facebook links and *Sponsor My Walkathon* email pleas flooded his mind with details about unexpected deaths, early-onset illnesses, it-could-happen-to-you disasters.

He looked at the people around him, obliviously chatting and eating and sipping coffee. He glanced at the breakfast congealing on his plate, the fork quivering beside it, his coffee jumping in the cup as if electrified.

His fingers ached as they clutched the edge of the table. His body compressed in on itself—collarbone into ribs, ribs into waist, waist into hips—like a giant wave pressing down on his shoulders, squishing him into a smaller and smaller square, like the paper-covered blocks his parents used to get out of their trash compactor.

Except he got smaller still, down to a shoe box, then a milk carton, until finally . . . *finally* . . .

He was inhaled by his smartphone. *Into* his smartphone.

It was like getting flushed down a toilet, or being sucked out an airplane window at thirty-five thousand feet.

He could only tell what was happening because, while everything else shrank, the cell phone got bigger and bigger, eventually looming like a skyscraper in front of him, until finally he was drawn into its center, tumbling down a darkened hallway until he ended up where he was now: an enormous cubicle-filled room.

The carpet beneath his feet was of the gray industrial type, the exact shade and texture of the cubicle walls, which were fabric with thick plastic supports. They were just like the cube he'd had in his first job out of college as a copyeditor. He tipped his head to look into the one directly in front of him. Just like those at his first job, a desktop wrapped the inside of three of the walls, a rolling chair in front of it. There appeared to be nothing else there, no computer, no printer, no in- or outbox, no paper, pen, nothing. It was a brand-new cube waiting for a brand-new employee.

It was so far from the sunny café patio, from the clatter of plates and the honking of horns, the slamming of car doors and the passing of pedestrians, the exodus of Macy . . . that he thought he must have passed out and be dreaming.

Except it didn't feel like a dream.

For a moment the floor seemed to dip beneath his feet. Then he remembered to breathe, and shoved aside the ache in the center of his chest brought on by the thought of Macy. His hand reached for the phone holster at his belt and found it empty.

What had *happened*? Had he died?

He turned his head, looked down a mile-long hallway lined with cubes, the doorless entries expressing nothing, and saw only a row of cavities in an oversized mouth. He walked a few steps over and peered into the next cubicle. An Asian guy wearing a plaid shirt and a thick black watch was hunched over his desk, gazing at a wall full of screens.

Thank god, he thought, the human presence calming him.

"Excuse me," he said, moving toward the opening. "Hello? Excuse me."

The guy didn't respond, just moved his head fractionally from side to side as his gaze jumped from one screen to another. Had he not heard, or had he heard and decided to ignore him? Jeremy's attention shifted to the wall of screens. They were like nothing he'd ever seen before. They had no edges, no glass, no seeming substance at all, except for the myriad images, charts, documents and moving pictures they seemed to be displaying. And there were dozens of them, some larger than others; a few were as large as televisions.

"I'm sorry," he said louder, unnerved by the guy's absorption. "Can I ask you something?" Ordinarily he wouldn't bother someone so deep in concentration, but panic was building inside him. What *was* this place?

Still no response. Jeremy moved to the next cubicle. Another guy, this one heavyset and impeccably dressed in a medium-gray suit with white shirt and blue tie. He wore fashionable glasses, and he too stared at his wall full of screens.

Jeremy cleared his throat. "Hi," he said. "I'm sorry to bother you, but can I ask you something?"

Same thing. No response. Could he be invisible? Was this some kind of Ghost of Workplace Future–type experience? He touched the man's shoulder. It *felt* real. But the suited man did little more than blink and reach up to brush the spot that Jeremy had touched as if ridding himself of a spider.

Jeremy moved on. A woman inhabited the next one, brown hair, business attire, good posture, deaf as a post. Two more men, equally oblivious. He halted then, listening more closely. There seemed to be people in every cube, but there was not a sound to be heard. He walked the outer hallway created by cubicles on one side and a wall of the room on the other, passing one cubicle after another, all of them occupied by someone—man or woman, young or old, black or white, fat or thin, neat or messy—none of whom paid him one iota of attention. It freaked him out.

After walking the length of the hall—which took no small amount of time—he stood on tiptoe, only to see a static sea of zigzagging cubicle walls. Above them lay an endless expanse of rectangular fluorescent lights; in front of him, an endless gray hallway. It was dizzying.

His heart raced, and sweat broke out along his hairline. He turned to go back to where he started, hoping to find the way out, but all he discovered when he arrived back at the empty cube was a name tag attached to the outer wall.

Jeremy Abbott

The sight of his own name caught him in the solar plexus like a punch.

He gasped, then forced an exhale.

He was in hell. He had to be. Or some really, *really* weird dream. But he hadn't fallen asleep and he felt more lucid than he had in years. Also more terrified.

His hand reached again for the cell phone case on his belt, but the moment he touched it he remembered it was empty. He'd only wanted to know the time. He looked around the room again, this time for a clock, and realized with a sinking feeling that there was none. In hell, he thought, time probably didn't exist.

His heart climbed into his throat, deciding to pound furiously there and block his windpipe. Fearing he might faint, he grabbed for the chair in "his" cubicle and plopped into it. It rolled and struck the desk with its back. Jeremy planted his feet and put his head between his knees, breathing deeply. A sound like a computer booting up had him rising nearly as swiftly.

Suddenly, on what had been the plain gray fabric walls of his cube, appeared the same collection of screens he'd seen on the other people's walls.

His eyes took in the sight, flicking from one to the other, and only a moment passed before he recognized what he was looking at. Apps! More specifically, smartphone apps. There were the calendar, settings, maps, messages, email, phone, web browser. The stock market. And then there were Redfin, Facebook, Twitter, TV Guide, NFL, Soccer, Tennis Channel—all the personal apps he had on his phone—and as he looked at them, they opened. He was controlling his iPhone with his mind! He looked around, wanting to tell someone, because this was freaking *awesome*. A mind-controlled smartphone!

But of course all those other people already knew it. No wonder they'd been too absorbed to hear him. Either that or they had *literally* been absorbed.

Was that what had happened? Had he been transported into the future, where—where what? He *was* his cell phone?

Novelty turned into nausea.

Then he remembered the words Macy had said just before standing up and dumping him: *Someday you're going to get sucked right into that thing and nobody will ever see you again.*

MACY STRODE DOWN THE STREET, SWALLOWING OVER THE lump in her throat and blinking to stop tears from overflowing her eyelids. She paused and looked up at the sky, willing them back into her tear ducts even as another wave of regret washed over her.

She was crying, on the street, over a guy. What had become of her?

She remembered the first time she'd noticed the problem—or rather, noticed how big of a problem it was. She and Jeremy had taken a hike to the top of Sugarloaf Mountain. The air had been soft with summer's last breath and the leaves were falling, crunching under their feet as they walked. They made it to the top, bursting out of the woods onto a rocky outcropping that showed nothing but rolling hills and a carpet of trees transitioning from green to orange, yellow and red. The breeze had kicked up, gently moving her hair from her forehead, and she'd gasped at the beauty before her, feeling as if the whole world was a magical place. It was a moment of such sublime happiness that she couldn't think of another place on the planet she'd rather be.

This is it, she'd thought. *This is the guy. This is what I've been searching for my whole life.*

She'd turned to Jeremy, buoyant to be sharing it with him,

convinced he had to be feeling it too, the profound connection, the *certainty* that this was something special, only to find him looking at his phone, thumb pushing screens aside, eyes riveted.

It struck her so hard, she couldn't help it; she'd wanted to cry. She felt crushed. Had she fallen into the classic trap of believing that because *she* felt something, *he* did too? Was he here just to placate her? Was this the kind of moment, the kind of shared activity, that would disappear completely as the relationship aged? Would they end up at the same kitchen table inhabiting completely different worlds?

After a minute, perhaps sensing her silence, he looked up with an oblivious grin and said, "Can you believe it? I've got a signal up here!"

She'd turned away quickly, blinking back tears of disillusionment, and said something about the view, at which point he had joined her on the rock. But she could tell he wasn't where she was, that he had no conception of the magic he had squelched.

By the time they'd gone to their respective homes, changed clothes and gotten back together for dinner that night she'd shaken most of it off, and the next morning he'd been charming at breakfast. Though he'd been checking work emails when she came downstairs, he'd put the phone down the moment he became aware of her.

"She's alive!" he'd joked, and those sleepy gray eyes of his smiled. He wore a faded sweatshirt and well-worn jeans, his wavy hair tumbled wildly on his head like he hadn't even glanced in a mirror, and she felt her heart lurch at the beauty of him.

She, on the other hand, had scrubbed her face, applied emergency makeup from her purse, and tried to casual-ize the outfit she'd worn the night before by going barefoot in her black skinny jeans and leaving her white shirt untucked.

"We've got to get you a pair of sweats to keep here," he said, rising to wrap her in a good-morning hug.

She put her arms around him and breathed in the laundry-fresh scent of his T-shirt. The feeling of rightness returned, and she pictured them sitting around in their pj's on Sunday mornings, reading the paper and sharing the interesting bits. She didn't need to hike; they'd find other things to do together, things that he found special.

"How did you sleep?" His voice was intimately low, vibrating against her cheek where her face pressed against his chest.

"Like a coma patient."

The sound of his chuckle, and the feel of it against her body, made her toes curl. She squeezed him tighter.

"Let me get you some coffee."

"Coffee," she breathed, starting to let go of him.

But he held her tighter and said, "Nope, we can do this. Trust me. Follow my lead." And he shuffled her over to the coffeemaker, where he poured her a cup one-handed and then prepared it exactly the way she liked it: dollop of cream, spoonful of sugar.

Laughing, she took it from him with one hand and sipped. "Perfect. But this could get awkward when you make me breakfast. How are you going to peel the potatoes for the hash browns?"

He laughed. "Madam, you underestimate me." He shuffled them over to the freezer, pulled it open, extracted a box of Bob Evans breakfast sandwiches and tossed it toward the microwave. "Voilà. Breakfast."

She laughed, her smile feeling unquenchable, and said, "Mr. Abbott, you're an amazing man."

Those ridiculously lashed eyes gazed down at her for a long moment, making her feel every kind of beautiful. "You've got it backward," he said softly. "I'm an *amazed* man, Ms. Serafini. Every day more amazed, by you." And he'd kissed her. Kissed her with the gentle finesse of a man falling in love.

She had swan-dived off the edge then, and felt herself willing to give everything for the man who made her feel like this. He was present for *this* magic, she'd thought, and that was enough.

She'd been so happy she hadn't even minded when, three minutes later as she was opening the box of Bob Evans breakfast sandwiches, he'd been back at the table, absorbed in his iPad.

Now, remembering how she'd duped herself made her feel even sadder. She was *just like* all the girls in those anti-smartphone videos, the girls looking lost as their boyfriends ignored them for their phones. The girls she'd chalked up as having chosen to love rather than *be* loved, like wallflowers satisfied with a wink from the cute guy, or spinsters secretly in love with their married bosses.

She wasn't like that. She *refused* to be. And so she'd made the only decision she could: to leave the man she cared about because she'd rather be alone than love a man who was not in love with her. Because since that lovely morning it had become increasingly clear that what she felt was a thousand percent more intense than what he did. How else to explain his ever-decreasing attention, the diminishing eye contact, the dwindling ability to pay attention to the moment for more than five minutes at a time? How else to reconcile that instead of her presence in his life lessening his phone/tablet/screen obsession, he had instead gotten more comfortable indulging it around her?

So she steeled herself, willed the tears away, and reminded herself she'd done the right thing. As she turned up her street, eyes on her apartment building, she remembered countless other times she'd tried to talk to him, only to end up addressing the top of his head as he scrolled through his phone's many offerings. And she knew that more and more lately she'd found herself talking more quickly, so as to hold his interest long enough to finish her story before he reached for the holster at his belt. And then there was the fact that she'd started making it a point not to ask any question that could be looked up online, so as not to lose him to the Internet for the next five minutes. And how many zillions of minutes had she wasted waiting while he searched for some answer, some inconsequential detail, before the conversation could resume?

The evidence was overwhelming.

He didn't even look at her anymore. The soulful eye contact from their early relationship was now a thing of the past.

She would estimate fifty percent of the time they were to-gether he was looking down at the phone in his hands. It was like competing with another woman who was *always* with them, inertly smug with her ability to know all, provide all and triumph over anything Macy had to offer.

Almost anything. Sex could still win.

But that was not enough. Not for her. She'd held on as long as she could. She'd made the point to him as many times as she was able without humiliating herself. And she'd come to the unhappy conclusion that she just wasn't enough for Jeremy Abbott.

CHAPTER TWO

The apps appeared to be his, so Jeremy checked his email, text messages, Twitter and Facebook. He hadn't missed much in the cyber world. A normal amount of time had passed, which he knew because the clock on the screens seemed to be accurate, so he found himself finally able to take a few normal, deep breaths. If he were really in hell, would he be able to check his email?

Despite himself, and knowing he had far more important considerations that should be occupying the front burner, he scanned his inbox again for anything from Macy. Also despite himself, considering he could be dead and in hell, he was disappointed to find nothing. No apology for dumping him out of the blue, no follow-up explanation, nothing to offer hope that they might be able to talk this thing out. It seemed to be . . . over.

A twisting began in his chest. Could he be having a heart attack—in hell?

He had to stop thinking about Macy. He had enough problems right now without dwelling on heartbreak, and just thinking about Macy made his insides turn into something cramped and painful, so he turned his mind to the safe haven of work. He managed to answer several client emails, making sure he'd still have a job if and when he ever returned, and included one to his administrative assistant asking for a reply on some inconsequential issue. If she wrote back he'd know something more bizarre than dying had taken place.

Then he sent one to his boss—just in case—telling him he had to be out for a few days. A family emergency.

He closed out his email and looked around the cubicle. There seemed to be screens for every app—or rather each app was an illuminated area in his cubicle—all in the same order as on his phone. Except . . . he leaned closer to a small one on the lower right. It was a bright yellow sun, with a red heart inside. As he looked close, the app opened into a larger screen in front of him. Find a Girl, Contact a Girl, See the Girls Looking at You.

Great, he thought, closing the app immediately. Just what he needed right now, a dating site. He hoped it wasn't a sign that things with Macy were well and truly finished.

He turned the chair away from the screens and looked out at the empty hall. "His" cubicle was on the edge of the farm, so his view out was a white wall. It might have been the cubicle where he'd started his career, except that the wall was not dinged up by people racing office chairs down the hallway for late-night stress relief.

In fact, the whole place seemed recently built and sterile as an operating room. He listened again, straining his ears against the silence. Not even the tapping of keyboards could be heard. It was a weird sort of solitary confinement, being among hundreds but completely alone and seemingly invisible. Rising from his chair, he lifted his chin, then stood on tiptoe, to try to see across the sea of cubicles. He was about to dip back down onto his feet when another head popped up ten or fifteen yards to his right.

His toes went numb and he dropped to his soles, heart pounding rapidly. He immediately went up on tiptoe again and didn't see the first guy, but a few yards to the left, another head appeared. It was like a life-sized game of Whack-A-Mole.

"Yo!" the second guy said, waving a hand. "Can you see me?"

Jeremy's heart leapt. He raised a hand in return. "Hey. Can you see *me*?"

"Yeah! Yeah, I can! And you can hear me, right? And see me?" He continued to wave his hand. He had a thick, dark thatch of hair and a broad forehead.

"Loud and clear, and I'm looking right at you."

"Finally!" It was hard to tell the guy's expression, since only the top of his head and his eyes were visible, but he seemed to be smiling.

"Where *are* we?" Jeremy called.

The guy's eyebrows fell. "You don't know?"

Jeremy shook his head. "You don't either?"

The guy disappeared, and Jeremy heard a small, discouraged "No."

"How about you?" Jeremy called. "The other guy—there was another guy over there. Hey!"

Nobody answered. Had the other guy left, or been a figment of his imagination?

"Hey, did you see that other guy? Are you still there?"

"What?"

Jeremy took the moment to drop back to his feet, then exited the cubicle. "Hang on!" he called. "I'm coming to find you."

He turned right and headed down the long hallway. He passed multiple cubbyholes just like his, all occupied by people staring at their screens, until finally he reached the corner. He turned and started down another interminable row.

He should have reached the one who'd spoken to him by now, but nobody seemed the least bit aware of their surroundings, let alone to be looking for him, so he stopped, hands on his hips, and called, "Are you still there?"

No answer.

Disappointment threatened to swamp him. He was crazy. Someone had put him in an institution and he was imagining the cube farm, the silent preoccupied people, the colorful screens. The only real things were the four white walls and he was actually in a straitjacket. Or he was wandering around some giant man-made rat maze, perhaps observed, perhaps failing this test, failing all the tests.

"Hello!" he yelled, fear giving his voice volume. He began to jog down the aisle, arms out to either side slapping the wall, the cubicles, the wall, the cubicles. "Answer me!"

The industrial carpet, the fabric-lined cubicles all conspired to suck his voice into an abyss. The room was huge, and there was no echo, just the dead thumping of his feet on the rug. He ran until his breath ripped audibly from his throat and his chest burned.

"Dude!"

The voice from behind him made Jeremy damn near jump out of his skin. He spun around to see a short, dark-haired, square-headed guy in a shirt and tie and wrinkled khakis. He was built like a wrestler and stood with his arms out from his sides as if about to draw in a gunfight. It might have been aggressive except he looked he like might cry.

He panted as he took the guy in. "Are you the one I was just talking to?"

"I was gonna ask you the same thing! Where the fuck are we, man?"

Jeremy started to laugh—hysteria, doubtless—when the guy launched himself forward and he found himself being hugged tight around the waist.

Just as abruptly the guy let go. "Sorry, man. I'm just so glad to see someone. I mean, Jesus, this place, it's huge, and I haven't talked to anyone since I got here."

"So all these other people can't see you either, huh? How long have you been here?"

"I don't know, man, *days*. One minute I was sitting in a meeting, checking my emails, and the next minute I'm like *here*, you know? It was okay at first, but now, I mean, what the hell, right? At least we got our stuff." He gestured back into his cube and Jeremy saw an array of screens similar to those that he had. "I'd really be batshit otherwise."

Jeremy's breath was slowly getting back to normal, but "days" threatened to make him hyperventilate.

"What's your name?" he asked.

"Brian. Yours?" He held out a hand.

"Jeremy." They shook. "So how'd you get here, Brian?"

Brian's face clouded. "Oh, man, it was awful." He went on to describe sensations that were eerily similar to the ones Jeremy'd experienced.

"And you said you were . . . what, checking your email? On your phone?"

"That's right. I just got this new Samsung, thing is fucking awesome. If I had it here I'd blow your mind with it. I'm talking hashtag-phone-gasm, right? I mean, I don't even know what all it can do yet and I'm on it *all the time*. You know?"

Jeremy nodded slowly. "Did anybody say anything to you before you, uh, before you ended up here?"

"What do you mean? I was in a meeting."

"I mean did anybody tell you to get off your phone, or ask you to listen up or anything like that?"

Brian shrugged. "Hell, I don't know. I was watching this video my buddy Ev sent, with this *sweet chick* in it wearing nothing but—"

Something from inside his cubicle dinged and Brian's head whipped around for all the world like the dog in *Up* when it saw a squirrel. Brian turned without finishing his sentence and bent toward the screen.

"Brian," Jeremy said, "did you see that other guy who popped up? Reddish hair? Looked annoyed?"

"Pay *attention*, boys and girls! Are you paying attention?" a female voice boomed over the cubicles. You could hear the smile in her voice but at the same time she sounded far from benevolent. "That's why you're here, boys and girls, to Pay. Attention. Get what I'm saying?"

The voice was getting closer. Jeremy glanced at Brian, who turned from his screens and looked at Jeremy with wide-eyed terror.

"What?" Jeremy asked. "Who is that?"

"Oh man," Brian said, dropping into his seat. "Oh man. It's *her*. Mrs. Hartz. Quick! Pay attention!" And with that, he turned back to his screens, hunching like all the rest of them, eyes riveted.

"Why? Who is it? What's she going to do? Brian?"

But the guy was trembling in his seat, ignoring him.

Jeremy turned toward the voice. What the hell? What on earth could anybody do to them *now*? They were already in hell.

He watched the hall to see if she would come this way, and he didn't have to wait long. She swung around the corner like the Stay Puft Marshmallow Man in *Ghostbusters*—about eight feet tall with a spherical body clothed completely in red, from her dress to her hose to her sensible shoes. Incongruously perched atop her fire-engine red hair was a tiara that did its best to sparkle despite being outgunned by the sheer massive proportions of the wearer. With her smallish head, thin legs, and colossal torso, she looked like a gigantic walking aneurysm.

"What is *this*?" she boomed, spying Jeremy. As she approached, her yellow eyes became eerily clear and narrowed with displeasure. "You're not in your office! You're not *paying attention*!"

It was hard to miss the malevolent gleam in her eye, as if his noncompliance might give her permission to do something awful.

"I'm paying attention to you," he said. He found himself sweating, despite his confidence that there was little she could do to hurt him.

"*I'm* not the point," she said.

"There's a point?" The question sounded sarcastic but he meant it. In fact the idea that there was a point gave him hope.

"That question *proves* you're not paying attention!" Her voice was piercing, especially at close range, but it was the waves of hostility and impatience that were most unnerving. "Look at all the other boys and girls; are you doing what they're doing?" She bent from the waist to peer in at Brian.

Though his back was to her, Jeremy could tell his trembling had increased from the force of her attention.

She laughed—a gruesome sound—and her eyes shifted to Jeremy, conspiratorial. "I don't think he's truly paying attention, do *you*?"

"Actually, yeah. I do."

"Well, that shows what *you* know. Get back to your office now and pay close attention—all the answers you seek are there. Go on. *Now.*" She made shooing motions with her hands, moving toward him. "Go on!"

As if pushed by an invisible force field, he backed away from her.

"Wait," he said, before she propelled him any faster. "Who are you?"

She stopped, her yellow eyes going wide and her red-lipped mouth gaping into a smile. As she bent toward him, her hands on her hips, his nervous glance fell on her tiara, upon which a large rhinestone heart anchored the center position, flanked by dozens of smaller heart-shaped glittery things, some of them on springs and bouncing with tiny ineffectual glee.

"Who *am* I?" She reared up, her hands on her hips, and boomed a laugh. Next to them, a mousy-haired girl in a cubicle looked over her shoulder. Spotting Jeremy, she turned in her seat, eyes alive with interest.

"Hi," she said, her lipsticked mouth broadening into a smile.

"Not *him*, you idiot," Mrs. Hartz snarled. "He's not real. Get back to work."

The girl flushed and snapped back to her computer.

Mrs. Hartz crossed her arms over her chest and regarded him. "I am Queenie Hartz—that's *Mrs.* Hartz to you—and I run this place. You'd do best to listen to me or else . . ."

Her eyes—brows raised, impish smile—demanded that he ask.

"Or else what?" he complied.

"Or else . . . *off with your head!*" she crowed. With another flick of her hands he was tumbled backward down the hall until he reached the corner, bumped off the adjacent wall, and then rolled another dozen feet or more and found himself sprawled in front of his own cubicle.

"Pay attention, boys and girls!" her voice said, much farther off now. "You know what happens if you don't pay attention!"

Angry, he picked himself up and brushed himself off. "No!" he called back. "What happens?"

There was an unnerving moment of silence before a peal of maniacal laughter shivered through the air-conditioned room. *"Nothing!"*

"IT WAS JUST . . ." MACY SWEPT HER HAIR BACK BEHIND HER ear and concentrated on her menu, hoping her inner turmoil did not show on her face. "Disappointing. That's all. I thought there was more to him."

"You were with him for seven months, Macy," her sister-in-law, Carolyn, said. "That's longer than, like, anyone in your history of dating. Are you trying to tell me you were looking for something more all that time and couldn't find it?"

"No." Macy looked up, wondering how to make herself clear without revealing the humiliating truth that she'd lost a guy to a phone. "There was a lot there, I'll admit it. But when it came down to it he just wasn't everything I wanted him to be. And it was just under seven months. Enough time to spot the flaws."

Carolyn slapped her menu down on the table. Macy noted a flush creep into her pale cheeks and felt terrible. She understood Carolyn's disbelief. He had seemed perfect for her. She had thought so too.

"I'm sorry," Carolyn said. "I just don't understand you. Surely you know that everybody has flaws."

"Of course. But they have to match up, you know? They have to be flaws you can live with."

"Sure, but . . ." Carolyn made a frustrated sound. "We liked him! Even your obnoxiously overprotective brother liked him. And believe me, when Lute likes someone you're dating, things are a lot easier at our house, I can tell you."

Macy lay the menu in her lap and smiled at her. "Then I'm sorry. I truly didn't intend to disrupt your home life."

Carolyn sighed. "It's not that, and you know it. Something must have happened, because the last time I saw you, you were head over heels."

Macy snorted, then took a sip of her water, eyes skittering away from her sister-in-law's too-perceptive gaze.

"Hey, it was subtle but I spotted it." Carolyn jabbed a finger into the table. "I've known you since you were ten, okay? And now you tell me you've dumped him. I have to say I'm shocked. And a little skeptical that he just *wasn't everything you wanted him to be.*" This last she said in a voice intended to imitate Macy's, but it smacked dangerously of Minnie Mouse.

"See?" Macy sat forward. "*This* is why I don't like dinner parties. If I hadn't brought him to your little shindig you'd have never known him, never liked him, and peace would reign again in the world. Instead, this little ripple in my pond has your boat rocking. But okay, we went. Did you not *notice* how absent he was half the time?"

"It wasn't just *our little shindig.* It was Thanksgiving too." Carolyn's brows drew together. "What do you mean, absent? Oh, well, he did take that phone call."

"*And* he spent the whole evening checking his email. He did that on Thanksgiving too, remember?"

"But he was expecting something, right? A contract or something?"

Macy waved a hand. "Whatever. What about the time Lute caught him checking Facebook?"

"He did?" Carolyn was starting to look doubtful. Then her face cleared. "Wasn't he trying to get in touch with his niece? Or sister? Or someone like that?"

"His cousin." She sighed heavily, giving Carolyn a helpless look. "But there was always something like that. Something he had to pick that damn thing up for—maybe something valid, maybe not—but either way, he'd look and then he'd get sucked into it and *poof!* He'd be gone."

"What do you mean, he'd be gone? He leaves?"

"Mentally!" Macy picked up her water glass. The agitation was beginning again. She took a few quick swallows. "You know, I spent months feeling like it must be me. That I must be boring. So I upped the chatter, tried to engage him, felt bad about myself and why he couldn't seem to focus on me for more than five minutes at a time. And you know what I finally realized?"

Carolyn looked at her, probably surprised by the heat in her voice. "What?"

"That *I* was bored. *Me!* Not him. For the longest time I was sure that I was the problem, that if I were smarter, prettier, more interesting, he'd put the damn phone down. But no. The problem wasn't me, it was him. Sitting at a table watching someone look at their phone is *boring*. So one day I'd just had enough. See ya!" She flipped a hand and shrugged, letting her gaze slip past Carolyn so she couldn't read the hurt in it.

Carolyn nodded. "Yeah, okay. I can see that."

The waiter arrived and took their orders. When he was gone, Macy added, "Besides, my life coach says it's inefficient to spend time with people you're hoping will change, that it's a surefire way to derail your future."

"Life coach." Carolyn snorted.

"Stop it, I *told* you how much he's helped me. I'm focused now. I'm clearing my life of anything that doesn't serve my goals, and it's working. The fact is, if love is not adding value to my life, it has no place in it. Letting things without value take up space in your life drains your energy for fulfilling yourself with what's really important."

Carolyn frowned for a long moment, then, as if she hadn't even heard what Macy had just said, asked, "But couldn't you have talked about it? Did you *tell* him the phone thing was a problem? You know, relationships are hard work. It's a cliché, but everybody says it for a reason. Not everything's going to be perfect right—"

Macy held up a hand. "Carolyn, I love you. But if you continue down that conversational path my head *will* explode.

C'mon, I'm not an idiot. I'm twenty-nine years old. I *know* a relationship takes work."

"Okay, sorry."

"I did talk to him. First I joked about it. Then a couple of times I asked him to put the phone away."

"And did he?"

"Of course. But the thing was, the next time we were out it was the same problem. And I don't want to be that woman, the one who's always nagging about not getting any attention. If he isn't into me enough now, at seven months in, to keep the phone holstered, what'll he be like in five years? Ten?" She poked listlessly at the tablecloth with her fork. "God forbid I'm ever in one of *those* dead relationships."

She spoke with assurance, but inside that knot was forming again, the one that tightened every time she thought about Jeremy. There'd been so many things *right* about him . . . except for the one very wrong fact that he wasn't into her enough.

That was what it came down to, every time. And it was that which caused the doors of her heart to slam closed. She'd rather be alone than be with someone who loved her less than she loved him.

"Well, all I know is I don't want to be the one to tell Luther Serafini his baby sister's on the prowl again." Carolyn shook her head as she loosed her silverware from its rolled-up napkin.

Macy jerked her eyes to Carolyn. "On the prowl!" she protested.

"Before you met Jeremy you were using a spreadsheet to keep track of your dates, remember?"

Her face went hot. "There was a reason for that!"

"Of course there was." Carolyn laughed.

"Look," she said, leaning forward, "here's the thing. My life coach had me make a life plan, which was great, because it's only when you know where you're going that you can make the right decisions to get you there. But I felt like, until I found the right guy I couldn't get the rest of my life in order.

I know, I know, I don't need a guy to be whole and all that. And I don't! But I *want* a guy, I want the *right* guy. But until I find him I can't get the whole rest of the show on the road. Do you know what I mean?"

Carolyn looked at her like she had three heads. "The whole rest of the show?"

"Yeah, you know, making sure I'm in the right job, the one with the best benefits, maternity leave and career track. Planning exactly where I want to be on that track when I decide to have children, so I won't lose ground. Then I can start looking at neighborhoods, think about buying a house, calculate the down payment needed and the payments we can afford. I can research new cars that would be family friendly and could be paid for by the time we have to start contributing to college savings accounts, figure out how to adjust our retirement savings, stuff like that, you know? Just make sure my priorities reflect my goals, the future I'm going to manifest for myself."

Carolyn was quiet a long moment, fingering one earring, a grave look on her face. "And you say *you* broke up with *Jeremy*? Not the other way around?"

She knew she shouldn't have confided all that. "What?"

"You just scared the crap out of *me*, and I'm not even dating you. So, that little speech? Save that for the losers, because it's the perfect formula to make a guy run screaming."

"Not the *right* guy. Not a *practical* guy."

"Not a *boring* guy."

Macy sat back, conviction warring with confusion. "But that's who I am, Carolyn. I'm a planner, you know that."

"Honey," Carolyn continued, "there's planning, and there's crafting a prison sentence. In your plan, the guy doesn't seem to matter much, beyond setting that whole unbelievably dull-sounding machinery in motion."

"Of course the guy matters! He's at the crux of the whole thing!" She bunched her hands together illustratively. Then she looked up. "What do you mean, dull? You're married, you've got kids, you must have thought about all this stuff."

"Yeah, right." Carolyn rolled her eyes. "We got together

in high school, remember? Back when planning was *Hey, who's getting the keg for this weekend?*"

"Huh. You were lucky. You got the whole thing settled early. My trouble is I keep meeting guys who don't live up to their billing. They *seem* great on the outside, and they can maintain that facade for a few dates—or, like in Jeremy's case, a few months—but then, inevitably, the Problem shows up." She leaned back. "There's always a Problem. With Jeremy it was the freaking phone. I mean, who wants to look across the table at the top of someone's head for the rest of their life?"

"If you're lucky, it'll have hair on it."

"Oh, it'll have hair. I require pictures of parents and grand-parents on the second date."

Carolyn closed her mouth, gathered her napkin and rose from the table.

Macy laughed. "Carolyn, stop! I was *kidding*!"

"I'll be right back. I have to think about an adequate re-sponse to all that"—she rolled a hand—"stuff." She walked off.

Chuckling, Macy pulled her phone from her purse, think-ing, *See? It's okay when someone leaves the table to check the phone. There is proper cell phone etiquette, and there is cell phone rudeness.* A sigh escaped her as she slid her finger across the screen, entered her passcode and saw that nobody had emailed or texted. She'd sort of expected something from Jeremy, a *What's going on?* or *Can't we talk about this?* But there was nothing. He must have agreed with her decision . . .

She gazed at the familiar checkerboard of apps. Familiar, that was, except for one yellow icon in the lower right corner that seemed to be throbbing.

She looked closer. iLove, it read underneath it. Inside the box was a red heart, surrounded by a bright yellow sun, which was the thing that seemed to be pulsating. She put her finger to the icon and the app burst into a bright full-screen sun, and then up popped what looked like a dating website. Find a Guy, Contact a Guy, See the Guys Looking at You—all with little red heart icons.

Her mouth dropped open. She hadn't downloaded *that*. What, were apps just self-installing now? That'll be the day, she thought, when she used a dating website. It was scary enough going out with someone you'd already laid eyes on. Setting yourself up on a blind date was an idea beyond horrifying.

She closed the application and deleted it.

CHAPTER THREE

Macy's phone rang again and she nearly threw it against the wall. All day the phone had been ringing, and not once had it been Jeremy.

"Macy Serafini." She tucked the phone between her shoulder and ear, identified the caller and pulled up the account file on her computer. She was nodding over the client's points when her coworker April appeared in her doorway. She held up a finger.

"Yes," she said, nodding, "yes. We can try that." She waved April in. "Let me put something together on that and I'll email you Monday, how's that?"

April settled herself in the armchair across from Macy's desk and began examining her fingernails.

Macy leaned her head back on her chair and gave a silent scream as the client droned on about things they had discussed multiple times already.

Bud Forester, she mouthed to April, identifying the client who drove them all crazy. April smirked.

If StockSolutions weren't such an important client, she'd hand the account off to her assistant.

As usual, the conversation went on way too long. Also as usual, he finished by asking her out—even though she'd told him multiple times she was seeing someone. The fact that she wasn't anymore was something she didn't even consider telling him.

"I'm sorry, Bud, but I have plans with my boyfriend this weekend. Let me know how the concert is, though, okay?"

He took the news as he always did—with cheerful resignation—and they hung up.

April drew her long blonde hair around her shoulder and twisted it with one hand. "Didn't you break up with your boyfriend?"

"Yes." Macy frowned at the phone. "And it seems to have stuck."

April dropped her hair. "What do you mean?"

"I don't know. I thought I'd hear from him." She swiveled her chair and put her hand on the computer mouse, opening up her work email.

"Why?"

She glanced at the list of impersonal messages, not one of them from Jeremy. "Well, because I was kind of abrupt about it."

"No kidding." Deadpan.

Macy grimaced and closed the program. "I know, it's stupid. I just thought he might call. God knows he's never very far from a phone!"

"What, to chat about the breakup?"

"No. But you'd think he'd want to know what brought me to that point, since it obviously took him by surprise. Why wouldn't he want to know that? Did he really not care?"

"So you dump the guy out of the blue and you're upset because *he* hasn't called *you*. Isn't that considered having your cake and eating it too? Why don't you call him, if you've got something you want to explain?"

Macy shook her head, rested her elbows on her desk and put her chin in her hands. She felt so tired. It was exhausting not thinking about Jeremy, and she'd been at it for a week now. "No, don't you see? That would defeat the purpose. I was going for shock and awe, but he didn't even notice."

"I understand. You were going for the quick fix. Don't you know you should never break up with a guy unless you really mean it? Otherwise, karma makes it so that the next time you see him he's with some ridiculously hot chick."

Macy's throat closed at the thought. She picked up a pen and tapped it on the desk blotter. "I wouldn't be a bit surprised. Jeremy's perfect when he's paying attention. Unfortunately that's only about forty percent of the time. The other sixty you spend watching him look at his phone."

"That might be enough for some women."

At the mention of cell phones Macy picked hers up, slid her thumb across the screen to look for texts or messages, and found nothing yet again. Yep, Jeremy was just fine with the breakup.

"And yeah, I see what you mean," April said drily.

Macy put her phone aside. "Sorry. I was just checking . . . See, if he'd called me it would mean he'd woken up to the problem, or would be open to hearing what the problem was. But if I call him it'll just be me telling him *one more time* that his constant distraction bothers me. And that hasn't worked."

"Which means it was a good thing you broke up with him. If this is all the notice he's taken of it he was probably done anyway, right?"

The blunt words struck her hard, and she picked up her phone again. She looked at it blindly a moment before something penetrated. "What the heck? I thought I deleted this."

"What?" April leaned forward.

The pulsating yellow icon was back in the bottom right corner of her screen—iLove. She pressed the icon and held it with the intention of deleting it, then changed her mind.

"Wait a minute." She cancelled the delete function. "Have you ever heard of a dating site called iLove?"

April shook her head. "It must be new, because I've heard of *all* the dating sites." She got up and came around the desk, leaning over Macy's shoulder. "Jeez, is that suggestive or what? Look at it, it's *throbbing*, for god's sake. Open it!"

Macy tapped the icon and the app sprang to life. Find a Guy, Contact a Guy, See the Guys Looking at You . . .

"'See the Guys Looking at You,'" Macy read. "How stalkery is *that*?"

"Go up, go up, go up." April pointed, moving her finger like it was on the screen. "Go to Find a Guy. Let's just see who they've got. How have I not seen this site?"

Macy tapped the red heart, which was also throbbing, and up came a screen that read What Are You Looking For?

"Ooh, this is fun." April straightened, grabbed the chair placed against the wall and dragged it over. "Let's join."

"April!" Macy laughed. "No way. Besides, look at the time. I have to get *some* work done today, you know."

"It'll only take a minute. Besides, it's Friday."

"Your point being? You actually think I'm going to find a guy for tonight?" Macy scoffed.

April shot her a raised eyebrow. "My point being that you can work all weekend since you're not seeing anybody anymore."

She scrolled down the page, scanning the questions.

Your guy is:

☐ *Tall*
☐ *Short*
☐ *Either, as long as he's taller than me*
☐ *Size doesn't matter*

Your guy likes:

☐ *Books*
☐ *Movies*
☐ *Museums*
☐ *Artsy-fartsy stuff nobody understands*
☐ *An* NCIS *marathon on his big-ass TV*

"I notice they don't say 'anything happening on the two-by-five screen in his palm,'" Macy quipped.

"Quiet. We're getting to the essay portion." April took the

phone from her hand and held it so they both could see while she scrolled faster. "What are you going to tell them about you? 'Hates technology. Wants undivided attention. Will dump you at the drop of a hat.'"

April laughed, but Macy folded her arms. "Hey. That's not fair. I don't think it's too much to ask to not play second fiddle to an electronic device."

April rolled her eyes. "Enough with the cell phone stuff. There had to be other stuff wrong with Jeremy or you wouldn't have dumped him, right?"

Macy paused, considering for the hundredth time that she might have been hasty. Then she recalled the feeling of sitting there while he searched for someone or something more interesting than her to interact with.

"Right?" April insisted, suddenly looking appalled.

"Of course! The phone was indicative of so many things. It meant . . ." She didn't want to put it into words.

"It meant . . . ?" April insisted.

"Well, that he couldn't sustain a conversation. That he didn't understand proper etiquette. That he was inconsiderate, rude, oblivious."

"He didn't understand *proper etiquette*?" April's brows were at her hairline. "You're kidding, right?"

Macy paused, feeling the words back up in her throat. "All right, here it is. He couldn't stop going for his phone because he wasn't interested in me. Okay? You said it yourself before. The fact that he hasn't called means he was done too."

She took the phone back, moving her thumb up and down on the screen and once again fighting the urge to cry. She couldn't remember ever feeling this upset over a breakup. They were usually a relief. Where was the *relief*?

"Hey, careful, you're going to lose our place." April took the phone from her again, smiling gently when Macy looked at her. "We can do this like an interview, okay? I'll ask questions and you answer them, and I'll put them in. What the heck, it could be fun. And you never know. You lost a guy because of a phone—who's to say you can't find a guy because of one too?"

* * *

JEREMY RETREATED TO HIS CUBICLE, PONDERING MRS.
Hartz's response to his question. If you don't pay attention,
nothing happens. True enough, in general.

He sank down into his office chair, wondering if it was
supposed to be a meaningful message, like something that
should be helpful. He gazed at his screens. Was sitting in this
box surrounded by his virtual life considered paying attention? The others all seemed to think so.

It was good in one way. He could contact people, maintain
his work, make sure people didn't think he was dead so his
life wouldn't be a total mess if he ever got out of here and
back to it. Which would be when? How long could he have
purely virtual relationships before his real life started breaking down? He couldn't even consider the question without
freaking.

Had Macy really done this to him?

Okay, he *was* crazy. Macy couldn't have done this to him,
because it was clearly some psychotic episode going on inside
his brain. It couldn't be *real*. And if it wasn't real then Macy
couldn't have done it. Not that he believed she would have
even if she could.

But she *could* have been the reason for his psychotic break.
How could he have gotten things so wrong? He'd thought they
were . . . falling in love.

What a sap he was for getting choked up. He stood up and
bounced on the balls of his feet a few times, then brought his
hands up to boxing position and jabbed at the air, once, twice,
threefourfive. *Get a grip. Be strong. You can get over this—
over her. And hopefully that'll get you back to reality.*

He reached for his phone again, then rolled his eyes at how
slow he was to break the habit when he *knew* it wasn't there.
It was like constantly flipping light switches when the power
was out.

He decided to leave his cubicle—Mrs. Hartz be damned—
and, on a whim, started to jog. He sprinted for ten cubicles
and slowed for ten, going back and forth between the two

while keeping an eye on what was inside each cube as he passed. Which was still one hypnotized person after another. But the exercise was invigorating, made him feel more like himself, so he continued running.

Jeremy's heart was just beginning to race again with anxiety when a break in the wall suddenly opened up on his left. He stumbled to a halt in front of it and found himself looking into a marbled alcove that housed a bank of elevators.

"Yes." He moved swiftly to the call buttons, pressed the down arrow, and looked above the sets of doors for illuminated numbers. *Nothing,* he thought, *figures.* Still, elevators went to ground floors and ground floors led outside. If he could get out onto the street, he could figure out where he was.

After several minutes with no change in elevator status, Jeremy pressed the "up" arrow so that both were lit. Immediately he heard movement behind one of the bays, the familiar lurch and roll of an elevator car moving in the shaft. Finally there was a *ding* and the far left doors opened, the up arrow shining red in the dim alcove.

Squelching a moment of fear that this might not be an improvement over his current situation, he boarded the elevator. After all, any change would be a good thing, wouldn't it? He wasn't going to get anywhere trapped in that cube farm with the Queen of Hartz breathing down his neck.

The elevator offered thirteen floors, something he decided to scoff at instead of hyperventilate over, and he pressed 1. So what if the elevator said it was going up? He stood back, waiting for the doors to close. When they did nothing, he moved forward and pressed 2. The elevator indicated that he was on the fifth floor, so anything below him would be a step in the right direction, but it didn't take long to realize nothing was going to happen if he kept pressing the lower numbers. So he tried 6. Still nothing. Frustrated, he pressed them all—all thirteen of them lit up except for 5, the one he was on—and the door groaned shut.

The trip was short, the doors moaning open again on 7. He stepped into an alcove just like the one on the fifth floor and turned, fully expecting to see a cube farm exactly like the one he'd just left. What met his eyes, however, was more like a giant, humming casino. There were cubes, all right, but each one was brightly lit and pulsing with color and sound. He walked slowly forward, into the din, squinting against the glare of the lights. Apart from being the circus version of his floor, these cubes had aisles between each one so it was easy to walk to whichever blinding set of lights most intrigued you.

For some reason he glanced up, and his mouth dropped open. The ceiling was mirrored, so that the entire room's cubes were visible at once, and the sight of it was unmistakable. The layout was exactly like the apps on a smartphone, each cubicle representing an app.

Could this be *his* phone?

As it happened, the Mail app was just in front of him to the left, so he turned toward it. If it wasn't his, he might be able to find out who was contacting whom from this giant phonelike warehouse, and what they were saying. Maybe this was the brains behind the whole operation.

With a bracing breath, he stepped into the cubicle—and was immediately assailed by visions of folders and envelopes and one half-written message on a large screen right in front of him.

Bud, following up on our conversation earlier today, I've done some research and it seems StockSolutions has made virtually no changes to their logo, website, advertising or visibility in the market in the sixteen years they've been in business. I believe this could explain their lackluster performance with the public, their approach being the same—

Whoever had been writing the note had left off in the middle of it. Either that or they were still working on it. In any case, the note didn't seem to have any bearing on this room or this building or the poor beleaguered souls trapped here.

He left the mail app and walked down the line. There was

a music app—like a radio stuck between stations, multiple songs played at once—and a clothing app, with hologram models slouching and sauntering about the cubicle. Shoes walked themselves around in another. Hotel rooms drifted across cubicle walls in yet another. And on and on past You-Tube and Amazon and real estate sites. One app whispered Spanish phrases as he went by. Another played tinkly music and urged him to relax. The Candy Crush game nearly deafened him, its cartoon characters waving flags at him to play, and the *New York Times* crossword demanded a three-letter word for a mythical Persian bird. He'd bet Macy knew the answer to that.

Some of the apps he passed weren't open, but they were all lit up like pinball machines waiting for a quarter. He kept going until he got to one wreathed in a blinding yellow light. Squinting, he peered into the cubicle and saw a pulsing red center. He took a tentative step toward the door and was immediately yanked inside and swept into a chair. A screen opened up in front of him proclaiming itself to be the *iLove Profile Page*. Someone was typing.

Who I'm looking for . . .

I'm looking for a man who's paying attention—

The phrase "paying attention" jerked him upright in his seat. Was this what he was supposed to be looking at? Should he have investigated that app on his own screen more closely? He continued reading.

. . . who knows the value of eye contact and asking questions. He has to be sincere, not just going through the motions, and he should be genuinely interested in people. He should be strong and smart, but confident enough to admit when he's wrong or when the woman he's with is right. He must be ethical, conscientious, generous and not petty. He should know how to make a girl feel special.

"He should be a boy scout," Jeremy told the screen. "Don't forget 'Be prepared'!"

He should not be afraid of powerful women. The man I'm looking for is comfortable in his own skin and sure of his place in the world. He should also have a very large penis—

Jeremy blinked. Then the cursor rapidly backed up over the last sentence.

"DELETE DELETE DELETE!" MACY SQUEALED.

April cackled like a witch over a cauldron, pecking at the backspace key. She had moved from the phone to the computer for ease of typing.

"What if you'd accidentally uploaded that?" Macy couldn't help a burst of laughter. "I'd be swarmed by perverts!"

"You think there are that many big penises out there?" April scoffed.

"I think there are that many men who *think* they have big penises out there."

The two of them cracked up again, and April poured another slug of wine into Macy's coffee mug. They'd stayed late to write the profile—April running out to get wine and Chinese food—and Macy was getting just tipsy enough to think that maybe this was worth trying. After all, she could sit at the privacy of her own computer and flip through scads of men without ever having to leave her chair. The filtering aspects of it were awesome. You could knock out guys who smoked with the click of the mouse. You could choose them by political party. You could search by age, status, college degree—even hair or eye color, if you were that picky.

"I've never really liked blond guys," Macy admitted when they got to that section.

"Give me a *break*," April said. "Ruling out blonds is like men ruling out women with small breasts. Tell me you're not that person."

"Of course not." She waved the suggestion off with her mug. "I was only saying. It's weird, what you look for and what you don't, what's attractive and what's not. It's so . . . inexplicable. It's a wonder anybody finds anybody. Don't put that in there." She clasped her mug in both hands, elbows on armrests and lips on the rim. "Though maybe you should add something about not being in love with technology . . ."

"Calling all Luddites," April typed. "That'll be our headline. You'll end up with a guy who's been living under a rock. With an illicit computer."

They'd gotten through the multiple choice questions quickly and were halfway through the essay. April had typed in a few positive things about Macy and was racing through what she wanted in a guy.

"What else?" April sat with her hands poised over the computer keyboard. Taking another sip of her wine, Macy leaned over to see what she'd written so far. It all sounded pretty cliché, but she thought it best not to mention that to April. She was, after all, just trying to help.

"He should be funny, and well-read," Macy added. "With a goofy sense of humor." She smiled, remembering Jeremy doing an impromptu dance while taking off his boxers in the middle of her bedroom. "And he should have kick-ass shoulders. Dreamy eyes, and long fingers . . ." Fingers that caressed with just the right amount of pressure, not tickling, yet not poking. A touch that sent shivers not just down a girl's spine but into her toes, melting her insides . . .

"Yeah, we all know what *long fingers* means."

Macy snorted. "That's not what I meant."

"I'm not putting all that. Especially not 'goofy.' You'll end up with some loser bodybuilder with a kick-ass comic book collection."

April laughed hard at her own joke, but Macy suddenly felt depressed. She put her mug down, blinking at the top of her desk.

"What? It was funny!" April protested. "Okay I'm putting down here that you want someone fit, with a good sense of humor . . ."

"I think I've made a terrible mistake."

April looked over at her, then down at the desk where Macy was gazing. "What do you mean? Did you forget to do something?"

"No." She looked up at her friend, her stomach in her throat, the conviction of having let something slip through her fingers filling her. How had she lost it? What had she been *thinking*?

"About Jeremy, I mean," she continued, her voice reedy. "I think I've made a mistake. I can't stop thinking about him. He was perfect, except for that one thing."

April's face lost its glee. "That one thing being that he didn't pay any attention to you."

She pictured Jeremy's eyes gazing down at her as his body moved over hers, their breath mingling while their torsos arched and flexed together, legs tangling. "He paid attention to me sometimes."

April made a sound in the back of her throat. "Sometimes. Listen to yourself. You're a powerful woman, Mace. Look, it says so right here." She jabbed at a place on the screen. "Come on, don't get all maudlin on me now, or I'm taking my Three-Buck Chuck back. Jeremy was an addict, and like with any addict, you were number two. Is that what you want?"

It was true. At times, it was true.

"Remember that time you told me he spent the entire evening on his phone while you were trapped in a conversation with Weird Mildred at Rob and Frank's?"

"*Ugh.*" Macy shuddered. She'd tried and tried to catch his eye, but not once did he look up to see where she was; and when she finally had escaped Weird Mildred, she'd gotten caught by the woman who ran the co-op, who went *on* and *on* about organic carrots. Something about how they shouldn't be grown on farms, but in people's backyards because that soil doesn't usually have a history of pesticides— Could that be true?

"And he waited in the car with his phone one time, didn't he? Instead of going in to your cousin's baby shower?"

She tapped her fingers on her desk. "I had to go get him. To be fair, it was a baby shower. Most of the guys there looked miserable."

"Sure, but if you say you'll go, you *go*. You don't sit in the freaking car."

Macy turned to her. "I thought you liked Jeremy."

"I did!" She lifted a shoulder, let it drop, continued to scroll down the profile page. "But, I don't know, it just seemed like . . ."

Macy waited, but April didn't finish.

"Seemed like what?" she pushed.

April exhaled and took her hand off the mouse. She turned the swivel chair toward her. "Don't get mad."

A bad feeling erupted in Macy's stomach. "I never get mad at you."

"Well, okay, don't get upset, then."

"Just spit it out," Macy said, feeling ill. "Was he cheating on me? Did he make a pass at you? Oh my god, it's not one of those things like Suzanne's boyfriend where you all took an oath not to tell—"

"Oh for god's sake, no! To be honest, I started thinking it wasn't right when you told me about that time he answered a text in the middle of having sex with you."

Macy's cheeks flamed. "That was a work thing. It was really important. And we weren't supposed to be having sex, actually. We were at the tennis club, in one of those unisex bathrooms near the pro shop."

April laughed and rustled Macy's hair. "That's right! I was so proud of you, thinking outside the box like that. A public restroom! That was a first for you, wasn't it?"

But he *had* taken the text, she was thinking now. He must have had one eye on the phone the whole time . . .

"Seriously," April said, "and I'll only say this once, in case you end up back together with him."

Macy's eyes shifted to hers, knowing it was hopeless. He'd *texted* during *sex*. You didn't come back from that. Granted, that had been months ago, but in light of all the evidence since then, it was significant now.

"What?" Macy was uncomfortable under April's scrutinizing gaze.

"He just wasn't that into you," she said finally, looking at her sorrowfully. "I hate to say it, but if you have to fight for a guy's attention, that's the bottom line."

"You don't . . . ?" April's words were injury enough, but she steeled herself and forced the question. "You don't think he was in love with me?"

April's expression got sadder, and it was so unfamiliar a look that it, more than anything else, convinced Macy she must be right. Then April shrugged and her face retrieved some wryness. "Eh, love. Maybe it was his version of love. I'm not calling him a liar. But I know you, and it wasn't *your* version."

Macy slumped and put her hands over her face. "I know," she said in a small voice. Emotion threatened to swallow her, but she pushed it back. It was the wine making her weak. She'd broken up with the guy because she'd known that what April said was true.

After a moment she straightened her spine, pushed her hair back off her face, and said, far more confidently than she felt, "All right, let's do it. Let's finish this stupid thing and post it. I'm moving on."

April's expression was instantly delighted. *"Yesss!"* She lifted a fist in the air, then lowered it to Macy. "Fist bump, sister. You are on your way!"

"On my way to what?" Macy fist-bumped April's ring with a wince.

"To happiness, my friend." April turned back to the computer. "Now, choose a picture . . ."

CHAPTER FOUR

Jeremy looked back up at the ceiling. Stuff was going on here, emails being written, that iLove profile page being worked on. As hard as it was to believe—though really, no harder than all the rest of it—he was starting to think the seventh floor was somebody else's cell phone. Each cube was an app, some of the apps were being used, and he could do nothing but watch.

But it wasn't his phone. Certainly he hadn't filled out a profile looking for a man. Nor had he written an email to anybody named Bud.

Was being here a message that he should be paying attention to that heart-throbbing app? He watched as the typist finished the essay with some blahblah about having a sense of humor and a sensitive side and whatever.

He stood up and left the cubicle, the forces that had sucked him in apparently having had enough of him. He looked up at the ceiling again, saw the face of the giant phone, and decided to check out the photos. If this place made any sense at all—and that was in some doubt—he'd be in this person's cell phone for a reason. Pictures might be the quickest way to figure out whose it was.

He went straight down the aisle from iLove to Photos, where he was once again immediately zapped inside. On the large screen in front of him was Macy's gorgeous face.

His breath left him in a whoosh. He should have suspected, but he'd felt so hopeless it hadn't even occurred to him—he was in *Macy's* phone. That email was to one of her PR clients. *She was filling out a dating profile.*

His heart twisted.

Most of the recent photos were of the two of them, or just him, and he had a moment of feeling glad she hadn't deleted them. Then again, it hadn't been very long. As he scrolled through the photos, he began to notice how many of the ones of him showed him bent over his cell phone—at restaurant tables, on city streets, in her living room, his kitchen, *in bed* . . .

He scanned the folders, opening a video. Immediately he heard her laughter, then the shaking screen revealed her face. God, she was beautiful—her eyes wet with laughter and sparkling as they looked at him holding the camera.

He remembered the day. They'd gone hiking, her hair was windblown, her cheeks pink, and they'd gotten to laughing over something. Her laugh was so infectious, her face so brilliant with joy, that he'd wanted to capture it. Of course he hadn't told *her* that, or she'd have gotten embarrassed and cynical. She never believed compliments.

They'd hiked one of the steeper trails that day, tramping through old fallen leaves, though the colors hadn't quite changed yet. Macy had said she loved fall the best because its breezes were summer heat wrapped in cold, as opposed to spring, which was winter cold veneered with warmth.

"Two old ladies," she said, marching up the path ahead of him, her booted feet picking their way over roots and rocks with confidence, "one with a feather duster, the other a knife."

"That's—visual," he said, thinking he could use something like that in an ad. "But why two old ladies? I'd think spring would be a young woman."

"Because every season is wise. But they're not all kind." She tossed a smile over her shoulder at him. "Do you think I'm crazy now?"

"Did you make that up?" he asked.

She dropped back as the trail widened so they could walk side by side. "Years ago, when I was a kid."

"Then yes." He grinned down at her and put an arm around her shoulders.

She stopped, her hands going to his waist, fingers through two side belt loops, and looked up at him. Her eyes shone as she pulled him close. "And you still like me?"

His heart had caught in his throat. He couldn't speak, so he only nodded, bringing one hand up to smooth strands of hair from her face.

She sighed. "Good. Because I *really* like you."

They kissed, and the fire that always burned between them flared to life. They'd said they loved each other that night, as they curled up under the warmth of her down comforter, sated from food and fresh air and vigorous exercise. Jeremy couldn't remember ever being happier.

Sitting in the cubicle of Macy's photos, he watched the video of her laughing over and over and over, until finally he rose, knowing he had to do something. He had to get out, he had to talk to her. He had to tell her how much she meant to him, even if she still wanted to let him go. What a *fool* he'd been, taking her for granted. Not that he'd realized it at the time, but now he did. Noticing how many times he reached for his phone, how often he wanted to turn from the "now" of this place to the "maybe" of a message from her—even if the "now" was whacked and the "maybe" not happening—he realized that the retreat into his apps was habitual. Even here, *inside a smartphone*, he reached for his phone.

But even if that weren't enough, the countless pictures of him looking at his phone, reaching for his phone, holding his phone, would have convinced him. He was appalled with himself. If he never saw another smartphone screen again he'd be happy, if only he could get out of here and back to her. But right now all he *had* were smartphone screens, and he had to use them the best way he knew how.

As he moved back down the hallway toward the elevators he was suddenly arrested by the sound of her voice. He stopped and listened. "Don't forget eggs again!" "Call Mom." "Tell Lute he was right."

Had to be her Reminders app. He moved on to Messages, heard what had to be audio texts. "I don't know how to get his attention! I must be the most boring person on the planet. Do you think it's me?" Then the sound of her laughter again—clearly in a different conversation—and finally, "I don't think I can do this anymore . . ."

The elevators, thank god, were right where he'd left them. He pushed the down arrow and waited, one shoulder leaning against the wall. He was exhausted and upset. He wished he could go to sleep and wake up back at home. He would run to Macy's apartment and beg her to give him another chance. He'd reform. He'd get a dumb phone. He'd learn to *pay attention*.

He felt the penny drop—the truth of the matter suddenly glaringly obvious. He got it now. It was about him, his lack of presence. And he could fix that! Shouldn't that get him out of here? Because once he was free he was going straight to Macy to tell her he understood at last.

She had left behind an enormous void within him. He wasn't the sentimental sort, so he wasn't getting mawkish on himself, but as things had progressed he had felt somehow less alone in the world. Safer. Like everything had a point. It wasn't that the rest of his life was bad. His job was great, his friends were top notch, and numerous, but there was something about Macy that had completed the puzzle. She fit, and with her he'd felt whole.

And then he'd blown it.

She'd tried to warn him, but he hadn't listened to her. Thinking back on it he recalled multiple conversations about his phone use. Most of them joking—he'd *thought*—but some of them serious. Heartfelt.

Why hadn't he *paid more attention*?

Why hadn't he realized that if she left him, he'd be heartbroken—even in the face of an apparent psychotic break?

The elevator doors opened with a clamor of hinges and electronics. He pushed himself off the wall and stepped inside. Just for the hell of it he pressed all the buttons again, but was not surprised when he ended up back on 5. The doors eased open, and he was back in the sterile world of non-glowing, non-throbbing, non-dinging cubicles.

Just outside of the elevator alcove he stopped and listened. Still silent. He glanced left, the route he believed went to his cubicle, then right, and nearly jumped out of his skin at the appearance of the elusive red-haired guy. The one he'd seen just before spotting Brian.

Impossibly tall and stooped with self-consciousness, he was thin, with a hangdog look to go with his past-due haircut and indoorsy complexion. He was older than Jeremy by probably ten years, and his eyes looked faded.

He addressed Jeremy with a dead gaze. "Hey."

Jeremy looked up—way up—and held out a hand. Between the giant Mrs. Hartz and now this guy, he wondered if he'd accidentally ingested something that said *Drink Me* on it. Or was it the *Eat Me* that had made Alice small?

"It's you!" Jeremy beamed. "I've been looking for you. Did you hear me calling earlier?"

"Yeah." The red-haired guy glanced down, then offered his hand. It felt like a collection of popsicle sticks in Jeremy's.

"I'm Jeremy Abbott."

"Kyle."

"Listen, I'm glad to meet you. Do you mind answering some questions? What *is* this place? Do you know? Have you been here long? Have you got *any* idea how we get out?"

Kyle nodded his shaggy head. "Yeah, so, we got, uh, sent here by stuff we did, you know?"

Jeremy raised his brows. Kyle seemed to think that was enough information. "Sent here? By who? What stuff? How do we find out? Is this some kind of purgatory?"

Kyle took a deep breath and let it out, as if fatigued by the questions. "Yeah, so, I'm not sure? But it seems like some-body, maybe some kind of witch or alien? Or maybe God? Sent us here." His arms flopped up and down in a bizarre expression of ignorance. "Yeah, so we need to work on our-selves, fix stuff, and then we can go home."

Jeremy's heartbeat accelerated. "So we're not dead?"

Kyle gave an incredulous look. "No, we're not *dead*."

Jeremy had no idea how much he'd feared the opposite answer until he got this one. Muscles he didn't know he'd tensed let go and relaxed. "Okay, good. So we did stuff we need to fix. I think I figured out what I did. So how do we get out once we know?"

"Yeah, so, um, I know I need to get better with girls? Uh, *women*. Stupid," he muttered to himself. "And I know 'cause I'm here. This is some stupid dating app, where we are, and we can only get out when we get dates."

Jeremy held out his hands. "Hold on. You're saying this here is an app?" He spread his arms out to encompass the room. Why wasn't it dinging and flashing and whirring like the apps upstairs? "The whole floor?"

Kyle nodded.

"For people who need to get better with *girls*?" This wasn't what he'd expected. It was the phone thing—it had to be. Jeremy had never had women problems. Not until Macy dumped him. Unless . . . "Or with a *certain* girl?"

Kyle did that thing with his arms again. "Whatever. Some people have, like, money problems or whatever, and they go somewhere else. Other places like this. Rehabilitation apps."

Jeremy rapidly put the pieces together in his head. "So you're saying I'm here because I've got relationship problems."

Kyle's mouth turned down. "I don't know. I think it's, like, online problems. I think it all has to do with the device, you know?"

"Ah. The device." It was all coming together, his thoughts, the photos on Macy's phone, that poignant note in her voice when she'd said to someone in an audio text, *I must be the most boring person on the planet.*

He could kick himself.

Macy's last words flew through his mind again. *Someday you're going to get sucked right into that thing . . .*

"Yeah, like if you like being on your phone or your tablet or computer or whatever a lot you can do that here. It's like device heaven, you know? I loved it, at first."

"Here," Jeremy reiterated, to be sure. "You loved it here."

"Yeah. Except for the other people. I hate it when there's noise. Like that day you got here, yelling across to Brian over there."

"Wait, that day I got here—that was *today*. Right? That was earlier today." Sweat broke out on his brow, under his arms.

Kyle wheezed a short laugh. "No, that was, like, a week ago. Look at your calendar."

A sudden dizzy spell had him searching for the wall with one hand.

"Look, so, I got a question for you," Kyle continued.

He'd lost a week. A week! He pressed his fingers to the bridge of his nose and squeezed his eyes shut. Maybe he *hadn't* figured everything out.

"Where'd you go?" Kyle continued. "Because, I think I've decided to go home now. I been here, I dunno, months, and it was great, but now . . . I think I discovered I want someone. Like a girlfriend."

Jeremy looked up. "Months?" He thought Kyle might be blushing, because his wan face suddenly looked alive.

Kyle shifted, pushed his hands farther into his pockets and stepped closer. "Yeah. So where'd you go, how'd you get out?"

"I took an elevator." He swung an arm back toward the elevator alcove, only to see a blank wall where it once had been. "Oh shit."

Kyle looked at where Jeremy gestured, then looked back. "Uh-huh."

"It was there. I swear it."

"Uh-huh." Kyle was nodding. "I meant how'd you get a date? Cuz I can't get one."

"A *date*?" Jeremy's neck was starting to hurt from looking up to see Kyle's face. "*No*. What are you talking about?"

"You gotta get a date, man. That's how you get out."

"*That's* how we get out?" Kyle had just given him the magic formula! He could have kissed him. "We get out!" He laughed, somewhat hysterically. "Come with me back to my cubicle, okay? Let's figure this thing out. We'll *both* get out of here."

They walked down the hallway, Jeremy—who wasn't short—taking twice the steps that Kyle did with his never-ending legs. His mind was spinning, thinking about how often he went for his cell phone, and how many times Macy had mentioned that he might want to put it away. The key to this whole thing was there somewhere, he was sure of it. Did he need to do some actual rehab? Was that how to mitigate this prison sentence and get back to Macy?

In a sudden flash he remembered what she'd said shortly before she'd walked off—what he'd *thought* was a joke. "I can't compete with your phone. I'll never be able to give you what it gives you."

Hah. What a jerk he'd been.

The thing was, it wasn't *her*! He did it to everybody. Hell, he remembered hearing his text alert go off and checking the phone *in the shower* one time. Damn near ruined the thing—but he'd answered! Thank god for the talk-to-text feature.

By the time they'd found Jeremy's cubicle, Kyle was panting for breath and looking paler than ever. Jeremy looked at him in concern. "This isn't a moment too soon for you, buddy. You need some fresh air and exercise. You've been sitting in front of these computers too long."

Kyle gazed at the array of screens in Jeremy's cube. "Naw, this is normal. I do the same thing at home."

Jeremy sighed, but a vague chill swept up his spine as he realized he was not that much different from Kyle. He just always had his screen with him.

He glanced at his email program, noting that he had 422 emails. As he looked at the app it opened, the first email being from his administrative assistant asking, Where the hell ARE you? Harrison's shitting bricks!

He'd have to sort that out later. Maybe tell them some kind of virus had knocked him out, sent him to the hospital . . .

He looked at his phone app, but it was the one square that never opened, no matter how long he looked at it.

"I don't suppose we can call anyone, can we?" he asked Kyle.

Kyle laughed, a dopey-dog laugh. "Yeah, right. Naw, we can text and email and tweet and post to Facebook and pretty much everything else, but we can't use the actual phone part. You can dial any number you want and it won't go through. I've tried. It's great."

Great. Jeremy sighed. He mentally shut off the mail and plopped himself in his chair. "Okay, so we need to go *here*, right?" He opened the iLove app. A large welcome screen appeared.

Macy was on this site, he thought.

"What'd they say about you?" Kyle asked.

Jeremy was clicking around the site. Find a Girl, Contact a Girl, See the Girls Looking at You . . .

"Who?"

"On your profile. Haven't you *looked*? Why do you think you haven't gotten any mail?"

"Kyle, I'm not on this site. This is the first time I've even opened the app."

"Oh man." Kyle shook his head slowly. "Then how'd you get out?"

He craned his neck to look up at the towering Kyle. "I didn't get out. I just went upstairs. You're saying I have to do this to get out?"

"Upstairs?" Kyle repeated. "I thought there was only a downstairs."

It took half a lifetime but Jeremy finally bled Kyle of all the information he had on the subject. According to him, to get out of here Jeremy had to get a date with a woman (or man or whatever, depending on who you were) on this site, at which time he could get out to go on the date. Afterward, he'd end up back here. The only way to stop this cycle was to establish a *real* relationship with the *right* woman. Then he would get out permanently.

Macy, he thought again. If he could find her on here, maybe he could get a date and actually get to *see* her. He wouldn't have to send her any emotional email bombs, or make up reasons why they couldn't get together to talk . . . A flutter of hope bounced around in his chest. If he saw her he could convince her to give him another chance. Maybe.

If that didn't work he didn't know *what* he'd do. Because how in the world could he start a *real* relationship with a new woman when he was still in love with the last one?

"That could take forever," he thought out loud. Then, to Kyle, "Relationships take time, you know? And in the meantime, what? I lose my job and go broke? Who makes the rules around here?"

"They don't let that happen," Kyle said. "Look at me, I've been here for months and I still have my job."

"How do you even *know*?" Jeremy threw up his hands. "You've been trapped in here like a mouse with a big block of cheese."

"Yeah, well, online banking. They're still paying me, so I'm still working."

"This is crazy," Jeremy muttered, dropping his elbow on the desk and putting his head in his hand. How would he even find Macy? Nobody used their real name on here, just those cutesy "handles."

"Yeah, well, we're not the only ones. People who get into trouble gambling, or in the stock market, or watching too much porn, or whatever, on their phones are sent to places like this too. Same kinda rules."

"And how do you know that?" Jeremy sat up straight.

"Queenie Hartz told me. She thought I didn't get it. But, see, I did get it, I just didn't want to go out on any dates. Not that *that's* been a problem, not with what they wrote about me."

"What do you mean, 'they'?"

"Look, you got mail." Kyle reached over and took the mouse, dragging it swiftly across the page to Jeremy's mailbox. It contained one note from someone named Serious-Fun844.

> Dear GnatMan: Are you kidding with this profile? Do you actually think someone's going to think it's cute? Why don't you write something serious? Share something of yourself. We don't bite, you know. You're a good-looking guy, if that's really your picture. But if you're actually the jerk portrayed in the essay, forget it. Telling people you're an asshole up front still doesn't make it okay to be an asshole.
>
> Let me know. I'm serious.
>
> And I'm fun. :-) Gina

Jeremy stared at the words. "I'm portrayed as an *asshole*?"

"Probably." Kyle moved the mouse over to the profile and clicked. "That's what they do, list all your worst qualities. And don't even think about changing it, it doesn't work. It just adds more bad stuff."

The first problem was the picture. It was him, all right, and not a bad shot, but it had been a photo of him and Macy at a restaurant last summer, out of which she had been rather obviously and ungracefully cropped.

Then, to cap it off were the words:

> I'm fresh out of a relationship and in desperate need of a new one. I always have to be with someone—even if it's just for arm candy. Though I would love to fall head over heels for someone, for most of my life I believed love was impossible, if not simply a delusional dream of the desperate. Well, count me in now!
>
> I'm self-centered and self-gratifying. I pay minimal attention to my dates unless they're wearing something hot and we're about to have sex. Sometimes superficial and regularly overconfident, I can be an insensitive bastard to those who can do nothing for me.

The thing went on in the same vein, ringing just enough bells of veracity to sink Jeremy's spirits. Was that really who he was? He certainly recognized some of the base impulses, but he hadn't acted on them, had he? He tried his best to be a decent guy. No, he *was* a decent guy.

Wasn't he?

Jesus, if Macy saw that . . . how could he write to her now? Even if he could find her?

"So if everybody on here has a crappy profile, why would anyone *not* in this crazy place use the app?" Jeremy asked, scrolling through the litany of horrors that was his dating profile. "Who wants to pick out a jerk to date?"

"Oh the site's open to everybody. We're a really small percentage overall. You can look around and see. Most people are normal."

Which would make it even harder to attract someone—and even easier for Macy to find someone better than him. Losing hope rapidly, he looked up at his own handle.

"Why am I called 'GnatMan'?" he asked, hoping it showed a kind of appealing self-deprecation, some awareness of his place in the universe, or maybe some clue that the profile was a big joke.

But, like the grim reaper, Kyle reached out one long finger and pointed at a line in the essay: *I have the attention span of a gnat.*

MACY COULD HARDLY BELIEVE HER EYES. TWO WEEKS AFTER breaking up with Jeremy and then hearing absolutely nothing from him, she was sitting in her office after hours looking at his grinning face on an iLove dating profile. He'd actually come up in her *Guys You Should Look At* section!

Her entire body flushed with mortification. He'd certainly gotten over *her* in a hurry.

She leaned close. *She had taken that photo!* They'd been waiting for a table at Captain Newick's and he'd been smiling so big—he had a *killer* smile—that she told him he looked like the picture of the cartoon captain on the wall behind him. He'd gathered her in close and they took a selfie with the sign. But only she knew it was behind him now, as it—

along with herself—had been unceremoniously cropped out of the picture.

Memories of that day, when they'd driven out to the bay in search of bushels of crabs and cold beers, the sun hot on their heads in Jeremy's convertible, enveloped her like mid-August humidity. She too had worn a grin that threatened to crack her face wide open, and she hadn't even cared that her hair was blowing like a willow in a tornado and was likely to look like a tumbleweed before it was all over. Jeremy was laughing and glancing at her so often it was as if he couldn't believe his luck, and they were singing together to the music, unself-conscious and electric. Neither one of them had had a care in the world beyond finding the elusive Captain Newick's, which instead of being on the bay was on a back road by a river that fed into it, and boasted the best steamed blue crabs within reach of the city.

He hadn't been on his phone at all that day. In fact she hadn't even been aware of the problem yet. She'd still had the wild intoxicating idea that there *weren't* any problems between them.

Every woman on here would want *that* guy, she knew. The one who was totally there, undistracted, happy, in tune. The guy who seemed like he'd be there forever, making up for everything you'd ever lost in your life.

Until he disappeared and you became the superfluous doll across the table from the guy making love to his cell phone.

Had he seen her profile?

She hoped if he had that he took it as a sign that *she* was over *him*, even though she was as far from that as she could be. She may have broken up with him, but that didn't mean the dream had died—the dream that she'd found the right one, that he was all he'd seemed to be, that she had stumbled upon nirvana. It was the dream that was so very hard to let go of. At least that was what she had been telling herself.

She knew better now. Staring down the barrel of the dating gun, she was afraid she wanted nobody but Jeremy. Even the Jeremy who listened with half an ear and couldn't drag his eyes from a backlit screen.

She flipped a pen through her fingers, chewing on the inside of her cheek. Then, despite herself, she clicked on his profile. It might make her feel worse, but if she didn't look she'd spend too much time wondering what he'd said.

As she'd learned to do on the other profiles, she skipped quickly over the multiple-choice section and went straight to the personal essay.

Sometimes superficial and regularly overconfident, I can be an insensitive bastard to those who can do nothing for me. I like things my own way and am persuasive enough to get them. I use my charm to make people like me, and am lost when it doesn't work. I do not trust my own substance. I occasionally use people. I tend to disappear on women I've lost interest in. I have a bad habit of not paying attention to people, of only hearing what I want to hear, of taking people for granted. I want love but have no idea what it actually is. If I'm with you, I'll likely only spend ten minutes out of every hour actually focused on you. The rest of the time I'll be carrying on conversations with others who are potentially more interesting on my phone because I have the attention span of a gnat. I have an insatiable need to be entertained at every moment. I blame others for my boredom.

What the heck—?

Was this a joke? Was it aimed *at her*? She was the one who'd complained about his inattention, his phone dependence and, yes, maybe she'd accused him of needing to be entertained all the damn time—but she didn't say any of that other stuff. Is that what he'd thought? Or was it just true?

Was he going for some kind of sympathy? Did he hope people would take it as a joke? It wasn't funny to her.

She leaned forward and reread it. *I tend to disappear on women I've lost interest in.* He'd disappeared on her, that was for sure.

She sat back in her chair, gripping the pen in her fingers. It was here in black-and-white—he'd lost interest in her. She had broken up with him, but there was obviously no going back. She considered writing to him, asking him what he was doing there. Had he known she was on iLove too, and was he making fun of her, the site or himself? Or maybe all three? But it would be too humiliating. If he saw her profile at all, let him think she was far too busy with other men to be looking at him.

She clicked on See the Guys Looking at You and up came a screen of head shots of smiling men, short paragraphs listing their vitals next to them. Here was HardLovinMan22 in a blurry shot wearing a cowboy hat, thirty-four years old, Aries, nonsmoker, in a suburb not far from hers. And Waiting4You, balding, sweet-smiled, thirty-eight, Pisces, nonsmoker, closer to downtown. ReelMeIn was posed, not surprisingly, with a fishing rod.

But Jeremy gnawed at her, and she scrolled down through the several pages of guys who'd looked at her, searching for his photo in the lineup.

He wasn't there.

And now she was wasting time second-guessing herself again. He was *not that into her*. Even April had seen it. It was time to let go—especially since she'd already let him go.

She glanced again at the guy in the cowboy hat. He looked nice. She wasn't into cowboys, especially, but she wouldn't mind a simple, uncomplicated date. She clicked, read the pleasant essay and decided to write. It was time to get off the computer and out on a date. There'd be no getting over Jeremy sitting here in her office.

She dropped the pen on the desk and started typing.

CHAPTER FIVE

Macy's hands were sweating, and she was having trouble taking a deep breath. Her mouth was dry and her smile felt stiff as she asked the restaurant's hostess if anybody had mentioned that they were meeting someone here.

The blonde was wearing earrings the size of handcuffs, and she pointed a manicured hand toward the front of the dining room. "Yes, are you looking for that gentleman by the window?"

Macy glanced over, took in the thirtysomething man in the blue button-down shirt with no tie and a pale complexion, and tried to match his features to the guy in the T-shirt and cowboy hat online. Because she was already nervous, this test nearly undid her. Despite the fact that she'd printed out and studied his profile like an SAT primer, she couldn't tell if it was the same person or not. She'd thought he was more rugged-looking, but then a cowboy hat would do that, wouldn't it? The chin *could* be the same, but . . .

She'd have to admit to the stylish young hostess—who probably never in her life would have to resort to online dating—that she did not know what her date looked like.

"Actually, ahhh . . ." As she leaned toward the girl, a couple tried to inch around her to put their name on the wait list, adding two more sets of ears to the problem.

The girl leaned toward her as the guy said something about a table for two. "I'm sorry?"

"Did he say he was waiting for someone named Macy?" she asked as quietly as she could.

The girl's finely arched brows drew down and, bless her heart, she moved around the hostess stand toward Macy. "He didn't say, I'm sorry. Would you like me to go ask him?"

Macy would have liked nothing better, but the line of people behind her was growing, and she didn't want to hold everyone up. "It's okay, I'll do it. But thank you."

The blonde gave her an understanding smile; she probably saw blind dates all the time. "Good luck."

Macy gave a short laugh and wound through the tables toward the man by the window. He was kind of cute, she thought, nicely dressed in khakis and that blue Oxford shirt, square jaw, thick hair. No cowboy hat.

He stood as she approached, looking uncertain. He was taller than her, but not by much. Maybe five-eight.

"Are you Bill?" she asked.

His face cleared as if he'd had the same worries she had. "Yes, yes, I am. It's nice to meet you." He held out his hand and she took it in one of those wimpy girl-handshakes for fear of his noting her damp palms.

She let her purse slide down off her shoulder and reached for the chair, but he leprechauned around her with a smile. "Let me get that!"

"Oh! Thank you." She gave a faint laugh and sat, hoping the waiter would arrive immediately to take her drink order.

Bill returned to his seat, leaning onto his forearms and clasping his hands, looking at her intently. He had a glass of something with a lime in it in front of him.

"You look just like your pictures!" he enthused.

She smoothed the back of her hair down with one hand—it had been breezy outside, and she imagined herself obliviously sitting there with it beehived around her head.

"Thanks, uh . . ." She couldn't say the same. He looked like the kind of guy who wouldn't put on a cowboy hat if you held a six-shooter to his head and made him. "You look . . . a little different from yours."

He wilted. "I know. It's the hat."

"Do you, ah, wear cowboy hats often? Are you a country and western guy?" She tried to imagine the two of them two-stepping around a dance floor.

"Actually, no." He appeared to be blushing. "I never wear hats, and I'm much more of a classical music guy. But there was this one time . . . I went to Houston with my, my, my, well, my ex-girlfriend, if you must know, and she took the picture. So . . . I don't know why I used it." He tried to chuckle and shrugged.

"Oh," she said, a picture of the situation materializing. She gave him a smile. "You looked really happy. In the picture."

"I do?" He looked at her. "I—I guess I was. We were both—or at least I thought we both were, on that trip."

The waiter arrived, and she ordered a red wine. Bill ordered another gin and tonic.

"How long were you two together?" Macy asked, mostly to fill the silence that remained after the waiter left.

"Almost a year." He said it with a note of pride in his voice. "We were doing great too, until I screwed up."

"What did you do?"

He polished off what was left of his drink and looked at her ruefully. "I canceled on some plans we made for Thanksgiving. It was the stupidest thing. I had lost my job and I wasn't feeling good about myself—I just couldn't meet her family like that. You know?" His face suddenly cleared. "But it's okay, I have a job now. No worries about that!" He laughed nervously. "Doing just fine now, it was a temporary problem, a layoff."

"Hey, a lot of people have gone through that. But good for you for getting back on your feet!"

He nodded absently. "Yeah, yeah I did. But it was too late. See, my girlfriend—I'm sorry, *ex*-girlfriend, she's a great girl, but she tends to make snap decisions. That's why we were good together. I'm the deliberate one, she's impulsive. I thought we brought out the best in each other."

It crossed Macy's mind that it probably wasn't a good sign to be talking about a guy's ex-girlfriend right off the bat on a first date, but she wasn't feeling any immediate attraction anyway, so she figured they might as well have a genuine conversation.

"So you canceled on Thanksgiving and she broke up with you?"

"Yeah." He nodded to himself again. "Yeah."

"Did you explain why you canceled?"

He took a deep breath. "Yeah, I did. But she . . . she didn't think that was a good enough reason. I guess she thought I was being weak, or something."

"Really? It's a big deal to meet someone's family. You want to be confident."

"That's what I said. But she said I needed to *man up*."

"Man up? She said that?"

He tipped his head. "But hey, enough about me. Jeez, sorry. Tell me about you! Have you got an ex-boyfriend we can talk about?"

Macy laughed. "Sure, we can talk about me, but I have one last question. How long ago did you break up?"

"Just a couple weeks ago."

"And you're online dating *already*?" She thought of Jeremy, online after only a couple of weeks. Then again, so was she. She held up her hands. "Sorry! That sounded really judgmental."

He leaned forward. "No, it's okay. In fact, I want to explain. I had thought, initially, that in order to 'man up' in the wake of the breakup I should get right back on the horse."

"Hence the cowboy hat?"

"Oh, hey, I never thought of that! No, see, I got online, found iLove, and who do you think popped up in my *Girls You Should Look At* list?"

"Your ex-girlfriend."

"That's right. So I put the hat picture up as a sign. To her. A reminder that we had something, that I could be someone else for a minute. Or something like that." He gripped his head with his hands and gave a mock growl. "Argh, I don't know. Maybe I just wanted to remind her I'm still here. Like I said, she makes snap decisions. Guess I was hoping I'd be one of the ones she regretted."

Macy thought about Jeremy's picture. He had zillions of pictures of himself, several of them professional head shots for his job. Why had he chosen that one when there were dozens he wouldn't have to crop? Was it meant as a signal to her?

Then she thought about his essay. It had been full of things she'd said to him, criticisms and complaints and cynical observations. She spent a horrified moment wondering if that was all she'd ever said to him, negative, complaining things. But maybe he was trying to tell her *he got it*. That he understood the problem she had with him.

But if that were the case, why wouldn't he simply call her?

Because she'd broken up with him. She'd pulled the plug, suddenly and without mercy. Certainly Jeremy had no manning up to do—if he was thrown out, he would move right on.

"I'm sorry," Bill said, the sincerity in his voice breaking through her reverie. "I've gone on and on about me and my ex-girlfriend. That's like number one on the 'don't' list for first dates. I'm sure you're thinking I'm not ready to date, aren't you?"

It took her a minute to refocus on Bill. "No, no. It's okay. I . . . To be honest, I'm pretty fresh out of a relationship myself," she said, thinking, *I make snap decisions too.* "Why don't we treat this as a dinner between friends, huh? No pressure."

He smiled. "You're on. Though I may live to regret getting caught in the friend zone."

As it turned out Bill was every bit as nice as he seemed, but he was so agreeable about everything, taking on every opinion that she had no matter what the topic, that Macy started to understand a little of what the ex-girlfriend might have had a problem with. It would bother her too, she thought, mentally putting an X next to his name. Then she caught herself. Was she being—once again—too picky?

The thought made her try harder to see him as a romantic candidate. She upped her energy level, made jokes, looked him in the eye, tried to imagine kissing him, but the more of an effort she made, the more defeated she felt. There was absolutely nothing wrong with Bill, but she was pretty sure that by the end of the evening she'd have no desire to see him again. There simply was no spark.

She was sagging under the thought when a familiar laugh caught her ear. She jerked her head to the left to see, just beyond the near table, another two-top, where a pretty brunette sat holding a glass of wine across from, and gazing into the eyes of, Jeremy.

Her stomach plummeted to the floor as her wine threatened to launch in the opposite direction. Jeremy was leaning forward, seemingly hanging on the brunette's every word, and the brunette was eating it up. Just as Macy had, when she'd had his full attention. She wondered how long it would be before Jeremy reached for his phone, but when her gaze dropped to his belt, where the ubiquitous holster resided, she was shocked to see it wasn't there.

Macy got abruptly to her feet, causing Bill to stop midsentence. "Is something wrong? I've been talking too much, haven't I? I always do that. I'm *sor*—"

But before he could get the apology out she excused herself to go to the restroom. She couldn't do this, she thought. It was too soon. Or too late. Or *something*.

She'd screwed up. She'd mistakenly condemned Jeremy as imperfect and so she'd bailed—just as she had on dozens of other occasions. The difference was, she hadn't been in love with all those other people she'd judged and found wanting.

But Jeremy had been different.

Jeremy had been the one. And she'd thrown him away.

JEREMY'S FINGERS DROPPED TO HIS BELT ONLY TO FIND FOR the one millionth time that his cell phone was not there. He thought he'd noticed the addiction when he was in bizarro world, but now, out in reality, it was so much worse. He'd had no idea how many times he went for the phone in the course of a conversation—and he wasn't even bored. He was far too anxious to be bored.

It had come to him in a flash, the way to find Macy, the details aligning themselves quickly. Jeremy had access to Macy's cell phone. Hadn't he seen the beginnings of her essay as she'd been writing it? So why couldn't he go back up there and find out when and where her next date was going to be? Then he could line up a date and see her there. Voilà! They could run into each other accidentally and he could talk to her, face-to-face, without having to wait until he figured out how to get out of bizarro world.

He couldn't pause to think about whether it was ethical or fair or, hell, even creepy, cyberstalking her that way. But hey, it wasn't fair that he was trapped in his mobile either, so *Eat that, ethics,* he thought savagely. And he'd done it. He'd found the place and the time, and then he'd groveled his way into a date, thanking god that the rules of bizarro allowed him to at least write his own emails.

He looked across the table at Gina. He'd answered her note, saying that his profile wasn't a joke but more a kind of atonement. He'd listed all of the awful flaws he could think of and exposed them. It was as close to the truth as he could get, and something told him that the iLove universe would accept nothing less. Still, somehow, miraculously, she'd agreed to go out with him.

The problem was he was only here to find Macy. Gina was a very nice woman. Attractive too. But looking into this woman's blue eyes only made him want to see Macy's brown ones. And watching this woman's high-heeled sashay made him want to see Macy's resolute walk in flats. And hearing this woman's breathy explanations of what made her tick made him want to hear Macy's teasing banter.

The fact was he wasn't going to get over Macy, so while lying to Gina was wrong, it was his only option. Unless he wanted to live in that room full of damaged cubicle dwellers forever.

His hand went for his phone with half a notion of checking out Macy's Facebook picture again—maybe she'd do a check-in at the restaurant—but it still wasn't there, so he brought his elbow back to the table, his eyes riveted to his date's face, feigning interest.

Gina, he reminded himself. What was she talking about? Her job? He let his eyes wander a bit to the scene behind her, but there was no sign of Macy.

He was just wondering how he could make this night last as long as necessary in order to find her when his eye was caught by shining auburn hair on a petite woman moving with swift determination across the dining room. His heart swooped upward. He'd know the set of those shoulders anywhere, the bob of those curls, the curve of that hip.

Without realizing he'd moved he was on his feet. Gina looked up at him in surprise. He smiled, apologized and said he'd be right back, then he took off after Macy.

He caught up to her in the wood-paneled hallway leading to the restrooms.

"Macy!" Just saying her name out loud made him feel like the wind had finally caught his sails.

She turned, clearly unsurprised to see him.

Her mouth was set, but her eyes looked tragic.

"Are you okay?" he asked, taking an involuntary step toward her. He reached for her, one hand out, before remembering he wasn't allowed to touch her anymore, their being broken up and all.

"Yes. Fine," she said, with a forced smile. "How are you, Jeremy? It's nice to see you."

His brows dropped. Was she angry? Because of the time warp of bizarro he knew it had been longer for her than for him. He'd have hoped that would make her happier to see him, but it seemed to have had the opposite effect.

"I'm—well, I'm glad to see you too. Are you— How have you been?" The meaninglessness of the words made him want to weep. But what to say? How to tell her he was sorry, how to beg for another chance? Just leap right in?

It didn't feel right.

She took a breath; he could see her chest rise with the effort and he wished he could hug her. A futile longing stabbed him.

"I've been fine," she said. "Really, just great. And you?"

He hunched into his shoulders, pressing his hands in his pockets. "Not . . . I wouldn't say 'fine.'" He tried another smile, wondering at the look in her eyes, so at odds with the detached tone of her voice. "Pretty *not* fine, actually. But—but you, you're okay?"

"Sure." She nodded with that tight smile, but he knew her, and he could've sworn she was trying not to cry. "I'm sorry you haven't been fine. You seem to have a nice new, um . . . your date looks nice."

"To be honest, I have no idea if she is or she isn't," he said, dropping his shoulders—along with all efforts at concealment.

"Oh." That startled her. "First date?"

"Yeah. Are you here with someone?"

She flushed red. "Yes."

There was a tense moment where they simply stood there, looking at each other. Then she did the most unexpected thing. Clasping her hands together, she stepped toward him. "Jeremy, I just want to say, I'm so sorry. And I'm sorry to do this to you while you're on a date with"—she swept an arm out toward the dining room—"that nice woman. But I just—I have to say I'm sorry. About the whole . . ." She swirled her hand in a circle, looking down, shaking her head. "Breaking-up thing."

The breaking-up thing?

"The breaking-up thing?" he asked out loud.

"I know I probably just beat you to the punch, but the way I did it!" She put her hands over her eyes. "I'm so ashamed. I'm impulsive and make snap decisions and I act on them too quickly, before I've thought. I'm just like Bill's ex-girlfriend!"

"Bill?"

"And I hope to god she's sorry too, because he's a really nice guy." She looked up and wagged a finger. Then she flushed and put a hand over her mouth, gazing at him. "But you. God, Jeremy, you didn't deserve me. I mean the awful me, just walking out like that. And I understand why you didn't call or anything. You were done anyway, but I wish we—"

"*There* you are!" a male voice said. "I was just beginning to wonder if . . ." The guy's voice trailed off as he took in Jeremy. "Oh," he said, with an expression like a smacked child. "Have I interrupted something?"

Yes, Jeremy wanted to say, *a thousand times yes.* What on earth was she talking about, beating him to the punch? She thought he was *done*? With what?

Macy's eyes darted from Jeremy to her date and back. She seemed on the verge of saying more, but she stopped herself and said, "No, not at all. I just ran into an old friend. Bill, this is Jeremy. Jeremy, Bill."

Bill stepped up and shook his hand. "Good to meet you." His eyes shifted to Macy. "Uh, I'll just meet you back out there. I wanted to be sure you were okay, is all." He nodded at her, waiting.

"Okay," she said. "Sure. I'll be right back."

But Bill lingered another minute, so she turned a falsely bright look on him and said, "Jeremy, great to see you. Hope you have a nice evening." Then she disappeared into the ladies' room.

Jeremy leaned back against the hall wall, then noticed Bill still standing there, hands in his pockets, head cocked like a spaniel awaiting a treat.

"Are you the ex-boyfriend?" he asked.

Jeremy spent a moment adjusting to the title. "Yeah, I guess I am."

"She mentioned she was getting over someone."

"Did she?" *Getting over.* Not over. Was this some kind of test? Was Mrs. Hartz watching even now?

"Yeah." The guy smiled and looked down, thinking. "To be honest I don't think she's let go yet. Hope I'm not out of line telling you that."

Jeremy straightened. "No. No, not at all." He gave a short laugh. "Really?"

Bill raised his hands and eyebrows, then turned back to the dining room.

Jeremy looked to the ladies' room door. How weird would it be if he were still out here when she came back?

CHAPTER SIX

Macy had trouble catching her breath. What had she said? She couldn't even remember. There were so many things she'd wanted to say but couldn't. And they'd been standing outside the bathrooms. And he was there with another woman! She was pretty sure she'd been inappropriate.

She hadn't even let him say anything. And he'd been about to say something, hadn't he? She wished it were a tape she could rewind. Oh, *if only* Bill hadn't shown up when he did!

She pulled her purse up and pawed through it for her phone.

"Carolyn?" she said, grateful that her sister-in-law had answered and not her brother.

"Macy, hi! I've been meaning to call you. Lute and I were just talking about it. There's a guy in my office—"

"Wait. I need to ask you something," she said, lowering her voice at the sound of someone entering the restroom.

"Where are you?" Carolyn asked, her voice taking on the same hushed tone as Macy's.

"I'm on a date."

"Great!" Her voice bounced through the phone.

"No, it's not like that. I'm in the restroom. I just ran into Jeremy."

"Oohhhh."

"Yeah. And oh god, Carolyn, I made the *biggest* mistake. You were so right about me. I judged him too fast, too harshly, I shouldn't have judged him at all! I *loved* him. Why did I give up on him?"

"'Cause that's what you do, hon," she said, not without sympathy. "I've been thinking about this, and I actually think *you're* the one who's afraid of commitment. All that talk about planning for kids and houses and career tracks, all that stuff I said would chase a guy off in half a second? I think it backfired. You freaked *yourself* out, Macy. You chased yourself off."

Macy paused, the ring of truth echoing through the phone. "Oh my god," she said, mostly to herself. She *had* freaked herself out. She'd looked at Jeremy's phone use and she hadn't seen a temporary problem, she'd seen a lifetime of neglect. She had loved him, that was for sure, but not as much as she'd feared for herself in light of him.

"I know," Carolyn said. "But here's the thing, Mace. You can change that. You don't have to have everything planned out and all the little boxes checked the moment you fall in love, or even when you get married. A relationship's a path, not a room. Let it wind around the forest for a little while."

Tears clogged Macy's throat. "That's really beautiful," she said, unrolling some toilet paper and pressing it to her eyes.

"Then, when you get to a clearing, you decide what comes next, which new path to take. Maybe it's one that's been well traveled, maybe one the deer have made. Maybe it's not even a path yet and you have to *hack* your way through, like Michael Douglas in, shoot, what was that movie?"

"*Romancing the Stone*," Macy said, pulling bits of toilet paper off her eyelashes.

"Right. Well, sometimes that's what relationships take, a little hacking through the underbrush—"

"Uh, Care? I think you've taken that analogy about as far as it'll go," Macy said, choking back a laugh.

"Fine, okay. But my point stands."

"You're right, you're absolutely right. But my question is, what do I do *now*? Do I go back out there and try to talk to him?"

"No no no. You're on a date, right? Where is he?"

"I don't know. At the table, I guess. I'm in the ladies' room." On cue, the woman in the other stall flushed the toilet.

"Right. So you go out, finish your date, then you call Jeremy tomorrow. Arrange a place to talk, because you shouldn't have important conversations like that on the phone if you can help it."

"But he's right here now. I feel like if I let him go I . . . I don't know, I might not be able to find him again."

"Why?"

"I don't know. Just a feeling." She shook her head. She was thinking superstitious and talking crazy. "I'm sorry, you're right. I'll wait and talk to him tomorrow."

"Good girl." She heard the smile in Carolyn's voice. "I'm glad you ran into him. I always thought it was a mistake to break up."

Macy heard the other woman finish washing her hands and leave the restroom.

"I know. Okay," Macy said, unlocking the stall door to move to the mirror. "I'm good now. *Thank* you."

"And call me after you've talked to him."

"I will." She smiled, hung up, then caught sight of herself. Her mascara was all over her face and strands of her hair were stuck to her cheeks. *Yeah,* she thought, *it'll be better to call . . .*

JEREMY WAS STILL STANDING NEAR THE RESTROOM WHEN HE saw Gina coming toward him.

"Is everything all right?" she asked, her tone somewhere between concern and suspicion.

"Fine," Jeremy said brightly, trying to act as if he'd been heading back to the table. "I ran into an old friend, that's all. I'm thinking of having another drink. How about you? Maybe move to the bar for a Bailey's or something?"

Gina looked surprised. "Sure, I guess so. I mean, there's always the chance of overdoing a good thing on a first date, but . . ." She looked at him, eyebrows raised.

He squelched a grimace. He was using her, there were no two ways about it. But if the date ended he'd end up back in bizarro, and without being able to actually *talk* to Macy, he wasn't sure he'd be able to straighten things out with her.

"A quick one. If we see evidence of damage we'll leave immediately." He gave her his most charming smile and she giggled and acquiesced, then continued on to the restroom.

He settled up with the waiter at the table, then picked two seats at the end of the bar closest to the restrooms, figuring Macy would probably be out before Gina. But minutes later it was Gina who emerged, and the look on her face was dark and wooden. She spotted him immediately and moved toward him, eyes steady on his face.

He became aware of a deep feeling of dread, like what he imagined animals must feel when faced with a gun, despite not knowing exactly what damage a gun could do.

"What can I get for you?" he asked in his most oblivious-guy way.

"Nothing," she said. "And I don't appreciate being *used*."

"What are you talking about?" Had Macy said something to her? Was Macy still somehow mad at him—had she told Gina something bad?

"I guess I understand now why you wrote the profile you wrote. You really *are* an asshole, aren't you? All that stuff about confessing your sins in order to get rid of them—"

"Well—"

"That was all just a load of crap, wasn't it?" she continued.

"Gina," he said calmly, patting the chair next to him. "What's going on? You went into the restroom just fine, and now you're mad. Did something happen?"

She crossed her arms over her chest and glared at him. "Are you going to tell me that you *didn't* pick these seats so you could see your ex-girlfriend again? Are you using me to make her jealous or what?"

"My ex-girlfriend?" he repeated, but he couldn't muster the tone to make confusion believable.

"Yes, your ex-girlfriend. Don't play dumb with me. I just heard her on the phone in the bathroom talking about you. You were dead set on coming to this restaurant too. Was it because you knew *she'd* be here? You were never interested in me for one second, were you? Admit it."

She had him pegged. What could he say? All of it was true.

He had visions of Queenie Hartz giving him the evil eye when he returned to his cubicle, so he said, "All right. It's true, at least partly. And I'm *really, truly* sorry. But the circumstances aren't what you think."

Her color had risen along with her eyebrows. "Oh yeah? I think I ended up on a date with a stalker, that's the only circumstances I'm seeing."

"Please sit down," he pleaded, low. Out of the corner of his eye he saw Macy exit the hallway down which the restrooms lay, glancing at him as she made her way back to her table.

His date, apparently, barely heard him.

"If I were your ex-girlfriend—and if I were *ever* your girlfriend I can guaran-damn-tee I *would* be an ex—I'd run screaming for the hills if I saw you. *You* are one *twisted* son of a bitch." She leaned forward and poked him in the chest on the word "twisted." Heads were beginning to turn in their direction. "I've got half a mind to report you to iLove at the very least, if not the police. Or maybe I'll just clue your ex in when she comes out."

"Please don't say anything to iLove," Jeremy said, rising.

"Why? Are you already in trouble with them? Have others complained too?" She shook her head. "Damn it. I knew you'd be too good to be true. First I thought you'd probably used someone else's picture, but then I saw you and you were that same good-looking guy. Well. Now I understand. You're *sick*. You're—"

"Yeah, I know, you're absolutely right. Let's just go." He tried to take her elbow to guide her toward the door, but she jerked away from him.

"Take your hands off me!"

The bartender was approaching, a disturbed look on his face.

Jeremy held up his hands. "Okay, whatever you say. I'm sorry. Do you want to leave first, or should I?"

"And don't try to contact me ever again, even to apologize or anything, because I am blocking you, buddy. You're the worst bad news I've had for a long time, and if I see you again I *will* report you." With that, she stalked out of the restaurant, leaving a long bar full of curious faces to gawk at him.

He swallowed and chuckled impotently, feeling his face go hot. Then he glanced over to where Macy sat with her date. Both of them had turned to see what the commotion was. Macy's face was confused, but her date looked decidedly wary.

Could it be any worse if he walked over to her and asked to talk for a minute? He could try to explain, though what he could possibly say at this moment eluded him. He could at least request another time to talk—surely bizarro would let him out if he had a bona fide date, even if it wasn't through iLove. Then again, it would be more of an appointment than a date. And making an appointment with her and not showing would be the death knell for his chances of winning her back.

No, he had to talk to her now. He tried to take a step in her direction, but when he picked up his foot it got yanked to the side. He looked down, expecting to see himself caught on something, maybe someone's coat that had fallen off their chair. But there was nothing, and in another instant his other foot was jerked in the same direction. Then as if someone were pushing on his back he was propelled straight toward the door. He tried to resist but it was futile, and as he pushed through the door, tilting and flailing, he felt that weird suction and instead of finding himself outside on the sidewalk his feet felt the industrial-grade carpeting beneath them and he stumbled into the corridor just across from his cubicle.

Despair hit him like an anvil from a high window. He wanted to scream, but was afraid he would scare himself with the lunacy of it.

Then it got worse. The floor trembled and a loud voice called out, "Where is he? Where's my boy Jeremy? A little birdie told me he hasn't been *paying attention*! And you know what happens when we don't pay attention?" Queenie Hartz turned the corner at the end of the hallway and lumbered toward him, her eyes gleaming red like a dog's in a flash photo.

Nothing, he wanted to say, but the dread in his gut turned into outright fear, and he launched himself into his cubicle, locking his eyes on his screens.

A second later she loomed in the doorway.

"We get your type in here *allll* the time," she said in a voice low and silky. "Trying to buck the system. Thinking they can outsmart the game. And you know what happens to them?"

Jeremy gritted his teeth. "They get dragged back here against their will?"

"Time and again."

He could see her grinning from the corner of his eye.

"Have you learned anything today, young man?"

He frowned, staring sightlessly at his email inbox. "Actually, no." He turned toward her, and looked up, up, up to her broad, maniacal face. The tiara twinkled in the fluorescent lighting.

"And *why not*?" Her tone gained a harder edge.

"Because, here's the thing. We're supposed to find a real relationship, right? That's the point of iLove? Well, that's what I was doing."

"Is. That. Right."

"Yeah, it was. Not with Gina, of course, but Macy. You know, the one whose phone I get to wander around in upstairs? So I must be here to get back together with her, right? Or else why would one entire floor of this building be dedicated to my accessing her cell phone?"

"Upstairs?" she scoffed. "There *is no* upstairs. Whatever you think is up there is in your very own head, young man. And I guess it doesn't surprise me any that what you got up there is nothing but another cellular phone."

Could he be so crazy that he was crazy even here? Or was

the place just built to make him think so? "Okay, sure. But listen, if there's one thing I know, it's that Macy is the girl for me. I'm not going to find anyone on iLove unless it's her. So if you let me out of here I *will* build a relationship with her, a *real* relationship."

"Just let you out, huh?"

"Look, you took away all of my tools to make this right. I can't see her, I can't *talk* to her, even on the phone. I can't even find her on iLove, at least not the way things are set up here. So I had to resort to . . . something else."

"We didn't take away your tools. You *have* all of your tools." She swept a hand toward his array of screens. "You have everything you thought you needed when you were out before. What's different now?"

"What's different? I could *see* people before, touch them, have face-to-face relationships."

"Honey," she said, leaning an elbow on the top of his cubicle wall, "that is exactly the point. You saw people, touched people, had face-to-face relationships, but all you were facing was your smartphone."

"I *get* that now," he said eagerly. "I do. I swear I do. Look, if you let me email her, let me get out of here for a date with her, I know I can make everything right."

"You want special rules, just for you?"

He exhaled in frustration. "All right, then, just tell me how to find her on iLove. If I make a date that way can I get out and see her?"

"Sure, you know the rules. So that's what you want? Me to tell you how to find her on iLove?" she asked sweetly.

"Yes!"

"And you'll do everything else the right way?"

"Yes. Absolutely. I promise." He gave her his sincerest smile, then held up three fingers. "Scout's honor."

"What a load of BS, mister. Here you are asking me out of one side of your mouth to break the rules, while out of the other side you're promising to do everything the right way. You've got to get your head on straight, that's what you've got to do. And start *paying attention*!"

CHAPTER SEVEN

Macy picked up her phone for the dozenth time and looked for the little red 1 that would tell her she had a text or an email or a voice mail. She even checked her Facebook page to see if Jeremy might have messaged her there, but there was nothing.

Two days ago, right after she'd seen him at the restaurant, she'd called him. His voice mail had picked up immediately and she hadn't wanted to leave a message. Then she'd tried again the next day. Same thing. She tried once more yesterday but she figured by then he *must* have seen her in his missed call list and was simply not calling back. The many possible reasons for this made her want to cry, but that didn't stop her from hoping he'd get in touch.

"Jeez, I'm really starting to see what you mean about Jeremy," April said, pushing through a rack of spandex yoga pants and eyeing her skeptically.

Macy looked up, her heart leaping at the possibility that April had spotted him. "About Jeremy? What do you mean?"

"About how annoying it is to be with someone constantly looking at their phone. You've barely taken your eyes off that thing the last few days. Not since you saw him at that restaurant. You're not still thinking you'll hear from him, are you? He was on a *date*, for pity's sake."

Macy smarted at the words. "You don't have to be so blunt about it."

"I'm sorry. But you've been mooning around for weeks now, and it's time to move on. I'm worried about you." April sighed and pushed away from the clothing rack. "Come on, let's get out of here. They never put the good stuff on sale and I'm just not the type to do yoga in leopard-print tights."

Macy shot her a look. "Yes you are."

"Well, yeah, but only if they really *look* like a leopard, not some cheesy pattern in green and orange."

"What, like made of fur?" Macy said absently, thinking all of life was pointless when you couldn't reach the one you loved. She felt as if she were the one who'd been dumped, and frankly, spending time in the faux-friendly world of her cell phone was a lot more comfortable than walking around like a dead extra in somebody else's movie.

The inanity of her conversation with April was making her tired. She wished she hadn't agreed to go out after work—she'd rather be home in bed—but April was right. She'd done nothing the last few weeks but angst about Jeremy. It was time to get out. But even that wasn't working.

She'd been holed up in her head so long she could barely make conversation. It was so bad she'd been afraid to see her life coach for fear of being outed as one of the fools done in by love. He'd already pointed out how her relationship was not adding value to her life; if he discovered that the relationship was over and she had descended into life immobility because of it he'd probably drop her as a client. She'd been pretty lax at work too. Where was this going to end? How was she supposed to get over him? Things had only gotten *worse* as time had passed.

They zipped up their coats and pulled on their gloves and headed for the exit. In a heavy-handed bit of symbolism, winter had descended suddenly and without mercy that week. She pulled her collar up, anticipating the icy wind.

"Why don't you just call him, then?" April said, turning to her once they were outside. "You want to talk to him, so take the bull by the horns. What the hell, right? If it takes that to get him out of your system then just do it!"

"I have called him. Several times. He doesn't pick up."

April's face went from frustration to comprehension. "Oh, honey," she said, putting an arm around Macy's shoulders. "I get it now. Come on, let's go get a drink somewhere."

Macy held the phone in the palm of her hand and gazed at it helplessly. "Do you think my phone could be broken?"

As if on cue, the thing chimed.

April laughed. "I guess not."

"That's not my ring tone. What is that?" She unlocked the phone, and Jeremy's face popped up on her screen.

"Oh my god, he's FaceTiming you!" April leapt away from Macy's side so she wouldn't be visible in the screen. "Take it take it take it," she hissed.

Macy flushed, and her finger trembled as she tapped the phone to take the call. "Hey," she said, with a shaking voice.

In her peripheral vision April seemed to be gesturing something to her, moving her hands emphatically up and down.

"Macy!" His face could not have looked more delighted to see her. "Is that really you?"

She laughed, confused. "Of course it's me." Then she frowned. "Did you mean to call someone else?"

"No!" He looked stricken. "It's just—I haven't been able to get through on the regular phone. The phone part of my phone doesn't work, see, but then I remembered FaceTime. It's not actually the *phone* so it works. I'm sure there's some metaphor in there somewhere," he muttered, rolling his eyes. "But then I wasn't sure it was allowed—well, anyway, never mind. It's a long story. Have you got a minute to talk?"

She had no idea what he was talking about, but her heart began to soar anyway. "Yes! Yes, I'm just—I just got out of work. What's up?" She tried to sound casual and glanced at April, who was still doing that movement.

"Macy . . ." He looked at her a long moment.

She caught sight of herself in the little box in the corner, the one that showed how *she* looked to *him*, and realized why April was gesturing. She looked *awful*. She jerked the phone up to face level and farther away, so it wasn't looking at her from below, and she instantly looked less ghoulish. April popped herself theatrically on the forehead as if to say, *Finally.*

"Hey, can I call you right back?" she asked, thinking she should also get into some better lighting. "I'm out on the street and—"

"No!" he shouted. "No, no, don't hang up. Please don't hang up. Can you hear me?"

She looked around at the people looking at her and turned the phone down a notch, but she didn't want to miss anything he said so she turned it back up. "Yes, but so can a lot of other people."

"I don't care. I don't want to risk not being able to call back. Listen, I've come to a realization. What you were trying to say the other night, that you thought I was done? What did you mean by that?"

She looked around again. Several people at a bus stop were looking at her curiously. She dropped her voice. "Oh, you know. That you . . . you obviously didn't feel the same way about me that I felt about you."

"What?" he said loudly, as if by increasing his volume he could increase hers. "I didn't catch that."

"I said, that I know you wanted out of the relationship," she nearly shouted, "that you didn't love me anymore."

"That's what I thought you meant!" He looked happy about this. "But Macy, here's the thing. I mean, I know I was a jerk about the phone. I get that now. Believe me, I *really* understand now. But I've been thinking all this time that it was about me, my problem, my . . . addiction, I guess you could call it. So I've been frustrated about what to do. How to get out of here—of the mess I made, that is. It's hard to explain."

"No, but Jeremy, it *wasn't* about that at all. It was *me*. I was so intolerant. And I'm so sorry I made you feel like it was you. The problem is that I'm spoiled and impulsive—"

"Stop it. No, you're not. But I did realize that the problem was *about* you."

"I know! I *was* the problem. I have no patience! I could have given you another chance. Heck, I could have just gotten over it."

"That's not what I'm saying. I thought the problem was mine, that it was something that I needed to change but hadn't gotten around to working on yet. What I didn't realize was not that I had become a jerk, or an idiot, or a guy who was a lousy boyfriend—all of those things were true, but they were still all about *me*. I finally realized that I wasn't truly *paying attention* to anybody but *me*. The phone was just a symptom. And all the rest of this stuff happened because of what that was doing to *you*!" He paused, shaking his head. "Did you honestly think I didn't *love* you?"

Macy gripped the phone in both hands, looking deeply into his eyes, drinking in his full-blown and distraught attention. "Well . . . yes. I mean, I don't blame you. If I wasn't interesting, why wouldn't you tune out? But you know, now that you say all of that I think I was doing the same thing. I was only thinking about *me* and what I wanted."

He ran a hand through his hair in a gesture so dear to her that her breath caught. "Macy, oh, Macy. That is *so far* from the truth. You were right there with me and I was always somewhere else. I can't believe I did that to you. The number one thing in a relationship has to be emotional security, and I gave you none of that. I was such an idiot, Mace."

She swallowed hard over the lump in her throat and gave a light laugh. "The number one thing in a relationship? Did you Google that?"

He looked sheepish and laughed. "Actually I did. I've been . . . uh . . . working on things. On myself. Or rather, *not* myself. Trying to figure out what went wrong."

"You were? Then . . . are you saying . . . ?" She couldn't get the words out. She could not ask him if he still loved her, because even after all of this, she was scared to death he might say no.

"Macy, I've never loved anyone like I love you. And it

wasn't about the phone, or the iPad or whatever, it was about *me* not knowing how to love. Not knowing how to nurture love, and build it, and take care of it the way it should be taken care of."

A tear slipped down her face and she smiled. "Google again?"

He gave her a look she hadn't seen since one of their earliest moments in bed. "Just the vocabulary, Mace. The feelings are all mine. And I'm so, so sorry. I ruined everything."

She swiped at her cheeks to dry them with her gloves and gave him a watery smile. "But I did the same thing. I made snap judgments and then—then I *bailed* on you. And in the cruelest way!"

His lips were pressed together, and his eyes looked as if they might be wet too. She gripped the phone harder, brought it closer to try to see if he was tearing up, then realized that her face was getting huge on his screen. She yanked it back.

"I miss you, Macy," he said. "God, I miss you so much. I wish . . . I wish I could go back in time, back to when I was lucky enough to have your love."

"Jeremy, I still love you! You don't know how much I wish I could undo it all, the misunderstanding, the breakup—" As she said the words the screen went blank. Then her phone vibrated and the app closed itself down. "No!" she wailed, shaking the phone in her hands. She took the finger of one glove in her teeth and pulled it off, then started poking the app with her finger. But instead of opening back up, the entire phone shut itself off. *"No!"*

"Macy," April said, coming closer.

Macy looked up and saw a crowd of people near the bus stop watching her, their faces looking as devastated as she felt, like they were watching the sad ending of her life's movie.

"Macy, turn around," April said.

Macy caught the smile on April's face and spun to look behind her. Weaving through the crowd on the sidewalk, Jeremy was moving toward her, his eyes scanning the people all around until his gaze landed on hers.

Her mouth dropped open, the glove fell to the ground and he stopped.

"You were right here?" she asked, not knowing what else to say. "All along? Why didn't you just—?"

But instead of speaking he moved swiftly toward her. Before she could get another word out his arms were around her and he was kissing her.

She didn't hear the applause from the group of tired commuters waiting for the bus. And she missed it when April said that she'd call her later. She didn't even hear her cell phone dropping to the ground.

The only things she was aware of were Jeremy's arms tight around her and his lips on hers. When the kiss broke he pulled her closer, one hand on the back of her head. "I'm not letting you go again. I'm never going to be that fool again, Macy, I promise. Doubtless I'll be some other kind of fool somewhere along the line, but don't you *ever* doubt that I love you."

She pulled back, her eyes capturing his. "*I* was the fool. And I've learned my lesson."

He smiled, and his eyes *were* wet this time, she was sure.

"Marry me," he said.

She gasped.

"I know. It's crazy. It hasn't even been a year, so it's probably too soon, but I know what I want. Just tell me I have a shot, that you'll think about it, that we can move in that direction. And when the time comes I promise I'll do it right," he continued. "I'll get a ring, get down on one knee, all that stuff, but please tell me now, so I can breathe, that you still love me. Tell me I have a shot at making you mine forever, my wonderful, patient, loving girl."

She could barely speak for the smile on her face, but as a tear of joy dribbled out the corner of her eye, she said, "Oh, Jeremy. I do still love you. And you have way more than a shot."

Something brushed against her leg, and she looked down.

"Hey!" Jeremy pulled her gently to the side and confronted the kid who was scooping up her phone from the ground.

The boy flushed and held it out to him. "I was just picking it up for her."

"Hang on." Jeremy took Macy's phone back and handed the boy his own. "Take this one instead. I don't want it anymore."

"Cool!" The kid grinned and took off.

Macy laughed. "That was *not* necessary."

"Trust me, I have my reasons." He gazed at her warmly. "I never want to lose you again, Macy."

She shook her head. "You never really lost me before. I was yours all along." She smiled. "And I always will be."

A TRUE HEART

MARY KAY McCOMAS

For my granddaughter and copilot on this one,
Allyson Elizabeth McComas

Love takes off masks that we fear we cannot live
without and know we cannot live within.

—JAMES A. BALDWIN

Our differences are only skin deep,
but our sames go down to the bone.

—MARGE SIMPSON

CHAPTER ONE

"I am *so* late!" Elise muttered, bursting through the doors of Candy's Costumes on the north end of State Street. Catching sight of her brother's wife, Molly, standing before a mannequin dressed as Bo Peep, she added, "And I'm so sorry! I had the hardest time finding this place. I thought it would be bigger."

Looking around, she could see that the space required to contain Candy's *colossal collection of costumes* was in the length of the building, not the narrow forty-foot width of the storefront. It was cavernous, with an overstuffed appearance that made her feel a little claustrophobic.

"That's okay." Molly's attention was on Bo Peep. "I've been standing here trying to decide if I want to go cutesy, creepy or cheap flashy floozy."

Elise mulled it over for a moment. She did adore her big brother, but . . .

"What about Roger? If you go as Bo Peep, will he go as a sheep or a big bad wolf?" They looked at each other, squinting in thought, and came to the same conclusion—Bo's problem was forgetfulness, not a wolf. There was love in her laughter. "So, Roger as a sheep. I might reconsider and go just to see that."

"Reconsider anyway. I want you to come." Molly started picking through a row of neatly hung storybook costumes. "Look at these costumes! They're fantastic. I can't wait to see what everyone else wears. Liz thinks you can tell a lot about a person by the sort of costume they pick; more than you can if they're wearing regular street clothes."

Elise was considering a mermaid's tail for Molly and Roger as a starfish, or maybe a seahorse, when something occurred to her and stirred suspicion. She glanced over her shoulder. "I wonder what Liz's cousin Bill will come as—do they have a nice-guy-with-a-great-personality costume, do you think?"

Molly flinched, but didn't turn away from the fantasy costumes she was browsing through. "Going by this place, I'm guessing they do."

"Ah." She chuckled, good-natured. "The truth reveals itself: Cousin Bill needs a date."

"*And* so do you."

"*Not* if I'm not going."

"Elise."

"Molly."

"Liz is counting on you."

"To be Bill's date?" This time Elise gave her a slightly longer glance over her shoulder . . . with an appalled expression.

"No . . . Well, yes . . . but not entirely." She took a deep breath. "She's hired the nice little dance band that played at Patty Morrison's wedding—she got lucky there, because they're super busy. But since so many people will be dressed as characters of some sort, she thought you might be willing to play piano between their sets."

"Me? Why? How does she even know I could?"

"We've talked about it. You know, about your lessons and how much the boys love it when you play 'Happy Birthday' for them. And it wouldn't be anything huge. A few short snippets of show tunes and funny little character jingles like . . . Oh! '*Muppet Babies, we make our dreams come true. Muppet Babies, we'll do the same for you,*'" she sang quietly. Then, as an afterthought, she added, "No, I hate that one. Reruns, every afternoon at one thirty—sticks in your head until you want to blow it off. But maybe '*Scooby Dooby Doo, where are you?*'" She chuckled. "Or *Batman!*—everyone knows the lyrics to that one: '*Nana, nana, nana, nana.*'" Suddenly, her right fist shot into the air. "'*Thunder, thunder, Thundercats, ho!*' Best ever. Super motivational for little boys under the age of six." She went back to the fantasy fashions. "I don't know what I'd do without it. Maybe 'Tomorrow' . . . there's bound to be at least one Annie there. *The Pink Panther . . .*"

Elise's expression was frozen in horror.

Piano lessons were her special treat for sticking with her day job—revenue officer for the IRS. Someone had to do it. The lessons were an indulgence, not a new career choice, and not for public consumption. She was doing pretty well, and proud of it, but she could barely play for family—she'd practiced 'Happy Birthday' so often she could also play it backward.

"Short snippets of show tunes? Have you lost your mind?"

Molly finally turned to face her. "I only said I'd bring it up and see what happens—and I can see it isn't happening. I pretty much assumed it wouldn't, but Liz . . . well, you know how she gets carried away sometimes."

Elise barely knew Liz. Liz was Molly's friend. She'd only agreed to go to the party because Molly had insisted and she'd had a date—at the time.

Now she didn't—so she wasn't.

Oh sure, there were worse things than a blind date. And there were more embarrassing situations than tagging along with your brother and his wife to a party—like having your credit card declined during a rush hour at the Piggly Wiggly or mistaking your boss's daughter for his son or producing a freight train fart in church—but honestly, who wouldn't avoid all those things given the choice?

A wall of masks caught her eye. Hundreds of masks—from plain domino masks like the ones Green Lantern and the Lone Ranger wear to intricate and beautiful Venetian Carnival masks that looked like works of art. Gaudy half-face Mardi

Gras masks to full-face rubber head masks of Freddy Krueger . . . and others more horrifying. Feathers and rhinestones. Glitter and lace. Plastic, ceramic and papier-mâché. Some were universal, others more specific . . .

She reached high to retrieve one with a six-inch nose. "This would be a good one for Jeremy."

Molly turned, confused. But only for a moment.

"Oh, right. Pinocchio. The liar." Her voice had an edge to it. She crossed the aisle to the action/adventure outfits. "You're talking about the Jeremy we haven't seen or heard from in almost three years? The Jeremy you married—the one who wanted to give you the world and then lied and cheated on you before he finally left you up to your eyeballs in debt? The Jeremy who could, at this very moment, be burning in hell for all we know, and yet he still manages to destroy every chance you get at a happy, healthy relationship? That Jeremy?" She yanked a dress from the crush of clothes and snapped, "Princess Leia?"

Elise bobbed her head. "With Luke, Han or Darth Vader . . . or a Stormtrooper?"

They both looked at an endcap display of the fallen Jedi knight and shuddered at the thought of how effectively Roger's voice would resonate from inside Vader's mask.

"Not Darth," they agreed.

Elise shrugged; there were better costumes. Not one that would involve the grizzly hockey mask of Jason Voorhees—which she quickly diverted her gaze from—but maybe something more wistful, like Erik's mask from *The Phantom of the Opera*.

"Jeremy's gone." Molly's voice went gentle and concerned. "He can't hurt you anymore."

"I know that." What about a Catwoman or V mask?

"Do you? Or do you compare every man who crosses your path to him?"

So what if she did? Who wouldn't? People aren't graded and tagged like cattle at auction. It was more like buying baskets from a snake charmer—who knows what's inside?

Her laugh was soft and quick. "Luckily, I limit the number

of men who cross my path, or I wouldn't have time to do anything *but* compare them all."

"I'm serious."

"I know."

Her fingers grazed a female Noh theater mask—beautiful in its flawless simplicity and mystery; steeped in history and tradition. She once read that they were an optical illusion; that the neutral expression of the woman changed to fear or sadness by angling the head down and to joy or happiness by lifting the chin up toward the light. She wanted to see it for herself, and lifted the mask off the hook, looking for a mirror.

"I don't understand," Molly said. "Max is really nice. Roger and I both like him . . . a lot . . . We liked John, too. He was charming. Not so much the one before Max—Dillon? But we told you that; we were honest with you, weren't we? I'm telling you: Max is a sweetie. He's really smart and he's funny. And I think he's serious. He likes you. You can see it when he looks at you." She glanced over as her sister-in-law stepped up to a strategically located mirror among the masks. "Why do you keep pushing these guys away?"

Elise covered her face with the mask.

"It's safe." Darth Vader's empty, echoing voice came from behind them. Elise screamed and dropped the mask; it shattered on the floor as she turned. He stepped lightly from his perch—she screamed again, jumped and pressed closer to . . . Molly wasn't there.

"Ah, God! Where's . . . What's happening? Where's Molly? Who are you?" Frantic, she managed to scan the area without actually looking away. "What have you done with Molly? Don't hurt her . . . or me. Please. What's going on?"

"Sorry." It wasn't just the voice changer in the mask that made his apology sound flat and hollow. "Startling you was going to happen no matter when I did it—so knowing the answer to her question seemed as good a time as any to introduce myself."

"What?"

"Which what? What is the answer to her question? What

are the answers to the five questions you just asked? Or what is my name?"

"What?"

"I said, which what? What—"

"Who are you?"

"Call me Martin." He did an about-face, stepped over the broken Noh mask and started walking briskly away, black cape billowing. "You smash it, you trash it. I'm not cleaning that up."

"What? Wait a second." Jumping the shards and overriding every instinct telling her it was a bad idea to follow him anywhere, she did so. He didn't seem intent, or even interested, in doing her harm . . . plus, there was no one else around. "Where's Molly? What have you done with her?" She wondered if the helmet was soundproof; she spoke louder. "I don't understand. What's happening?" Anger was inching up on her fear. "Is that it, then? That's all I'm getting? Your name?"

"That's a lot." He took a sharp right turn on the far end of the military uniforms. Rounding blindly behind him she came up short—Zorro turned to face her. "But I will give you so much more, *querida mea*, if you let me."

"Wha—" She took a step back, gaping at the flowing black Spanish cape, the flat-brimmed sombrero cordobes and the black cloth Domino mask that covered the top of his head from eye level up . . . from his sparkling and seductive gold-green eyes up. "Am I dead?"

"No, *bella damisela*."

"Stroke?"

His grin was roguish . . . and dazzling, set in a strong dimpled chin. Any other day she might have said it was sexy; that his soft Latin accent was dreamy—but clearly it wasn't any other day.

And truth be told, the pencil-thin mustache was distracting. How hard was it to shave and shape something like that? How long did it take him? And the obvious question: Why bother? Come to think of it, didn't Don Diego de la Vega have an identical 'stache? Who wouldn't notice that? A peculiarity like that on the face of both men? No wonder . . .

See? Distracting.

"So, it's a brain tumor, then—a big one." Elise sighed, downcast. "Inoperable?"

"Physically, you are perfectly well." With a wicked twinkle in his eyes, he added, "And perfectly safe. Molly, too."

"Where is she?"

"Where you left her."

"Where's that? Take me there." He sidled by in front of her, then swept off in the opposite direction. "No. Wait. You said physically." He slowed to a stop. "I'm well and safe physically. So mentally . . . I'm screwed. Insane. I'm hallucinating."

"No." He turned to her, took a few steps back in her direction. She found it comforting—he wasn't trying to elude her. "No, you are not hallucinating—not exactly. Candy's Costumes is, let us say, an unconventional establishment." He studied her. "You are more astute than most, I will say that about you. That is surprising, considering your lack of self-awareness. And you are not screaming and weeping—that is another good thing, *querida mea*."

"That doesn't mean I don't want to, you know."

He turned again and slowly ambled off—slowly, as if he was inviting her to follow.

"Of course," he said. "But you have no idea how hard it is to get tearstains out of these costumes. And also, the only apparel suitable for someone with puffy eyes and a red nose are clown suits or the two-piece Rudolf, which requires a second person, and I am *sick* of being the ass-end of a reindeer."

A smile twitched across her lips—she couldn't help it.

He veered left into a relatively short collection of animal costumes—moose mask, beaver head, alligator face . . . fur. Where was he going? What was he looking for? She stretched her spine, searching for a way out—the dividers were too high. And each end of the aisle opened to another wall of costumes. Who knew there could be so many?

"And clowns, as you well know, are *inquietante* . . . disturbing. Very disturbing." Yes, but how did he know she thought so? "Truly, I am worn to the bone by the time the crying stops. They are exhausting—men and women alike. And then we must waste more time on the inevitable confusion and reluctance that quite naturally accompanies a journey such as this—all of which you seem to be handling well, *mi belleza.*"

"Thanks?" He was bound to pass a door eventually, right? "So, where are we going on this journey?"

"That's up to you."

"Back to Molly."

"Possibly. Eventually."

"No, I mean: back to Molly. If this journey is up to me that's where I want to go. Back to Molly."

From somewhere deep in the bowels of Candy's Costumes came a muffled growling noise—caged beast or ancient furnace, it was hard to tell. A disturbing, worrisome sound no matter its source, though Zorro seemed unconcerned.

"Then let us begin. We must hurry." He swerved left again at the end of the rack. She followed.

CHAPTER TWO

"Ah!" Elise came face-to-face with a giant Cat in the Hat—very authentic looking and much taller than Zorro. "Oh no."

"Oh yes! And, I guess, you must know what this means. We mix your dreams and my schemes, with some baffling talk. But before you can run, you must first learn to walk."

"Rhymes? Seriously?"

"For as long as it takes, and with lots of mistakes."

"That's not makeup . . . or a mask."

He did a couple of facial contortions and then waggled his brows—it looked pretty real to her. "It's a magical face, like this magical place."

"Are you . . ." She couldn't make herself say it, and so took another track. "Are you still Martin? Can . . . can I still call you Martin?"

"Or Bill or Will or Jon or Don; if you want me to I'll try them all on. But if one is the same as all the rest, Martin's the one that I like the best."

"Is that part of the deal, then? Do you have to keep changing?"

"I do. So do you. It's just part of life. We do it to handle the pain and the strife." Her stare was vapid. He chuckled. "Come on, get in gear. You've nothing to fear. Together we'll figure your way out of here."

"God, that's annoying."

"I know and it's slow. It's a tough way to learn. Just follow directions; it's your turn to turn."

"My turn to turn . . . into that? I don't think so."

"I'm already taken, there's just one of me. First feel it—then think it, and soon you will see, it's all up to you as to who you will be."

She squinted at him, thoughtful. It was startling to realize how clearly she was thinking inside her not-damaged, not-insane, not-hallucinating but clearly not-normal state of mind.

"So, I decide on what I'm feeling and then I think about it—and I'll change. Like you do." She looked him up and down. "What on earth were you thinking?"

"Of you, that's who. To get your attention and to add some dimension. What you feel is the deal; you must know it is real."

"If this really works will you change into something that doesn't rhyme or talk in riddles?"

"If you will it, I will."

"Okay." Elise looked down, searched for her strongest emotion—and when nothing changed, she lifted her gaze back to his. "Is this a joke?"

"Think and blink."

She blinked instinctively, several times, before she could stop thinking about blinking and settle down to concentrate on what she was feeling. It helped to not look at him . . . or his big hairy cat feet. Her lids slid slowly over her eyes to close them out.

"No better than that, for the Cat in the Hat?" There was disappointment in his voice.

She opened her eyes and gasped at the black and white convict stripes that covered her all the way down to the ugly low-top, canvas, triple-Velcro prison sneakers on her feet. She huffed out an astonished laugh and glanced at his annoyed expression.

"What. It worked. I feel like a prisoner. What did you expect?"

He put his hand over his heart. "The real questions you keep, have answers more deep. The better you ask, the shorter the task."

"If it takes me more time, will you run out of rhyme?"

His cat brow furrowed darkly; she grinned at him. He folded his arms across his chest, clearly expecting her to try again, to do better.

"Okay. Okay." Elise closed her eyes for a heartbeat, then opened them. He was scowling at her. Following his line of vision downward, she pressed her lips together at the sight of a ball and chain latched to her ankle. She snorted laughter through her nose; then released it with great amusement.

"The longer it takes, the longer it takes." He turned and strode away. She watched him turn another corner, saw him glare at her over the partition and then followed the sight of his hat getting lower and lower like a setting sun.

"No. No. Wait." She started forward; her ball rattled and clanked against the chain as she dragged it along behind her. "I'll try again. Come on. Give me another chance. I think I've got it now." She bent, picked up the ball and carried it like a baby. It was heavier than she thought it would be. She was a little out of breath when she caught up to him.

"Neeh . . . What's up, doc?"

Elise stared at Bugs, lounging casually, chomping on a carrot, and then slowly closed her eyes. In less than a hiccup the weight in her arms changed shape.

"Oh!" To her great delight she wore a jacket and pants of tobacco brown canvas trimmed in red, with a matching trapper hat and russet boots. She had a rifle cradled in her arms . . . which she automatically lowered and leveled straight at him. "I want to weave, wabbit."

His gaze traveled slowly from hers to the Elmer Fudd rifle and back again—it held a challenge. Unfortunately . . . or fortunately . . . she wasn't about to take even a toy gun for granted, and so rotated wide of her target and pulled the trigger. A cloud of gray billowed upward as a cork popped from the muzzle, landing on the floor between them.

Their eyes met through the smoke—dancing and twinkling. They laughed.

And just like that Martin had gently and cleverly gotten her out of her prisoner frame of mind and broken the precarious ice between them. He could have killed her at any time, she realized. Maybe not with a lightsaber, but certainly a sword . . . or his bare hands . . . and yet he hadn't once touched her.

"I'm beginning to wike this," she said.

Nodding, he pushed himself into an upright position. Reaching out, he took hold of the rifle barrel and gave it a gentle tug—she released it to him. He put it and his carrot on the floor, and when he stood up he was Abraham Lincoln . . . stovepipe hat in hand.

Always described as being *a tall man* didn't really cover the extent of his height, in Elise's opinion. He was bend-your-neck-back tall. He was stare-at-the-top-button-on-his-vest tall. He was . . .

"Pwesident Wincoln. Howwy cow!" Elise covered her mouth immediately, appalled.

His smile was close-lipped and gentle. All manner of emotions existed in his fine eyes as they changed from gray to a golden-green hazel. Sadness and kindness were most notable . . . until amusement sparked.

"Martin."

"Feeling not quite yourself today?" he asked, making his voice soft but clear and Lincoln-like—once again immersing himself in the character. She shook her head. "Go ahead, take a moment and gather your wits. I am in no hurry at all." While searching the inside of his hat, he added, "I have no gun to my head today."

She gasped softly at his wordplay and he looked up . . . then down. It was his turn to be startled. He swept his gaze over her, nodded once and muttered, "Interesting."

Elise looked like Curious George. She sighed, dismayed. "Ahhh."

"Take heart. We are in a costume shop, after all—magic and make-believe live here. And who would not be curious in a situation such as this? At least you are not the cat that curiosity killed." The president smiled. "And while I died before reading the book, I understand the intensely curious Alice of Wonderland was foul-tempered and exceedingly bossy, which I would have found tedious in the extreme. So all in all, an inquisitive monkey is not so bad."

"Ooo-ooo ah-ah."

Mr. Lincoln grimaced. "Yes, I see. Conversing will be difficult. But perhaps, just for a moment or two, I can speak and you can listen." He paused. "It would never work in the Congress, of course, but I believe you're a different breed of monkey."

She rolled her eyes and he chuckled.

"So, shall I come down to you or will you come up to me?" Martin or not, she couldn't ask Abraham Lincoln to sit on the floor. She pointed up with her thumb. He reached down to wrap his long fingers around her hand and gave it a little yank—the ability to quickly climb a president's body came with the costume, apparently. He seemed willing to hold her in his arms, but she couldn't have borne it—she sprang to the lip at the top of the partition, squatted and curled her toes around the dowel below. They were almost eye to eye now—she just a smidgeon higher.

"Are you comfortable?" Bemused and tentative, she nodded. While he looked inside his hat once again she scanned for an exit. Her disappointment was unexpectedly bearable.

Mr. Lincoln removed and replaced several different-sized pieces of paper and at least one envelope from the lining in his hat until he found the note he was after—then he set it on the floor.

Rising slowly, he read the memo, clearly perplexed. "I must be honest with you; I am surprised by this report."

"Ooo?" Elise craned her short monkey neck to make out the words.

"It says you are cynical and judgmental and unwilling to balance your checkbook." He looked as perplexed as she was.

Their eyes met and held; observant and reflective—hers wavered first.

Okay, so the checkbook thing was true. And sometimes she was a little pessimistic, who wasn't?—aside from yoga instructors and Jamaicans, of course. But judgmental? *And* with that disapproving undertone?

She wasn't very curious anymore. Elise became an Angry Bird, soaring over rows of costumes with a head-on trajectory to the far wall at the back of the store. She was about to crash and disintegrate . . . and there was no pig in sight to make her trip worthwhile.

Terrified, she squeezed her eyes shut tight, held her breath, felt herself falling and landed on her feet with a jolt.

At first, it was hard to see beyond her new bulbous nose, but the long white beard, the red jacket, the soft leather booties . . . and her still short stature left little doubt of her present emotions—or who she now appeared to be. She stomped down the aisle and around the corner to the next to confront Mr. Lincoln with her hands fisted on her hips.

"Grumpy." The light in his eyes danced. "Perhaps you should run for Congress after all."

"Humph." Her eyebrows formed a near perfect V on her forehead. In a deep, rough voice she asked, "Who'd you expect? Sneezy? Dopey?"

"It is the gap between our assumptions and expectations that deliver most of the surprises to our life—and would not our lives be abysmally dull without them?"

"Hah! I hate surprises. They make life sloppy and unstable. Not for me, no, sir. A fine kettle of fish, they are." Elise started pacing back and forth, agitated. Abe watched her until she stopped in front of him and asked, "What were we talking about?"

"I was reporting to you that there are certain people who believe you are the skeptical sort and an atrocious book-keeper, despite your profession. But I believe it was the assertion that you are also judgmental that had you flying off the handle . . . in a manner of speaking."

"Right." She made a gruff noise, clearing her throat.

Her language was full of contractions and almost completely g-less. "Judgmental. Molly told you that, didn't she? Of course I'm judgmental." She threw up her arms. "Everyone is judgmental. It's how we mark people and places, things and ideas, as right or wrong, good or bad, healthy or not.

"But here's this about that: No one ever says you're being judgmental if you think something is right or good or healthy. Only the opposite—only if you don't like it and only if they *do* like it. And there's something else . . ." She filled her lungs with air. "If they don't agree with what you decide is right or good, they got no problem telling you how wrong you are about it. But they're just expressing their opinion, not being judgmental of my choices. Fact is, if that's the way Molly wants it, then she's being judgmental by calling *me* judgmental. What do you think of that?"

The tall man stared down at her thoughtfully—considering, not judging, her perspective.

"Pfft. Molly is the patient sort—everyone she meets is her best friend. She's everybody's pal. I love that about her. I'm more discriminating is all; private-like and choosy in my friends. We aren't all the same." She hesitated. "And I think you're more like me."

"I am."

"She's always saying I can't judge a book by its cover. And maybe I can't, but reading the first couple pages will tell me if I want to waste more of my time on it. A gooseberry pie can come out of the oven looking perfect and taste so bitter it'll take a week for your face to unpucker. Why would I take another bite? And people—what we're really talking about— well, people are the same. They can look as normal as me and you but it doesn't take long to know if you want them always in your life."

Mr. Lincoln considered this. "But people are not books and they are not pies. People are never fully cooked or completely written. What if the first time you encounter a person they are not at their best?"

Elise turned her hands palms up. "So what if they aren't?

They'll be out of my life in two swings of a pickax—why would I care?"

"But what if it is someone you will encounter again?"

"Are they back to being their normal self?" Abe's nod was provisional. "Then I'd say I still got at least a fifty-fifty chance of liking them. Same as the first time I met them. I can't always be my usual charming self either. Most everyone deserves a second chance. I believe that. I do. Ask Molly."

"And if they happen to not be at their best . . . again? What if it is a particularly bad time in their life?" One corner of Elise's mouth tilted upward in dissent—the odds had already diminished. "But what if they are truly charming and exciting people once—"

"Once they aren't around me?"

"No. Just . . . once you have had more time to warm up to each other."

"Eh. I'm to keep rubbing up against people I don't give a lick for until I can love them like my brother? To make everyone else happy? To make them stop judging me as judgmental?" She folded her arms across her chest and tapped her right foot. "In a pig's eye! I'm not mean and I'm not uncaring. But I'm also not the type to be making friends with those I've got no interest in."

Martin/Abraham sighed. "But if you do not give them all the chances they need to connect with you, how will you ever know for sure?"

"I won't." A Grumpy Elise bobbled her oversized head loosely on her shoulders. "Now I reckon I'm supposed to lose sleep over not knowing about all the things I don't know about?"

His smile was kind, but not convinced and not discouraged. He opened his mouth to speak—

The muffled growling noise came again, vibrating the floorboards beneath their feet; distant and close at once. It furrowed the president's brow and alarmed Elise nearly as much as becoming an Angry Bird had.

"What *is* that?" she asked.

"It's time. We must hurry."

CHAPTER THREE

For a second time, President Lincoln bent to take hold of her hand—not to pull her up into his arms but to draw her around another endcap, this one featuring a large Shrek. Once there he stepped behind her and placed his hands lightly on her shoulders; then slowly pushed her forward.

The brightly colored costumes on both sides of the aisle began to fade—first to gray, then completely away, to reveal a filmy image of a woman she knew.

"Molly."

Abruptly, the figure turned toward the sound of a voice saying, "Ready?"

"Yes," Molly said.

Elise—looking very much herself—emerged from a cloudy dressing area in the beautiful red cocktail dress she bought four weeks earlier on one of their late-afternoon shopping trips. With a short gossamer skirt and spaghetti straps that crossed over the low-cut back, it had the wow-power to burn her image into Max's brain until the day he died . . . maybe a little longer.

Molly gasped her approval. "Now *that* is a six-month an-niversary dress!"

"You think so?"

"Lord, yes! It's fabulous."

"Not too . . . red?" She twirled before a mirror, looking concerned, but not about the dress.

Her mind began the slow rotation of thoughts that would—too often of late—spin out of control . . .

Pretty red. What if Max hates red? Do I care if he hates red? And what about this special need-a-new-dress-for-it anniversary dinner? It was his idea . . . so obviously he's been keeping track of our days together. What does that mean? Is it romantic or weird? Or is there a six-month expiration date on the women he dates? Is the dinner a setup to let me down easy? Maybe I should dump him first. Maybe black would be a better color . . . something long and shrouded. No, no. He likes me. I know he does—I feel it. But I thought and felt the same thing about Jeremy. What did I miss in the first six months with Jeremy that I might be missing now with Max? Hell, it took me five years to figure out he was a liar and a cheat. Maybe Max would consider having nine more six-month anniversary dinners . . .

Her sigh was loud and discouraged as she swished the lovely red skirt back and forth around her knees. *That would mean nine more amazing dresses I can't really afford—and five more wasted years of my life. Maybe I should just ask him: Max? Are you planning to stomp on my pride and break my heart?*

"I don't think a sexy red dress can be too red," Molly said, curbing Elise's mental debate mid-spin. "Wanna borrow my Judith Leiber knockoff?"

Elise smiled. "Perfect. Thanks."

"One down, one to go."

"What?"

"We have a spectacular dress for your special dinner, and now we have to decide on costumes for Liz Gurney's party."

"Today?"

"If we wait until the last minute all the good costumes

will be gone. I was thinking of Scarlett and Rhett." She used a thicker-than-thick Southern accent and placed a limp wrist on her forehead, prostrate—then quickly discarded the pose. "But Liz took them for her and the birthday boy. Then I thought of Sonny and Cher, but Roger's too tall. The kids thought of Bert and Ernie, but I see them all day long—and in my sleep—I'd rather swallow LEGOs. Antony and Cleopatra—there'll be a dozen sets of those. What do you think?"

Molly gravitated to a nearby sales rack and automatically started to sort through her size. Unable to afford another dress, even on sale, Elise kept close to the mirror, primping.

"How about Pebbles and Bamm-Bamm?"

"For us? That's more you and Max—still lusty and eager to mate. Rog and I mate plenty, and we have three boys to show for it. Not to mention freezing our fannies off in little furry cave outfits."

"We have freezable fannies, too, you know. I was thinking Raggedy Ann and Andy for us. That is, if I can't get us out of it altogether."

"You said you'd go and bring Max." Using the mirror to follow Molly around, Elise watched a stubborn streak settle into her features. She'd witnessed her brother cower like a timid puppy at the same expression. "You did."

"I know."

"You promised."

"I know."

Elise's Grumpy-self glanced up at the president and rolled her eyes. She couldn't remember the last time she won an argument with her sister-in-law.

"I bought extra tickets," said Molly.

"I know! But see there?" Elise seized the key word. "What's that about? Why would you sell tickets to a birthday party? Who does that?"

"It's *in lieu* of a gift." Molly's endorsement was unmistakable as she worked her way to the other side of the rack. "It's to help defray the cost of the venue. And, frankly, I'd much rather do that than try to decide on what to get a forty-year-old man whose sole mission in life is to fish all day, every day, for his birthday." That didn't exactly answer Elise's question. "And Liz couldn't very well entertain two hundred guests in costumes at their house, could she?"

"Then why costumes?"

"Why not?" Molly stopped and went thoughtful. "In summer maybe . . . that might work . . . we could wander around outside, eat catered barbecue, but in February—"

"That's another thing: Two hundred people? I'm not sure I know two hundred people well enough to invite them to a birthday party. Do you? Two hundred people who'd come . . . and pay for the venue, as well? Maybe a wedding or a charity thing, but . . . It reminds me of that time she tried to sell CD recordings of her singing 'Jolly Old Saint Nicholas' in Pig Latin at the mall for the Dyslexia Research Trust. Remember that?"

"It's a good cause—her son is dyslexic."

"Sure it is, but don't you think her methods are a little . . . unusual? . . . if not just wacky? What about a car wash or . . . or a lemonade stand? Raffles are always good."

"She was making a point." Molly replaced a pretty blue sheath on the stand. "It was symbolic: The jumbled letters in Pig Latin and the jumble of letters a dyslexic kid sees. Clever, really—just disastrously unmarketable."

"Mmm. You think?"

Wandering off topic briefly, Elise pondered lip-smacking new shoes for her scrumptious new dress versus a pair of old, bland, stale pumps from last year and had barely arrived at the most obvious course of action when something occurred to her . . .

"Liz posted the party invitation on Facebook, didn't she?"

Molly cringed, but didn't look up. "To save money on party invitations that could then go toward an open bar."

"And two hundred people accepted."

"Only one hundred ninety-two . . ."

"That's one hundred ninety-two friends, acquaintances and virtual strangers?"

"Within driving distance, yes." Then she had to admit it. "That's why she needed the bigger venue . . . and a cash bar."

"That woman is industrial-strength weird."

The wavy image dissipated, and Elise felt suddenly alone again without Molly. When she turned back to the president, he looked . . . expectant.

"What? You don't think she's as strange as a cow jumping over the moon?"

"Jumping to conclusions makes more sense to you?"

"What?"

Hands on her shoulders, Mr. Lincoln directed her attention back to the murky passage—it pictured Molly and Liz having lunch at Ferdinand's, *her* favorite restaurant.

"Hey! I found Ferdinand's. I was the one who told Molly about it. We go there all the time. It's our place. What's she doing there with Liz?"

Shocked, she pressed her fingers to her lips. Did she say that? Out loud? The acerbic tone of her voice jarred her. The words were petty and spiteful. And while she did, on occasion—like now—think and feel exactly that way, *not* saying so kept it a secret. It allowed her to pretend she was above such socially unacceptable emotions as dejection, jealousy and resentment.

Moreover, the silence protected her from the disapproval of others—those who appeared to have the enviable ability of making the best out of everything; who never had a negative point of view or reaction . . . or at the very least had the talent of giving that impression.

No, prudent people didn't leave their feelings hanging out; didn't leave themselves vulnerable. She sighed, resigned to keeping her most unbecoming thoughts and emotions to herself.

"You don't, you know." The president spoke softly at her ear.

She tipped her head his way, still watching Molly and the interloper. "I don't what?"

"Keep your thoughts and emotions to yourself."

"Yes, I do." Elise frowned. Her low Grumpy voice felt scratchy . . . and she hated him messing around in her mind. " 'Course, I do—the not-so-nice ones, I do. I don't scream at the little kids running wild at the grocery store—or club their mothers for blocking the aisle with their carts."

The smile on his lips was soft; the perception in his eyes was hard to take.

"Okay, so . . . so I'm still steamed that Nick Basserman got promoted over me. Especially after I mustered the courage, and the pride, to go in and plead my case to that old pinhead Winston. Three years it's been. I'm still crushed. I've had to act like a good sport, a team player, all along knowing I'm more qualified. *Crushed.* But I don't talk about it. I keep it to myself. It still hurts, but I haven't let anyone see none of that."

"You do not talk about it, but that does not mean your disappointment goes unspoken. You are less enthusiastic about your work and withdrawn among your coworkers; you smile less and your posture has gone lax with disinterest. The way you are feeling is very much hanging out, as you say."

She scowled, considering. "Well, what about the time my mother completely forgot my twenty-fourth birthday—the year she went back to Italy to visit my grandparents? My own mother. No card, no call, no T-shirt, nothing. I said nothing, and I didn't let her see how much it hurt me."

Abe nodded. "Your mother was remorseful—you saw it in her eyes. But you played indifference, you cut her off short and you did not give her a chance to apologize. Do you know why?"

If she didn't at the time, she did now. To punish, to teach her mother a lesson, to have stowage to barter with, tit for tat, for any future transgression of her own. Her heart tipped. That wasn't the way she was raised, it wasn't the example her mother set for her. Everyone deserved a second chance—isn't that what she'd said? Didn't they also deserve the opportunity to ask forgiveness?

"And with no apology to sooth your wound it remains sore and unable to mend," he said.

Elise shuffled her weight from foot to foot uncomfortably, searching for a good excuse or a reasonable explanation. A chronically overdrawn, cynical, judgmental hypocrite was not what she'd set out to become.

"Look," he said, reclaiming her attention; his slim-fingered hands still resting on her shoulders. "Their food has arrived."

"Oh! Good choice!" Elise smacked her lips. "Ferdinand's Crab Louie never gets old."

"Thank you for this, Molly," said Liz Gurney, picking up her fork and knife to cut her salad into manageable pieces. A chink in her voice suggested her emotions were raw and near the surface. "I need . . . You're a good friend."

"Nonsense. We mothers need to stick together. We may not have all the right answers, but we do have all the same questions, I think. It helps to know we're not alone." She sipped on a sweet tea, still watching her beleaguered friend. "You know, if kids were cake mixes we'd have all the instructions on the back of their boxes with baking tips and low-fat alternatives. But they aren't, so we don't. All we can do is our best and hope it's enough."

Liz shook her head slowly and left the utensils resting on her plate. "My best is suffocating him. I know it. I see it. And I can't seem to stop it.

"I look at Cody and I see him struggling to carry a heavy burden that I've forced on him—without thinking; without intending to. I've been too overprotective, too involved in every second, every aspect of his life . . . holding him too tight, fearful of losing him, too."

"But that's perfectly understandable, Liz, losing Lucas the way you did. Cody understands. And he's not going to blame you for loving him too much."

"No, of course not, but that's not what I mean. I see him trying to be *more*, you know? More than what he is already, which is more than enough. Way more. I see him trying to fill the empty space Lucas left. And I've seen the fear in his eyes that he might not be enough."

Her voice finally cracked, and a tear spilled onto her cheek. "The 'Jolly Old Saint Nicholas' recording?—that's when I started to notice it. Cody was so patient and supportive the whole time Lucas was sick. He's such a great kid.

"But then after . . . we decided we needed to get away; to do something fun, just the three of us. We took him to Disney World. It was a trip we'd always meant to take—you know, before—but then there was no time and . . .

"I should have realized the first time he said it . . ." She tapped on her forehead with the tips of her fingers. "I should have seen it then. I should have seen it coming. All those stupid books I read on dealing with the death of a child . . . I didn't see it." She looked away, and then back again. "We were leery at first, thinking the trip might remind him of Lucas too much. You know, more painful than pleasant for him, for all of us. Finally, Cody just blurted out that the trip was something Lucas would have liked. He said Lucas, not him. It didn't click."

"But what twelve-year-old boy wouldn't want to go to Disney World?" Then, recognizing that there might be a few exceptions, Molly added, "And even if he didn't, how were you supposed to know?"

"Because it got worse." She took a draw from her water glass. "He kept pushing himself. Rides that would have scared him to death normally, he rode because 'Lucas would want me to.' I look back now, I see his face and he *was* scared to death. Terrified. But then he'd go find another—a ride Lucas would have ridden over and over—and he'd ride that one. He'd get off pale, trembling and forcing himself to laugh. And all I saw was what I wanted to see."

"What you needed to see, too, I think. You were all hurting."

Liz's nod was slow and tired. "I think the whole trip was like a punishment for him. You know, that survivor's guilt they talk about?" Her chin quivered. "I can't bear to think that he, even once, wished he'd been the one to die instead of Lucas. The books say it's common, but I can't . . . I hope it isn't true."

"But what about his therapy? I thought you were all in therapy."

"He is now, but that's only been recently. In the beginning, we were all going to support groups. We went to the parents' group, of course, but there was a special one for siblings that Cody went to. He always said he liked it, that he was learning a lot, that he thought it helped—he said everything he thought I wanted to hear. Then last fall he turned out for middle school football. We couldn't believe it; he'd never shown any interest in it before. Lucas was the athlete, and school was easy for him. Cody struggled with his dyslexia to be a good student. He was the laid-back one, the daydreamer who loved to draw the most amazing pictures—his attention to detail is startling . . ." She hesitated, then sighed. "Last year he ran cross-country. It seemed like the perfect sport for him—running alone with just his thoughts, competing against his own best times. He loved it. Football, though, that should have been another red flag."

"He didn't like it."

Liz shrugged her bewilderment. "He never said he didn't. He went to practice. He sat on the bench during most of the games, and when they did play him, he spent most of his time facedown on the ground. He'd come home at night scraped and bruised and forcing an enthusiasm he clearly didn't have. His father tried to help him, give him a few tips, but he had no aptitude for it. And again, I missed it. I missed seeing that he was trying to be both himself and Lucas for us. I only saw him failing at things that had been so easy for Lucas, without a clue as to why he'd bothered to try them in the first place."

Molly reached across the table to cover her friend's hand with hers.

"The recording." Liz shook her head. "The dyslexia is so frustrating for him. The tutor has helped, but he still needs some special ed at school. Kids tease him. I wanted to do something just for him. Something important. I wanted to show him that I love him; that I love everything about him— his talents and his limitations—and I wanted to do it in a big way. I wanted . . ." Her voice trailed away in defeat. "Well, let's just say Elise wasn't the only person who walked by looking like I was trying to sell vials of Ebola."

"Oh no, I'm sure—"

"Oh yes. I could see it all over her face. So could Cody."

From the wings, a horrified gasp escaped Elise, and she closed her eyes in deep and sincere regret.

Liz went on. "But to be fair, he was embarrassed to begin with. He said it was a bad idea. He said that he didn't want me to go to so much trouble. He said, in every polite way possible, that he didn't want me to do it. But did I listen? Did I hear him?

"The reactions I got at the mall were only the last straw for him. He finally broke down and told us everything. How he felt, what he was trying to do for us . . . why." Her soft chuckle was ironic. "Maybe I should thank Elise after all."

"Listen. I love my sister-in-law to death, I really do. But she can be very cynical sometimes. I was there that day. I knew what you were doing . . . Not that you'd made the recording, but I knew it was for Cody. I didn't think to mention it to her, but if I had I know she . . . well, she probably wouldn't have bought a recording, I'll be honest with you, but I do know she'd have donated money. She has a soft heart, but she's skeptical, and so intolerant of things she doesn't understand."

This time Liz's chuckle was amused. "Wait until she hears that I accidentally spam-invited everyone I've friended on Facebook to Tom's birthday party."

CHAPTER FOUR

As the picture cleared, the growling and grumbling noise came again. The sound seemed to roil around inside her like leaves in a tea cup, but Elise barely noticed. She sighed and lowered her gaze to the floor.

She was intolerant. She knew it. Mockery was another defect she'd allowed to take up residence in her life.

She knew, too, that she could wither a stone with a single stare when called for. She used to practice in the mirror to look not frightened, not helpless, less caring—for protection, to defend herself. The downside was that the same expression could come across as fearsome, aggressive or unfeeling.

She never meant to hurt anyone, but she knew she could. She'd seen furtive glances before—fleeting looks that were *about* her, but not meant for her to see. They hurt. Terribly. Then they made her angry.

"I'm sorry about the boy—and his brother. I didn't know," she said, her voice thick in her throat. "I never meant to hurt him."

"Not meaning to hit a dog with your automobile doesn't make its pain any less, doesn't make it less dead." The words slapped, burned—so much she didn't detect the odd pitch to his new voice.

She bowed her head in disgrace . . . and would have proceeded on to feel like a miserable wretch had she not at that moment noticed she was now wearing bright yellow socks and a matching shirt—with a black zigzag pattern at the hem.

"Good grief," she said, though an angst-filled Charlie Brown felt like a good fit just then. She turned quickly to see that her favorite president was now Dorothy Gale's Tin Woodman. She moaned. "Great. You don't need to tell me I have no heart—I am well aware."

"Don't be dense. Of course you have a heart. Everyone has a heart. Even I have a heart."

"I didn't mean it literally."

"Neither did I," he said. He turned slowly and started walking down another aisle . . . of fruit and vegetable costumes.

"No. I meant . . ." She stopped, once again distracted. "I can never remember: Is a peanut a fruit or a vegetable?"

His clanking steps stopped and he turned. "In botanical terms, since the seeds are contained within a pod, it is considered a legume, which is a fruit. In culinary terms, since the pods develop underground, it is considered to be a plant cultivated for an edible part, therefore a vegetable. The debate of fruit versus vegetable is an old one with various outcomes." He went on in a brainy fashion, "For instance, in eighteen ninety-three, the United States Supreme Court ruled unanimously that an imported tomato should be taxed as a vegetable, rather than a fruit, which was taxed at a lower rate. The court agreed that a tomato is technically a botanical fruit, but a vegetable in its function—it's served in salads, soups and main courses, where fruits are eaten in hand or in a dessert. It's complicated."

Elise frowned at him, considering. "It's been a while, but . . . were you smart in the movie?"

"I'm hollow, not shallow." He turned away—his steps seemed louder than before. "And the movie is based on Dorothy's story, not mine. My story starts well in advance of her finding me the woods."

"Really?" she asked, staying close on his heels as he turned into sporting uniforms. This was a story she wanted to hear.

"Yes. I had problems of my own with the Wicked Witch of the East long before Dorothy's house landed on her."

"Really?"

"Yes, really. You don't remember? Gamma read you all the Oz books when you were young." Elise squinted, trying to recall—Gamma read her lots of stories. "And everyone knows the books are always better—and more informative—than the movies based on them." True; she nodded. He sighed, resigned. "Anyway, I did once have brains and a heart as well. I was as human as you are . . . except that I was a character in a book."

"Really?"

"Yes, really." He turned around to face her. "My name was Nick Chopper then, and I had a sweetheart. She was a beautiful Munchkin maiden named Nimmie Amee, and I loved her very much."

"Really?"

"Yes, really. We were going to marry, but the witch decided Nimmie was to remain a housemaid. She enchanted my ax, and it began chopping off my limbs, one at a time. One by one, I got the tinsmith to replace each extremity as best he could, but in restoring my head and chest, he forgot to add a brain and a heart."

"Uh-huh." This part she knew.

"Now, I admit that for a time I was afraid I could no longer love my lovely Nimmie Amee without a heart. I was broken-hearted about it. And with no heart to guide me, to keep me from doing wrong, I knew I needed to be extra careful not to be cruel or unkind to anything. So in the end, well, it turned out I was a better man; a more caring man without a beating heart than I was when I had one." He grinned. "You might say I had more heart when I didn't have any."

This was something Elise had never considered, so she did it now.

"You know," he went on. "It isn't the brain in your head or the heart in your chest that you make choices with. They aren't what you feel and care and empathize with. You know it's more than muscles and impulses. It's something *you* control. It's you choosing who to be; you deciding how to live your life."

He gave her a long, steady . . . Martin-like stare. His golden-green eyes found what he was looking for inside her and gently let go. She understood what he was telling her.

"And that *no heart* nonsense?" he said, his tone more upbeat. "That came from a discussion Scarecrow and I had on the merits of brain versus heart—he having no more of either than I did . . . physically. I told him that if having one or the other made the difference between being smart and being able to love, that a heart would be my choice, because being smart doesn't make you happy, and happiness is what makes life worth living." He smiled. "He was young at the time and his straw was still fresh. He hadn't had the time to learn, which is why he thought he was dim-witted and brainless, and yet in the end it turned out he was the wisest man in all of Oz all along."

Elise glanced at a football balanced prominently on a rack with other sporting equipment . . . and the Charlie Brown inside her pined wistfully.

She looked away. "And the lion was actually brave, right? He just didn't realize that courage is acting in spite of his fears. And he did that a lot." She sighed, easily empathizing with the lion's lack of self-confidence. "So, none of you knew that you already were what you wanted to be?"

"We didn't believe in ourselves."

"And Dorothy needed all three of you—heart, wisdom and courage—to find her way home; to find happiness."

He nodded, pleased with her acumen. "To find herself."

He directed her to the gap between two more rows of costumes. Cowboy hats and chaps; fringed shirts, Indian leathers and brightly colored prairie skirts began to fade away to gray . . .

A fog drifted apart to reveal a diorama of the afternoon she and Molly crossed paths with Liz Gurney at the mall.

Knowing now the ramifications of her original reaction to

the scene, Elise was inclined to take a more objective view of it—taking the time to notice that great effort had been taken to ensure that the CD cover and the charity poster looked appealing and professional, that Liz was dressed in a serious businesslike skirt and jacket, that her expression was both friendly and hopeful . . . and that her own expression was, at best, snotty and condescending.

And yes, though completely oblivious to him the first time, she now saw a dark-haired boy sitting across the way—head down, shoulders hunched and clearly in pain of the worse kind.

"Oh no," Elise said, miserable in a way Charlie Brown couldn't imagine. There was a sickening tightness in her chest. "That poor kid. And look at my face—could I look more soured or hateful? Why do I do things like that? I mean, I do things and hear myself say things and I don't even know why . . . not specifically. I'm kind and generous and loving—most of the time. I am. And I never would have hurt that little boy like that. Ever. I'm just so—"

"Lacking in self-awareness?"

"You said that before, as Zorro. You said I was pretty astute for someone with so little self-awareness. But I am aware. I know when I do or say things that aren't very nice. And afterward, I'm almost always sorry. I can even see that it took more time and thought and energy to be harsh and insulting than it would have if I'd simply been polite and respectful and moved on—I don't know why I bothered. I don't enjoy it. It's like an unsatisfying habit." She tipped her head to the diorama. "I didn't even try to understand what Liz was doing that afternoon."

He smiled at her kindly. "Acknowledging your inferior behavior is a beginning, but for true insight you must also know why you behave as you do. Remember, the way you treat people affects them, but it isn't necessarily about them. It is, however, *always* about you."

He looked into the stationary setting, and she followed his gaze. There was a quick blip in the scene, and she and Molly started walking backward into Macy's. Liz took back the CD she'd handed to Molly, took back the wave she'd used to get her friend's attention and went back to staring at the boy across the way who seemed suddenly very restless on the bench. Rapidly, she and Molly reversed their lazy mosey through the store—perfume was sucked back into bottles, Molly put down and picked up dress shirts for Roger, and Elise closed and opened at least fifty purses before Molly sped past her and vanished through the street entrance. Momentarily, Elise backed out the door as well, unwound her way up two flights of stairs to Parking Level Green. Without so much as a glance out the rear window she pulled out of her parking space . . . but then continued to drive backward all the way to her building; she zigzagged the halls to her office, where she lowered her head onto her arms, which were folded in front of her on the desk. She jumped up suddenly and backed her way into the conference room, where several other collection officers sat. They were looking directly at her, while Cooper Winston did the same with a scowl. The rerun slowed down . . . slower and slower, then started forward again.

"Haven't we been over this before, Elise?" Cooper Winston wasn't shouting at her, but the tone of his voice made it seem so. "We have regulations. We have rules for *everyone* to follow—not everyone except you! Your job is to collect the taxes people owe. If they didn't *owe* the taxes you wouldn't be here. All you need to do—all you are authorized to do— is get the money owed to the IRS by any means possible: liens, levies, wage garnishments, property seizure. That's it."

"I know what my job is." And she knew she was mortified at being berated in front of her coworkers. She also knew she was being dressed down for an act of kindness; for being understanding and compassionate . . . and stupid, because she'd known she'd get caught eventually. "But you can't get blood from a rock. The Sheldons have no money, Cooper."

"It's not your job to audit these people—just get the money."

"It's my job to get it in a fair and reasonable manner. Fair and reasonable, Cooper, that's what it says in the manual. Fair and reasonable."

"According to whose standards? Yours? Are you making them up as you go along or what? Because you're the only person I know who takes it upon herself to unilaterally decide to ignore the standard rules and regulations to—"

"They have two sick kids with some odd genetic disorder . . . that I verified as real, by the way . . . and the hospital bills are sucking them dry. He works a good job, but it's not enough. They called and explained the situation; they told me they were trying to sell their house to pay off their bills—the IRS included—but needed the lien on it lifted to do that. They also asked for a waiver on the penalty and interest charges on their installment agreement for six months . . . or less, if they sell their house. Being fair and reasonable, I agreed."

"And you got that authority how?"

She sighed, defeated. "They're good people, Cooper. They're trying. They're doing the best they can. I cut them a break."

"Rules and regulations, Elise. Rules and regulations." He tipped his thumb at the computerized display of the Sheldons' financial information on the wall behind him. "That's twice you've stepped over the line. Just do your job."

She pushed her chair back and started to stand when he asked, "Why didn't you come to me first?"

Elise didn't normally go out of her way to live her life dangerously, but she was already in for a penny. "I knew you'd say no."

The piercing glare she turned and walked away from added a frightened, insecure feeling to the embarrassment and anger that was presently overpowering her inclination to be sympathetic ever again. No good deed went unpunished, right? Who were the Sheldons to her? Would they send her a Christmas card? If she lost her job for helping them she wouldn't be able to pay her own taxes—and who'd take mercy on her? Cooper Winston? People suck.

Elise and the Tin Woodman watched the events of that afternoon take on a faster pace.

"And see there?" she said, pointing. "Every purse I looked

at while I waited for Molly was as ugly as my mood. Not to mention the disrespect I felt when she couldn't even manage to get there on time." She hesitated and looked up at her companion. "Normally, it doesn't matter. She's a late person. I'm an early person. Most people are one or the other, which is why it's such a surprise when someone shows up at the exact right time. Who does that?"

A tin finger directed her attention back to the show of that wretched afternoon. She and Molly were just approaching the exit.

"Stop. Please. Can we stop it there? Look at my face. My expression is rotten and foul before we even see Liz. She could have been Mother Teresa and I wouldn't have had a single good thought in my head for her. Liz didn't stand a chance . . . no matter what she was trying to sell."

The fog closed in around the picture and it vanished. It was a long minute before she could look into the Tin Woodman's . . . well, Martin's golden-green hazel eyes.

"I get it. It's not them, it's me."

"Only sometimes," he said kindly. "Cooper Winston should be flying monkey bait for calling you out in public. And the regulations are soulless. Still, no matter how much you couldn't regret it, in the end you knew you'd broken a rule."

"And none of it had anything to do with Molly or Liz or that poor little boy."

"No. But it still doesn't mean you have no brain and no heart." He grinned at her. "The trick is to be more aware of what you're doing, as well as *why* you're doing it. Emotions can create problems that don't need to exist. Express them to the right person at the right time and then let go of them. That's my advice," he said, with a judicious nod.

They looked at each other, and then the muffled rumbling returned—a distant racket, but getting closer; echoing, vibrating like a train on a track heading their way . . .

CHAPTER FIVE

"Don't tell me. That's the sound of the train I missed to a life less ordinary." Elise frowned at the flat affect of her voice. "Not that I'd know what to do once I got there."

She looked down at the grass-green jacket and black skirt she was wearing . . . then at the sticklike legs in gaping black boots. She shook her head as she stood up straight again.

She was Daria Morgendorffer. Instantly she felt the cynical, pessimistic and sardonic connection and, despite her recent revelations, she had to admit it was the most comfortable costume yet. She used both hands to feel and examine the large round glasses set nerdishly on her face, then turned around slowly.

As a rule, this persona never smiled unless she had a good reason—a really good reason. Elise had a really good reason.

"Hank Hill," she droned in Daria's happy-as-she-ever-got monotone. "My brother from another mother." Hank stared at her as if she'd just asked what propane was. "Same father, different mothers? Mike Judge and MTV?" She pointed to herself, referring to her character creator and television network, then at him and his. "Mike Judge and Fox."

"Oh. I see what you mean. I thought you were telling me we were relatives." He looked relieved. "It wouldn't be impossible. My extended family is already stretched as broad as daylight—nothing about it surprises me anymore."

"My family, on the other hand, is as ordinary as white paper," said Elise. "Father. Mother. Sister. Strangers who clearly carried the wrong baby home from the hospital."

"Aha."

"In my dream life I'm the only child of stationary characters, like high-end mannequins, who accept that I'm plain, unfashionable and aloof; arrogant, cynical and cranky. They also travel a lot."

"You forgot smart, sensitive and logical."

"Also realistic, honest and doomed to live a lonely life."

Hank tipped his head to one side, and after a moment she saw the twinkle of Martin's humor in his green-hazel eyes. "Big fan?"

"Huge. I love Daria. I am Daria . . . Well, before I looked like her. The real me is like her."

"Yep. I can see that," he said, in a short, clipped, Hank-like manner. "You both avoid people because they make you feel vulnerable. Those you can't avoid you push away because it's hard for you to trust. You're defensive in a way that makes people dislike you—so you're not surprised or confused when they do. You mock the world so it's less likely to disappoint you. The only difference is that she's a child learning to cope with her life; you're an adult who should have managed to find more mature methods by now."

"What?" Elise hadn't expected the awkward, introverted Hank to be so direct—she'd forgotten about Martin.

"Shutting down and running is no way to deal with your life, Elise."

"I don't shut down and run."

"The hell you don't."

"I don't."

Hank stepped back to reveal a different point of view.

Costumes on both sides of the aisle lost their color and their shapes melted away . . . and suddenly there was Jeremy, sitting at their dining room table, his laptop open in front of him.

Elise remembered the occasion.

He didn't look up when she entered the room, but she was relieved to see him shuffling though their unpaid bills—her credit card had been declined at the Piggly Wiggly that morning.

"I'm brewing tea, want some?" she asked.

"No." He startled her when his fist hit the table and he shouted, "Where the hell is all the money going?"

"What?"

"The money, Elise, the money! Where's it going?"

"I don't know," she shouted back, automatically feeling guilty for keeping them perpetually on the precipice of financial ruin—though she didn't know why. "My paychecks go straight into our account. You know I'm not having anything withheld."

"This." He waved a statement at her. "Bobby's Hobbies?"

"I bought a couple new tubes of paint and three brushes a few weeks ago."

"Budget. We have a budget."

"And they're miscellaneous entertainment—hardly enough to break us."

"What's this . . . Nordstrom?"

"Shoes, but—"

"But I thought we agreed you'd cut back on buying shoes for a while. I remember us laughing about it when you promised to cut back to shoe emergencies only." He looked at her askance.

"They're a gift."

"A gift? For who?"

"For you, if you must know. The Ferragamo oxfords that you liked, I bought them for your birthday. I haven't bought a new pair for myself in months."

He had to take in a deep calming breath before he could speak to her again. "The money has to be going somewhere, Elise."

"Maybe if I take a look . . . I deal with numbers all day, maybe it's something simple that—"

"What, you're the only one here who can add and subtract? Look, if you think I'm doing a shit job with our finances you can do them. Here!" Instantly angry again, he shoved a pile of papers across the table to her. "You do them."

She slowly pushed them back, saying, "I don't think you're doing a shit job. I was just offering to help, to take a second look. I'm sure it must be something simple . . . a stray decimal point."

Mostly mollified, he sighed. "I've checked and rechecked." He shook his head in deep regret. "I'm afraid we're going to have to dip into your inheritance again."

"Really?" Her half of the money her grandmother left was not a great fortune, but it was a sizable sum held in a trust that her mother controlled until she turned twenty-five in two years. Her mother, however, was an extremely generous and lax guardian who barely blinked twice whenever Elise asked to draw on the funds. "Again? It's that bad?"

His expression read: *I wouldn't have brought it up if it wasn't.*

She sighed. "I'll call Mom later; ask her to transfer more money into our savings account. It should only take a day or two, so I'll call the bank first thing Monday—"

"*I'll* call the bank on Monday. You need to march yourself into Winston's office on Monday and tell him you deserve that promotion. Be firm, sweetheart. You're better qualified, you have more experience, you've been there longer . . . Tell him you deserve it." He flipped his hands palms up. "There's no reason for you not to get it, Elise. And the way money disappears around here, we're going to need the raise."

He closed the laptop and gathered up the rest of their accounting materials and left her sitting there.

Elise turned to Hank Hill and pushed her big black Daria glasses up against the bridge of her nose. "I didn't know how to tell him I'd already lost the promotion—that took me another week." She lowered her gaze to the floor . . . where her pride was. "Took a lot longer for me to figure out where the money was going."

He was sympathetic. "The bastard. I wouldn't mind kicking his ass for you."

She shook her head. "I was stupid. I know it's a sick, sad world out there. I should have known. I should have seen it. That's what makes me mad. I trusted him." She hesitated, then her eyes closed and her shoulders drooped. "Maybe I did know. I think I suspected. Maybe. I just . . . I wanted to believe him. I wanted to believe in him. Is that so bad? I loved him. He loved me. It was through thick and thin, good and bad, all that stuff. I never imagined he'd leave me—much less actively position himself to leave me penniless."

"Dagnabit! Having a heart as big as Texas is never a bad thing. And trusting the people you love should be as easy and safe as using propane for all your residential and commercial needs. And just as natural, too, come to think of it. You've got good instincts, Elise. You just need to listen to them and then not overthink what you're hearing."

Hank directed her attention back to the gap between the rack of costumes and another scene from her life with Jeremy.

She recognized the expression on Jeremy's face as he followed her through the blurry image of their kitchen into a much clearer picture of their dining room after work—and from the look on her own face, she knew that a heavy ball of tension was coiling in her abdomen.

"I cooked your favorite tonight—coq au vin."

"Great. Hopefully it'll be better than the last time you made it. I'd like one good thing to happen to me today."

She knew better than to ask about the not-so-good parts of his day, but did so anyway. "Rough one, huh?"

"Rough? That's mild."

"What happened?" she asked, turning to light the candles she kept centered on the table—mostly to create a relaxed atmosphere, as opposed to anything romantic.

"Stop. Blow it out. I'm not in the mood for that shit."

"I thought—"

"Well don't." He took his seat at the table. "I'm not in the mood for that either."

That stung. Bad.

But she understood days that could drain every ounce of happiness from your life. And she was aware that lashing out at the people who love you best happens because they are the most likely to tolerate and forgive your bad behavior. Plus it was her experience with Jeremy that he simply needed a little time to calm down and center himself. Her sweet, funny Jeremy would come back around.

So she swallowed her own harsh retort, pressed her lips together and poured his wine.

Generally, it didn't seem to bother him that she didn't drink with him—preferring water to the blistering headaches even small amounts of alcohol delivered. But on other occasions . . .

"There it is again."

"What?" she asked.

"That smug, superior look you get when I drink."

"What? I don't. I don't care if you drink." Her smile was tight and hopeful—she didn't want to fight with him. "I envy you. I could use a drink once in a while."

"Once in a while? But not as often as I have them."

"I didn't say that . . . or mean that. Look, I'm sorry you had a bad day, but don't take it out on me. It's not fair."

He appeared to back off a bit—but it was only to form a new line of attack.

"Sorry." He heaved a long-suffering sigh. "You're right. It's not fair. But do you think it's fair since you didn't get your promotion, I have to work longer hours *and* work them all with Barry Levine?" He took another gulp of his wine. "We could have used your pay raise to buy us some time while I tried to find a better, more fulfilling job that would benefit both of us in the long run. I'm frustrated. Can't you see that?"

She nodded, though she didn't see his frustration being any greater than her own.

They finished their meal in silence. She did kitchen duty alone that night, then joined him in the living room to watch television—so to speak. The television was simply background noise while Jeremy, sporting earbuds, disappeared to wherever the computer on his lap took him and she escaped into Elizabeth Moon's new novel.

Until it was time for bed . . .

She heard him close his laptop; listened while he prepared for bed. She knew when he left the bathroom and went down the hall to their bedroom. Then she pretended to be engrossed in her book when he returned in his pajama bottoms to stare at her from across the room.

Normally, she would have looked up expecting to see that spark of desire that promised the hot, sweaty sex she was accustomed to with her husband.

But her sweet, funny Jeremy had not returned . . . and the other one had offered no apology for his surly conduct earlier in the evening. His resentment and her hurt feelings from dinner lingered in the air like the scent of coq au vin.

There was a time, not so long ago, when she would have been grateful to see that he still wanted her at the end of a miserable day. A time when she cut him slack with apologies; told herself that the intimacy of making love would fill the empty spaces that the lack of respect and kindness and friendship the rest of the night had created. A time when she could still pretend she didn't feel used.

There was also a time when all the books she read said she needed to open a dialogue with him. She needed to let him know how she felt and express her concerns. After several attempts at communicating her distress didn't go as well as she'd hoped, the books suggested marriage counseling as an opportunity to rekindle their relationship.

Jeremy was surprised—shocked, even—to hear that she thought their relationship needed to be rejuvenated. It cut him to the quick; he was devastated for three solid days.

Yes, there was a time for all of that and then some—like the niggling notion of other women. And if she was truthful, there were also times when she gave as good as she got in feeble attempts to take back her self-esteem. But it became harder and harder to flip the switch between overjoyed and offended; between joining in and faking it; between faking it and making no effort at all.

"Are you bringing that sexy bod to bed anytime soon?"

She looked up at him and smiled; her cheeks felt stiff. "Absolutely. I just want to finish this chapter real quick, okay?"

"Sure." He turned to walk back down the hall. "But don't be long. I'm beat. I may pass out."

Please do, she thought and then she turned the page and started chapter twelve.

She didn't get through the second page before she shoved her candy wrapper bookmark into the crease of her book and tossed it onto the end table.

She covered her face in shame. "What am I doing?"

She wanted to follow him; she loved making love with him. But her feelings were hurt and her expectations had deflated. Was she pouting like a child; a stubborn, grudge-holding child . . . or was she a woman cocooning herself in a protective shell?

She knew that doing nothing changed nothing, and yet she couldn't make herself get up and go to him—not this time. Her mind and emotions snapped back and forth so fast she went numb. It was her marriage, her life, and she was disengaging, withdrawing and shutting down. She felt it.

Elise crossed her thin Daria arms across her chest, but couldn't meet the look in Hank Hill's eyes . . . Martin's look. "You're right. I do shut down and run . . . Well, if he hadn't run first, I probably would have. But I still wonder, if he hadn't taken all the money and left, if I could have—"

"Uuuuuuuaaaaaagh!" he said, showing his teeth. "You're chasing your tail, girl. No number of *if*s will change what is. Slow down, step back and just think." He tipped his head to the space where outfits were coming back into view. Strawberries, lemons and grapes—fruit suits. "That's when you did all the right things; when your instincts were telling you something was wrong. That boy ain't right. And deep down you knew it. But you didn't want it to be true, so you didn't listen to what your gut was telling you—that he needed to be taken out behind the barn and shot. And I'll tell you what, that ain't the worst part of it. No, the worst part is that when all was said and done, and you knew you were right about Jeremy, you suddenly got giblets for brains and decided you couldn't trust yourself to trust your own good sense anymore. And that's overthinking to the point of not thinking at all."

"Yeah, well, where was my amazing intuition when I first met him? Or the whole time we dated . . . or during the first year of our marriage?"

"It was there—it's always there, watching for yellow flags. Maybe there was just nothing to see. What if he wasn't looking to fleece you in the beginning? Could be that didn't occur to him until after he took up with that floozy—and that's when his game started falling apart. He got sloppy, took too many chances, made too many fouls, and flags started falling all over the place." He raised his hands palms up. "Maybe not. Maybe he was a rat bastard all along. *Maybe* you made a mistake. Hell, even Tom Landry made mistakes from time to time."

"What if I keep making mistakes?"

"What if you do? And what if the mistake is seeing red flags where there aren't any? What if it's choking under the slightest pressure? What if it's shutting down and running in the opposite direction if someone tries to . . . well, you know . . . love you? What if you keep living in fear or you quit and never play the game again? Isn't that like scoring for the other team? Who wins then?"

Daria wasn't a huge fan of sports analogies, but when Hank Hill used them they made sense. Alas.

He turned and walked into the next row of getups—nature costumes. Trees and mushrooms; fall leaves and rainbows; butterflies and snowflakes.

"I hate being lonely," she said, barely noticing the large yellow sun partially blocking the path. "I do. Also I'm allergic to cats. So I'll probably end up being a crazy bird woman—the one who talks to herself and feeds the pigeons in the park all day? But I'm so afraid of being hurt again that it might not be so bad if—"

This time the loud rumbling noise came from deep inside—of *her*. Churning, vibrating, uneven. More confused than frightened, she put her hands on her stomach and looked down, but as quickly as it had come, the reverberating and stirring died away to nothing.

"Okay. Are you ever going to tell me what that sound is, or—" She looked up and frowned for several long seconds. "Who are you supposed to be?"

CHAPTER SIX

Martin looked like da Vinci's Vitruvian Man . . . with clothes on. Legs apart, arms out, he looked like a human kaleidoscope of what appeared to be superheroes.

His arms and legs presented random bursts of green or black or red or blue sleeves and leggings; some limbs were scaled, some hairy, some metallic. Frosty, flaming and electrified. There were some with contrasting gloves and boots and some without, and some looked distinctly . . . well, turtle-like. His head and torso popped, hit and miss, body armor, mammoth muscles and capes with various caps, masks and helmets.

"I appear to be having an identity crisis," he said, his voice a booming whisper mix that was creepier than it was cool. "Pick your favorite. Please."

"Do I have to?"

The light in his eyes changed from uncertain to unamused. "Yes. And quickly, I feel nauseous."

Elise offered him another rare Daria smile. It was friendly and fond. "Spidey then, I suppose. No! Wait! Superman." She wrinkled her nose and gave her head a shake. "I don't know . . . those Spidey-eyes . . . and Superman is, taken as a whole, less bizarre, more emotionally available and socially adept, I think."

Immediately his hands fisted on his splendid red trunks and his crimson cape billowed—without a breeze—behind him. Superman . . . though his face was quickly morphing from DC Comics to George Reeves to the Christopher Reeves version that was her personal favorite. Even after his laser-blue eyes faded to Martin's lively golden-green, he was still the Superman by which all other contemporary Supermans were measured.

"You're a pain in the neck, you know that?"

"I've been told before," she said.

"It bears repeating."

She agreed with a lopsided smile, then she went serious and worried. "Why haven't I changed?"

"Maybe your feelings haven't changed." He dazzled her with his supersmile. "Or maybe I'm here because you need a new perspective on an old problem."

She thought about it briefly. "Are we back to the book and its cover again?"

"I love working with people I don't have to drag every inch of the way. And yes, we're back to your extraordinary ability to be judgmental and arrive at false assumptions."

Hadn't she already admitted to those unflattering flaws in her character? She looked away, disappointed that Superman would kick a sad little IRS agent when she was down.

But then he added, "Except this time, instead of polarizing people and ideas you barely know or understand, let's take a look at some you do know."

"Some what? Some people I know? My friends? My family?" Tears pricked at Elise's eyes, her throat got tight and her remote, dispassionate Daria-shield slipped a bit. "I'm alienating my family? And my friends? Hurting them? No one's said—and Roger would say . . ." Now she was feeling nauseous. She took a deep breath and let it out slow and dazed. "I didn't know. My family is stuck with me, I guess, but how can my friends stand me if . . . Why do they stay?"

Her hands were trembling. She clenched them, open and closed, looking up at the iconic champion of truth, justice and the American way—he didn't lie.

"Your friends love you, Elise," he said with understanding and compassion in his handsome face. "They accept and cherish what you've allowed them to see in you—the good and the not so good."

"I love them, too. Fay and Trudy know me better than my mother. Carol Ann, she's the best; she drove me everywhere for three weeks after I sprained my right ankle last year. Abby and Leigh . . . and Molly and . . . all of them. I have great friends. I'd jump in front of a locomotive for any of them. They know that, right?"

"They know you."

"So they think and agree that I'm . . . Daria Downer? That I'm fault-finding; that I take a lot for granted?"

"*All* about you." He held up a finger. "I'm not saying they approve of the practice or that it doesn't bother them at times—only that they accept it as a part of you. And they do *that* because there's so much more about you that is worthy of their friendship and love." He stopped at another four-way aisle intersection. "Their primary concern is that you're not seeing the damage it's doing *to you*. They're afraid that you don't know how self-destructive it is."

The gray shadows fell across period costumes—Colonial gentleman and Southern belle; flapper, pilgrim and disco dancer—and then scattered away from a scene that had played repeatedly in her mind for weeks. For three weeks and two days, to be exact.

"It's that night, after our six-month anniversary dinner," Elise muttered, watching intently.

She'd let Max park his car, turn off the engine, get out, take the elevator and walk her all the way to her apartment door knowing full well what he was anticipating and equally as certain that she had no intention of letting him in.

She had come to a decision; she just didn't know how to tell him.

"Max." It was an odd moment to note how perfect he was

to hold hands with. He wasn't so tall and she wasn't so short that either one of them had to compensate for the length of their arms—their hands were just right, back to back then palm to palm, coming together easily and inevitably.

"Hmm?" He smiled at her.

"We need to talk."

"Good." She could barely glance at him. "You've been acting . . . not yourself all night. Is something wrong?"

Her tongue felt stuck to the roof of her mouth, and she was too aware that they were still holding hands. She let go and turned to face him.

"This isn't going to work," she said, blurting out words that were closer to the end of her prepared speech than the beginning.

"What?"

"Eh. That's not how I meant to say it."

"Say what?" He had the deepest, warmest brown eyes she'd ever seen. They were confused and cautious.

"I'm saying that this, you and me, it isn't going to work. I've known for a while and I'm sorry now that I didn't put an end to it sooner. Certainly before tonight." She waved her fingers back and forth between them and their elegant attire. "All your plans and . . . the flowers and . . . I'm sorry."

He studied her face. "What's happened? What triggered this?"

"Nothing. Not one specific thing. And it's nothing you've done. You're great. I like you a lot. I'm just not ready for more than a friendship right now. My life is complicated and—"

"It isn't any more complicated than mine, Elise." He wasn't angry, just stating a fact. "You're scared."

She was. It might save a lot of time if she just owned it.

"Okay. I'm scared."

He nodded, like he'd known for a while. "So am I. I get it. Life's scary." He recaptured her hand. "And love is the scariest part of all. It's supposed to be. If love was as easy and free as everyone says it should be it would hold no value. It would be as ordinary and objective as . . . getting hungry. But it isn't easy and it isn't free; it's rare and fragile." He secured her other hand. "Don't let your fear force you to turn your back on something so special and out of the ordinary."

"Yeah. Extraordinary. I saw what loving someone can do to you when my dad left my mom. She suffered. It broke something inside of her . . . and me. I knew better. But then Jeremy came along and I thought: *Oh wow. This is real love, not what my parents had. This is something extraordinary.*"

"And it was." His frown was worried, his sigh was sympathetic. "Loving someone is never wrong. It's what you live for. It's . . . it's *why* you live; how you should live. But it takes two people to keep it alive, Elise. If one person gives up on it, it dies—and it's a painful death."

"With a new girlfriend and all my money, I don't think Jeremy's feeling much pain."

"I'm not talking about Jeremy. I couldn't care less about Jeremy. People have shit in their lives—you scrape it off your shoes and keep walking." He stooped to look into her downcast eyes. "I'm talking about you, Elise. About us. Right here. Right now. You're the one I care about."

She looked up, knowing she'd see everything he was saying with his voice set solid in his eyes. It terrified her.

His smile was small, sweet, endearing. "Besides, it's too late to run away from me now. You're crazy about me." She frowned and his smile grew, but only a bit. "You can deny it if it makes you feel safer, but I know when someone loves me, the same way I know when someone doesn't. I can see it in your eyes; hear it in your voice. I can feel it when we touch . . . and when we kiss.

"And you feel it, too. That's why you're afraid, isn't it? Because it feels like you're exposing your underbelly to me. Because you're feeling weak and vulnerable." He brought her hands up between them, kissed the back of one and then the other. "That's not what I want you to feel. I want you to trust me. But I'll take it—for now—because I know what it means."

"How can you be so certain?" It was very unfair. "How do you know I haven't met someone else?"

"Have you?"

"That's not the point. How do you know you can trust *me*?

This could be revenge love . . . Maybe I'm using you to get back at your entire gender."

"Are you?"

"No! That's not it either. What I need to know is—"

"What you need is a guarantee." He tipped her a sly look. "They don't even have those in your romance novels. Love is a leap of faith . . . and hope and determination . . . and you know that already. You're just afraid and—while I am prepared and very willing to hammer at it until we're old and gray—you're the only one who can do anything about it."

He stepped back. Having presented his argument, he didn't seem to have much more to say. He stood quietly, giving her time to speak, to reconsider, to look him in the eye and reiterate her case. When she didn't, and when the silence between them grew awkward, he spoke again.

"Look, I was sort of prepared for this—sometimes the gears in your head squeak really loud," he said, trying to lighten the mood. "Maybe you weren't prepared for me to fight back—you underestimated that in me, too, I think. So just for the record, I do know you're serious. I know you want out. But I also know that panic and fear can make us do stupid things. Disastrous things. So I'll give you a little time, and some space, to reevaluate our situation." He knuckled her chin up to look into her face. "I'm not going to beg you to admit that you love me. Not my style. But I will be around if you change your mind."

Her heart felt like an egg—cracked, everything inside spilling out. She watched him walk away, taking the stairs for expedience, not quite running. She wanted to scream.

The scene blurred and slipped away.

THE FEW WEEKS THAT FOLLOWED WERE TORTURE, AND SHE was exhausted. Elise vacillated in the tiny breath between *feeling* stupid for putting her heart in peril again and *being* stupid by throwing away what could be the love of a lifetime.

"Tough one," Superman said, though there didn't seem to be any pity in his voice.

"No kidding. And I still don't know what to do. I . . . I think I love him. I'm ninety-nine percent sure he'd never deliberately hurt me, but that one percent, I can't get around it. People fall down all the time, you know? But after the first time they're more careful and take extra precautions because they know how bad it's going to hurt if it happens again."

"But don't you think that standing in one place and going nowhere is extreme?"

"I'm not standing in one place," she said, miffed. "I just think I'll have better balance if I walk alone."

"I might have to agree." He had her attention now. He was tall enough to bend an arm across the top of the framed divider and lean on it. "Maybe Max is deluded. Maybe you don't love him at all."

"Why? I do. Of course I do. Who wouldn't? He's . . . We fit, you know?" Every inch of her ached for him. She missed him. "He's wonderful. And smart and funny. And real. Kind." She let out a deep, wistful breath. "He's the calm to my crazy. He listens to me—even when I'm not saying much of anything. And *hot*! He's hot, don't you think?" He raised his superbrows. "He is, trust me. I think he's amazing. I just don't know—"

"And that's why I'm wondering: Do you really love him?"

"What?"

"In this conversation alone there have been twice as many *I*s and *me*s than *he*s and *him*s. It's all about you. It's always all about you. What you want, how you feel. What about him?"

He motioned with his head toward the Medieval tunics, hippie dashiki shirts and polka-dot poodle skirts as another episode commenced . . .

CHAPTER SEVEN

"Relax. She's sweating. She'll fold. Just a matter of time." Her brother, Roger, looked as unconcerned as Max looked gloomy and miserable. "She's scared, not stupid." He hesitated. "She can be stupid . . . I just don't think this is one of those times."

Slouching in a booth at some bar she didn't recognize, Max's sigh was deep and loud. "It's been two weeks. And six days. That's almost three weeks. I should at least call her; send a text . . . just *hi*. I need to do something. What if she's forgotten about me?"

The wrist under the fist supporting Roger's cheek went limp in disbelief. "Do you need a slap or something? I'm telling you, she's in bad shape." His pause was dramatic. "Not as bad as *you*, clearly, but I have it from a reliable source that she's been calling in sick to work and then spending the whole day in bed. My source caught her a couple of times with puffy red eyes and a stuffed-up nose, which—and you should take my word on this, too—once seen can never be unseen or mistaken for anything but crying."

"No. I don't ever want to see her cry." Max took a swig of

his beer. "Happy crying would be okay. I could handle that. But I don't ever want to see her as unhappy as she was the last time I saw her. I swear to God, it was all I could do to walk away from her. She looked so hurt and confused."

"I still say stubborn." Roger finished off his beer and motioned to someone for two more. "I know how my wife and my sister work, but I have no idea what drives them to do what they do. If I say no to Molly all she hears is *Oh sure, sweetie pie, do whatever you want.* Elise is really good at overanalyzing everything. Her mantra is *Yes, but.* It can drive you completely insane, but eventually she gets to the point where everything *yes* is bigger or better than whatever comes after the *but.*" He took two beers off a waitress's tray and handed one to his companion. "It just takes time. What?"

Max caught himself staring, gape-mouthed. "I can't believe I understood that."

"Well, that's because you've spent more than ten minutes with her. In thirty years you'll have an owner's manual full of female gibberish. The thing you have to remember is that nothing you do is going to change anything. See, with Elise, you can give her all the answers, write them down for her and show her scientific evidence, and she still has to stubbornly go through her whole weird process until she comes to the conclusion you gave her in the first place." He tipped his head and squinted at Max. "Come to think of it, you should probably run away while you still can."

Max chuckled. "Too late. I am hopelessly in love with your sister."

Roger shook his head in commiseration. "Why do we do this to ourselves?"

"I don't know. One minute I'm standing behind her at the grocery store. She's reading the *Cook's Illustrated* magazine while she waits for the people ahead of her to finish. Her feet hurt, I guess, because she steps out of one shoe and then the other and stands there in her bare feet, reading, waiting, curling her toes. I was mesmerized. And the minute there was movement in the line she was back in her shoes and returning the magazine . . . then she changed her mind and put it in her cart." He sighed again and met Roger's sympathetic gaze. "I wanted to follow her home like a puppy."

"Molly backed into my practically new, *parked* Cherokee Trailhawk with her Mazda piece-of-crap car and the whole time she was standing there trying to be apologetic and responsible she had tears in her eyes. She never cried and her voice never cracked. We did the insurance thing and the cops came; the tears stayed and they never spilled, not one. I thought she was trying to kill me. I did follow her home, but only because I didn't know if she could see well enough not to hit someone else." He grimaced. "We're pathetic."

Max smiled. "Maybe. Probably. But I don't feel that way when I'm with her. She does things that—"

"Is this going to get weird? This is my sister we're talking about. I don't want to have to knock you out."

Max chuckled. "Pathetic, not insane." Roger played relief. "I was going to say that she makes me feel like I belong. And awake. I feel so awake around her . . . and I didn't feel asleep before." Another forlorn sigh. "We fit, you know? Why can't she feel it, too?"

"She does."

"Really? She has an odd way of showing it."

"I told you. It's a process. She's *yes, but*–ing." He bobbed his head. "It doesn't usually take this long, I'll admit that, but she's not exactly buying a new car. The good news is that once she makes up her mind about something it becomes a forever thing . . . like a Twinkie."

Max laughed again—Roger had a way about him.

"I hope so. It's been six months and I can't imagine my life without her anymore." He pushed both hands through his thick black hair, front to back, then looked up suddenly with an epiphany. "Love sucks, man."

The both laughed then—agreeing, bonding, deciding to order burgers.

Elise watched, transfixed, as a vanishing Max forced forward a jovial demeanor for Roger when clearly, behind it, he was anxious and unhappy. "He loves me."

"Yes, he does."

"I'm a dope."

"Yeah, you are."

"He never said it to me. Not like that."

"Then why didn't you say it to him? Too afraid? Too proud?" She was both, and he knew it. "Did you know that historically it took forty years for Lois to discover that Clark Kent was Superman? Two people in a love triangle? All that time loving each other—him saving her life a dozen times a week, not knowing if she loved him or his superpowers and being super-insecure about it. And all it took in the end was trust and the truth. Think of all the time *they* wasted."

These words came in a different tone of voice and from far above her. Things had changed again. She looked at her hands and touched her face . . . then touched it again to be sure.

"Oh." A two-letter word filled with more relief than one would think possible. "I'm me again . . . I look like me again." It then occurred to her: "I feel like a fool and I'm back to being me again?"

"Apparently that shoe fits."

Elise sighed and started to turn to see who Martin planned to foil her with this time—she hesitated briefly, hoping it wasn't God speaking from on high.

She saw it peripherally first—smooth, striped cyan-colored skin, a long sweeping tail—and eventually came around fully to face the lower hem of a . . . loincloth. Automatically stepping back, twice, her gaze traveled steadily up the slender ten-foot body of Jake Sully's avatar, Toruk Makto, resplendent in native cuffs, bands and ties; hair braided with beads, bones and bright feathers.

God might have been a little less disquieting.

"I know." He stretched out his arms, and his lemurlike eyes of golden-green danced. "Is this cool or what? I tried it once before on a guy from Philadelphia, but he fainted." Bobbing his head and admiring himself, he added, "He was pretty much hysterical the whole time anyway. I should have known better, I guess—but *Avatar* had just come out and everyone was talking about it and I was really eager to try it out. Still, you know what they say: There's no point trying to dazzle someone who's out of their mind with fear. Right?"

"I can't think of one, no."

"So now I keep this one for special people who've made the most of this experience and are on their way out."

"I'm on my way out?"

"If you think you've made the most of this experience, you are." The beautiful blue Na'vi came down on one knee and sat back on his calf, making him more accessible but no less mind-blowing. His wide, muscled shoulders rustled costumes and barely fit between the partitions. He curled his tail around himself, and then he grinned at her. "I told you I'd help you find your way back."

She stared at him. "So all this, just to tell me I'm an idiot? A suspicious, neurotic, hypercritical, misanthropic idiot who takes for granted all the wonderful people in her life who love her in spite of that. You couldn't have just told me?"

He shrugged. "Would you have believed me? They say it's more about the message than the magic, but I think there's more bang in the buck with the magic; it's more fun, and the message is less likely to be forgotten too soon."

"Yeah, forgetting this isn't likely."

He tipped his head to one side. "It happens. And don't beat yourself up when it does. You're going to keep screwing up and reverting back to those safe, dark, life-wasting caverns in your mind, because you're just like everyone else, Elise. You're human."

"Then what's the point of all this?"

"You tell me," he said, distracted by the long black queue hanging over his shoulder. It looked like a long braid of hair with many little pink, hairy, wormlike neural tendrils on the end—an extension of the Na'vi nervous system. He gently poked at it, quivered and then tossed it away to hang down his back again. He looked at her. "If you were me, what would I tell you next?"

Her stare was blank; she had no idea. So many things had come up and gone down in ways she'd never dreamed of— what could possibly be next?

In mild desperation, she closed her eyes, hoping to become Waldo—he was perpetually lost, and that's exactly how she felt.

"He isn't lost; he's a traveler," the lovely blue avatar said, getting in her head again. "Wherever Waldo happens to be, he chose to be there."

Dashed but still hoping, she sought out an omniscient character, all-knowing and wise. The *Matrix* Oracle maybe—she'd know plenty, and cookies would be involved.

Abruptly, she opened her eyes. "I'm not changing."

"Of course you are."

"No, I'm still me."

"Of course you are."

"No, I mean, I'm not becoming something new."

"Why would you want to?" He grinned at her confusion. "You only get to choose what you feel, Elise. It's the magic in this enchanted space that decides how best to show it to you—a picture worth a thousand words and all that."

"And now I feel like me?"

"Now you're feeling what there is no costume for; what lives naturally inside you, always." He turned his long-fingered hand palm up. "Always."

"What is it?" she asked. His brow rose—it wasn't his question to answer. "If I were you what would I tell me?" She spoke slowly, thinking. Rewinding, rolling forward and re-winding recent events. Her gaze came to rest on the large golden-green eyes that shown Martin, through and through, encouraging her. "I'd say: Go back to the last time I felt . . . not myself. What changed? How? Why? When did I feel completely myself again?"

"And?"

"And it was when Max said he loved me."

He shook his head, no. "No one, no matter how much they love you—or don't love you—has the power to change you, Elise. That's all you. You choose to be happy or bitter or cruel or kind. Max loving you is a damn nice thing, but it can't make you feel whole."

"But my accepting that I love him can. Right? That's it,

isn't it? It's not about his love, it's about mine. It isn't him loving me. This is about me trusting him enough to let him. All this, and it isn't about all the garbage that piles up in my life; it's what I decide to do with it—the choices I make. Good or bad. I choose. Max, Jeremy, Liz Gurney, Cooper Winston . . . even the costume I want for Liz's ridiculous party. I choose."

He smacked his lips. "I do enjoy the smart ones, I really do." He stretched his arms out over the dividing walls. "And me? What am I here to tell you now, in this disguise?"

"How should I know?" But then—and with a distinct sadness in her heart—she said, "How to get out of here? How to find Molly?"

"Before I do that." His smile was gentle, but then he wagged his head and teased her. "Think of something insightful and profound; something more in keeping with my previous incarnations, which, let's face it, had considerably more wisdom and dignity than all of yours put together."

"Yeah right, the Cat in the Hat."

"Curious George." He looked at her pointedly—then used his finger to point to himself. "Abe Lincoln." He aimed the finger at her. "Angry Bird, Grumpy and Charlie Brown." There was a swagger on his face. "Hank Hill and Superman to your Daria. And now you as . . . well, you, and me as this magnificent and way too cool ten-foot blue avatar? Who's winning this one?"

"Tsk. You are so annoying." He grinned. She considered him carefully. "So . . . Jake Sully. He's all about leaving the past behind; about changing and reinventing himself and then deciding how he wants to live the rest of his life. You're about choosing new adventures over wallowing in self-pity." She laughed, uncomfortably. "Not too shabby for wise and dignified advice, my friend. The last of it, I'm guessing."

Before he could speak, the rumbling came again; a thundering like a stampede of Pandoran thanator plowing through the jungle. And then it went silent.

CHAPTER EIGHT

"Okay. Enough now! Tell me what that is. It's driving me crazy."

"You're hungry."

"What?"

"You're hungry. It's your stomach, it's growling."

"Seriously?"

"A lot of things can make your stomach growl, of course, but in this case it's hunger. You skipped lunch to have an early supper with Molly after helping her decide on costumes."

"You're right, I did. And that's been my stomach growling this whole time?"

"Well, you haven't actually been here a *whole time*; it's only been a tiny bit of time."

"What is a tiny bit of time to you?"

"Same as you: a couple of seconds."

"What?"

"When you first got here you asked if you were dead or in a coma or hallucinating and I said *No, not exactly.* You didn't ask about dreaming, and I avoided the subject of *day-dreaming.*"

"What?"

"Daydreaming. Wandering around inside your own head, thinking, fantasizing—"

"Fantasizing?"

"Trying to decide what you want to be, who you want to be, how you'll go about—"

"Fantasizing? I made you up? I made it all up? *Me?* It's been me all along?"

"Of course." He looked like he wanted to tickle under her chin and call her a *silly button*. "Who knows you better than you know yourself?"

"I—"

"That's right. You. You're in control."

She stood perfectly still. "So you, Martin, you're not magic? You're just . . . me?"

His smile was lopsided and lovable. "Elise. We make our own magic, you know that." He gazed deep into her eyes and sighed. "Time for you to go."

Her reluctance surprised her.

"Will I forget all this?" He turned his head first to one side, then slowly to the other; then did it again when she asked, "Can I come back if I do?"

"You need to go now. Molly will start to worry about you."

"How?" She turned in a circle. "Where?"

"Just put the mask down."

"What? No, wait . . ."

"Put the mask down, Elise."

Martin and the corral of costumes around them started to fade away. But slowly, growing clearer and clearer into focus, was a reflection of a Noh theater mask with golden-green hazel eyes peering through from behind. Her eyes.

". . . Max is a sweetie. He's really smart and he's funny. And I think he's serious. He likes you. You can see it when he looks at you," Molly was saying. "Why do you keep pushing these guys away?"

Elise lowered the mask from her face, bit by bit. She pressed a cool hand to her flushed cheek and blinked back tears—a combination of the relief to be back and sadness for the loss of Martin. She turned the mask over, examined it, saw nothing askew.

"Elise?"

"Yes?" She turned with a start. "What?"

"I don't understand why you keep pushing these guys away."

Lifting her gaze to Darth Vader's mask, she waited for him to speak.

"Elise!"

"Yes." She looked straight at Molly this time, delighted to see her. "It's safe. I push men away to feel safe. But in truth, all I feel is empty and alone."

"What?" Molly couldn't have looked more shocked if she'd been hit by a bus.

"And you're right, by the way—about that guy, John? He was sort of charming, but he texts during movies. It made me crazy. And Max—you're right about him, too. He is nice and sweet and smart and funny and serious. He does like me—I can see it when he looks at me, too. He loves me, in fact. And I love him."

"What?"

"Look, I know you left Roger at home to feed the kids tonight so you and I could eat at Ferdinand's, but I need to take a rain check. I'll buy. But I have to leave right now. I have to find Max and tell him that I'm not a dope anymore. I've never been much of a groveler, but . . . well, it'll be a new adventure, won't it?"

"What?" Apparently, she'd stunned Molly speechless.

Elise laughed and hurried over to take Molly's face between her palms—then laughed again, threw her arms around her and squeezed tight. "I love you, too! I know I don't say it often enough—but that's going to change. And I want you to know that while I'll never understand why you married Roger, I'm so very, very glad you did." She giggled at Molly's wide-eyed expression and kissed her cheek. "Give my love to him and the kids and tell him thanks for being a great brother. And—ha! Do you hear that? My stomach's growling. I'll take Max out to eat . . . I can be dessert."

"Elise, honey, are you feeling all right? I can drive you home if—"

She chuckled and started to leave, but then stopped. She looked back at the dark display of the dishonored Jedi knight and, despite what she knew to be the truth, she felt a deep and warm gratitude. Risking a tacky straitjacket in a shade outside her color wheel, she walked over to stand before him and murmur softly, "Thanks, Martin."

"Elise?"

When she turned back to Molly's fretful expression, she paused a moment to calm down and gather her wits.

"Listen," she said. "Tell your friend Liz that I'd rather swallow a piano than play one at her party but I am looking forward to attending the event. And tell her, too, that if she can think of something reasonably sane . . . er, more traditional, more inside the box or . . . dull, probably. I don't know. Just tell her if she decides to do another fund-raiser for dyslexia research I'd like to help."

"What?"

"Ha! Poor Molly. I promise you, I'm fine. I'm better than fine. I'll explain everything later, but right now I have to find Max." She stopped short. "Oh! I have it! I'm brilliant! Your costumes are Roger and Jessica Rabbit—goofy and gorgeous. Max should be Dick Tracy—intelligent, steadfast and fearless. And I'll be his Tess Trueheart—because I am."

FALLEN

R. C. RYAN

For all who believe.

And for Tom, who believed in me always.

PROLOGUE

"Highlands?" The four-year-old girl lifted wide, trusting eyes to her grandmother. "Why do they call it that, Gram?"

"It is high country, and very rugged. It's where my ancestors in Scotland lived, my darling. It's also wild and grand and beautiful."

"I love your story about the Beast of the Highlands. Why was he called that?"

"A spell had been cast upon him. At the dawn of each new moon the man was turned into a huge, wild stag, with great, punishing antlers. No one ever saw the creature, though many claimed to have heard his dangerous hooves pounding the earth as he raced through their villages. Of course, it was all a myth." The old woman smiled. "Now, to finish the story. Thanks to the wonder of magic, the beast was once more turned into a handsome man who embraced the lovely woman who saved him, and they lived happily ever after." Evelyn Campbell's voice lowered to a purr as she glanced down to see her little granddaughter's eyes closing.

As she started to get up, little Beth's hand shot out, stopping her. "More, Gram. Did the beast ever return?"

"No more tonight, my darling. It's time for dreamland."

"Do you think Mommy and Daddy are living happily ever after in heaven?"

The simple question had the old woman blinking back a rush of scalding tears. The loss of her son and his wife on the slick, curving highway in California was a hole in her heart that would never close. "I'm sure of it, love."

"When I grow up I'm going to tame a beast who is really a handsome prince and we'll live happily ever after like Mommy and Daddy."

Evelyn bent over to kiss her granddaughter, looking like a tiny princess in the pretty canopied bed. "That is my hope for you, too. But remember, darling girl, that handsome isn't what matters. He must have a good heart."

"How will I know if his heart is good?"

"As we get to know people, they reveal their true selves. Our job is to listen and learn all we can, and then we must trust our own heart."

"I will, Gram. I promise. 'Night."

"Good night, my darling Beth."

"I love the stories you make up, Gram."

The old woman stood a moment beside the bed, watching as her granddaughter drifted into sleep.

If only she could do the same. But sleep, as well as peace of mind, had eluded her since the accident and the arrival of her precious grandchild.

To add to her pain, just today the doctor had confirmed the dreadful diagnosis, telling her she had little time left. And when she was gone, her son's last wish would be denied.

He had left behind a letter, written shortly after the birth of his child, asking that his mother assume custody of Beth should anything happen to him and his wife. He had specifically requested that his daughter never fall into the hands of his sister, Darda, with whom he'd had an explosive relationship his entire life.

Richard had been a loyal, loving son. An athlete who also embraced academics. A lawyer who championed the down-and-out. His wife, Cybil, had supported his causes and had

worked tirelessly alongside him in the law firm that carried
their name.

Darda, on the other hand, was the pampered darling of her
father and his first wife. From an early age she'd shown a
tendency toward cruelty, and had learned how to wrap her
weak father around her finger and obtain her every wish. And,
oh, the exotic, outrageous, selfish things she'd wished for.
Despite Evelyn's repeated pleas to her husband to stop giving
in to his daughter's demands, he had adamantly refused. It
had brought a painful end to their marriage, and Darda had
grown up a spoiled, self-absorbed, bitter young woman.

Evelyn Campbell sighed as she walked from the room.
When her illness became too advanced to care for little Beth,
she feared what would happen to this sweet, innocent child,
since there was no other family member to care for her. She
couldn't bring herself to consider offering her only grandchild
up for adoption. There seemed to her only one road left open.
As distant as they had become, Darda was all the family left
to her.

Evelyn could only hope that the years had changed the
spoiled, mean-spirited girl Darda had been into a more compassionate, caring woman who would see the goodness in this
child. In the meantime, Evelyn vowed to spend whatever time
she had left preparing Beth to resist the temptations of this
sometimes selfish world to become a fine woman her parents
would be proud of.

She fervently hoped the lessons of childhood would stay
with the girl for a lifetime.

CHAPTER ONE

"Beth." Darda Campbell ushered her niece into an exquisitely appointed office. "I'd like you to meet Alan Connifer."

Beth's eyes widened. "Of Connifer-Goldrich?"

"The same." The handsome, prematurely gray-haired man offered a handshake before indicating a pair of chairs across from his desk.

Following her aunt's lead, Beth sat.

She could feel the top executive studying her. "Darda and I have had several long, intense meetings, both here in New York and at my firm in London."

Beth folded her hands primly in her lap. Since joining her aunt's firm, she'd worked harder than any of her contemporaries, hoping to prove to Darda that she was worthy of the position. Darda had taken over her late brother's small law firm and turned it into one of the most prestigious in the state. As president and sole owner of the Darda Campbell Agency, Darda had a reputation for being a tough, take-no-prisoners negotiator who showed not a drop of mercy. Now, with a contingent of top foreign firms paying court, rumors were rampant that they were about to be swallowed up by a giant conglomerate and half the firm would be sent packing. A second rumor speculated that they would all receive promotions and huge bonus checks to go along with the firm's expansion.

Beth figured the truth lay somewhere in the middle.

Without preamble Alan announced, "The Darda Campbell Agency has accepted our offer to merge with Connifer-Goldrich."

Beth blinked. So, it was true. Her father's once-tiny firm would now be part of a multibillion-dollar international conglomerate that specialized in negotiating impossible deals for developers coveting exotic properties around the globe.

Alan fixed Beth with a look. "I'm sorry to say we'll be cutting back on your department, since we already have enough in-house lawyers."

Beth braced herself for the ax that was about to fall on her head.

Instead, Alan's next words had her looking up in surprise.

"But, since you're part of Darda's family, we'd like to keep you on."

He turned to Darda. "Why don't you tell her the rest?"

Darda's lips were carved into her famous ice-princess smile. A smile that never reached her eyes. "You're being offered the deal of a lifetime. The firm is sending you to Scotland to meet with a . . . difficult client. He happens to own a huge tract of land that a client of Connifer-Goldrich wishes to develop. There are stepsiblings, I understand, who very much want to sell, as the will states that they will be given one-third of any profit from a sale. But the client has sole discretion on the entire estate, and right now he's resistant to any sale. If you can get him to sign a contract, you'll be given a title with our new firm and a very generous bonus."

Beth didn't bother to ask what would happen if her impossible mission failed. One fact had been drilled into her from the time she was a little girl: If she wished to please Darda Campbell, failure was not an option. "Do you have the particulars?"

Alan picked up a USB flash drive and passed it across the desk. "This is everything we have on Colin Gordon, whose nickname is the Beast of the Highlands. He's called that because he's known as an angry, no-nonsense loner who would rather hike the mountains or fish in an icy stream than sit by the fire in his grand lodge. We've tried in the past to entice him to sell, but he has no need of more money, and he's impossible to deal with."

"The stepsiblings?" Beth looked hopeful. "Can they be counted on to persuade him?"

Alan shrugged. "Let's hope so. Though Colin Gordon calls his estate a humble hunting lodge, it's actually a palatial estate set in the heart of the Highlands, where the people are often as fierce as the land and the weather."

"Why would anyone want to plan a development in such a place?"

Alan looked over. "It's a privately owned paradise for sportsmen. Lakes teeming with fish. A forest, closed to hunters for hundreds of years, that is home to many rare species, including red deer and even the occasional Scottish wildcat. Quaint villages nearby would be snapped up by upscale retailers, eager for a new venue." He paused a moment before asking, "So? Think you're the one who can make this happen?"

Beth felt the weight of the world descending upon her shoulders. This was a test. She would have the opportunity to prove that she could be as shrewd a businesswoman as Darda. Winning at any price was Rule One in Darda's world.

She pasted on her best smile. "I've always wanted to visit the Highlands. My grandmother was born there. Besides, you had me at . . . title and bonus."

Darda shot Alan a smug smile before turning to Beth to offer a handshake. There had been no hugs in her household. And here at work, she wouldn't permit her niece to even hint at anything personal. Whether at home or at work, she was ma'am or Darda. Never Aunt Darda.

"The firm is counting on you, Beth. I've spent a lifetime playing hardball with the best of them. Now it's your turn to show me that you can do whatever it takes to close this deal."

"I won't let you down."

"Of course you won't. Your place with the firm is depending on it."

Darda turned to Alan. "If we're finished here, I have some details to see to."

Beth winced, certain that the "details" involved giving notice to dozens of young lawyers like herself that their jobs had just disappeared.

When they were alone, Alan sat back, looking relaxed and relieved to have finished with his business.

"I knew your father. He and I were in law school together."

At that, Beth brightened considerably. "Oh, how grand. What was he like?"

She had no idea of the absolute hunger in her voice, in her eyes.

Alan gave her a gentle smile. "Darda told me about her brother's accident. How old were you?"

"Four. I lived with my grandmother for almost two years before she passed away, and then I was taken to live with my au . . . with Darda."

Hearing the slight hesitation, he nodded. "I'm sure you were too young to remember much about your father. He was positively brilliant. The rest of us had to work twice as hard just to keep up. But what struck me most was his compassion. I do believe Richard Campbell was the kindest man I've ever met. And your mother, Cybil, suited him perfectly. The two of them made the title 'lawyer' not only respected, but revered. They took on impossible cases, often pro bono, and won against all the big dogs. They were known as dragon-slayers."

"I'd heard this firm was well-regarded in his day, even though it was quite small." Beth was positively beaming. "I wish I could have been a part of it then."

Alan looked away. "You have your aunt. And now you have the power of Connifer-Goldrich behind you."

"Yes. Well . . ." Beth got to her feet, clutching the flash drive. "I'll familiarize myself with the details of this client, and, as Darda promised, I'll close the deal for you."

As she turned away, Alan Connifer said, "Beth."

"Yes?" She turned back.

He merely looked at her for long moments. Then, shrugging, he smiled. "You remind me of Richard."

"Thank you. I can't think of a finer compliment." Beth floated away on a cloud. But minutes later she began to wonder if it had been meant as a compliment, or if Alan Connifer considered her to be, as Darda had often complained, too softhearted to fit into the corporate world.

She would show him. She would show all of them.

AS SOON AS THE PLANE FROM LAGUARDIA TO EDINBURGH landed, Beth phoned Stag's Head Lodge to report when she'd be arriving. She settled into the rental car and programmed the GPS, noting the estimated time before reaching her destination.

As she steered the car away from the town and toward the Highlands, she went over in her mind all the information she'd learned about her formidable opponent.

Colin Gordon had been educated like royalty. After attending boarding school at Eton, then moving on to Oxford and the University of Edinburgh, he'd returned to Stag's Head Lodge, where his father had remarried after the death of Colin's mother. Not long after, his father had died, followed shortly by his stepmother. As heir, Colin had taken the necessary steps to clean up an estate riddled with debt. It would seem his stern father had chosen to look the other way as his wife's son and daughter by a previous marriage had partied like rock stars. Both were now married, but despite their established place in wealthy, titled society, rumors persisted that they were living beyond their means and were urging their stepbrother to sell Stag's Head in order to erase their debt.

At Darda's insistence, Beth had already notified all parties concerned of her pending arrival, in the hope that the step-siblings could add a little weight to the deal.

Before leaving the country, Darda had given her niece her marching orders.

"Our firm has authorized you to offer one hundred million."

Beth's eyes widened. "So much?"

"Too much." Darda's tone hardened. "Start the offer at half. That way you have some bargaining room if he balks. For every million you shave off his price, the firm will add to your bonus."

"Do you think that's wise? What if he's insulted by a low-ball figure and flatly refuses to even deal with me?"

"That's all part of the art of negotiating. You need to know just how far you can push the client before he loses interest." Darda clapped a hand on her niece's shoulder. "But I should add that I've found a lovely villa in the south of France that could be ours for just under five million."

Ours. The very word registered as alien to Beth's ears. Though Darda was responsible for raising her, she'd never felt any bond of kinship between them. In truth, Darda had always deliberately held Beth at arm's length, sharing nothing but their name.

"Not bad for a few days of having to put up with a stuffy Highland lord. Did I mention that the firm arranged for you to stay on at Stag's Head Lodge?"

"But why? If the negotiations should stall, don't you think it would be a lot less awkward if I had a room in a nearby village?"

"Awkward for you or the client?" Darda's eyes narrowed. "Your comfort isn't important. You always want to remain close to the client. That way, whenever the opportunity presents itself, you're there to press him." Darda's carefully cultured voice played through Beth's mind. "Let me remind you. Not only is your job on the line here, but my reputation, as well. I expect you to do whatever it takes to land this deal. Do I make myself clear?"

Beth struggled to put aside any lingering guilt at the thought of separating a Highland lord from his ancestral estate. She knew she had to land this for the firm, no matter the cost to her conscience. After a lifetime of being told she was too tenderhearted, or, as Darda liked to say, too warm and fuzzy, to ever succeed in the hard-knock world of business and finance, she intended to finally win her aunt's approval and guarantee a place with this new firm.

While she finalized her mental strategy for dealing with her hard-nosed client, she peered at the gunmetal gray clouds spitting rain over the gloomy countryside. In a strange way she welcomed the bleakness of the day. She needed no distractions as she went over in her mind the moves that Darda had so carefully planned and plotted.

As she drove through the village of Stag's Head, she decided to make a stop, noting the clean streets, the smiling faces. It would be her last chance to be alone until the deal was finalized.

Though she hadn't planned this, she found herself drawn to a little shop offering late-afternoon tea and scones.

The shopkeeper brought her order to a small round table for two and paused to pour tea.

After a few pointed questions about her reason for the visit to his town, he smiled, giving him the look of an ancient, gnarled cherub.

"Ye've business with the laird, have ye? A finer man ye'll never meet. 'Tis thanks to him that I'm still in business. Most of the folks in town will tell ye the same. Unlike some who've inherited land and titles, our Laird Gordon truly cares about the lot of us. This town wouldn't survive without the laird's generosity."

Beth considered his words as she enjoyed the scone, still warm from the oven, and strong, hot tea. Fortified for the rest of her journey, she walked to the doorway where the old shopkeeper stood.

"Thank you. I'm glad I made a stop here. The tea and scones were lovely. Now I'm off."

"Aye. It's just up the road a bit, lass. No more than a few kilometers and ye're there. Take care, now. It isn't safe to be out of doors after dark, or . . ."

A customer stepped between them, placing a hand on the old man's arm and engaging him in small talk.

Beth glanced at the old man, who waved a hand before continuing his conversation with his customer.

Fortified by that brief respite, Beth settled into the rental car. She couldn't wait for her first glimpse of Stag's Head Lodge.

As the car followed the twists and turns of the narrow road, she could just make out the stark outline of a fortresslike castle up ahead before it was hidden from view by ominous clouds.

She smiled. Only the very rich would consider calling a castle of that size a hunting lodge.

She was still smiling when, without warning, her car's engine suddenly died.

Puzzled, Beth tried the ignition. Nothing happened. She sat for a moment before trying again.

The engine was completely dead.

Darda's first rule popped into her head: Punctuality. In order to impress her clients, it was necessary that she reach her destination on time.

Annoyed, Beth slung her bag over her shoulder and dug into the backseat for her small overnight case. The rest of her luggage would have to remain with the car until she came back for it. Locking the doors, she started on foot, determined to walk the final mile. As she trudged, she questioned the wisdom of having worn such fashionable heels. She'd wanted to make a good first impression, but her choice had been frivolous. Still, her walking shoes were in her suitcase. There was no time to turn back to the car and rummage around for them.

She pushed aside her doubts. She'd walked much farther than this in the city. What woman hadn't sacrificed comfort for style, especially when the stakes were so high?

Dusk was settling over the countryside, and she had begun to accelerate her pace when she suddenly stumbled. The weight of her overnight bag added to the momentum. With nothing to grab on to, she fell face forward. Instead of hitting the ground, she could feel herself continuing to fall down a long, dark tunnel.

As the darkness rushed by she let out a piercing scream before landing hard and hitting her head, causing a shower of stars to dance through her brain.

Such pretty, spinning stars, in bright neon colors.

It was her last thought before losing consciousness.

CHAPTER TWO

"Well now. What have we here?"

At the strange voice, Beth opened her eyes.

Standing over her was a plump little groundhog wearing a chef's hat and a long white apron, and peering at her as though she had two heads. In the animal's front paw was a giant wooden spoon that could have easily served as a paddle for a boat.

How was this possible? A talking groundhog? Dressed as a chef? The fall must have been much more serious than she'd thought. Her brain was muddled.

Still . . . she'd seen his face somewhere before, though she couldn't recall where. "Who are . . . ?"

"I have baking to see to. Bones and phones to add to my scones." He abruptly turned.

"Wait. Please don't leave me."

"I mustn't be out at the start of a new moon or I might encounter . . ." He never even gave her a backward glance as he hobbled away.

She was left alone, with only silence.

Of course she was alone. She'd only dreamed her visitor.

She eased to a sitting position and felt her head swim. Touching a hand to the spot, she could feel the sticky warmth of blood.

Very slowly she picked up her purse and overnight bag before getting to her feet. She started walking in the direction the funny little groundhog had gone, though she had no idea where she was, or what might lie ahead. Dream or no dream, that creature was her only guide.

Why was the countryside so dark? Where were the street lights? Had the fall affected her vision? And where had she been headed? Oh yes. Stag's Head Lodge. Thank heaven she had enough brainpower to remember that much.

As she came up over a rise she spotted a light up ahead. A light that seemed to be swaying, before abruptly moving away. Alarmed that she would be left behind in the dark, she started running and stumbling until she could make out the figure of a giant stag up ahead.

Hearing her footsteps, it turned, and twin beams of blazing red light were fixed on her with a look so fearsome, she covered her eyes and looked away.

When she looked up she realized her mistake. It wasn't a stag, but a horseman holding a lantern as he headed away from her.

"Wait. Stop." Dazed, confused, she began to run after him. "Can you help me? I seem to have lost my way."

"Who are you? What are you doing here?" In the darkness, the heavily accented Scottish voice was low with anger.

"I'm expected at the lodge. I'm Beth Campbell from New York."

"A Campbell? On Gordon land? How dare—"

"I phoned to say I was on my . . ."

Feeling herself fading, she began to sway as the sky above her slowly circled.

The man was out of the saddle and managed to catch her before she hit the ground. With little effort he swung her up into his arms and mounted his horse.

"Thank y—" Her throat was so dry, she couldn't seem to make her mouth work.

His breath was hot against her cheek. "It's not thanks I want. I'd much prefer to see the back of you as you take your leave of my land. But for now, I suppose, I have no choice but to take you with me."

He flicked the reins, and the great black horse started toward a darkened fortress in the distance.

Beth found herself in a most awkward position, being held in the strongest arms she'd ever known, her face nearly buried in the hollow between his neck and shoulder. She breathed in the scent of forest and evergreen, making her think of a wild, dangerous, primitive creature. She felt small and insignificant in his arms.

A feeling of sheer terror rose up and had her by the throat, but she couldn't make a sound.

He was dressed in a rough woolen cloak, with the hood lowered, allowing his shoulder-length hair to flow out behind him.

As the horse's hooves ate up the distance, he spoke not a word, leaving Beth to hear nothing but the pounding of her own heartbeat mingling with his. A strong, steady drumbeat that had her own pulse speeding up.

At last they arrived in some sort of courtyard. A dozen hounds swarmed around the horse, setting up a chorus of baying until the man gave a single command. At once they dropped to their haunches and remained still as statues, tongues lolling. He dismounted, still holding Beth in his arms as easily as if she weighed no more than a feather.

In the blink of an eye the hounds disappeared, to be replaced by a cluster of men, all dressed in similar fashion to her rescuer, in rough woolen cloaks, hair and beards long and unkempt.

A stooped, furry groundhog, a twin of the one in the chef's hat and apron, caught the reins and led the horse away. The men formed a circle around the man holding Beth.

"What have ye here?" one of them asked.

"A Campbell. She seems ill or wounded. Possibly demented, by the odd way she speaks. I'll have Maura see to her."

Her rescuer carried her through a doorway and into a cavernous room lit only by the roaring flames of an enormous stone fireplace. The log ablaze on the grate was as big as a tree trunk.

The man lowered her to a fur-covered chaise set in front of the fire.

A plump gray rabbit hurried toward them. "Ye've need of me, m'laird?"

"Aye. This female seems to be in distress. See if she is injured, and minister to her needs."

"Aye, m'laird. Will ye have ale?"

"I will, Maura. It's been a long journey."

The rabbit hopped away.

Minutes later Beth felt a cool, damp cloth on her forehead. She opened her eyes to see an old woman kneeling beside her, holding a bowl of steaming broth and a goblet of something warm and red.

"Are ye strong enough to drink this, lass?"

"What is it?"

"A bit of broth and some mead, lass. They'll ease yer pain and give ye strength."

Beth managed to sit up, taking several sips of broth before tasting the sweet, pungent, fermented mead. She managed only a few swallows before setting it on a side table. "Thank you. I'm sure I'll be all right. My car's engine died, and I started walking when suddenly I tripped and fell down some kind of black hole."

The woman was staring at her as though she'd just spoken gibberish.

"Could you contact someone at Stag's Head Lodge and ask them to send a driver to fetch me?"

The woman began to press her backward against the chaise. "You lie down now, lass, and rest a bit until yer mind clears."

"My mind is clear. My name is—"

The old woman gave a quick shake of her head. "The laird told us yer name. Ye'd be wise not to speak the name Campbell here at Stag's Head Lodge."

"This is Stag's Head?" Beth was up and on her feet, visibly swaying. "Then they're expecting me. I phoned and told them I was on my way."

The old woman glanced across the room. "Ye can see she's not herself yet, m'laird."

Beth turned and saw the man who'd carried her standing in front of the massive fireplace, holding a tankard of ale.

The men standing in a cluster around him were talking in low tones until he waved a hand, dismissing them. They walked to the far end of the room, where they stood watching and listening.

The man had shed his cloak and now wore a length of plaid tossed over his shoulder in a rakish manner and tied around his waist like a kilt. On his feet were leather boots. Other than that, his legs and chest were naked.

On any other man this whole pose of an ancient warrior would look phony. Like some cover model or actor hoping for his fifteen seconds of fame. But there was something about this man. Something dark and rough and dangerous that had him looking like the real thing, and had Beth's breath backing up in her throat.

He shot her an angry look. "Now you'll tell me what a Campbell is doing on Gordon soil."

"I have an appointment with Colin Gordon."

He set down his tankard with enough temper to have the ale sloshing over the rim. "I am Laird Colin Gordon, woman. And I've never before met you."

Beth swallowed and decided to try a reasonable approach. "I can see that I've crashed your masquerade party. I'm truly sorry. But my firm arranged this meeting, and nobody told me about the party." She tried a tentative smile. "If you'd rather, we can certainly postpone our meeting until tomorrow, at your convenience."

The man looked beyond her to the old woman. "It's as I feared. Demented, she is. Take her above stairs and see that she's made comfortable until I figure out what's to be done with her."

"Aye, m'laird."

As the old woman began to lead Beth away, the man added, "And, Maura, see that she's not left alone."

"Aye. I'll see to it, m'laird."

Stung by his insults, it was on the tip of Beth's tongue to protest, but she realized she didn't have enough energy for even that small effort.

As she began to sway and drop to the floor, she was once again lifted in those strong arms. She heard the man's muttered oath as she was carried up a rough, winding staircase and into a room with massive wooden beams overhead and a long balcony offering a view of a midnight sky sprinkled with millions of stars.

"I don't know what's wrong with me." Her voice sounded strange in her ears, like a child whispering down a long, hollow tube. "I've never fainted before."

"'Tis the bump on her head, m'laird."

"Let's hope so. More likely, she's escaped from some poor fool's tower, where she's been hidden away because of her affliction."

"I'm not mad." Beth wanted to stomp her foot, but being in the man's arms, all she could do was thump her fist against his shoulder.

He looked down at her, and she could see a glint of humor in his eyes.

Was he laughing at her? That thought only added to her fury.

"Ah, Glenna." The man spoke to an orange-and-white kitten who was busy setting a fire on the grate. "Fetch a nightdress for my . . . guest."

"Aye, m'laird." The kitten hurried away and a young, redhaired serving lass returned with a soft woolen gown with a high, prim neckline, long, tapered sleeves, and a skirt that fell to Beth's toes.

The man stood facing the fire, allowing the lass and housekeeper to minister to Beth until she was settled into a soft pallet. Then he walked to her side.

His tone was gentler than before. As though he'd decided upon a temporary truce. "Sleep now. Tomorrow will be soon enough to explain your reason for being here."

She could feel his eyes, dark and fierce, pinning her with that look that seemed to see clear through to her soul.

Her own eyes felt heavy. And though she had a hundred questions still unanswered, she was too weary to ask them. Where had she landed? What sort of place had rabbits and kittens that turned into human form? Why was everyone here treating her as the odd one, when it was clear that she was the only sane one among them? Or could it be that this castle was in some other dimension? An alternate universe? Could she be suffering some sort of mental breakdown?

Snug and warm, her head still pounding from the fall, she drifted into a restless, dream-filled sleep in which the apron-clad groundhog was offering her tea and scones and telling her to beware, and a plump gray rabbit was sponging the blood from her head and pouring it into a tankard for her to drink, insisting it was good for her.

The whole world had gone mad.

BETH LAY PERFECTLY STILL, LISTENING TO THE SOUND THAT had wakened her. The whispering of the wind? Or voices? Voices, she decided. They sounded very near, but when she looked around, the room was in darkness except for the dim light from the hot coals on the grate.

"You promised to find someone to do the deed." A woman's whisper, low with anger, drifted on the breeze.

"I found a hunter." The man's tone was soft, placating. "I've secured a place for him here with the other guests. But I don't trust him."

"Why?"

"Now that he has seen the splendor of this place, he is demanding more gold than he'd first agreed upon. He threatens to reveal our secret unless we double our offer. I need to find another to do the deed."

"Fool! There's no time left. It must be done before we

leave. If my debts are made public, my husband will refuse to pay. I fear he'll leave me this time. I'll be a pauper."

"As will I, if I don't soon make good on my promise to Judith's father."

"What foolish promises have you made now?"

"He learned that I've been neglecting her in favor of gambling and . . . other women. If he should tell her, and she leaves, all will be lost. I've given my word to give up my vices and become a dutiful husband."

The woman's voice lowered to a hiss. "Your hunter must finish this."

"For double the price?"

"What do we care what price he demands?" There was a hint of smile in the woman's words. "Once the deed is done, we'll see that he takes his secret to his grave. That way, we get to keep it all. Ours, as well as what he demanded."

There was a long stretch of silence before the man's voice sounded hushed. "How clever of you. You're right, of course. He leaves us no choice. If we're ever to be free, we must rid ourselves of all obstacles."

"There will be a new moon rising soon. Send your man to Stag's Head Peak as soon as it appears in the sky."

"'Twill serve the beast right. All his grand talk about honor. He values his family lands more than his family's needs. I'd gladly trade both honor and land for the gold it will bring us." The man's voice was chilling. "Soon it will all be ours. And no one will be the wiser. Even while they mourn their loss, our clansmen will cheer the death of a beast that fills all their hearts with terror."

"And all will hail the day that they were finally set free of the Beast of the Highlands."

CHAPTER THREE

Beth jolted upright and felt a moment of panic at the shadows leaping and dancing across the walls of her room. When she realized they were caused by the flames on the grate, she let out a sigh of relief.

Had she really overheard a plot to kill Colin Gordon? Or had it all been a bad dream? After that fall, and the crazy night she'd put in, she couldn't be certain of anything. She decided that, at least for now, she would store it away, along with all the other strange nightmares that had plagued her sleep. They'd been so disjointed, so terrifying, they couldn't possibly be anything more than bits and pieces of nonsense. It had to be as Colin Gordon had told his housekeeper. The fall had affected her mind.

The dawn sky outside the balcony was awash with ribbons of pink and gold and mauve. If she moved quickly she might still be able to repair the damage she'd caused by her embarrassing introduction. That awkward fall on the way to the lodge had ruined any hope of making a grand entrance. On the contrary, she'd made a complete fool of herself the previous evening. She'd not only barged in on a party, but had angered her host.

At least he'd been gracious enough to permit her to stay the night. But he'd been angry enough to let her know he felt he had no choice. No matter what arrangements had been made by the firm, she feared she would not be welcome to remain another day. She needed to meet with him as soon as possible and present the firm's offer, before she lost her best, her only, chance to make a deal.

She touched a hand to her head, where a dull ache was a reminder of just how hard she'd fallen.

She shoved aside the bed linens and got to her feet.

She could find no light switch. What in the world . . . ? Could Colin Gordon be so determined to honor his family's history that he'd refused to switch his hunting lodge over to electricity?

And where were her clothes? Apparently the housekeeper had taken them away to be cleaned. In their place lay a very old-fashioned costume. Some sort of gown of unbleached ivory wool, along with a soft chemise and knee-length drawers that appeared to be hand-embroidered with delicate rosebuds.

Was this intentional? Was she being informed that the masquerade party would last the entire weekend?

Feeling foolish, Beth washed herself in a basin of rose water she found on a nightstand and dressed in the costume the old woman had provided, then pulled on a pair of soft kid boots. She crossed to a mirror and couldn't help laughing at the sight that greeted her. She looked like one of those characters in the fairy tales her grandmother had enjoyed reading to her. It was a far cry from the chic image she'd learned to project at work.

Without hairspray and pins, she wasn't able to fasten her hair in its usual no-nonsense knot at the back of her head. Instead she was forced to run her fingers through it and let it fall long and loose to spill past her shoulders.

"All right, all you lords and ladies," she said to her reflection in the mirror. "Two can play this game."

She stepped out of her room.

A youth was lounging against the wall. At the sound of her door opening he straightened, while his hand went to the sword at his waist.

Beth tried to cover her surprise. "Good morning. I wasn't expecting to see anyone up at this hour. And in full costume, too."

The boy looked around rather wide-eyed before saying, "The laird's belowstairs. He said I was to report to him as soon as ye showed yerself."

"Fine. I'll let you lead the way."

Instead of walking in front of her, he waited until she reached the staircase before falling into step beside her, darting quick glances as they walked.

"And just where is the . . . laird?"

"In the library, m'lady." As they reached the lower level he indicated a hallway, and Beth moved along at his side until they came to huge, intricately carved double doors.

The lad knocked and the voice from within called, "Come."

"The lady is here, m'laird." The youth stood aside, allowing Beth to precede him.

"Thank you, Jamie." Colin Gordon appeared distracted, staring out a window and frowning.

In the dancing light from the fire on the hearth he was even more darkly handsome than he'd seemed the previous night. He wore the same length of plaid over some sort of full-sleeved, saffron shirt. His long hair was tied back with a narrow strip of hide.

His eyes reflected the firelight, gleaming like a cat's as he turned to study Beth. He looked, she thought, exactly like a Highland warrior about to do battle. He was perfectly suited to play the role of lord of the manor.

"Shall I wait, m'laird?" Jamie stood just inside the door, his hand at his sword, shooting nervous glances at the young woman beside him.

"Nay. I'll summon you when we've finished."

When the door closed behind the lad, Colin Gordon

watched in silence as Beth crossed the room to stand in front of him.

He was wearing the same frown he'd worn last night every time he looked at her. Still, with so many guests here, this may be the only time she would have his undivided attention. She seized the opportunity.

"Thank you for the clothes."

"You may thank old Maura."

"I will, when I see her. I'm sorry for that awkward scene last night." She managed a smile, though her heart was racing. "I fell and hit my head on my way here, and I'm afraid it left me a bit muddled. But now, after a good night's sleep, I'm feeling much better. I'd like to fill you in on the offer my firm is prepared to make."

"Offer? Firm? I know not these words."

Oh, the man was good. His face had gone deliberately blank, as though he hadn't a care in the world about the offer. Or maybe millions of dollars didn't matter to an already wealthy man. Still, since he'd been alerted to her arrival, and the reason for her visit, he had to be aware of what her firm was planning.

Beth realized that Colin Gordon wasn't going to make this easy for her. If she wanted to seal this deal, she would have to be every bit as cagey as he.

She pasted on her best professional smile and held out the packet of documents she'd prepared before leaving New York. "Maybe we could sit and go over these point by point."

He led the way to a massive hand-carved desk.

Before either of them could take a seat, the door was opened and a pack of hounds burst into the room, barking, howling, and slathering as they formed a circle around their host and his guest.

Beth let out a cry of terror and cowered against the desk.

Colin gave a quiet command, and the hounds turned into a cluster of men, laughing, talking among themselves.

Beth clutched her arms to her chest, on the verge of tears. It was clear to her that the bump to her head had been much more serious than she'd first thought. She was still seeing impossible visions. And though the vision had cleared, revealing humans, she found herself questioning her sanity.

One of the men slapped a second man on the back. "Hamish here wants to bet me a hundred gold pieces that he'll be the last man standing if ye'll agree to a contest."

Their host's head came up sharply. "What sort of contest, Ian?"

Ian's ruddy young companion was grinning from ear to ear. A toothy smile so wide, it seemed to stretch his face to the limit.

"I know ye're planning a hunt. Hamish can best any man here."

"Except you, m'laird," the grinning young man added with a slight bow.

"So I've heard, Hamish. I am told you are the master with both dirk and longbow."

Hamish's smile stretched even wider. "With enough ale in me, I might even beat ye, m'laird. And I'd dearly love to double my money with Ian here."

"What you two choose to wager is your own business." Colin shot a knowing look at the one called Ian. "But I've already warned you that I'll not pay your debts, brother."

At his use of that term, Beth shot him a look of surprise, before reality dawned. Ian would be Colin's stepbrother.

Colin set aside the documents Beth had given him and walked around the desk. "Since you're dressed and eager for the day, I suggest we go to the refectory and see what Mistress MacKay has prepared."

Beth's heart sank. Her one moment was gone, and with it, perhaps her only chance to speak privately with Colin Gordon.

Her host turned to her. "You're welcome to join us as we break our fast, though I assure you the other ladies are still abovestairs, as is their custom."

Perhaps food would restore a clear mind. "Thank you. I'll join you."

The noisy revelers led the way from the room, and her host

approached and offered his arm, indicating that he would escort her. Tentatively Beth placed a hand on his sleeve.

The heat that danced along her flesh had her looking up at him. He looked down at her in the same instant, and the feeling intensified. As if little fires were being set up and down her spine.

She saw the flash of something dark and dangerous in his eyes, and her throat went suddenly dry.

"Will you honor me by joining us in the hunt, my lady?"

There was no way she could graciously refuse her host's offer. "I would be delighted."

He closed a hand over hers. "I am honored."

Walking ahead, Hamish said something before punching Ian in the arm.

Colin's stepbrother swore good-naturedly before returning the blow to his friend's shoulder, sending the taller man bumping against the wall.

Hamish was still rubbing a hand over the tender spot as they entered a room lined with rough wooden tables and benches. Several young women were dashing about, setting out platters piled high with slices of meat and joints of fowl. In the middle of the room stood old Maura, calling out orders and chastising any server who happened to move too slowly.

When the group of men entered, Maura called out a greeting before disappearing. Minutes later she appeared alongside a tall blue crane, its beady eyes unblinking, its head making jerking movements as it walked stiff-legged toward their host.

Beth blinked and the tall bird turned into a stick-thin woman in a long white apron, her dark hair pulled into a severe bun at the back of her head.

"Ah, Mistress MacKay." Colin stopped, and his entire company paused at either side of a long table. "What have you prepared for my guests this morrow?"

"Fowl, m'laird. And yer favorite, warm bread puddin'."

Beth watched as Colin's face creased into a smile, which completely transformed him from stern warrior to dangerously handsome rogue. She couldn't decide which one intrigued her more. She was prepared to stand toe-to-toe with the warrior.

The rogue, on the other hand, presented a much greater problem. She couldn't imagine any weapon she could use against that heart-melting smile.

"You do know how to please me, Mistress MacKay."

"And have, since ye were a wee bairn, m'laird."

Laughing, Colin walked to the head of the table and indicated a wooden bench to his right. He remained standing until Beth and his guests were seated.

Old Maura hurried over to ask, "Will ye have ale or mead, m'lady?"

Recalling her dream, Beth quickly discarded the idea of blood-red mead. "Ale, I believe, Maura." She noted with a sense of unease that her host had been right when he'd warned her that she would be the only female in the room, except for those who were serving the men. "Why are the other women not here, Maura?"

The old woman whispered, "'Tis too early for highborn ladies. They prefer to break their fast in their rooms, and then allow servants to help them prepare for the day."

"I see." Beth glanced around. "Will they mind that I've joined their men?"

The old woman gave a mirthless laugh. "They'll not give you a thought, m'lady."

The men seated around the table were too eager making plans for the test of skills to even acknowledge the presence of a lone woman in their midst. She could have been invisible for all the interest they paid her.

"Where will we hold the contest, Ian?" one of them asked.

Colin's stepbrother was quick to respond. "In the high meadow."

"So far? Just below Stag's Head Peak?" Hamish raised a brow. "We dare not tarry up there, or we could encounter the Beast."

Ian sent him a chilling look, and in that moment he became a sly, cunning fox, his eyes alight with sudden knowledge. "The forests around the high meadow are lush with game this time of year. 'Twill be an easy matter for the lads to scare up enough quail and pheasants to make the contest interesting."

Another man spoke up. "If the lads are busy shaking the bushes for game, we'll be scattered in every direction. Who's to fetch our game as we take it down?"

The fox merely smiled, as though anticipating the argument. "We're all honorable men. We need no judge riding alongside us to keep a tally of the kill." He turned to his brother. "Unless you've a better idea?"

Colin shrugged. "Murdoch has a right to question. We'll send as many lads as we can spare to retrieve the dead game when the contest is over. Since every man here has his own distinct feathers affixed to his arrows, it will be an easy matter to see who brought down the most."

The fox's eyes glittered. "There. The laird has spoken. Eat up, lads. Then we will make haste to the high meadow."

"And if we're delayed until darkness?" Hamish persisted.

The fox shot a meaningful glance at the others. "I'll send some lasses from the village to hold yer hand and help ye forget yer fear, coward."

The others around the table burst into gales of teasing laughter, and Hamish ducked his head, while the fox transformed from animal to human.

Beth had watched and listened in silence, too stunned by the quick transformation of Ian into both fox and man to pay close attention to his words. Either she was completely losing her mind, or she'd landed in a place that was both magical and dangerous. And for now, she would cling to the hope that, though she felt completely lucid, something otherworldly had taken over her life. Though a contest between warriors interested her not in the least, she felt a tingle at the base of her skull. She tried to recall the words from that frightening dream. Hadn't they mentioned Stag's Head Peak? Or was she merely inviting drama that didn't exist?

While the others enjoyed their fine meal, Beth vowed to herself to pay close attention, for there was evil in this place. And magic. Or else, she was going completely mad.

* *. *

BETH STOOD ON THE BALCONY OF HER ROOM AND WATCHED
Colin Gordon walking the garden path below. Since he was
alone, it seemed the perfect opportunity to try her luck with
him yet again.

Snatching up the hem of her skirt, she hurried across the
room and down the stairs.

Once outside, she paused a moment to catch her breath
before walking quickly toward the figure moving along the
pathway.

"Would you mind some company?"

At her words, the figure paused before turning. His head
was bent, his hands behind his back. A man, it seemed, with
much on his mind. But once he spotted her, he forced a smile
to his lips.

"My lady Campbell. I'd be pleased for your company."

She flushed at his courtliness. "I know I'm intruding on
your privacy, but I'd like to discuss the terms of the sale, if
you're willing to listen."

Distracted, he merely nodded before starting along the
stone pathway, with Beth doing her best to keep up.

"Connifer-Goldrich would like to offer you . . ."

He paused, placing a hand on her arm to halt her words.
"I know not this name."

For the space of a heartbeat, she couldn't find her voice.
Her entire being was concentrated on the flood of heat radiat-
ing from his touch to every part of her body.

She stepped back, away from the heat, and waited for her
heart to settle.

"I work for them. I'm here to present their offer for"—she
swept a hand to indicate the lovely view before them—"all
of this."

"They desire my gardens?"

She smiled. "And all that goes along with them. Your
lodge. Your land. These glorious hills. The lake."

"Aye. The land. The hills. The loch." His smile was gone.

"The Campbells have always wanted what is mine. 'Tis not for sale, at any price."

"But . . ."

He was already several steps ahead of her. She moved quickly to match his pace.

He never once stopped to admire the lovely roses in full bloom or the birds fluttering their wings around the sculpture of a goddess in the center of a fountain. He strode straight and sure on the stone pathways between the hedgerows.

But as she struggled to keep up, Beth found herself enchanted by the view. The fragrance of roses hung heavy in the air. The sound of water flowing from the sculptured fountain was a balm to her troubled soul.

"I can understand why you would be loath to consider selling all this. Now that I'm here, I think it may be the loveliest place on earth."

He stopped then, and though his frown remained, he allowed himself to look around, as though seeing it through her eyes.

His own eyes softened. "Aye. 'Tis a bonny place. We stand on hallowed ground." He pointed to a small chapel across the garden and started toward it, with Beth trailing behind.

When they came to a fenced area, dotted with stone markers and sculpted angels, he paused. "My ancestors lie here. Those who died in battle, and those who mourned them. One day I'll join them as well. Until then, I see it as my duty to nurture the land and the life they left in my care."

Without thinking, Beth touched a hand to his. "I can't think of a more peaceful place to spend eternity."

He glanced at her small hand, and then up into her eyes with a fierce look that had her heart racing.

Before she could pull away, he closed both hands over hers. "Are you telling me a Campbell can understand what this place means to me?"

She swallowed. "Please don't judge me by my name."

"How else am I to judge you?"

"Judge me by my character. By my behavior. By the

choices I make." She ran her tongue over suddenly dry lips. "I'm more than a name."

"As am I."

She nodded and managed a small smile. "Maybe . . ." She sighed. "Maybe we could start over. I know I made a bad impression when I . . ."

He touched a finger to her mouth to stop her. Just the merest touch, but she felt the fire all the way to her toes.

"My lady Campbell . . ."

"Beth," she corrected.

"Beth is not a name. I shall call you by your full name. Bethany."

She was caught by surprise. "How did you guess? Most people think it's Elizabeth."

"Nay. It could only be Bethany." He spoke the word in a harsh whisper. "For 'tis truly a bonny name."

And then there were no words as he lowered his face to hers and kissed her full on the mouth.

An earthquake would have been less devastating than the kiss, which seemed to spin on and on, catching them both by complete surprise.

His arms came around her, drawing her against him, while his warm, firm lips moved over hers with a thoroughness that had her trembling.

She was so caught up in the moment, she found her arms around his neck, though she didn't recall how they got there. And when his hair brushed the backs of her fingers, she absorbed a tingling sensation that raced through her veins.

When at last he lifted his head, he stared down into her eyes with a look that was devouring her. "Are you a witch then, Bethany Campbell? For I know of no other reason I should behave so boldly with a woman I've only just met."

Though she knew her cheeks were flushed and her eyes wide with surprise, she couldn't look away. "I'm no witch, my lord."

He reached out a big, rough palm to cup her cheek. His voice was husky with emotion. "Perhaps not, but I'm bewitched all the same."

"I'm the one bewitched." Her tone was low. Breathless. Troubled. "Ever since arriving here my world has turned upside down. Nothing is as it should be."

" 'Tis true for me, as well. You've brought a candle to my darkness." He bent to brush a soft, butterfly kiss over her lips. "Now, my sweet, fair Bethany, you must leave me. This very moment. Before I do something that would shame us both."

She stared mutely as the meaning of his harshly whispered words sank in. She caught up the hem of her gown and turned away.

She knew she was taking the coward's way when she ran as fast as she could from the garden.

And all the while she could feel the heat of his gaze fixed on her as she made her escape.

CHAPTER FOUR

Beth paced the length of her room and back before pausing at the balcony to see Colin pacing the garden like a caged animal. Even from so great a distance it was clear that he was as tormented as she.

What in the world had she been thinking? How could she expect to conduct business, for heaven's sake, to negotiate terms of a sale with a man after allowing him to kiss her like that?

Allow? That was too mild a word. She'd been a full participant in that kiss. And it shamed her to realize that if he hadn't been the one to call a halt to it, she would still be in his arms, taking pleasure in the amazing feelings his touch aroused in her.

Though it was completely out of character for her, she'd welcomed the unexpected rush of passion. Had embraced it. And even now, just thinking about his kiss had her trembling like one of the silly, lovesick heroines in the novels she'd kept hidden from her aunt in her teens.

She turned away from the balcony when the door to her

room was opened and old Maura stepped in, her arms filled with fresh clothing.

"If yer to ride to the hunt, m'lady, ye'll need proper clothes." She set her burden down in the middle of the bed and began to sort through them. "We keep a store of the lady Catherine's clothes."

"Lady Catherine?"

"The laird's mother. Though she's been gone these many years, the old Laird Collier kept her gowns in a small room abovestairs. Since she was near your size, I thought they would do, though I'm sure Edwina will sulk."

"How kind of you, Maura. Who is Edwina?"

"Why, the laird's stepsister. She and Ian are the product of the old laird's second wife and her first husband. Laird Collier Gordon wed her after Lady Catherine died." Under her breath she muttered, "May God rest her dear soul."

"You cared for her."

"The lady Catherine? Aye. She was loved by all who knew her, my lady."

"And Laird Collier and his second wife?"

"Both gone to the grave now. Our affection for the old laird never wavered, though we all questioned his wisdom. He lies buried beside the chapel, next to Lady Catherine." Her smile turned to a frown. Her voice lowered with a trace of scorn. "His second wife was taken by her children to be laid to rest with those of her clan."

"Do Ian and Edwina live here?"

The old woman shook her head. "They live among their mother's people. She first wed a wealthy laird from the clan Campbell . . ." She stopped, her eyes wide as she realized what she'd revealed. "Begging your pardon, my lady. Ye probably know of yer kinswoman? The lady Darda Campbell."

"Darda . . . ?" Beth turned away to hide her shock. Her aunt's name was uncommon enough that she'd never before heard it. And now, to hear it in this place seemed unimaginable.

"Was she as beloved as the Lady Catherine?"

The old woman's voice was icy. "She was undeserving. All she loved, all she coveted, was the old laird's gold and lands. There now, my lady. I've spoken ill of your kinswoman, and may my Maker smote me for it."

Beth managed a smile. "You're free to say whatever you wish. My clan is far from here, Maura. In a land across the sea."

"Across the sea? 'Tis more than the mind can imagine." The old woman shivered at the thought of it and shook her head in amazement before holding up a gorgeous long skirt and fitted jacket in lush green velvet. "This will keep ye warm as ye join the hunt." She began helping Beth out of her wool gown and into the riding clothes.

When Beth was dressed, Maura held up a jaunty green hat adorned with a veil and a jewel-toned peacock feather. Placing it just so on Beth's head, the old woman stood back to admire her handiwork. "There now, m'lady. Take these." She offered a pair of softest kid gloves. "The laird instructed me to tell ye yer groom will be waiting at the stables with your mount. Mistress MacKay is preparing a picnic luncheon to be served in the meadow."

"Will the other women be joining the hunt?"

Maura shook her head. "They care not for it. But they'll attend the meal in the meadow."

When Beth stepped from her room, Jamie stood waiting, and walked beside her down the stairs and across a sloping lawn to the stables.

It was clear to Beth that, even though she was being treated as a guest, she was not to be trusted. Colin Gordon wanted her where he could keep an eye on her. Which was no doubt the reason he'd invited her to join the hunt. And when he wasn't around, that duty would fall to this lad.

Colin was astride a spirited black stallion. He wore a woolen cape tossed rakishly over one shoulder. When he saw Beth striding toward him, his gaze fixed on her with such intensity, she felt the heat rise to her cheeks.

She paused beside a stable lad holding the reins of a horse

and looked up at Colin. "I hope you don't mind that Maura offered me the use of your mother's things?"

"Not at all." He was out of the saddle and striding toward her. "I'd instructed her to use whatever suited you."

"Thank you. That was very generous."

"It was necessary. You could hardly sit a horse in a day gown."

While the groom held her mount, Colin assisted Beth up a carpeted set of steps that made it possible for her to slide easily into the ornate sidesaddle.

When she was offered the reins, she felt a moment of panic. But the docile mare stood perfectly still, allowing Beth to relax.

Colin returned to his horse, mounted, and led the way from the stable area.

The horsemen fanned out in a wide circle, except for their host, who reined in his stallion so that he could easily ride alongside Beth.

Why had she worked herself up over this? What could she possibly have to fear on this lovely, sunny day?

At the end of the day, when the contest had been decided and the men were celebrating, she would find time to talk privately with her host and present the firm's offer once again.

She would close the deal, ride off into the sunset, and return to her firm to enjoy the spoils of victory.

And she would remember for a lifetime that memorable kiss from a Scottish nobleman.

Lulled by that thought, Beth let go of the last of her tension. She'd never seen a lovelier place. With the sun high above, and a field of heather all around, she decided to take the time to savor the view and simply enjoy the day.

"SO." COLIN'S VOICE WAS LOW, SO AS NOT TO BE OVERHEARD by his guests. "You seem clearer of head with each passing hour. Have you put aside whatever was troubling you last night, my lady?"

"I have, thank you. I know I caused quite a fuss when I crashed your party last night. Blame it on the fall." Beth touched a hand to her head. "I've got a nasty bump. But other than that, I'm fine."

"Fine indeed." He was studying her far too closely. "And fair of face."

At his words, his gaze moved over her with a thoroughness that had the heat rushing to her cheeks. Almost as if, she thought, he was replaying their kiss in his mind.

He cleared his throat. "You remind me not of any Campbell. Neither in looks nor demeanor."

"I'm told I take after my father, though I don't remember him. He died when I was very young. And I've seen pictures of my mother. I have her eyes. She was a Douglas. Cybil Douglas Campbell."

His eyes narrowed in thought. "You're a long way from either clan."

"Actually, I wasn't born in Scotland."

"England, then?"

She shook her head. "I'm from New York."

At his puzzled frown she added, "America."

"I know of it. I've heard it described as a primitive place." He glanced skyward, to watch the path of an eagle soaring toward a distant ridge of trees.

Beth felt a quick rush of alarm. Was he teasing her? Or could it be as she'd feared? Could that fall have pushed her into another dimension? Some strange, mythical world? In truth, hadn't she felt as though she'd traveled back in time to some long-ago place of her imagination, where animals walked upright and some even turned into noble heroes?

She arched a brow. "Tell me something. Do you invite your friends here often?"

"This is a rare respite. As you well know, the times are troubling. Our beloved Highlands are divided. Some of the clans have grown rich accepting favors from the English. They would swear fealty to the English queen, subjugate the surrounding clans and strip us of our ancient lands and titles unless we do the same. But we will stand by our beloved Mary. With our Highland warriors at her side, she will prevail, and all disputes will be settled."

Stunned, Beth thought about the Scottish history that she'd so loved in her college years. If what this man said was actually true, she'd somehow been thrust back to the sixteenth century, when Mary returned from France after the death of her young husband, Francis, and assumed the throne of Scotland, paving the way for a deadly duel with Elizabeth I of England.

A perilous time in history, with two powerful nations hovering on the brink of war.

Beth chose her words carefully. "And you don't doubt your loyalty, my lord?"

"Regardless of the outcome, I am loyal to our Mary Stuart, who deserves to sit upon the throne."

He saw the way her brow furrowed. "'Twould seem you disapprove."

"No. It's just that I know what will happen . . ."

At a shout, he looked up, before turning to her. "I must leave you." He turned back to Jamie, who rode a short distance behind them. "You'll stay with the lady while I see what Ian has found."

Beth watched in alarm as he nudged his horse into a run.

She remembered a great deal more about the history of this country than mere names and dates. She knew the outcome of this rebellion. And it spelled disaster for all who defied England. Many would lose their ancestral lands. Some would die in an English prison, or be hanged as traitors.

Sweet heaven. Now she was certain that this wasn't just a bad dream or a head injury. Somehow that fall had transported her back to Scotland's dark and dangerous past, where Highlanders were divided, and many would pay with their lives. As long as she was here, she had no way of escaping the fate of Colin Gordon and his clan.

These were very troubling times. And she was trapped, with no way out.

*   *   *

COLIN WATCHED AS HIS GUESTS CHEERED THE SIGHT OF HUN-
dreds of quail and pheasants lifting into the air as young lads
from the village raced through the brush, brandishing tree
branches to frighten the birds into flight.

He cupped his hands to his mouth. "Let the contest begin."

At once Ian and the others notched their arrows to their
bows and took aim.

Each Highlander used the feathers of a different bird to
balance his arrows. Thus it was an easy task to determine by
the arrow embedded in the dead bird just which hunter had
made the kill.

Ian turned to their host. "You're not joining us?"

"Aye. In time. I prefer to give my guests the honor of first
kill."

Ian's eyes narrowed. "You think yourself so much better
than the rest of us that you would hold back?"

Colin merely smiled. "I consider it my duty to be a good
host first, and to partake of the games only when my guests
are enjoying themselves."

As Ian wheeled his mount and began riding after the others, Colin reined in his horse and watched with a thoughtful
frown.

His thoughts weren't on the hunt, but rather on the female.
On that kiss in the garden, which had inflamed him as none
ever had.

Who was she, and why had she chosen this time to come
into their midst? Was she, as he feared, a spy, sent by the
Campbell clan to report on his intentions regarding Queen
Mary? After his stepmother's heavy-handed rule over his
father and his clan, he trusted no Campbell. Especially one
so young and fair.

Still, she seemed truly confused by her fall. Or addle-
brained.

Colin considered himself a good judge of character. And
though he intended to keep a watchful eye, he found himself
beginning to believe that she was as she appeared. Not so

much addled as injured. There seemed to be a goodness in her heart, a sweetness in her soul that called to him. A dangerous thing, he knew. Many a laird had failed to understand that a fair face could hide an evil heart. Had not his own father made such an error in judgment? The price paid for his father's folly was still being exacted today. Darda was not a woman to be trifled with. As she had so ably proven.

The stranger could be here to relieve him of the last of the Gordon legacy. Hadn't many a devious woman mastered the art of seducing a laird before betraying him?

Seeing the female and Jamie approaching, he put aside his troubling thoughts and forced himself to smile.

"Now that you're here, we'll observe the others."

Jamie looked surprised. "Yer not joining in the hunt, m'laird?"

"There's plenty of time, lad." Motioning for Jamie to give them some room, Colin guided his mount to fall into step alongside Beth's horse and found himself enjoying the way the sunlight turned her hair to spun gold.

"This place you spoke of. This New York. Do they all speak as you do?"

Beth nodded. "They do."

"And that strange manner of dress when you first arrived, baring your legs as a Highland warrior, but wearing on your feet small bits of calfskin with daggers at the heels? This is also something your kinsmen wear in your country?"

Beth found herself laughing. "The heels aren't really meant to be daggers, though I suppose they appear that way to someone who's never seen them before. They're considered fashionable in New York."

"Fashion?" Colin frowned. "I've heard the women in the English court are consumed by it. Here in the Highlands we're more concerned with surviving the cold and feeding our young. We are constantly at war, if not with neighboring clans, then with the English, who will never cease until we wear the yoke of oppression. We've no time for frivolous pursuits."

Beth instantly sobered. "I'm truly sorry for your hardship.

I hope it will give you some comfort to know that life will be easier for your heirs in generations to come."

He gave her a sharp look. "Are you one of those who can see the future?"

"I . . ." Unsure how to answer, she merely nodded before looking away.

"Ah." He drew the word out as he pondered this bit of wondrous news. "And do all your people in New York have this power?"

She swiveled her head. "I'm afraid not."

"So you are one of the few." He leaned close to place a hand on hers, lowering his voice so that Jamie wouldn't overhear. "Have you come here to warn me, or to use your power against me?"

Again she felt the most amazing rush of heat, which sparked up her arm and sizzled along her spine, and wondered if this man had some sort of strange power as well.

"I would never . . ." Her voice caught in her throat, and she struggled to remember why she had come to Stag's Head. To urge this man to sell that which was most revered by him. To persuade him to offer up his ancestral land for a modern development that would turn this idyllic paradise into a playground for the rich and famous. Her tone lowered. "No matter why I was sent, now that I'm here, my only wish is to help you in any way I can."

"I wonder . . ." He kept his hand on hers for long moments while he stared into her eyes.

At last, satisfied with what he saw, he straightened and looked across at Jamie. "My guests have had enough time to thin the flock." He removed his bow and reached into his quiver for an arrow, bearing the distinct eagle feathers adopted by his father and grandfather before him.

He watched the path of a bevy of quail and took aim. Once released, the arrow flew straight and true, and the bird fell to the earth, followed by another, and yet another.

Jamie was out of the saddle to fetch the game, which he tossed into a leather pouch before pulling himself back into the saddle, declaring, "A clean kill every time, m'laird."

"You'll see that all the game brought down this day is given to the villagers, Jamie. Enough to satisfy the hunger of every family."

"Aye, m'laird."

Colin gave a nod of his head before urging his mount forward, toward the cluster of men in the distance.

While Beth and Jamie watched from a nearby hillside, the hunters scattered across the verdant meadow, calling encouragement to one another and shouting triumphantly with each kill.

Though Beth abhorred the killing, she felt consoled by the fact that this contest would feed the poor villagers.

It was, she realized, another reason to admire Colin Gordon. He gave his guests a fair advantage, and he used the fruits of this contest to see to the needs of his people, who trusted him to look out for them.

CHAPTER FIVE

By the time the sun was high overhead, a line of horse carts had filed across the meadow, where, under the care of Mistress MacKay, a tent was erected, and tables groaned beneath the platters of fresh salmon and mutton, and even a whole roasted piglet. There were baskets of bread and sweetmeats, and flagons of ale and mead.

The women, who had remained at the lodge to be pampered and bathed, arrived in a wagon, their gowns fluttering in the breeze like pretty wildflowers.

Once there, old Maura took charge of their comfort, offering them cushioned chairs beneath the cover of a tent.

A tall, regal woman in a gown of rich, royal purple separated herself from the others. From a distance, she was every inch a queen. Even her hair, in a coronet of braids, was topped by a circle of diamonds and precious stones that caught and reflected the sunlight.

As she drew near, Beth could see her face. Though her skin was unlined and her features perfect, instead of beautiful, she was frightening to behold. Her eyes were without light. Dead eyes, Beth realized. When she opened her mouth, her teeth resembled fangs.

"So, this is our unwelcome guest." Her voice was the hiss of a snake. "You are the talk of the household. 'Tis said you are either mad or dangerous, and that you insinuated yourself into the laird's fortress by feigning illness."

Despite the woman's obvious attempt to be insulting, Beth decided to deflect her temper with a smile. "I don't believe we've met. My name is Beth Campbell."

The woman arched a brow. "So I have heard. A lie, of course. I am a Campbell, and I am familiar with every member of our clan."

"Not all your clan, or you would know me. You must be Edwina, the laird's stepsister."

"I know who I am." Edwina fixed her with a dark stare. "But I also know this. You are no Campbell."

Beth saw the women's heads turning as they easily overheard all that was being said. While she watched in amazement, before her very eyes the women turned into a flock of geese, their wings flapping, their beaks moving as though trying to speak, though no words came out.

By now she was accustomed to seeing these changes in the people here. But she couldn't help wondering if she was imagining these dreadful changes, or if it was something about this place. Was it magical, mystical, or purely evil?

Beth was grateful when Colin's horse stopped beside them and the laird slid from the saddle. Did he see geese as well? she wondered. Or was she the only one who saw these people as birds and other animals?

While Jamie took the reins, Colin smiled at Edwina, apparently unaware, or uncaring, of the transformation of the women. "I see you've met my guest."

"Guest? And wearing the precious clothes old Maura hoards as though they are rare treasures? I've never known the old crone to let anyone even touch the lady Catherine's gowns, let alone wear them."

"And that troubles you, Edwina?"

At Colin's question, her dead eyes narrowed. "Though this woman claims to be of our clan, I know her not. You'd be wise to send out riders to see who she really is, brother. Perhaps one of the neighboring crofters has misplaced an addled wife."

"I thank you for your concern for my guest." Colin made a slight bow before offering his arm to Beth. "Let us enjoy the food Mistress MacKay has prepared. The hunt always sharpens my appetite."

As they turned away, Beth caught sight of the anger flaring in Edwina's eyes as the silly geese surrounded her, heads bobbing, tails wriggling nervously, beaks flapping.

Beth was reminded again of her dream. There had been no geese. Only a man and a woman. The voices had been mere whispers. It wasn't possible to recognize them among these guests. And yet the obvious fury in Edwina's eyes could not be masked, making her suspect.

Beth pondered her problem. If she were to tell Colin about the words she'd overheard, would he be grateful for the warning? Or would it be one more reason for him to believe she was truly addled?

Could there possibly be others among this company who wanted Lord Colin Gordon dead? Was there an insidious plot to have him killed? Or had her fall, and her subsequent failure to represent her firm, made her want to believe in silly fairy tales, rather than concentrate on the true purpose of her visit? There was no denying that she wasn't looking forward to seeing Colin's face when that happened.

While she sorted out fact from fiction, she decided that for now she would watch and listen—and try not to draw any more attention to herself than necessary.

COLIN GLANCED AROUND THE CLUSTER OF GUESTS. "WHAT is your tally so far, Ian?"

"Ten and two quail. A score of pheasants. But I intend to double that before the day ends." Colin's stepbrother tossed back a tankard before holding it out for a refill.

A serving wench was quick to attend to his need.

The men stood in a circle, drinking ale and paying little attention to the women seated beneath the tent.

Perhaps, Beth thought, it was because their women, despite the fashionable gowns, still had webbed feet and feathered wings. But the men fared little better. As she watched, Ian once again became a sly fox, while Hamish seemed to hunch into himself, growing shorter and shorter until he more resembled a mouse than a man.

Beth blinked, hoping to dispel the image, but now she realized the other men had also changed back from human to animal form. Though most were hounds, one was a hawk, with sharp, knowing eyes, watching the others.

She turned to where Colin stood a little apart, talking quietly to Jamie. The lad was now a wolf pup, eyes bright, tail wagging in a sign of friendship, while Colin had been transformed into a sleek, proud stag, with powerful antlers that could take down an opponent with one deadly swipe.

While she watched, the animal fixed her with a look so fierce, she felt a prickling sensation along her back and arms. He'd looked the same after her fall, when he'd greeted her with such disdain.

Despite her fear, she couldn't bring herself to look away.

The beautiful animal pranced toward her, keeping her in its line of vision, and though she wanted to run in fear, she was rooted to the spot.

"You should eat something." Before her eyes the animal disappeared. In its place was her handsome host. "Mistress MacKay will take offense if you refuse to sample her cooking." He studied her pale face with a look of concern. "Are you feeling ill?"

She shook her head, desperately trying to keep up with the troubling transformations that had her believing she must surely be going mad. "I'm fine. And you're right. We mustn't offend the cook."

He smiled. "I've often referred to her as a better fisherman than any here. She always manages to catch the finest salmon, the largest trout in our Highland streams."

Beth looked over and saw the cook, transformed into a crane, standing as still as a statue, watching live fish swimming in a bucket of water. With split-second timing she dipped her head and caught several in her mouth before depositing them over hot coals.

Beth glanced around. Had no one else seen it?

Colin held Beth's chair, and she was grateful to let her weak legs fold under as she took a seat with the geese.

Colin sat beside her, and the hunters followed his lead, joining their women as the meal was served.

In the blink of an eye Beth watched all the guests return to their human forms. She took a calming drink of ale and gripped the edge of the table for support.

Edwina shot a quick look at her brother. "Who is winning the wager so far?"

Ian shrugged. "Hamish and I are even. But I've decided on yet another wager. A hundred gold coins to the first one to bring down a stag."

Colin's head came up sharply. "We are hunting pheasants and quail. You're not to disturb the deer in the forest."

"Why such concern, brother?"

"'Tis mating season. I'll not have the herds thinned for the sake of a handful of gold."

"We'll take care not to harm the females or their young." Ian eyed his stepbrother. "Surely the loss of one stag shouldn't matter to you." He looked around with a knowing smile. "As we all know, it takes but one rutting male to populate an entire forest of willing females."

Around the table the men nodded and joined in the laughter. Even the women covered their mouths to hide their smiles.

Seeing Colin's frown, Ian arched a brow before glancing at the others. "Or are you more concerned with one particular stag?"

Hamish shot him a puzzled look. "Are you suggesting the laird would protect the Beast?"

"Perhaps." Ian looked directly at Colin. "Or perhaps you merely wish to save that trophy for yourself?"

Hamish looked astonished. "Have you ever actually dared to hunt the Beast, m'laird?"

"I have not." Colin drained his tankard. "And I would ask that none of my guests dare to attempt such a dangerous thing."

"Because you fear for our lives?" Ian persisted. "Or is it the Beast you worry after?"

Colin's tone was brisk. "I have graciously provided you with enough fowl to satisfy your appetite for the hunt. I now command that you refrain from hunting the four-legged animals during this mating season, so that the forest will continue to feed our people for generations to come."

"Ye've heard it. The laird . . . commands." Ian's tone was sharp with sarcasm. "And we all know the laird's command must be obeyed without question. Without regard to the fact that this command will cost me one hundred gold coins."

Hamish flushed, as did several others, who were aware of the sting of anger in the young man's words, directed at their host.

"I'll choose to overlook that for now, brother." Colin pushed away from the table. "Let the hunt continue."

As the men mounted their eager steeds, the woman treated themselves to slices of rich brandied cake, dotted with currants and drizzled with honey, before facing their return by wagon to the lodge.

Colin turned to Beth. "If you are weary of the hunt, you may remain here with the ladies. They will soon be back in the comforting care of my servants."

She gave a quick shake of her head. "I'd prefer to ride with you."

He seemed pleased with her choice. "Very well." He offered his arm and she placed a hand on his. "Jamie, lad, fetch the lady's mount."

"Aye, m'laird." The boy raced off to separate Beth's horse from the others tethered nearby.

When they were away from the others, Colin leaned close to whisper, "Perhaps, once the hunt is underway, you would permit me to taste your lips again, my lady."

Caught by surprise, Beth knew he could see the heat that rushed to her cheeks. She tried to cover it by saying, "I don't think that would be wise."

"Perhaps not wise." As Jamie drew near, leading her mount, Colin leaned closer, the warmth of his breath feathering the hair at her temple. "But speaking for myself, 'twould surely bring me a great deal of pleasure, my sweet Bethany. And I would do my best to pleasure you, as well."

He lifted her to the sidesaddle, allowing his hands to linger at her waist before pulling himself onto the back of his stallion and leading the way toward the forest, with Beth and Jamie following behind.

And all the while, Beth's poor heart kept up a steady rhythm that matched the pounding hoofbeats of the hunters' horses as they raced into the thickets.

The mere touch of this man did the strangest things to her. She couldn't recall another man who had ever had this effect on her body, her heart, her very soul.

She wanted, more than anything, to taste his kiss again. Wanted, in fact, a whole lot more than a chaste kiss. But what she wanted would have to be sacrificed for what she needed to do here.

She would have to guard her heart carefully. Once their business was concluded, she had no doubt that Colin Gordon's feelings for her would equal his feelings for the woman he held most in contempt—Darda Campbell. Surely her reason for coming here was every bit as selfish as Darda's motive for marrying the old laird. They both wanted the same thing. Ancestral lands that were, to the men who cherished them, more precious than gold.

The thought of seeing the light go out of Colin's eyes when he realized what had brought her here sent a shaft of pain through Beth's poor heart.

CHAPTER SIX

For the next hours, as the sun slowly made its arc across the sky, the forest was filled with the voices of the hunters, directing the lads to their kill, or shouting in triumph as they boasted to their friends of their prowess.

Their host joined in, bringing down a bevy of quail and pheasants before setting aside his bow. With a smile he urged his horse across a meadow to the place where Beth and Jamie sat watching the hunt.

As he approached, he couldn't hide the smile of appreciation as he took in the sight of Beth, sitting in a patch of heather, her skin kissed by the sun, her hair dancing about her shoulders on the gentle breeze.

He dropped down beside her. "You look like a beautiful butterfly, my lady."

"And you look very much like the lord of the manor."

"I care not for the title. But I do care very much for my clansmen, who trust me to look out for their well-being."

"So I'm told." She glanced at Jamie, who had pulled himself into the saddle and, at a word from Colin, started off in search of the laird's fallen game. "Jamie has only praise for

his laird. He told me how you see that all in the village are
fed and clothed and protected from harm. He said when their
herds don't reproduce, or their crops fail, it is you who sees
to all their needs. And when invaders came, you herded every
villager inside the protection of your lodge, until the enemy
was driven off. And those who, like Jamie, or the little serving girl, Glenna, lost families in the battle were taken in by
you and given a home and a future."

"It is what a good laird does for his people." Colin studied
her. "Would you not do the same?"

"I'd like to think so. But I've never been tested."

He smiled then. "All of life is a test. I feel fortunate that
my father was a harsh taskmaster. Long before I faced difficult decisions, I was trained to be ready."

"What about Ian and Edwina?"

His smile faltered. "My stepbrother and his sister were not
so fortunate. Their mother spoiled and pampered them, and
when my father tried to intervene, she took them back to her
clan. But that is no excuse for the choices they make now. As
children, we can lay the blame at the feet of those who were
our elders. But there comes a time when we must step out of
their shadow and cast our own."

Beth thought about her beloved Gram, and the feeling of
love and peace she'd felt in that dear woman's arms. And then
about the years since, under the tutelage of Darda, where both
love and peace were absent. All that mattered, all that had
been drilled into her young mind, was winning at any price.
And that lesson continued to this very day. Because Darda
demanded it, Beth was willing to do all in her power to oblige
her. Perhaps it was time to think about what truly mattered
in her life.

There was no time to ponder such things now, when Colin
took her hands in his and stared into her eyes. "I have always
enjoyed a good hunt. But today I found myself distracted by
a certain fair lady. Did you miss me at least a little while I
rode with the others?"

At the wolfish look in his eyes, she swallowed before nodding. "I did." Her smile was quick and bright. "But only a little."

"I think you tease me, my lady. But even so, I must do my best to change your heart." He leaned close and brushed her mouth with his.

It was the merest touch of his lips, but she was forced to absorb a shocking jolt to her system.

"We shouldn't . . ." She reached out a hand to the front of his shirt, thinking to push him a little away.

"Ah, but we should, Bethany."

At his gentle, mocking laugh, feelings pulsed through her and, despite her intention to hold him at arm's length, her hand fisted in his shirt.

"Forgive me, my sweet Bethany, but I can wait no longer." His arms came around her and he dragged her close, while his mouth covered hers in a kiss so hot, so hungry, she could feel it vibrating through her entire body, all the way to her toes.

When at last they moved apart, his eyes narrowed on her with fierce concentration. "Tell me true, my lady. Are you using your special powers over me?"

"I have no powers."

His smile came then, and he gathered her close. Against her temple he whispered, "If you believe that, you are lying to yourself. There is something magical about what is happening between us."

He lifted his hands to frame her face. "All my life I have known that there would be one special woman who was meant to be mine alone. I knew that when I met her, I would know her. And now, though I know nothing at all about you, and though I fear that you have come here to betray me, I cannot deny what I know to be true. Even if I leave myself open to pain and betrayal, I must have you, Bethany Campbell. We are meant to be together."

"Colin . . ."

The protest died in her throat when he laid her down in the heather and drew her into the circle of his arms, kissing her with a thoroughness that had them both sighing.

His hands moved over her, lighting fires wherever they touched. Their kisses grew more heated, their breathing labored, their lungs straining. They were practically crawling into each other's skin, and still it wasn't enough. Nothing could satisfy the need that was building, heating their blood, threatening to consume them.

As he reached for the buttons of her riding jacket, a great shout went up from the hunters.

Colin and Beth sat up, looking around in surprise.

A line of village lads stepped out of the forest, staggering under the weight of a stag. It had been skinned and gutted, and now its legs were secured to several saplings resting on the shoulders of the lads who had been ordered to transport it back to the lodge.

Colin stood and offered his hand to Beth, who got to her feet beside him.

His face was as dark as a thundercloud as he watched the procession of villagers, followed by the mounted hunters. In their midst rode Ian, laughing and slapping the others on their arms as he boasted of his trophy.

Without a word Colin helped Beth into the saddle and then mounted his own stallion, just as Jamie rode up with his leather pouch filled to overflowing with game.

Seeing the dark look on the laird's face, the lad drew back his mount, allowing Colin and Beth to lead the way.

In silence they rode side by side to the lodge, with the lad trailing behind.

When they arrived, the women spilled out of the hunting lodge and hurried down the lane toward the stables.

The mounted hunters drew near, and Ian came thundering up to the head of the procession, wearing a look of supreme satisfaction as he dismounted.

When Colin drew near, Ian held out the sack of coins to his stepbrother, calling in a loud voice, "I know I gave my word, but you must admit your command was unjust, since it would have cost me a fortune I could ill afford to lose. I was not about to let such a bounty pass me by."

Hamish, who rode up behind Ian, looked sheepish.

Colin's voice held a note of cold fury. "You gave your word, knowing you would not keep it? So now your word will mean nothing to all who know you. You prove to one and all that you revere gold more than our father's good name."

"He was not my father. And his precious name will not pay my debts, nor put food on my table."

"When the laird wed your mother, he offered her children his name. Yet you refused, and claimed that of your mother's clan instead."

Still hot with anger, Ian's voice rose. "I bear my mother's name proudly. And though she accepted your father's gold, she accepted neither his name nor his clan as her own."

Their guests wore looks that ranged from shock to horror.

"You think to dishonor me, Ian. But in truth, you dishonor yourself, along with the woman who bore you and the clan that sheltered you."

Edwina rushed to Ian's side and locked her hands on his arm, physically restraining him from reaching for the dirk at his waist. "You are distraught, brother. Go now and return your horse to the stable."

He looked at her as though she were mad.

Her voice rose. "And then you will ask forgiveness of our laird."

"He is not my—"

She silenced him with a hand on his mouth before leaning close enough to whisper in his ear.

He shot her a triumphant look before turning away.

She smiled up at Colin. "My brother's blood runs hot with the hunt. But when he has had time to cool his temper, he will realize how deeply he has hurt his brother-laird."

She turned to the lads, who continued to hold the bloody carcass of the stag, and dared to give orders like a queen. "Do with this as the laird instructs you."

She lifted her skirts and turned away, with the other women gathering around her and chattering like geese as they made their way to the lodge.

And all the while, Colin sat stone-faced on his horse, watching as Ian disappeared inside the stable.

When they were alone, Beth reached over to touch a hand to Colin's arm. "I fear for your safety. There is something I need to tell you. Something I overheard that troubles me . . ."

He seemed unaware of her words as he turned in the saddle to Jamie. "You will tally the kill, so that we may reward our hunters at the banquet this night."

Beth looked stunned. "After that scene with Ian, you would hold a banquet?"

"It is customary for the laird to offer his guests a feast and to reward those who deserve it."

"But . . ."

He silenced her with a wave of his hand before slipping from the saddle to take her reins. "Forgive me, my lady. I know you are troubled, as am I." He helped her dismount and closed a hand over hers, squeezing it gently as though to reassure her.

He leaned close to press a kiss to her cheek. "Go inside now and allow Maura and the servants to help you bathe and dress for tonight's banquet."

"And you?" She looked up into his eyes and saw something dark and dangerous before he managed to blink it away.

"I, also, must prepare."

He turned away.

While Jamie began leading the horses toward the stable, Colin turned toward the gardens, his head bowed, his manner thoughtful.

Though Beth yearned to go after him, she knew she had to respect his need for privacy.

As she entered the lodge and climbed the stairs to her room, her thoughts were in turmoil. She fully intended to warn Colin about the threat she'd overheard. If he chose to scoff at it, she would do whatever it took to convince him to take it seriously. She was more convinced than ever that his life was truly in danger.

Ian's hatred was now so out of control, he'd revealed it to the entire company. Only a man bent on violence would show such utter disrespect to a much-loved Highland laird.

The look in Ian's eyes in that moment before Edwina intervened spoke volumes about what was truly in his heart.

There was darkness in that young man's soul. He'd seemed, in that moment, the personification of evil.

Beth's hands were cold as she stepped into her room. She nearly groaned aloud at the number of people milling about. Old Maura was giving orders to the serving girls as they filled a round tub with steaming water and set folded linens to one side. The bed was piled high with brightly colored gowns and shawls and delicate underpinnings. Another servant stood beside a dressing table, where she would prepare the lady's hair for the evening's festivities.

As Beth allowed them to attend to her needs, she forced herself to smile and nod and pretend that all was fine. But her heart was heavy with the thought that at this very moment Colin could be facing great peril.

She was desperate to finish this charade and go to him. She needed to get him alone, so that she could share with him all the terrible secrets that were whirling around her mind, giving her such distress.

All she could see was the evil in Ian's eyes.

All she could hear were his hateful words, hurled like arrows straight to the laird's heart.

COLIN PACED THE GARDEN PATH LIKE A CAGED BEAST.

Though he'd seen evidence of Darda Campbell's evil magic before, this was the first time he'd witnessed just how deeply, how completely, she'd managed to control her children. Even in death, she continued to wield power over their minds and wills.

It was clear now that Ian had turned his back on all that was good and decent, and had somehow descended into a hell of hatred. And the choices he made going forward would affect not only him but everyone around him.

It pained Colin to acknowledge his father's folly. How easily the old laird had been manipulated by a woman's youth and beauty. When Darda was thwarted in her effort to control her new husband's estate, she had put a curse on him and on his only son.

At the time, Colin had scoffed at her attempt to manipulate him. And yet, the first half of the curse had already come to fruition, and it appeared that the rest of Darda Campbell's curse would prevail.

That knowledge made this night all the more important. Though he could not remove the curse, he could leave behind a legacy of his own heart. He would reward the friendship of his guests. And if the Fates were willing, he would taste the wine of true love before going into his final battle.

CHAPTER SEVEN

Old Maura stood back, admiring the work of the village lasses who'd been pressed into service.

"Ye look lovely, my lady. I've no doubt Lady Catherine would approve the use of her gown."

Beth ran a hand down the jewel-encrusted bodice. "I've never worn anything this fine, Maura. I feel like a princess in a fairy tale."

"I know not this tale of which ye speak, my lady. But ye surely look as fine as any lady who has ever graced Stag's Head Lodge."

"And all thanks to you and your helpers."

The old woman blushed while the serving girls smiled their appreciation at her words. It was apparent that none of them were accustomed to being thanked for the work they did for their visitors.

They all looked up at the knock on the door. Maura hurried over to admit the laird.

Colin paused in the open doorway. And though the room was filled with servants milling about, he had eyes only for the lovely young woman standing in front of the fireplace.

"You are a vision, my lady."

Beth smiled. "None of this could happen without Maura and these amazing women." She touched a hand to the jeweled gown. "I'm told this was your dear mother's. And look what they've done with my hair. It was all wind-tossed until they managed to tame it."

His eyes twinkled with laughter. "And will you give them credit for that lithe young body and beautiful face, as well?"

That had all of them laughing.

Maura cleared her throat and motioned for the women to leave. When the last one was gone, she paused, seeing the way the young woman and the laird were staring at each other with naked hunger.

The old woman was smiling as she silently closed the door and made her way along the hall.

COLIN REACHED A HAND FROM BEHIND HIS BACK AND handed Beth a nosegay of flowers. At her look of surprise, he touched a finger to her cheek. "I saw these in the garden and had to pick them. They reminded me of you, so sweet and so perfect."

She buried her face in the nosegay and fought a sudden rush of tears. "Thank you, my lord." She looked up. "Before we go to the banquet, there are things I must tell you. Important things that could—"

He gently shook his head and offered his arm. "There will be time later to talk. Now we must go belowstairs."

Seeing the set of his jaw, she took a deep breath and placed her hand on his sleeve. And as she moved along by his side, she prayed that she could remain strong and vigilant. For there was evil here. She could sense it. Could almost feel it vibrating in the very air.

THE GREAT ROOM WAS FILLED WITH VOICES AND LAUGHTER as the men strutted about, boasting of their hunting prowess,

while their ladies made a great show of displaying their finest
gowns.

Giant logs blazed on the hearth, warming the room and
perfuming it with the scent of evergreen. The tables were
groaning under the many dishes prepared by Mistress
MacKay and her serving wenches.

When Colin and Beth entered, there was a sudden silence
as the men and women looked over at the handsome couple.

Edwina's eyes narrowed. "Another of the Lady Catherine's
gowns? Have you nothing of your own?"

Beth gave a slight shake of her head. "I arrived at Stag's
Head with nothing but the clothes on my back."

"Which, as I recall, were strange garments reminiscent of
someone quite demented." Edwina shot a quick glance at her
friends, who looked embarrassed before laughing behind their
hands.

A handsome young man stepped up beside Edwina. "Mind
your manners, wife. I've only just arrived and already you've
had your fill of ale."

"Oh, I've had not nearly enough. But I've had my fill of
you, Muldore." At that, Edwina flounced away, leaving him
staring after her.

Beth's brow shot up as she turned to Colin. "That is Edwina's husband?"

"Aye. Muldore Campbell. Poor fool. She cared not about
his heart, but only for his gold. And he never looked beyond
the pretty face to see into the soul of Edwina, so now he pays
the price."

He led Beth toward the head table. As soon as they were
seated, the guests followed suit.

In no time, as servants scurried about filling platters and
goblets, the noise level rose to a fever pitch.

More than a few of the hunters were staggering about, the
result of too much ale. Their drunken laughter rang through
the room.

As if to further taunt her husband, Edwina openly flirted
with the men who returned her attention until they would

happen to take note of Muldore Campbell seated to one side, glaring, his hand on the dagger at his waist. Then they would step back, leaving Edwina to seek out another conquest for her dangerous game.

Beth caught a glimpse of Ian pulling one of the serving girls close to whisper in her ear. Whatever he said had the lass blushing before she hurried away. With a laugh he turned to another, younger lass, and boldly ran his hand down the front of her gown, causing Colin to give a hiss of anger.

Beth turned to him. "Ian's wife is not here with him?"

Colin's voice was low. "She could not make the journey, since she is soon to deliver their first child."

"Poor thing."

"Aye. She had little to say about the matter of marriage. It was decided between her father and Ian, and I'm told he promised the old man a great deal of gold in exchange for his daughter's hand."

"I hope her father thinks it was worth making a bargain with the devil."

At her words, Colin turned to her. "I see you are not deceived by Ian's handsome features."

"A very wise woman once told me that looks aren't enough. What matters most is a good heart."

"A wise woman, indeed." Colin got to his feet and held aloft a cup of ale.

Around the room voices were stilled as the laird began to speak.

"My friends, I am in your debt. Even now, as we feast, the villagers are also celebrating with a feast of their own. Because of your skill with bow and arrow, no man, woman, or child, even the oldest among them, will go hungry this night. For that, I thank you, my friends."

Hamish stood and lifted his own tankard. "It is we who salute you, my laird. These days spent in your company have been a special treat to all."

Colin smiled at the young man. "It is time to announce the winners of today's hunt."

At a signal, Jamie stepped up beside his laird and handed him a bundle of arrows, sorted by feathers.

Colin glanced around the hall until he spotted the red-bearded son of an old friend. "Adair, you brought down the most pheasants. Come forward and accept your reward."

As the young man paused before him, Colin clapped a hand on his shoulder before handing him a small sack of gold.

After accepting his prize, the young man knelt and declared loudly, "I thank you, my laird. And I declare my fealty to you forever."

Touched, Colin nodded. "Your laird thanks you, Adair."

He reached for the second set of arrows and called, "Bancroft. You brought down the greatest number of quail. Come forward and accept your reward."

Like Adair, the young hunter with pale blond hair stepped forward and was handed a small sack of gold. And, like Adair, he knelt and loudly declared his fealty to his laird, to much shouting and pounding of goblets on the wooden tables.

"Hamish." Colin picked up the largest bundle of arrows, bearing the soft, plumed feathers of an egret. "Yours was no idle boast. You have, indeed, proven yourself to be a most gifted bowman. When we combine the number of pheasants and quail brought down by your arrows, I declare you the winner of the entire hunt. In all, you provided my villagers with three score and five birds for a glorious feast."

To much shouting and pounding, the young man stepped forward to claim a much larger sack of gold.

Clearly humbled by the honor, he knelt before his laird and declared in a loud voice, "Though I was born to the Campbell clan, and have declared allegiance to my clansmen, I do declare my fealty to you, as well. If ever you need my strong arm, it is yours."

"I thank you, Hamish. You may walk freely among my clansmen, knowing they will never harm you."

Ian walked up to the head of the table, stepping in front of his friend Hamish and swaying slightly.

His words were slurred. "What of my reward?" He looked around at the others. "Since I was the only hunter to bring down a stag, I have earned the right to be declared winner of the hunt."

"I have not forgotten." Colin's expression never changed.

He nodded toward Jamie, who handed him a goblet of blood-red wine.

Colin held it out to his stepbrother. "Drink, Ian."

Incredulous, the young man stared at the cup, then up at Colin. "What of the gold you gave the others?"

"Gold is their reward. But this is made from our own vines, grown in our own hallowed soil. It is the drink of life that binds us one to the other."

With a look of absolute fury, Ian tossed the goblet against the stone fireplace, where it spattered and ran in rivers of red.

"You will pay dearly for this, brother." Without another word, Ian turned and stormed out of the great hall, his booted feet beating an ominous tattoo on the scarred wooden floor.

In the silence that followed, Edwina hurried forward. "My brother is drunk and knows not what he is doing. On the morrow, he will apologize to you, brother-laird."

In a low voice, for her alone, Colin muttered, "No more lies, sister. We both know the morrow will not come. And we know why."

For a moment she was so startled, she could find no words. Then, with a last glance at the others, she turned and lifted her skirts before racing after Ian.

With the joy of the evening now gone, the guests made ready to return to their chambers for the night.

A murmur ran through the room, and Beth caught snatches of the conversation as the men and their ladies hurried away. It was something she'd heard before, though she couldn't seem to recall where.

Remember, with a new moon, it isn't safe to be out after dark.

Before she could ask Colin about the meaning of their words, he had his arm around her waist as he escorted her up the stairs to her chambers.

Her body felt practically scorched from his touch.

At the door, he turned to Jamie, who had trailed them.

"You'll not be needed this night, lad. You may go to your chambers."

"Aye, m'laird." The lad bowed to Beth. "Good even', m'lady."

"Good night, Jamie."

As Colin opened the door she stepped into her room and turned to him. "Before you leave, I want to tell you something very important."

"I have much to tell you, also, my lady." He stepped inside her room and closed the door before leaning against it.

On his face was a look that had Beth's heart racing.

"You're in danger." She spoke the words quickly, since she'd been holding them back for so long.

He gave her a wolfish smile as he lifted a hand to her cheek. "Aye. Grave danger indeed, my sweet Bethany. For the greatest risk of all is giving one's heart. But that is what has happened to me. I've already lost my heart to you. And now, before you say another word, I must taste your lips."

He drew her into his arms and kissed her with a thoroughness that had all her breath backing up in her lungs. A kiss that had her blood running hot through her veins. So hot, she could barely breathe.

His mouth moved over hers until she had no choice but to wrap her arms around his waist and hold on as he took her on a dizzying ride that had her mind spinning, her heart soaring.

And then, as his lips continued to weave their magic, she was lost. Whatever she'd been about to say was forgotten as she gave herself up completely to all that he was offering.

"I fear I've lost my heart, too, Colin. Completely."

"Oh, my sweet, beautiful Bethany."

And then there were no words as he lifted her in his arms while his mouth, that wonderful, clever mouth, continued weaving its magic, clouding her mind, heating her blood until all she could taste was Colin. And as he carried her across the room, all she could feel was this incredible hard, driving need to show him, in every way possible, all the things that were in her heart.

CHAPTER EIGHT

"My bonny, bonny Bethany."

In front of the fireplace, Colin set her on her feet and continued kissing her.

She wrapped her arms around his neck and returned his kisses with a hunger she'd never known. This was more than hunger. It was a desperate, driving need that clouded her mind and stole her will. A need that only this man could fill.

How had this happened? When had this Highland laird become so important to her?

There was no time to consider as his mouth pressed kisses to her ear while he murmured endearments, and his hands, those clever warrior's hands, moved over her at will, driving her closer and closer to the edge of insanity.

With a sudden sigh of frustration, he grasped the top of her gown and tore it from her, sending silken threads and sparkling jewels dropping to the floor at their feet like pebbles.

She let out a cry of consternation. "Your mother's beautiful gown . . ."

"It is mere cloth, and can be replaced. But I'm desperate to see you, Bethany. Now. All of you . . ."

His words died in his throat at the sight of her. "You are so lovely, my lady. Please don't torture me. I must lie with you, Bethany, now, or die from this wanting."

In answer, she framed his face with her hands and lifted herself on tiptoe to press a kiss to his mouth.

It was all the response he needed.

He groaned and gathered her into his arms, lifting her off her feet and carrying her the last few steps to her pallet.

There he laid her down as gently as though she were made of spun glass. And then, tossing aside his plaid, he joined her on the pallet and began raining kisses across her face, down her throat, and then lower, to her breasts.

Her breathing quickened, and her heart was racing as though she'd been running for miles.

"Colin. Wait. I need a moment."

He lifted his head, his eyes blazing. "A moment feels like eternity when the very sight of you has me on fire."

"I just need to catch my breath."

"You may have mine, my lady, for I have no need of anything, even my very breath, without you." He brushed her lips with his, and she breathed him in, loving the familiar scent of Highland forest that clung to him.

And then, with teeth and tongue, with lips and fingertips, he began leading her higher and higher, until her entire world narrowed to this man, his kiss, his touch, and the paradise he promised.

Outside her balcony the wind sighed, matching her sighs. A night bird cried, and its mate answered. A dove cooed to its young in a nest. None of it mattered to the man and woman locked in a loving embrace.

As needs rose in her, Beth clutched at Colin, and the feel of his flesh had her palms tingling, her nerves quivering. Then, aware that she was free to touch him as he was touching her, she allowed her hands to move over him, tracing the solid ridge of muscled torso, the flat planes of his stomach.

He was so beautiful. A sculpted Highland warrior, a laird who wielded great power over his people, and yet he treated her with such care. As though afraid she would break if he but held her too tightly.

The thought emboldened her as she gave herself up completely to his loving ministrations.

"There is magic between us, Bethany." He whispered the words against her mouth, and then inside her mouth, as he kissed her long and slow and deep.

She absorbed the deep timbre of his voice inside her. She could do nothing more than cling to him, and sigh from the pure pleasure he offered.

"My sweet, bonny Bethany." He framed her face with his big hands and stared down into her eyes with a look so hot, so hungry, it had her shivering with anticipation. "I am completely captivated, my lady." He pressed moist kisses over her eyelids, her cheeks, the tip of her nose.

Was the room moving? Spinning? She could feel it dip and sway with each touch, each kiss, until she was forced to close her eyes and hold on to him for fear of falling.

He lowered his head, and his lips closed around one erect nipple.

A shaft of heat pierced her heart, and she gasped and clung to him as he took her on a wild, dizzying ride, taking her higher, then higher still. A fire of such desperate need began building inside her, she feared she would surely burn to ash.

"Colin, please . . ."

"Say the words, Bethany. I've longed to hear you speak of your heart's desire."

"I . . ." Her need was so great, the words lodged in her throat like a boulder.

"Then I'll say them for both of us. I love you, my beautiful, sweet Bethany."

He took her then, with a fierceness that staggered them both.

As he entered her, he paused, and pressed his lips to her ear. "I am yours, my lady. Forever."

Her body arched, her hands fisted in the bed linens. She stared blindly, a mist of passion clouding her vision. Her body was slick with the sheen that rose up between them. She could feel him struggling to be gentle, but the overwhelming need swamped him, making tenderness impossible.

It wasn't tenderness she craved now. It was a release from the fierce passion that was building, fighting to be free.

Lungs straining, hearts thundering, they began to move, to climb. Pleasure, bordering on pain, began to build, until at last, locked in a fierce embrace, they soared to the very center of a star-filled universe. For the space of a heartbeat they paused, then stepped into the unknown. And soared.

FOR THE LONGEST TIME THEY LAY, STILL JOINED, UNABLE TO move as they waited for their world to settle.

Against her throat he muttered thickly, "Forgive me, sweet Bethany. I was rough."

"You weren't." She touched a finger to his lips to still his apology. "You were . . . amazing."

He managed to rouse himself enough to lift his head. When he did, he caught the glint of moisture on her lashes. "Tears, my lady? I hurt you . . ."

She pressed a kiss to his lips to silence him. "These are tears of joy. I've never known anything like this before."

"Nor I." He gave a long, deep sigh of relief. "What we have found is something rare and special."

She couldn't help smiling. "Isn't that what men always say to women after lovemaking?"

"Is it?" He sounded genuinely surprised.

"Are you telling me that you've never said such a thing before?"

"Never, my lady. You are my one. My only."

He rolled to one side and drew her into the circle of his arms.

As she snuggled against his chest, she found herself believing him. Colin Gordon was unlike any man she'd ever met. A truly honorable man. Of that she had no doubt.

She ran a fingertip up his arm, lingering over the ridge of

muscle that was oddly comforting. This man was a warrior. He would know how to defend himself against whatever evil scheme was brewing.

Though she hated to shatter this tender mood that held them in its grip, the time had come to warn him about what she'd overheard.

She touched a hand to his face, as though to soften the blow of her words.

"I've tried so many times to warn you about the danger that threatens. Now, Colin, you must listen."

He went very still. "Say what you must, my lady."

As quickly as possible she told him about the voices she'd overheard outside her balcony.

"They were little more than whispers, and I can't identify the voices, but I'm convinced that they were plotting to kill you. And now that I've seen Ian's anger, and his sister's attempt to cover it up, I believe both Ian and Edwina want you dead." She paused, wondering just how much to reveal. But after what they'd just shared, there was no reason to hold anything back, no matter how difficult it would be to explain.

"There's more, Colin. I know it will sound crazy, but I need to be completely honest with you, no matter what you may think of me when you hear it."

He ran a hand gently down her arm. "You can tell me anything, love."

Love. It was the sweetest word she had ever heard.

She took in a deep breath. "Ever since coming here I've seen odd things. Things I have never seen in my world." She paused for only a moment before saying, "Several times the women here turned into geese." She looked up at him, then away, before going on quickly, so she wouldn't lose her nerve, "I know it's crazy. But it truly happened. And the men turned into animals. I'm not saying they merely reminded me of birds and animals. They actually turned into them."

She waited for him to laugh, or to insist that she'd been dreaming. Instead she felt him draw slightly away before he asked solemnly, "What animal did I become?"

"A deer. A very large deer, with huge antlers."

He gave her a sad smile before nodding. "Aye. A stag."

Her brows shot up. "You're not surprised by what I've told you? You know?"

"You weren't imagining such things. They are very real." It was Colin's turn to take in a deep breath before explaining. "My father was an old man who still mourned the loss of my mother, his soul mate, when he met Darda Campbell and was so dazzled by her youth and beauty, he married her within days of their meeting."

"Were you offended?"

He shook his head. "Though I cared not for her, I wanted only my father's happiness. When it became obvious that he was not happy, I took myself off to battle, in order to give them time alone. But when I returned, and Darda learned that her new husband had named me his only heir, she came to me with a proposition. Renounce my claim to my father's estate, and she would do all in her power to make his last years happy and peaceful. Refuse her offer, and she would place a curse on both of us."

"What did you say to her?"

"I could not, in good conscience, accept her terms, since I believed that she did not have the well-being of my clan in mind. As for her curse, I scoffed at her attempt to frighten me." His hand tightened on hers as his voice lowered to a whisper. "If only I had listened to her."

"Are you saying you believe in magic? You actually believe in Darda's curse?"

"How else to explain? Immediately after my refusal, my beloved father was dead."

"Could Darda have killed him, just to make you believe her?"

He nodded. "It is quite possible. But soon after, Darda died by her own hand. She left a note to me, sealed in wax and stained by her own blood, saying she was taking her life so that she could never be tortured into rescinding the second half of the curse, which she'd called down upon all within the confines of this castle, and upon me."

"Your people turn into birds or animals?"

He nodded.

"And they know it is happening?"

"They know. But they cannot change it."

Beth could barely breathe. Even as she asked the question, she feared she already knew the answer. "What is the curse on you?"

"You have heard of the Beast of the Highlands?"

She swallowed before nodding.

"On the first night of every new moon, I must leave this body and enter the body of a great stag. I am compelled to climb to the highest reaches of Stag's Head Peak until dawn. If I survive a hunter's arrow, I will live for another month. But with each new moon, the curse begins anew, until a shrewd hunter's arrow shall find me, and death shall surely claim me."

Her hand flew to her mouth. "That's why I was being warned to be indoors before dark. We are drawing near to the new moon."

"It is, in fact, upon us. Through the years many have spotted the great stag, known as the Beast of the Highlands. Many more have heard the fearsome sound of hooves racing through their villages. All who live here avoid going out after dark, especially on the night of a new moon. And each time, I am prepared to die. But this time, more than ever, I am convinced of it."

"There must be something we can do." She pushed away from him and began to pace. "What if I were to tie you up? Or lock you in the stables?"

He reached out a hand to stop her pacing and drew her back down into his arms. "Do you not think I have tried such things? But I am helpless to evade this curse. I am compelled to kick and bite and free myself, even though I know I should not. I am helpless to stop the curse. And tonight, at midnight, as the new moon rises, I believe I will face my final hunter. My executioner."

"Darda's son, Ian."

He nodded. "Or one of his accomplices."

Beth wrapped her arms around him, holding him tightly

to her. Against his temple she whispered, "This can't be. None of this makes any sense. There has to be a way to stop this madness."

"There is none. But until midnight, there is a way to distract ourselves from the horror that is to come." He laid her down and kissed her with a tenderness that said, more than any words, just what he was feeling.

And then, with a desperation born of the knowledge that this could be their last time together, they took each other beyond the fears and doubts and pain to a place of peace and tenderness.

A place where only lovers can go.

CHAPTER NINE

Beth lay in the darkness, feeling Colin's arms around her, his heartbeat as erratic as her own. During their time together they'd pushed away the fear in the only way they could. Now there was nothing left to do but face the fate decreed by Darda's curse.

Beth had shared with him every scheme she could imagine to evade this cruel outcome, but he'd assured her that he had already attempted everything imaginable through the years. Darda's curse was unbreakable.

As the new moon began to rise over their balcony, he brushed a soft kiss on her lips and slid from the pallet.

"Wait. You mustn't go. I can't let you." She caught his hand and clung fiercely.

His voice was an urgent whisper. "Understand, love, the call is so fierce, I would crush you beneath my hooves in my haste to get to Stag's Head Peak. Now that the time is upon me, nothing can stop this overwhelming need."

Tossing a cloak over his plaid, he strode from the room without a pause.

As the door closed, lightning streaked across the sky, followed moments later by a crash of thunder so close, it shook the rafters.

Chilled, Beth pulled on the woolen nightgown that had been left on the chaise. Turning to the fireplace, she stirred the ashes and added a log, but even the sudden blaze of flames couldn't warm her. The thought of what was about to happen to Colin left her chilled to the bone.

Shivering, she ran to the balcony, hoping for one last glimpse of his beloved face.

Lightning streaked, illuminating a great stag, its antlers as wide as a longbow as it raced across the courtyard and fled into the countryside beyond. Lightning flashed across Stag's Head Peak in the distance.

After a day watching the hunt, Beth knew that the landscape was every bit as wild and rugged as the tales her Gram had told. Looking out over the bleak countryside, she chewed her lower lip, considering her options.

Colin was convinced that nothing could change his fate. But she refused to stand idly by while he went to certain death. There had to be a way to intervene in Darda's hateful curse.

A search of the room found little to help. Beth's gaze was arrested by the ancient sword and knife hanging above the mantel. Standing on a settee, she was able to reach the sword, but when she tried to remove it, she realized that it probably weighed more than she. That left her no choice but to help herself to the knife, which she tucked into the pocket of her nightdress.

She had no plan in mind, except to find Colin. With that thought playing through her head, she snatched up a coarse woolen cloak and opened the door to her chambers before racing headlong down the stairs.

Once outside, she pulled the cloak over her and hiked the skirts of the ridiculous nightdress as she started walking, keeping the high peak in the distance clearly in her line of vision.

Maybe she really was crazy, she thought. What other explanation could there possibly be that would have her sneaking away in the middle of the night, crossing the wild, dangerous Highlands barefoot, and hoping to stop a dangerous hunter from killing the fictional Beast of the Highlands?

As if the wind blowing across the countryside wasn't enough, Beth's bare feet kept sliding over damp moss and slippery rocks, making her feel as unbalanced as many at Stag's Head Lodge believed her to be.

The climb to the peak seemed an impossible task. The howling wind was threatening to blow her away. Each lightning bolt, each boom of thunder, had her questioning her sanity. Still, she refused to turn back.

She scrambled from rock to rock, low branch to low branch, and found herself struggling for every breath. She'd never dreamed the climb to the top of these Highland peaks would be so daunting.

At the keening of the wind, the sky turned so dark, she looked up and saw the moon covered by a wall of thick, dark clouds. Perhaps she should be grateful for the wind and the clouds. Without them, she would have been as visible as if she were carrying a lantern.

As she came up over a rise, a sudden flash of lightning gave her a clear view of the scene before her.

A great stag stood on a shelf of rock, head high, standing as still as a statue.

Seeing a slight movement to one side, Beth caught sight of a man wearing a hooded cloak. In the blink of an eye he lifted his hands. Another flash of lightning showed an archer's bow in one hand, an arrow in the other.

As he took aim, she shouted, "Behind you!"

The night went dark, and she feared her words had been snatched away by the wicked wind. Straining, she thought she heard the flight of the arrow as it sang through the air. In the same instant the stag leapt down from the rock.

Instead of hitting the stag's throat, as intended, the arrow landed in the moving animal's side.

With a cry the great beast staggered and fought, rearing up on its hind legs before dropping to the ground, writhing in pain.

With a muttered oath at his bad timing, the man stepped out of his place of concealment. Following behind him was a woman dressed in an elegant fur-lined cloak.

The two headed toward the animal, prepared to finish the deed. In the man's hand was a sword. In the woman's hand, the razor-sharp blade of a knife glinted in the moonlight.

"No!" With a look of absolute horror, Beth raced across the distance that separated them and knelt beside the wounded creature.

With a look of surprise, the man halted for a moment.

Edwina took the lead and started forward. "Move away, woman, before you join the beast in death."

"You think to kill us both so no one will know the evil thing you did here?" Beth got to her feet and faced the man and woman.

"No, you fool," Ian shouted. "The Beast will take care of that for us. Before he dies, his antlers will rip you to shreds. If that isn't enough, those great hooves will crush you."

"Then you'll have your wish, won't you? The only witness to your cruel deed will be eliminated." Beth fixed them both with a look of fury. "What happened to the hunter you paid to do this evil thing?"

Ian looked stunned. "How did you know?"

"I overheard your evil scheme."

"Why, you . . ." As Ian rushed toward her, Beth pulled the knife from her waistband.

"Come any closer, Ian, and you'll be the one to suffer."

When he hesitated, Edwina tossed back the hood of her cloak and advanced. "Do you think you can kill both of us?"

"I'll die trying."

Hearing the sound of pain and fury emanating from the stag's throat, and seeing the feral gleam of its eyes, Edwina turned away with a sly smile. "This woman is a bigger fool than your friend Hamish." She shot a glance at Beth. "You asked about him. He refused to carry out the deed, saying the laird didn't deserve such a fate. Even now he lies in a pool of his own blood."

Beth looked in horror at Ian. "And you called him a friend?"

Edwina answered for her brother. "What we do is necessary to carry out the will of our mother. As for you, fool woman, you shall suffer an even harsher death, as you'll certainly be crushed beneath the hooves of the beast as he fights to the death. You both deserve what you will get."

As thunder crashed across the heavens, Edwina turned away. Her boot caught the edge of a rock and she lost her balance, falling into the rushing waters of a swollen Highland stream.

With a cry, Ian dropped his weapon and made a desperate attempt to save her, until he, too, was swept away.

Their cries filled the air.

Within minutes their voices were stilled.

Shuddering, Beth turned her attention to the great stag. But as she reached for the arrow protruding from its side, powerful hooves flailed at her hand, barely missing her flesh.

She watched as the animal's breath came in short bursts, indicating the amount of pain even that effort cost.

"You have to let me remove that arrow, or you'll surely bleed to death."

The stag turned to her with a look of terror.

"I know you mistrust humans. Especially now that one has caused you such pain. But you have to trust me. I'm here to help you."

While she kept her voice soft, she ran a hand along the creature's sleek hide and felt a quiver, and another low rumble deep in its throat. A warning to retreat? Or an admission of its fear?

"In order to help you, I'll be forced to inflict a little more pain as I withdraw the arrow. But then, if you'll let me, I'll bind your wounds and stay with you until you're able to find your way home." She touched a hand to the animal's head and stared into the pain-filled eyes. "Please let me help."

As she spoke she took hold of the shaft of the arrow and pulled it free in one quick motion.

The stag gave a howl of pain that could be heard echoing

and re-echoing across the Highlands, sending chills along the spine of every man, woman, and child who heard it in the villages below.

"I'm sorry, my love. I can't bear the thought of causing you any more pain than you've already experienced."

Beth tore the hem of her gown into strips, which she wrapped tightly around the animal's hide until they were drenched with blood. When she was finished, her hands, her body, even the ends of her hair were soaked with the creature's blood.

"If I could, I'd take away your pain. But all I can do now is hope that you're strong enough to recover from this horrible wound." Beth wrapped her arms around the animal's neck and pressed her mouth to its ear. "Try to sleep, love. To heal. And we'll hope that in the morning, you're strong enough to find your way home."

There was another growl, softer now, as the big stag trembled.

Exhausted from the climb and the emotional toll of her efforts, Beth huddled against the great beast, tucking the edges of her cloak around him, and fell into a deep sleep.

THE STORM HAD BLOWN OVER, LEAVING A FINE MIST FALLING from a sky tinged with dawn light. Beth awoke with a start. Instead of the great stag she'd been holding when she fell asleep, she looked down into the face of her beloved Colin.

"You're alive."

He made a slight movement, struggling to grasp her hand. "Nay, love. I am dying."

"But you've broken the curse. You've survived the night. You can't die, Colin. Please stay with me." His hands, she realized, were as cold as ice. His flesh was as pale as the snowcaps that dotted the peaks of the Highlands. "I can't bear to live without you. There has to be something I can do."

"It is too late to stop the curse. In order to fulfill Darda's promise, I must die. But there is a way to thwart her."

"How? Tell me what to do. I'll do anything."

His gaze was fixed on her. "You have already done it."

"I don't understand."

"Love, Bethany. Love is stronger than hate. A pure heart is stronger than any curse. If you love me, truly love me, you must know that I'll never leave you."

"But you said you're dying."

"I am. I must. But that does not mean I'll ever leave you, love."

"You're not making any sense. You're dying, and you say you'll never leave me?"

"I give you my word, my beloved Bethany. I will always be with you. And one day, I promise you, your grief will turn to joy."

She watched the uneven rise and fall of his chest, and knew that he was struggling to remain with her. But his life was slowly fading.

Though it pained her, she knew she needed to be completely truthful with him before death claimed him. "I need to tell you something. I hope you won't hate me when you hear this. I came here to persuade you, by any means I could, to sell your ancestral lands. I was told to do whatever necessary, to beg, buy, or steal. I even planned on enlisting the help of Ian and Edwina in order to trick you into selling."

"Is that why you made love with me?"

She felt the quick rush of tears and wiped furiously at them. "Of course not. What we shared was honest. And beautiful. And now that I understand what all this means to you, the price you paid to keep it, I would never make such an offer. I know now that this is, as you said, hallowed ground, and must remain in your possession for generations to come."

"Then love has truly transformed us both." A sad, haunted smile touched the corner of his mouth and, though it cost him, he drew her close and brushed a kiss to her lips. "You never said the words. Do you truly love me?"

"With all my heart." A sob caught in her throat. "I wish I had told you sooner. But please know how much I love you, Colin."

"I can die in peace now, my love."

"No! Oh, Colin, no."

"Though the curse must be fulfilled, I will never leave you. Believe that."

She felt him take a small breath. His hand went slack. His handsome face looked deceptively peaceful, as though he were merely at rest.

She couldn't contain her overwhelming grief. Great, wrenching sobs were torn from her throat. And as she gathered him into her arms, she wept until there were no tears left.

CHAPTER TEN

Beside the little chapel in the garden, Beth stood to one side as the villagers paused at the fresh mound of earth to whisper a prayer or drop a rose petal onto the moist soil.

The chapel had been abuzz with the murder of young Hamish Campbell, and the rumor that Ian and Edwina, running from the scene, had been caught up in the churning, swollen waters of a stream and had both perished. As yet, their bodies had not been recovered.

It mattered not to Beth. Colin was dead, and whatever the fate of his stepsiblings, it wouldn't bring him back to her.

When all the villagers had left, it was time for the staff of Stag's Head Lodge to pay their final respects. Old Maura leaned heavily on the arm of the young serving lass, Glenna, tears streaming down both their faces. Mistress MacKay knelt to place a bowl of the laird's favorite bread pudding on the grave. Poor Jamie could hardly contain the grief that had him rubbing at his eyes and turning away.

And then, finally, as the sun began to set and dusk settled over the land, Beth was alone. She dropped to her knees and allowed the tears to flow. Great choking sobs were torn from her throat as she knelt beside the grave, wishing with all her heart that she could join her love.

"How cruel of the Fates to give me a taste of true love, and then demand that I go on living alone," she whispered.

She was so caught up in grief, she could barely recall the events of the day. It had been Jamie who had found her, lying beside the laird on Stag's Head Peak, her arms locked around his still body, her face buried in his neck. The lad had to pry her arms free. Wrapping her in a dry woolen cloak, he'd helped her up to the saddle of his mount before draping the laird's body across the back of his favorite stallion.

Taking up the reins of the laird's horse, the lad pulled himself up behind Beth and was forced to hold tightly to her or she would have surely fallen, she was so limp and weakened by her grief and pain.

As they'd made their way back to the lodge, people in the village came out of their houses and stood in silence, watching the sad procession. All had known about the curse, and all had kept the laird's secret, out of love and devotion to him.

When they'd reached the courtyard of the lodge, every member of the laird's staff stood in a straight column, heads bowed, faces somber.

An old man hobbled forward and helped Jamie remove the laird's body from the horse. At once old Maura appeared with a length of ivory linen in which to wrap the body.

When that was done, Jamie indicated Beth. "The lady needs tending."

"No." She slid from the saddle and knelt on the stone paving to place a hand on the linen shroud. "My needs are not important now. First we must see to the laird, and give him a proper burial."

"Aye." Maura, grateful for the chance to do something, took charge. "We'll summon the old friar and send word to the village that the laird's funeral will be before dusk."

And so it had been done. Right now the villagers and the members of the laird's household retreated to the great hall, eating a meal in Colin's honor, and talking quietly among themselves about the good man they had lost, and what would happen to Stag's Head Lodge going forward. There was word that the old laird's brother had a son, a cousin near the age of Colin, whose quiet dignity and calm demeanor would continue the course set by his predecessors.

And now, Beth thought, her own future stretched out before her, empty and meaningless. She had found the great love of her life. And, just as quickly, had lost him.

Was it possible for her, after all this, to return to the life she'd known before Colin?

The thought of returning to the city, of struggling daily to please her stern, demanding aunt, of pretending that the work she did, the business she conducted, meant anything at all to her, was unimaginable.

How could she possibly go on?

Even though I must die, I will never leave you.

"But you have, Colin. Why did you make that impossible promise?" Her whispered words caused a fresh round of tears. "You've left me, and nothing will ever be the same."

She wished with all her heart that the world would just go away and leave her to this all-encompassing grief.

Drained beyond belief, she closed her eyes.

"HERE, NOW. WHAT'S THIS? WHAT'S HAPPENED?"

When Beth heard that much-loved voice, her eyes opened and she found herself staring into the familiar eyes of her beloved.

"Colin?"

"Aye. I'm Colin Gordon. And you'd be . . . ?"

"Beth. Beth Campbell." She struggled to sit up. "But you're . . ."

She blinked, and realized that this man, with Colin's face, was wearing corduroy slacks and a fisherman's knit sweater with patches at the elbows. His hair, though dark as midnight, was cut short. His voice was cultured, with the merest hint of a Scottish burr to it.

And then she realized that she was wearing her charcoal silk business suit and designer shoes, and lying along the side of the road.

"I was . . ." She swallowed. What was going on here? Had she actually lived in that other time and place? Or had she been having a hallucination, brought about by the bump to her head?

"I was on my way to Stag's Head Lodge when my car stalled, and when I started walking I fell and hit my head . . ."

"Indeed you did. And I can see why, wearing shoes with those stiletto heels." He put up his hands. "Wait. You musn't try to stand. Let me carry you."

He lifted her easily in his arms and started toward a waiting Rolls-Royce, where a handsome youth was seated behind the wheel. Beside him, setting up a chorus of barking, were several beautifully-groomed hounds.

"Hush now." At that single command, the dogs sat back, tongues lolling, as he settled her in the backseat before sitting beside her.

"Let's get our guest to the lodge, Jamie."

"Aye, m'lord."

As the car began rolling toward the lodge, Beth's host took her hand in his, sending the most delicious curls of heat along her spine. "I hope you don't mind that, after receiving your letter, I took the liberty of asking my stepsiblings to stay home this weekend."

"You did?"

He nodded. "I don't want any distractions while I show you around. There's so much to see. The lovely loch, where I've been fishing since I was a lad. All the quaint shops in the village."

"I stopped in Stag's Head Village on my way, and it was lovely. The old gentleman in the bake shop couldn't say enough good things about you."

"That would be Hanley. A sweet friend and a fine tenant." He smiled, and Beth felt her heart doing a strange dance in her chest.

"Not to mention an outstanding baker. I thoroughly enjoyed his scones."

"Wait until you taste Mrs. MacKay's bread pudding. There's no one around here who can match it."

Beth sighed. "I can't wait."

He continued holding her hand. "I hope this doesn't sound too presumptuous of me, but if I were to ask you to stay on for an extended visit, would you think me too bold?" Before she could respond, he added, "Though I suppose, if you did stay on, you would probably miss New York too much."

She gave a quick shake of her head. "At the moment, New York seems so very far away. I doubt I'll miss it at all. In fact, I don't know how anyone could ever bear to leave all this beauty to live in the city."

"Do you know how much it pleases me to hear you say that?" He lowered his voice. "I know you've come to negotiate the sale of my ancestral estate, but I should warn you that no amount of money will tempt me. It isn't for sale at any price."

"Then why did you agree to see me?"

"Why indeed? I think you know, sweet Bethany. I've been waiting for you for a very long time. It feels like hundreds of years, in fact."

She felt a quick hitch around her heart. "It's true, then? I didn't dream it?"

He squeezed her hand and stared at their joined hands before looking up into her eyes. "I hope you're prepared for a very long stay."

"How long?"

He caught a stray strand of her hair and watched as it sifted through his fingers. "I think you know."

As they pulled into a paved courtyard, she heard the pealing of bells, and caught a glimpse of a small chapel to one side of a lovely rose garden.

"Tomorrow I'll show you where my ancestors are buried."

"I'd like that very much. And I want you to know that I understand why you will never part with this estate. This is hallowed ground."

"Exactly. Our hearts and minds are in sync, Bethany. Come."

She accepted his hand and slid from the car to see a plump, gray-haired woman standing in the doorway, smiling in welcome.

Instead of merely leading the way, he dropped an arm around her shoulders, and she felt the warmth of his touch all the way to her toes. "It's time you say hello to old Maura. She's been on pins and needles ever since she learned you were on your way."

She paused to look up into his eyes. "Tell me the truth. Is this really happening? Or is it more magic?"

His smile was quick and easy. "Who can say what is real and what is magic? Instant attraction? Love at first sight? How to explain them? Many have tried. But only those who've experienced it can know for certain." He paused before adding, "This much I know, Bethany. You and I are real. And I do believe we're both ready to accept whatever . . . magic the Fates decree."

Beth looked around at the ancient castle, the beautifully tended gardens, the little chapel, with its cherubs and stone markers standing guard over the graves of Colin's ancestors.

Though this was her first trip to Scotland, she knew this place intimately. And whether she had lived here in ancient times, or it had all been a strange dream brought on by a fall, she knew, without a doubt, that her lonely heart had, at long last, found its home.